BATTLETECH
THE QUEST FOR JARDINE

BY HERBERT A. BEAS II

BATTLETECH: THE QUEST FOR JARDINE
By Herbert A. Beas II
Cover art by Tan Ho Sim
Interior art by Doug Chaffee, Harri Kallio, Chris Lewis, Duane Loose
Cover design by David Kerber

Printed in USA.

Published by Catalyst Game Labs,
an imprint of InMediaRes Productions, LLC
5003 Main St. #110 • Tacoma, WA 98407

CONTENTS

FOREWORD

Serendipity is often a wonderful thing. When I was younger, I tended chalk up beneficial events that seemed to happen by chance as random coincidences. Now that I'm a bit older, I know that while many events are not predestined, a lot times things fall into place that we don't realize were set up to happen from the start until we look back on them.

Take this collection, for example. Back with *BattleTech* was in the Jihad Era, there was very little fiction of that era published at that time, other than what appeared in various sourcebooks. The simple reason for this was that there was no Catalyst fiction department at that time; short fiction was assigned as part of the sourcebook program, and that's practically all there was. I'm sure there was the occasional Jihad Era short story that appeared on *BattleCorps*, but my point is there was no official fiction program for that era.

Fast forward to today, and I'm pleased to report *BattleTech* fiction is alive and well, with original novels, novellas, and short stories published across every era, from the Age of War (just a tiny bit right now, but with plans to grow) to our current IlClan Era. And yes, there has been the occasional Jihad Era story appearing in *Shrapnel* and elsewhere (one of the most recent being Craig A. Reed's excellent novella *Blood Rage*). However, for the most part, these stories have used the era as their setting, but haven't really delved into the true essence of the Jihad.

Which brings us to the collection you're holding right now. Written by Herb Beas, former *BattleTech* Line Developer and the architect of the Jihad Era, no one knows more about this time period than the person charged with creating it. As such, it made perfect sense for him to write what is essentially a three-part novel about what should be a simple search for a planet that fell off the interstellar maps that turns into the discovery of a massive conspiracy to conceal an impending galaxy-wide operation that will change the whole of the *BattleTech* universe forever.

And what a story it is! Told through the eyes of Brooklyn Stevens, a character who might not normally be a protagonist in a novel-length *BattleTech* story, but I can't think of anyone else who could be at the heart of this tale and take us on her journey, experiencing the trials she does, and discovering this vast secret along the way.

Of course, every hero needs a menacing villain, and Precentor Omicron Apollyon is one of the most terrifying ones we've seen in a long time. A true believer in his mission to carry out what he believes is the mission charged to the Word of Blake by ComStar's founder, Jerome Blake, to bring their beliefs to the rest of the Inner Sphere...by any means necessary. But the interloper Dr. Stevens has discovered the secret of Jardine, and she now threatens everything he holds dear.

And what a secret it is! If you're coming to this collection for the first time, and haven't read these three independently published stories before now, then I won't say much more other than you're in for a treat, a tale that answers several questions about the beginning of the Jihad, but also raises several more. And if you've already read the ebook stories and perhaps picked up this volume in a paperback edition for your *BattleTech* collection, thank you, and I hope you enjoy re-reading these tales again.

Finally, I'm pleased to announce that this volume is the first in a line of forthcoming Jihad-Era fiction Catalyst will be producing. Right now, we are creating a program to explore this era through more original fiction, expanding on the wealth of information, reports, rumors, and legends that run rampant about one of the bloodiest eras in the history of the Inner Sphere. So if you enjoy Dr. Stevens' adventures in *The Quest for Jardine*, I hope you'll come back to read more forthcoming fiction about the Jihad.

—John Helfers, Executive Editor
Catalyst Game Labs

THE HUNT FOR JARDINE

FORGOTTEN WORLDS, BOOK ONE

PROLOGUE

My dearest Tyler,

Well, we're here at last! I'm sure by now you've been getting bored with the usual in-transit messages, but I also know how much you worry during these field missions. What can I say but the usual assurances that I'm fine, I still love you, I miss you very, very much, and I hope to be home in just another few months?

It's a shame you couldn't come, by the way. From orbit, Rocky seems quite fascinating. Trouble says the scans he's getting so far reveal the planet slid back into an ice age, probably thanks to the nuclear winter from that last battle down there between the Davions and Steiners. Radiation levels now are fairly tolerable, of course—survivable, even without protection.

Better still, we think all that environmental damage played havoc with ocean currents after all these years; the Annie M *is now beached on the Obsidian Coast. I won't even need full arctic diving gear or the DrillerMech to get at the target.*

So it looks like everything on this job is working out right (for a change!). But don't worry, honey. I'll bundle up nice and warm in the heavy envirosuit, just for you.

And I'll play it safe, as always.

Love!

—Brooke

RSS *ANNIE M*
OBSIDIAN COAST
ROCKY
LYRAN ALLIANCE
13 FEBRUARY 3067

"Brooke, you better get your ass out of there!"

Its sound muffled only slightly through the insulation of her sealed helmet, a powerful blast emphasized the words barked in Brooke Stevens' ears. Shuddering the length of the ancient cargo ship, the explosion set free a brief cascade of long-dead barnacles, centuries-old stalactites of ice, and decayed minerals from the ceiling and walls around her. More powerful than the first explosion, this one shook the bowed, age-worn deck grates so violently that she had to reach out with her free hand, grasping at a corroded rail along the starboard bulkhead.

Not unexpectedly, the rail snapped free, denying any support—real or imagined—and leaving Brooke to fight a losing battle with gravity. Flailing, she fell back and knew an exquisite pain that shot along her left leg when it twisted almost completely out of joint. The heavy satchel, still clutched in her right hand, bounced against the grates with a muted clatter of metal on metal. Instinctively, she tightened her grip on its carrying strap, holding on for dear life even as her other hand let go of the useless rail fragment.

The shock of pain forced a short yelp from Brooke's lips that momentarily fogged the polarized faceplate of her heavy helmet and reflected back the stale stench of the mystery meat hash she'd had for breakfast this morning. She coughed as much from the odor as from the pain.

"Brooke?" Though robbed of emotion through the transmission, Marissa Boerefijn's voice nevertheless betrayed her worry.

"I *heard* you, Marie!" Brooke spat back, then bit her lip as she forced her left leg back underneath her.

"Are you okay?"

"Ask a stupid question," she hissed.

Another explosion shook the derelict vessel, and icy debris peppered her thick suit. Brooke pulled herself upright, sucking in a lungful of filtered air through grinding teeth as her leg screamed back in pain. Just ahead, barely illuminated by the (remaining) headlamps of her envirosuit helmet, the topside hatch was an oblong pool of blackness against the mottled gray and streaking shadows of the aft bulkhead. Burned away barely half an hour ago, the heavy door lay flat before the opening, an awkward step to the chamber beyond.

Still clutching the satchel, Brooke moved again, breathing heavily into her faceplate with each laborious, pain-wracked step...

It was all supposed to be so easy, she reminded herself again.

After all, the *Annie M* had rested on the bottom of Rocky's Obsidian Sea for the better part of three hundred years, survived a nuclear war, shifted shoreward by gross changes in local currents, and undergone a deep freeze as the planet's ice age plunged the average surface temperatures to -20 centigrade and below. Surely time and the elements would have rendered useless any of the booby traps left behind by the Rim Worlders who originally scuttled their secret prize for later retrieval.

That was what Brooke and her team had decided, anyway. Seemed reasonable enough—until she found those cargo holds piled high with ancient munitions. Chemical sensors linked to her suit fed data to Marissa, who enjoyed the relative comfort of the *McKenna.* The modified AstroLux star yacht remained parked somewhere just beyond the beaches-turned-tundra of the Obsidian Coast, a few kilometers northwest of here.

The data—and Tibor "Trouble" Mitternacht's lightning-fast analysis of it from his own post on the *McKenna*—quickly revealed the presence of chemical propellants and warhead leakage. Only semi-frozen on the flooring, where it all had spent the last century or so pooling up, the chemical cocktail was unstable in the extreme, a literal powder keg awaiting a match.

Fortunately, the cargo hold that was Brooke's destination was separated from the munitions holds by several badly rusted bulkheads and one deck encrusted with dead, frosted barnacles and other curious mineral remains.

Unfortunately, the hold—and the heavy stainless-steel safes within holding the *real* prize—lay just beneath the waterline, trapped in ice requiring a handful of incendiary charges to flash-melt.

Compared to other jobs Brooke had taken, dunking herself into a murky slush to blindly cut away corroded safe latches with a pocket plasma torch was a piece of cake, as was groping about to withdraw items by touch alone. But somewhere in all that effort, some spark or vibration she hadn't accounted for must have happened. Perhaps even a bit of a functional and ancient mechanical booby trap was to blame.

Whatever the cause, the result was a chain reaction that even now slowly ignited the *Annie M*'s explosive cargo, warhead by tri-centenarian warhead...

"Brooke!"

A thunderous blast followed Brooke as she hobble-ducked through another open hatchway and into a narrow spiral stairwell heavily cluttered with debris and remains. Half an hour ago, she had descended these very stairs slowly enough, mindful of the mummified ruins that might once have been living, breathing crewmen over three hundred years ago. Now, she raced, forcing pain-wracked legs—weighed down by an extra few kilograms of unidentified treasures and a partially frozen envirosuit—to pound the ancient metal steps, kicking up bits of ice, ancient metal, and perhaps even fragments of long-dead corpses.

"Brooke!" Marissa shouted again.

"I know! I *know*!"

As the blast all but tore open the deck below her, Brooke clutched the stair rail tightly, thanked the fates for its support, and made her way to the upper deck, catching a glimpse of dim daylight somewhere beyond the open hatch above.

Then the world spun at the sound of groaning metal, sending her sprawling back several steps to crash shoulder first onto the landing. The satchel, following her fall, slammed back and landed full on her chest. Another yelp of pain escaped through clenched teeth. Stars swam before her as she forced herself to roll back to her feet, all while dimly aware the ship itself continued to lurch and shift.

"Marie!" she snarled.

"She's capsizing, Brooke!" Marissa came back in a rush.

"We're *beached*, for Bast's sa—!"

"The *bow* was on the ice shelf, *dummkopf!*" Tibor's harsher voice cut in suddenly. "That last blast looks like it ruptured the outer hull, and you're on the half that *doesn't* have the support!"

"Oh, *terrific!*" Brooke spat. Hauling herself upward again, satchel in hand, she made for the upper decks, watching the gray shaft of daylight as it gradually, shakingly turned away. Each step became a challenge of balance—and pain management—as the *Annie M*'s aft continued to list, and it was onto a deck now half-sunken in partially frozen seawater slush that she finally emerged agonizing seconds later.

As ancient, oceangoing cargo vessels went, the 30,000-ton *Annie M* was a small beast, her length only about two hundred meters from bow to stern. Though technically beached, her final resting place after centuries of drift amounted to little more than a mere twenty meters of ruined bow settled into a beach of frozen, debris-flocked sediment. This left her wide aft section—including the decrepit superstructure from which Brooke just emerged—hanging in the water, only partially submerged.

That the ship never rested wholly on the bottom of the seabed only attested to the expert efforts of her engineers and—Brooke presumed—the equally stunning incompetence of her last occupants in failing to scuttle her properly.

But now, the aft quarter shook violently as the latest explosion rocked the ship once more. With a powerful lurch, ancient deck plates blasted skyward, and the forward-port cargo boom—the last survivor of five such booms once boasted by the venerable ship—toppled over the side.

The blast also drew Brooke's attention to the real problem. The *Annie M*'s fractured hull was now listing deeper to starboard, its aft section literally twisting away from the grounded fore...

...with Brooke still on it.

Another explosion, more powerful than the last dozen or so, blew apart the warped upper decks of the ancient cargo ship in a flash of golden fire. Tearing a neat line across the hull dead amidships, the blast rippled the surviving deck plates on both ends and scattered a spray of ice and debris in all directions. The shockwave hit Brooke instantly, tossing her against the superstructure walls and threatening to spill her back inside the ruins as the stern accelerated its lazy spin toward a final sideways rest in the shallow, murky seabed.

"*Scheiße!*"

"Shit, indeed," Tibor echoed in her ears. "I could see that blast from shore. Are you all right?"

Brooke suddenly found the need to suppress a laugh, despite the pain throbbing in her side and legs, and hooked her free arm around a twisted superstructure beam as the slope of the deck deepened. A lock of auburn hair, finally free of the tight bun she kept it in under the helmet, chose that moment to tumble across her left eye. She tried to blow it away and only succeeded in fogging up the faceplate again. "I'm all mixed up here, guys," she said instead. "Where's my damn skimmer?"

"Go left," Marissa told her.

Brooke looked left and sighed. The *Annie M*'s death roll forced that side of the ship higher and higher as Brooke's side spun lazily toward the sea. Getting to the skimmer meant climbing that rising slope while holding onto her satchel and accounting for any further explosions threatening to blow what remained of the ship into a cloud of rusted metal and dead sea life.

"Hell with that!" she shouted, and turned.

"Your *other* left!" Tibor yelled over the din of groaning metal and rumbling blasts.

Ignoring him, Brooke slung the satchel over one shoulder, grasped the strap with both hands, and lunged over the starboard rails. Eyes closed and tensed for the shock, she plunged into the murky, icy slush of the Obsidian Sea, just two meters below the sinking deck of the *Annie M*...

SHUTTLE *MCKENNA*
OUTBOUND TRAJECTORY
ROCKY
LYRAN ALLIANCE

Brooke loudly drew in a lungful of air through her nose and bit her lip as Marissa gently prodded her with thin, nervous fingers. In the mirror bolted to the bulkhead before them, Brooke could see the massive bruise that outlined every rib along her left side, vanishing under her sports bra. An even uglier blotch of black and blue peeked up from the preserving sleeve that now encased her left knee, revealing a nastier injury there that had already swollen her left ankle to twice its normal size, and gave the lower half of her leg an unhealthy purple cast.

"Christ, Brooke," Marissa muttered under her breath. "You're lucky that suit was padded..."

Brooke chewed her bottom lip as Marissa's pale fingers—a sharp contrast to the light bronze of her own skin—groped at her wounds, probing for broken bones. Though the cabin was heated to a comfortable 22 Celsius, sitting on the thin foam-lined table nearly naked, she felt chills with every gentle poke. A rash of gooseflesh spread along her arms and legs, and she shuddered involuntarily.

Marissa's chocolate brown eyes, framed by a pair of classic, brass-rimmed bifocals, widened slightly as they met hers. Though Marissa hadn't been in the field with her, her long locks of dirty-blond hair looked tousled and matted, and there were visible bags under her eyes. Brooke could easily guess why. As the team's researcher and a longtime spacer, Marissa rarely traveled to the mission sites any more; she had insisted this time, however, because she had grown to miss field operations.

And—as always—something had happened to nearly deprive the team of its leader. Looking into Marissa's startled and weary eyes, Brooke recognized an all-too-familiar concern.

"Well, consider yourself lucky," Marissa said. "Damned lucky, in fact, that you didn't dislocate or break something down there. If Tyler knew about this, you'd be grounded for sure."

"Oh, come on, Marie," Brooke said, shrugging on the loose-fitting T-shirt Marissa offered. "I've been through worse."

"Yeah, but jogging around under thirty meters of slush while a burning ship falls down around your head had to be the dumbest move I've ever witnessed from you in recent memory, and Tibor agrees."

"Oh, come on!" Brooke scoffed. "What about Svalstad?"

Marissa paused for a moment in thought. "Okay, *since* Svalstad, then."

"Hah!"

"Of course, as I recall, Tibor and Tyler were plenty fumed at you then, too."

"Well, what Ty doesn't know won't hurt, now will it?"

Marissa finally met Brooke's gaze again and smiled crookedly. "That still leaves you with Trouble."

"He's just broken up because we lost the skimmer," Brooke said with a wink.

"Maybe. It *was* a very nice skimmer. And do you realize how hard it is to adapt a B-90 for subarctic work? I had to listen to him complain about how that cost 'over a hundred man-hours and maybe an easy five grand in parts,' you know..."

"And it worked beautifully when I drove it there," Brooke admitted with a smirk.

Marissa matched her expression for a moment and shook her head. "You still could've gotten yourself killed out there. We said 'left,' you know."

"Blake's blood, Marie! 'Left' was a forty-degree slope by then! And in case you missed it, I was a little hard-pressed to make that jump."

Bending her left leg as much as the sleeve would allow just for emphasis, Brooke instantly paid for the act with a sharp, stabbing pain shooting up her thigh and numbing her toes.

Marissa's tired eyes narrowed slightly.

"Yeah, yeah," Brooke said with a roll of her eyes. Looking at the cabin floor, she pondered jumping down, but decided she'd better stay off the leg a little while longer. Even in the half gravity currently produced by the yacht's acceleration, a hard landing could further inflame the torn ligaments. Instead, she met the younger woman's gaze again and gave her a wolfish grin. "But the haul still ain't half bad, is it?"

Marissa finally smiled, with a real gleam in her eyes.

"Tibor's still scanning the bonus prizes for integrity and contamination, but I can't wait to see them up close and personal when we get back to the *Sacajawea*. It looks to be a small fortune, all right—even if your acrobatics banged up a few pieces a little."

"Hell, in that muck, I couldn't see what I was grabbing. How do we know those dents weren't there already?" Brooke winked, then added, "Of course, the big prize came through intact, didn't it?"

"*That* is where you got lucky, I'll admit." Marissa smiled. Turning away again, she retrieved a compad from the counter behind her, tapped the keys, and called up the image of an exquisite vessel of fine gold and platinum, bearing the clearly enameled crest of House Cameron, ringed with six brightly colored gemstones. The timestamp that scrolled across the bottom of the slowly rotating flatscreen image certified it had been scanned in a mere two hours ago.

"If that bloody chalice had been in another safe," Marissa told her, "or maybe stuffed deeper in the corner of the one it was in, you probably never would've found it before those bombs went off."

Brooke nodded sagely and used the keys to slowly rotate the chalice's image, watching as blue-green light reflected off the broad handle along one side of the artifact. Curiously asymmetrical in design, the cup easily could have been mistaken for the hilt of a nobleman's rapier from a certain angle—exactly as its crafter had likely intended.

A relic of a bygone era, but worth millions—perhaps even tens of millions—in kroner, if one knew the right museum or private collector to sell to.

And, of course, Brooklyn Stevens knew all the right ones.

"It's magnificent," Marissa breathed when Brooke handed the compad back to her. "A pity there are no DeKirks left to inherit it. Just doesn't seem right to hand it off to a man like Duke Robert."

"Now, now, Marie," Brooke said with a wink. "That's our employer you're talking about. You're starting to get as cynical as Trouble."

"Perish the thought!" Marissa winked back at her. "I just want to be sure that when you risk your neck like that, the payoff's worth it."

CHAPTER 1

Dearest Tyler,

 It's times like these I really wish you weren't so deathly afraid of space travel. It's bad enough I have to miss having you with me on missions, or that I had to worry about you through all that shooting back home. But you just haven't seen a high-class party like the ones they throw on Skye.

 Oh sure, now that the war's over, I'm sure you can waltz up the mountain back home and find a friend willing to get you into the really big spectacles at the Triad, where everyone and their brother is just dying to catch our soon-to-be Archon's eye. But because o`f all that politicking and deal-making, you just see so many stuffed suits, royal seals, and overinflated egos you have to know, deep down, that you aren't seeing anything but masks.

 On Skye, it's almost like those masks come off. Sure, Duke Robert and his pet, Colonel Dundee, are all smiles and pro-Alliance on the outside, but everyone knows they're up to something, and half the courtiers here aren't afraid to voice something positively scandalous about it.

 Better still, they'll find almost any excuse to party, and this time around, yours truly happens to have made the Guests of Honor list...all for a little trinket!

 Missing you deeply! (And, sorry; it seems Duchess Aten/Kelswa-Steiner is actually in your neck of the woods on some kind of business, so I won't be getting her autograph for you on this trip...)

 Love!

—Brooke

NEW GLASGOW
SKYE
SKYE PROVINCE
LYRAN ALLIANCE
24 APRIL 3067

"—And so, without further ado, allow me to present our lady of the hour, Dr. Brooklyn Stevens."

The grand ballroom in Duke Robert Kelswa-Steiner's estate was maybe half the size of the Royal Court on Tharkad—at least as far as Brooke could recall—but it shared many of the same medieval European features as that far distant palace serving as the seat of all Lyran government. The smaller area, however, made for a more intimate feeling, a closeness with the audience gathered beneath the soft, golden glow of almost a dozen crystal chandeliers.

The crowd was a mix of men and women of various ages ranging from twenty-something to the upper seventies, Brooke guessed. Their collective attire featured far less Steiner blue than a Royal Court gathering. Instead, more colorful tartans (and the occasional matching kilt) blended with a darker selection of tuxedos and evening gowns. Incidental flickers of light came from wall sconces, designed to mimic ancient torches for more of the classic feel while simultaneously drawing nearby eyes to the Scottish-style tapestries and beautifully executed holo-paintings of past members of Skye's upper nobility—all of which lined the walls between large oaken doors and cathedral windows.

Thunderous applause virtually deafened Brooke as she stepped behind the tartan-draped podium before the gathered Skye elite. Duke Robert's guest list claimed over three hundred of the province's most illustrious men and women, both noble born and otherwise, and his house staff added perhaps another hundred to the attendance figures for this latest soirée in the ducal palace. How some of them made the trip so quickly, with the war only days over, completely eluded Brooke.

But now, with all of their eyes focused on her, she simply hoped she was projecting the image they expected—that of a tall woman with elegance and poise...and a confident stride that defied the dull ache of her eight-centimeter heels.

Even as she quickly crossed the small stage to embrace her host for the benefit of the audience and the media cameras, Brooke made a mental note to ask Marissa why these shoes were supposed to be such a good idea when her feet were barely visible beneath the hem of her black-satin evening dress.

Beside the podium, a black silk sheet—strangely enough, matching the color and sheen of Brooke's dress—was draped across a rectangular glass case. Within sat the Chalice of Uston DeKirk, restored to its full glory and awaiting the light of a thousand stares. Were it not for that hidden treasure, Brooke knew full well she would hardly have merited an invitation to a gathering like this—physical charms and PhD in archaeology notwithstanding.

Her eyes flicked nervously across the audience and found Tibor Mitternacht. Watching her from the western bar, the rail-thin man with greasy black hair and mismatched eyes—one emerald and one jade—tried to look as casual as possible in his black Nehru-style tuxedo. To Brooke, he looked more like a cat ready to pounce and run. She threw him a reassuring smile, gently pulled her long auburn braid back over her right shoulder, and mouthed a *thank-you* to the audience as their applause died down.

Folding her hands out of sight on the podium, Brooke absentmindedly twisted the ring on her left hand and drew in a deep breath, filling her nostrils with the competing scents of several exotic perfumes, colognes, and cigars. Trying not to cough, she cleared her throat.

"Thank you, Your Grace," she finally began with a nod to Duke Robert Kelswa-Steiner. The words, picked up by wire-thin microphones sprouting up almost invisibly from the sides of the podium, were amplified across the room, yet left no echo in their wake. "It is indeed an honor to be here today."

Just within her peripheral vision, the Duke of Skye (by grace of his marriage to Duchess Hermione Aten, only surviving member of Skye's Aten family), Tamar (by virtue of his own mother's claim to the now Clan-held world), and Porrima (by his own father's blood claim to that Steiner holding) nodded pleasantly back at her. His black, slicked-back hair caught the light like polished steel, and his easy smile seemed both confident and fatherly. Although he wore the uniform of the Lyran Alliance Armed Forces, it eschewed all Steiner insignia. Instead, a green and blue tartan sash with hints of white crossed his broad chest and ended in a knot at the left side of his trim waist.

Dressing down for the occasion, no doubt, Brooke told herself.

"Um, forgive me," she said to the audience with a sheepish smile. "I usually give these kinds of speeches for museum staff and university students, so if I start sounding like a teacher, just bear with me for a few moments, and I'll try to make it all as painless as possible…"

Polite chuckles answered as she paused for breath, set her mind into neutral, surreptitiously licked some moisture back into her crimson-painted lips, and finally began describing the origins of the chalice that remained hidden beneath the black cloak beside her.

"The Cameron family," she began, "particularly its latter rulers in First Lord Simon Cameron and his son, Richard, put great stock in the heroic and chivalric ideals of those like the legendary King Arthur. But it was a host of so-called Modern Chivalrist writers, such as Uston DeKirk and Bonnie Cracken, who many historians believe truly inspired these men— contemporaries who brought these images back to life in vivid new terms during the late twenty-seventh to middle twenty-eighth centuries…"

Brooke *hated* giving lectures. Not because of the large crowds or the possibility of embarrassment and media misquotes. It was actually because of the *tedium* of it all, and the general apathy of her typical audience. Every time she stood before a group to explain her latest find or to make her latest sale of recovered artifacts from some forgotten world, the knowledge that—deep down—few of the people listening *truly* cared about what she was saying simply robbed the find of its thrill. It was like a mythology professor trying to brag to a bunch of corporate executives about some interesting new combination of fables they'd discovered from long ago, or the proverbial fisher's tale told to someone with no interest in the sport. The entire exercise was…anticlimactic.

That these thoughts crossed her mind at all annoyed Brooke, however. If there was one thing she couldn't stand, it was a snob, and here she was, underscoring how much she thought like those she hated. Still, none of that changed the fact that only a born-and-bred explorer—a problem solver of the most dedicated sort—could understand why talking about the discovery of such rare antiquities as this three-hundred-plus-year-old chalice would be so marvelous. And Brooke could see in this audience's eyes that any kindred spirits—as always—were few and far between.

Which was why, halfway through her lecture, she suddenly became aware of one pair of eyes—other than Tibor's—hanging on her every word, . Matching the man's stare for a moment, she took in his features. Pastel-blue eyes, a broad, almost flat face, fair skin, blond hair cut so short it almost disguised the fact that he was prematurely balding. Even before she finished explaining the origins of the chalice—how Uston DeKirk had personally received it from First Lord Simon Cameron during the waning years of the original Star League—Brooke found she recognized the man who gazed so intently at her. Seeing that recognition on her face, he smiled and nodded.

Henry Croft.

Brooke's stomach dropped, and a warm flush came to her face as she wrapped up her introduction. As "suggested" by her employer, she closed with a remark that the DeKirk family had carried on their famous luminary's commitment to honorable ideals ever since—seen today (of course) in the likes of Duke Robert's right-hand military aide, Colonel John Claverhouse Dundee. With that, she nodded slightly to the pageboy next to the stage. The young man pulled on a golden braided cord, lifting away the cloak at last so the assembled masses could *ooh* and *ah* over the giant, jewel-encrusted goblet she had brought back from Rocky.

Applause again filled the room as Duke Kelswa-Steiner and Colonel Dundee himself stepped beside Brooke, thanked her, and shook her hand, each in turn. The duke then reclaimed the limelight as Brooke smiled and stepped back with a feeling of sudden relief.

Looking out over the crowd, she found Croft again, still watching as she resumed her seat at the tables reserved behind the podium for Duke Robert's guests of honor.

And what brings you *here, I wonder?*

"Great speech," Tibor remarked with a dry smile as Brooke finally made her way to the bar for a fresh flute of Glengarry Rosé. A slight batting of her lashes at the bartender guaranteed she did not wait long, and she gave him a grateful wink and a smile as payment for the courtesy.

"Horseshit," she muttered back, just loud enough for Tibor to hear over the din of partygoers. "But thanks for the compliment."

"Well, I think it was that patented glazed look in your eyes that gave away your total disinterest," Tibor said, swirling the golden, foamy brew in his own glass. The odor of some cheap Skye-made knockoff of Timbiqui Light assailed Brooke's nostrils. "That is, of course, until you noticed your admirer."

"You saw him too, then?"

"These eyes don't miss much." Tibor nodded, giving Brooke a moment to draw a quick sip of bittersweet zinfandel while his eyes—one natural jade, the other artificial emerald—roamed the crowd.

"He talk to you yet?" she asked.

Another nod, this one punctuated by him draining the ale from his mug, foam and all. His eyes darted back to hers, then resumed sweeping the ballroom.

"And?"

"And I told him *you* make the decisions, so he could save the pitch for you."

"So it *is* a pitch then, eh?"

"Yup," Tibor said, as his eyes finally locked onto their invisible target. Pointing more with his blunt chin than anything else, he directed Brooke's gaze into the sea of humanity in fine evening wear. "And he's eager as hell to make it, too. His thermals jumped when I stalled him... Here he comes now. Want me to scatter?"

"Hell no," Brooke murmured as Croft finally emerged from the mob, paused for a moment to get his bearings, and smiled right at them. "At least not yet."

Croft had a husky build that, while not *too* bad for a man approaching his mid-forties, stretched the fabric of his black silk tuxedo. He walked with a slight limp, favoring his left leg in a way Brooke didn't remember from the last time she'd seen him. But then, it *was* almost five years now, and Croft was still a dedicated field man when she knew him then...

"Why, if it isn't Dr. Brooklyn M. Stevens, as I live and breathe," he said as he neared. His voice had the harsh rumble of a chain smoker who'd started far too early in life, but his smile was amiable and white enough, framed by a goatee almost as brutally short as his hair (and a few shades lighter). Brooke allowed him to come close enough for a friendly embrace, but noticed how Tibor shifted uneasily on his barstool.

"And if it isn't Dr. Henry J. Croft," she replied in a carefully neutral tone. "I understand you've already encountered our good friend Mr. Mitternacht?"

Croft turned his semi-charming smile on Tibor and executed an abbreviated bow toward him. "Yes, indeed I have. And— stubborn as ever—he told me not to bother with my 'usual spiel' until you'd had the chance to join us. Polite chap, I must say."

"Why, thanks, Hank," Tibor drawled, flashing the man a casual grin.

Brooke chuckled. "What can I say, Croft? Trouble, the others, and I all have our issues with you Interstellar Expeditions folks. When you don't exactly leave on the friendliest of terms, and then someone from the company comes a-calling, you don't just buy the first thing coming out of their mouth."

Croft's expression darkened, but only for a moment. "Ancient history," he said with a dismissive wave. "Since Dr. Wooden took the helm, there's been a bit of a shake-up in the ranks. The upper echelons now realize what happened on Vulture's Nest wasn't your fault."

"Small comfort, that," Brooke said, her expression hardening as she thought back on the disaster—and the outrageous treatment she and her crew had endured in its aftermath. "Tell me, at least, that Denderhoff finally took the fall for it."

Croft frowned. "In a manner of speaking," he said flatly. "They put him back in the field as an assistant dig director and sent him out to do a follow-up on the Nest... And that was the last we heard of him, or the rest of his team."

Brooke blinked, and caught a glimpse of the same shock in Tibor's face. Denderhoff was the lone wolf type, a rugged mercenary just one step removed from piracy—especially after Interstellar Expeditions promoted him to project director and gave him a couple of dig crews to supervise. His main problem, as Brooke remembered it, was his inability to listen to anyone else when he thought he knew the situation. When in doubt, he fought, and fought hard; he wasn't the kind who simply vanished in the void.

"The Ghosts?" she asked. It was the first possibility that crossed her mind.

Croft nodded and sighed. "What evidence we found— eventually—suggested as much."

The three lapsed into silence. The Green Ghosts were a mystery, even to the likes of Interstellar Expeditions, as well as the biggest threat to the organization. Their attack forces, including sophisticated BattleMechs—some even of Clan manufacture—had first appeared roughly seven years ago, and seemed to have a knack for showing up at IE-sponsored digs as if summoned there by the same sources. Naturally a leak was suspected, but to Brooke's knowledge none were ever found. Since then, the bandits had only grown stronger, their plague of piracy appearing mostly along the Lyran Periphery, but sometimes in other sectors, shadowing IE like a wolf pack stalking a herd of prey.

Brooke suddenly became aware of their surroundings again, the background noise of conversation and laughter from Skye's gathered elite set to the quiet harmony of a live string quartet whose music had resumed—at Duke Robert's command— just as soon as the unveiling ceremonies ended. The masses gathered, forming their cliques, mingling, networking, perhaps even courting.

She also realized her mouth was dry. Almost absently, she finished off the zinfandel, barely noticing the taste this time. As she quickly placed the crystal flute back on the bar, her motion snapped the others out of their own silent musings.

"At any rate," Croft blurted, "the point I was going for was this: IE wants to pass along its assurances that—should you desire it—there is always a home for you and your crew within our organization."

"Generous!" Tibor said. "Of course, there's a catch, *ja*?"

Croft raised a finger, and his lopsided smile returned. "More of an *opportunity* than a catch, my distrustful friend."

Brooke arched an eyebrow expectantly.

Croft's smile turned her way. "A mission," he said, practically beaming. "Your usual freelance work on your usual freelance terms...if you're interested."

Brooke scoffed. "That's how you suckered me into your organization the last time, Hank," she said. "What if we don't want to go back?"

Croft shrugged and briefly glanced out over the crowd. "Well," he said, "I could play hardball with you, Dr. Stevens. After all, you and your people *did* abscond with almost three hundred *million* kroner's worth of IE property and equipment—"

"Empty threat and you know it," Tibor grumbled.

"Still actionable," Croft snapped back, "but—as I said—while I *could* play that card, I know better than that. If you don't wish to return, then so be it. But the offer still stands, and IE *is* willing to pay well for this one."

Brooke glanced at Tibor and caught the same curiosity in his jade eye that she knew showed in her own. Folding her arms across her chest, she gave Croft another arched eyebrow look.

Croft's smile broadened. "If you want to hear more, I'd suggest we find someplace a bit more...intimate, Dr. Stevens. Some details of the mission are not for other ears."

"*Intimate*, is it?" Brooke countered with a playful smirk. "Why, Dr. Croft, you *do* recall I'm a married woman, don't you?"

Croft chuckled. "How could I ever forget?"

As it happened, Croft's desire for "someplace intimate" proved nearly as scandalous as Brooke had teased. When she asked one of Duke Robert's house servants for a private room for herself and a friend, the young man's gaze flicked between her and Croft and—with a grin bordering on lecherous—he led them both from the ballroom. Two corridors and one conspiratorial wink later, Brooke and Croft found themselves in a guest room most noteworthy for having the largest canopy bed Brooke had ever seen.

With bookshelves lining the east wall, dark green drapes (closed by the servant as an added "courtesy"), fine cherrywood trim that both matched the furnishings and nicely complemented the off-white stucco walls, the room was elegant enough. But the presence of that bed, two strategically placed mirrors, and the unmistakable scent of sandalwood incense combined to create an image that just screamed "royal rumpus room."

"If I were in different company," she said, "this would be hysterical."

Croft gave her a cockeyed smirk and reached into his jacket pocket. Producing a device no bigger than his palm, he activated it, scanned its display, then showed it to her with a polite smile. In the absence of sound, the white noise generator would remain silent, but the annoying effects of its counter-frequencies once they began talking would force Brooke to get closer to Croft than she otherwise preferred. Still, she nodded and stepped closer, catching a hint of the man's musky aftershave.

"Perhaps," Croft said, his voice clear enough, but rendered more alien by the strange non-echo the generator added to it. "But I'll try to make this as diverting as possible."

"All right, Doctor," Brooke said, "fire away."

"In this case, my dear, a file is worth a million words," Croft said as he reached into an inner pocket this time. "And it can do more justice than any sales pitch I might make."

His hand emerged with a compad so small it could have passed for a simple calculator, and his thumb switched it on as he handed it to Brooke. "Have a look at the latest zoological find from the Free Worlds League."

With a momentary glance at his eager expression, she took the device. Her eyes locked onto the heading: "*Panthera Ignus Jardinalis*—A New Link?"

With a sudden surge of curiosity, she devoured the first few paragraphs before she had to ask, "Is this for real?"

Croft nodded. "If not, it's a hell of a hoax. That file includes a detailed gene map of this 'new' species—one that hasn't been seen by human eyes in, oh, two hundred years or so?"

Brooke nodded numbly and kept reading. *Panthera ignus jardinalis* was the Latin nomenclature given to an alien feline species known for its scarlet coat and golden eyes that seemed to glow even in daylight. Since these creatures could spit a toxic venom that included enough acid to sear flesh and dissolve vegetation in seconds, it was little wonder its more traditional name so closely matched the literal Latin translation: the Jardinian firecat.

"Are they positive it has all the right markers?" Brooke asked, her eyes still glued to the display. "This beast really shares the same native ecosystem as the *tabiranth*?"

"Well," Croft said, "*we're* sure about that anyway. And the credentials of the discoverer, Dr. Amanda Holyfield, are unimpeachable. There's no motive for a hoax here, and the images you see there were analyzed by the best in the business. No forgery there either. We even matched the provided sample with a mummified carcass at the Regulan Historical Zoology Museum. The species is the same, even if the progeny indicates a distinctly different bloodline."

Brooke stared in awe at the miniaturized images scrolling up: a firecat and her cubs, lying and playing in a small rainforest clearing. The cranial features evident in the mother bore the closest obvious similarities to the *tabiranth*, a feline riding beast known across the Inner Sphere. For centuries, the *tabi*'s hardiness, adaptability, and regal grace had made the species a favorite among sophisticated nobles and professional animal trainers in the Successor States. Thriving exports and breeding enterprises perpetuated its existence on dozens of worlds, assuring that the species itself survived even as its native world had been lost to the nuclear fires of the First Succession War. They were the only surviving link to a lost, dead planet, as far as anyone knew.

Until now.

Then the full weight of the implication hit. The world of Jardine had not simply died in the First Succession War; it had *vanished*. Even archival maps dating back to the original Star League showed no such world in Free Worlds League space, where all accounts placed it. Nor did it appear in any of the neighboring states. If a "new" species from the planet's ecosystem had been discovered, then that meant, just maybe...

"Someone found Jardine?" she asked.

Croft smiled again. "That's what we had thought, at first, before a curious thing happened."

Brooke threw him a quizzical look.

"Less than one week after this report was published, it was yanked from every scientific journal in the League, and dismissed as a hoax by several prominent xenobiologists—including, apparently, Holyfield's own benefactors."

"What did Holyfield say about that?"

"Absolutely nothing," Croft said flatly. "She was killed in a freak laboratory explosion three days earlier."

"Sounds fishy."

"League authorities use the term 'accident,' but I like your assessment better."

"Are you asking me to follow up, then? Go to this world where the species was found?"

"If you like," Croft nodded. "As part of the greater mission, perhaps."

"Greater mission?"

"Why, my dear Dr. Stevens, surely you can see what we're asking here! Someone may have found Jardine recently enough to have brought a species thought long extinct back from there...

"And if someone managed to accomplish *that*, then surely someone like you and your crew might just be able to do so again."

CHAPTER 2

My dearest Tyler,

Think of it, Ty: Jardine! The Atlantis of our time!

And of all people to hire me for the hunt, it had to be IE, huh? Yeah, they have their own resources—vast ones—but in this case, it looks like they want to avoid too much attention. Fact is, ever since that Starling book came out, IE has become the hot ticket; their name pops up everywhere on the holovids and planetary net searches, like some new out-of-the-blue fad. I can see why Croft and the others would want to try outsourcing a job like this, even why they'd come looking for me to do it, considering our last encounters.

Of course, I'm no fool, either. Croft said someone took out the biologist who found a link to that world, then did their best to deny her work. So someone else is on this hunt. Could mean Ghosts, but I doubt it. Someone's always been messing with IE business when they sniff around a big mystery like this. House governments are more likely than Ghosts.

Whoever it is, it's someone IE wants to keep off their scent, so they came to me, and for missions like this you know I like to pack a little heavier. (Don't you just love it when the only person you can trust in the universe is an ex?)

Unfortunately, the offer had a short shelf life, and the mission had to start ASAP. The pay is enough to cover the entire crew and myself for a year, and we'll still be able to cover expenses. I won't blame you for being upset, but I promise when it's over and done, I'll spend every waking minute of that time with you, my love!

Forever thinking of you!

—Brooke

EXPLORER-CLASS JUMPSHIP *SACAJAWEA*
ZENITH JUMP POINT
SHASTA
FREE WORLDS LEAGUE
29 JULY 3067

As soon as she entered the *Sacajawea*'s launch bay, Brooke could feel the tension in the air almost as surely as she could the chamber's ambient chill.

The first thing she noticed in the half-lit bay was the sound, or rather the relative lack of it. Instead of their customary chatter as they loaded up the three-meter racks of equipment parked just outside the squat ovoid hull of a modified K-1 DropShuttle, Tibor and Marissa seemed silently lost in their work. Their magnetized boots tapped lightly on the deck, sending echoes across the bay. Punctuating these footsteps every few seconds came the harsher metal-on-metal clang announcing another sensor tripod locking firmly into place.

As the pair worked to load up two such racks—separately—Brooke caught the deliberate manner in which Marissa, her expression studiously blank, grabbed another collapsed tripod from the neat pile arranged on the deck, made sure its legs were secured, and brushed right past Tibor as though he weren't even in the room, her gray jumpsuit fluttering the folds along his own. Tibor responded in kind, barely acknowledging the action.

Brooke sighed and fixed her face into a scowl. *I swear,* she told herself, *sometimes, these two are no better than children...*

As she finally strode into the bay, her own boots tapping loudly on the polished steel, they both looked up. She caught each of their gazes in turn, folding her arms across her chest.

"I know a tiff when I see one, you two," she said, forcing a slight edge into her tone. "Don't you think this trip's going to be long enough without it?"

Tibor was the first to break. With a scoff and a shrug, he muttered, "It's nothing we haven't discussed before."

That figures...

"Indeed we have," Marissa added, deep brown eyes flashing at Tibor through her bifocals, "but you *need* me down there, damn it."

"Down there, yes," Tibor shot back, "but not in the field! The Mesozonia may be a natural preserve for the Shastans, but it's not a zoo. There won't be any carefully laid-out paths and fences. I know you're itching for field work, Marie, but—"

"Wow," Marissa said coldly, "you've been preparing for *this* one, haven't you?"

Brooke sighed again, "It isn't like Trouble hasn't got a point here, Marie..."

Marissa looked crestfallen, and her delicate cheeks flushed red as she turned on her. "Oh, you're not going to take *his* side now, are you? I told you, I'm ready! I can handle a gun, and I've studied the—"

Brooke held up a hand. "I said he had a point," she said. "I didn't say you couldn't go."

Tibor scoffed again and rolled his eyes.

"Now, look, Trouble. You're right. We *have* been through it. I need someone in the field with me, and someone to back us up who can monitor the readings and fly the shuttle. Marie has studied the local flora and fauna. She knows what we're looking for, and the best chance we have of finding it is with her eyes on the scene, rather than filtered through vid links.

"But," Brooke quickly added, leveling her gaze on Marissa, "*you* have to realize Trouble's got a real solid reason to be concerned, Marie. We've both shown you how to fire a pistol, but if there's a cause to do it for real, you have to know it's not like shooting holograms and paper targets. I'll be counting on you to watch my back down there."

"Then why not have me along, too?" Tibor asked. "We have Lawrence. He can watch the shuttle."

"*And* the sensors?" Brooke asked sweetly. They'd been through *that* before as well. In the final analysis, Tibor was always the master of sensors, electronics, and other technologies in this crew. With the shuttle parked at the nearest spaceport, he could easily monitor the situation, analyze the data, and help guide the expedition while also being ready to pilot the craft in and out of the vast Mesozonia rainforest should the need arise.

The problem, of course, was everyone *expected* the need to arise. The Shastan government initially denied permission for Brooke and her "ecological survey" to set foot near the Mesozonia. It was Marissa and her research on Shastan customs and laws that finally got them in (with a healthy dose of Tibor's computer savvy and the relatively poor public security of the Shastan interweb). It was also Marissa's practiced familiarity with the ecology of the Mesozonia—where Dr. Holyfield's Jardinian firecats were found—that forced Brooke to concede Marissa *had* to be in the field with her this time.

But whoever silenced Holyfield would naturally be interested in anyone wandering into those jungles again. And that meant going in without backup was tantamount to suicide. Marissa *could* handle a firearm, but Brooke knew she'd be lying to herself if she thought her number-one research assistant could handle a true firefight.

That left the third member of her shuttle crew for this expedition to accompany her in the field as an extra precaution: the *Sacajawea*'s captain, Lawrence Pohl. A spacer with combat training as part of the ComStar Explorer Corps (before that, even he rarely discussed), Lawrence preferred to get his "land legs" every few field missions or so. Keeping with tradition, he prescribed the same to all his crewmen, for health reasons. But knowing this expedition threatened combat action—even hypothetically—he had *insisted* he would take the normal crewman's rotation for the Shasta landing, saying he refused to put "his" people in any danger he wouldn't take on himself.

Brave words, of course, but Brooke also saw the wisdom in them; few of the chronically shorthanded *Sac*'s crew had the military training she preferred when she expected gunplay.

Tibor scowled.

"Exactly," Brooke said. There was no need for further discussion. "So, now that that's settled...again...how are we looking on the equipment?"

Marissa sighed. "We already loaded up most of the basics. Three field tents, six medkits, compads, discs, enough rechargeable packs to power a house, and the heavy comm-sets, so T can track us even through the growth..."

"I also stocked up on emergency rations," Tibor jumped in. "Just in case the local fare isn't to our liking. You'll have enough to cover a few weeks in the field after we make landfall."

"Cute," Brooke said as she started to study the racks. Swallowing dryly, she tallied the sensor pods herself. "Coffee, too?"

"Enough to keep *you* awake," Tibor grinned. "Even after another one of your own lectures."

Brooke rolled her eyes. "Weapons?"

"A couple knives for each of you," he said, his tone suddenly serious, "plus one vibroblade for you and Lawrence. Each of us—myself included—also gets a Python and a tranq gun, with a few mags each. Add the two G-150s, Lawrence's MP-20, and a couple sawed-offs, and we should be fine down there."

Brooke's eyes widened slightly. "They only assigned us one chaperone, Trouble!"

"Not a petting zoo, remember?" he came back with a smirk. "Besides, you were the one who said, 'pack heavy.' If I could, I would've put *Digger One* or *Forty-Niner* in there with you."

"Somehow I imagine the Shastans would've looked rather unkindly on seeing an armed WorkMech in our inventory."

"Well, all the same, I may throw in a couple lasers. The dampness in that jungle may not be best for them, but I'd feel better if I knew you ladies had something with more stopping power to work with."

"The sensor pods were the last of it," Marissa joined in again. "We only came up with forty-eight reliable ones, though. It's enough for two racks, and we shouldn't have any trouble getting a local ATV big enough to carry them, but it's still rather low for my liking."

"Don't look at me," Tibor muttered. "A certain Dr. Stevens promised me we'd have more before we needed to handle another wildlife op."

Brooke turned and grasped the cool metal of the tripods on the rack. Giving the rack a slight shake, she tested its security against bumps in transit. The delicate pods themselves would be stored in the well-padded central portion on the rolling frame, ringed by the tripods on which they would be fixed when used, but a hard collision—in whatever vehicle transported them—could be enough to send dozens of unsecured metal shafts flying. Even if they didn't harm any of her expedition, the game of "pick-up sticks" they would face after such an accident (not to mention the potential loss of multiple pods) would likely make a bad day ten times worse.

"We'll have to make do," Brooke told them. "Four dozen should be enough to cover a few kilometer stretches at a time, even in all that foliage. Well enough before we have to start leapfrogging them, anyway. Unless we'll need to daisy-chain them?"

Tibor shook his head. "No need. Shasta has a good enough satellite network that I can bounce signals and get a fix. Leapfrogging will be your only option to max out coverage, but it'll slow you down a bit with all that backtracking. I made sure all of the shafts have working pop-up flares, too. Fire one through the forest canopy, and I'll pick you guys up on thermals. Try not to get jumpy with them, though. I don't want to test the Shastans' air-patrol forces while running to your rescue."

"They won't be a problem," Marissa chimed in. "I already reviewed local air security."

"The *official* security rolls, Marie," Brooke cautioned, finally turning around to face them. "Leaguers like to understate their air patrols, even if they're only using a conventional aircraft force."

"Nothing *you* can't handle, though, Trouble!" came a new voice, deep yet almost fatherly. Lawrence Pohl was already halfway across the deck from the bay entrance, having chosen to float into the room, rather than walk. Smiling, the gray-haired spacer executed a graceful midair half-flip that placed his mag boots firmly on the deck with barely a tap. He threw them all a lopsided grin, twisting his salt-and-pepper goatee into a strange shape, but kept his ice-blue eyes focused mostly on Tibor.

"Uh, Cap?" Tibor began. "You *do* remember you'll be in the field, too, right?"

"'Course I do." Lawrence beamed. "You sayin' you can't fly *and* handle guns at the same time?"

"Not nearly as well as you, old-timer." Tibor grinned back, and turned to Brooke with one eyebrow arched.

"Ah-ah," she said quickly. "It's settled already."

"Trouble is what Trouble does, Doc." Lawrence shrugged. "I'm sure we can look forward to a whole week of this guy trying to talk you out of it."

"At the very least," Brooke agreed. "Do I gather by your presence that you're about ready to shove off with us, then?"

"All set, ma'am," Lawrence said with another smile. "I gave the helm to Juan and he'll beam us any signals he don't like from the local nets. He'll keep us apprised in the daily check-ins while the *Sac* recharges."

"Okay, then," Brooke said with a nod. "Looks like we're all done here. We have the sensor racks to load up, and then everyone can grab their bags and we'll hit space in one hour. The sooner we can get dirtside, the sooner this mission can begin. Sound fair, people?"

All three nodded. Brooke drew in a deep breath and let it out slowly. She could feel the pre-mission jitters settling in even now, putting her nerves on edge even though landfall would still be six long and hopefully monotonous days away.

And beyond that, she knew, things could get *very* dangerous *very* fast.

LEOPARD-CLASS DROPSHIP *KAYLIN*
NADIR JUMP POINT
ALTERF
MARIK COMMONWEALTH
FREE WORLDS LEAGUE

The intercom gave only the shortest of bleats, its sudden noise in the total silence virtually guaranteeing the cabin's sole occupant would tense in his restraints. Nearly dropping the compad reports he'd been reviewing, Anton Hara turned to face the small speaker beside his cot.

"Captain," his exec, Lenard Bryce, said, "we got a signal."

Hara's eyes narrowed. *A signal?* he wondered. *Or* the *signal?*

"General broadcast?" he asked aloud.

"No, sir. Targeted transmission. Scramble codes match."

About damned time! "Put it through."

"Aye, sir."

The intercom clicked off, and with a simple beep, the small video terminal bolted to Hara's cabin desk automatically sprang to life, even while he forced his own tired muscles into action. Undoing the restraints he'd strapped into only minutes before, anticipating another night of uneventful null-gravity sleep, he felt almost grateful for the intrusion.

Boredom, the perennial danger of modern space travel, had taken its toll not only on the crew, but on him as well. He heard the eager edge in Bryce's tone, and knew with absolute certainty the still-unknown contents of the incoming message would be the focus of gossip across the ship, probably even before he landed in his chair.

"Finally!" they would all be saying. "Orders!"

Hauling himself out of bed, he swam through the air to his desk and landed in the floor-anchored swivel chair with the grace of a seasoned spacer. A simple prompt awaited his code phrase. Hara typed quickly; voice codes could be recorded by any number of hidden bugs.

Not surprisingly, the accompanying video was little more than a local star map, a few lines of printed text, and coordinates. Nodding, Hara committed the lot to memory.

Upon wiping the message off his screen, he tapped the intercom's stud and punched in Bryce's personal code "Bryce."

"Tallyho, Lenard," Hara said. "Tell the JumpShip skipper to lay in coordinates for Shasta zenith, by way of Escobas nadir."

Bryce's tone was almost exuberant. "At once, Captain," he said, and closed the link.

Hara sat back in his chair and steepled his fingers. His eyes never left the now-blank monitor before him, even when the klaxons for jump stations sounded mere minutes later.

The hunt is on...

CHAPTER 3

Dearest Tyler,

I almost forgot how much easier exploring dead worlds could be compared to live ones.

Our entire journey to Shasta was spent in arguments, mostly between us and the Shastan authorities over the extent of our access to the Mesozonia. They may have bought the cover story T and M worked up (when those two weren't fighting), but they insisted on a local guide.

I'm not sure if I'd have been more or less suspicious if they hadn't, to tell the truth. Holyfield's work wasn't too long ago, meaning anyone who'd be out to silence her would likely be on guard for any follow-ups like us. Marie worked up our own excuse for being here, of course: an exobiology expedition, examining the hazards facing rare Terran-exported species. (She somehow found an obscure, recently noted decline in an introduced rat population that's endangering a special form of Amazonian rainforest tree the Shastans have cultivated here, and thinks the culprits may be a certain scavenger species newly introduced, like our furry firecat friends. So, our goal is to act like we're examining the ecological imbalance without any ideas as to the culprit. Clever, but maybe too abstract to convince the paranoids.)

Anyway, we have a guide assigned to us, Esok. He seems knowledgeable and provincial, and he's even helped us out of a few uncomfortable (and embarrassing) jams since we've been here over the past week. But, I don't know. Could be I'm the one being too paranoid...

At any rate, the real problem isn't the guide these days, but Marie. It seemed like such a good idea to have her along, but now I just can't be sure. Since coming into the field, she's become like a temperamental Eichhörnchen — moody one day, excited the next, and downright pissy the day after that. I hate to admit it, but maybe Trouble was right (Please don't tell him I said that!).

Love!

—BROOKE

**NORTH MESOZONIA RAIN FOREST
SHASTA
FREE WORLDS LEAGUE
14 SEPTEMBER 3067**

Brooke could tell just by glancing at Marissa it was going to be one of those days again. Her lips were drawn into a tight, thin line, neither smiling nor frowning. Her eyes had a predatory look lasing straight through her glasses, and her hair had been tied into a tight bun, pinned beneath a dusty green, wide-brimmed bush hat.

After more than a week in the rain forest, battling all manner of insects, setting and resetting sensor probes, flinching at every unfamiliar noise, and facing at least one close encounter with some six-armed thing Esok had called a "skatha ape," Marissa was in her ever-more-popular "let's just get this damned mission over with" mode again. Seated behind Esok, she turned away from her brooding stare out the clouded windows of the Ibex RV and caught Brooke's gaze for a moment. She flashed a weak smile as the Ibex lurched again before resuming her angry staring contest with the greenery beyond.

She almost looks like I feel, Brooke told herself, trying to ignore the irritating throbbing that had plagued her legs for the last few days.

Brooke turned a little farther in her harness and nodded slightly to Lawrence, who met her eyes with a smile and a subtle shrug. He also knew the signs of Marissa's foul moods by now—and had long since become accustomed to reading Brooke's own discomfort.

Settling back in her seat, Brooke adjusted the brim of her simple cap and drew in another long, deep breath of damp forest air, catching only the faintest whiff of gasoline from the modified RV's grumbling engine. The 2-ton, muddy-tan Ibex lurched violently as it drove on through the dense forest, shocking her spine with every bump and adding to the irritation she tried so hard to bottle up. Anything resembling a beaten path had vanished days ago. But the Shastans prided themselves on accurate maps of the "unmarked trails," one of which the dark-haired, dark-skinned Esok claimed this was. A clearing, he said, lay just ahead…somewhere.

Thank Bast for small favors!

"You should find many more samples here, Dr. Stevens," he promised once more, breaking the silence. His Shastan accent had a distinctly Asian style to it, and reminded Brooke of something she'd expect to hear a Kurita character say on some holovid picture.

"Yes, you mentioned that," she replied, fighting back a sarcastic snap. The man could still be someone's plant, and giving in to her own annoyance could only put him more on edge if he was waiting for a sign to do something rash.

"According to the map," she added, "this was one of the original groves, wasn't it?"

"Certainly was," Esok said proudly. "The first settlers dreamed of recreating the Amazon in this unspoiled wilderness. They succeeded beyond their wildest expectations with these woods."

Without any real warning, the thick walls of green and blue-green leaves parted ahead of the Ibex's blocky snout. As another pass of the vehicle's wiper blades cleared off the misty fog on the windshield, an irregular clearing of thick grass and patches of dark brown earth sprang into being before Brooke's eyes.

Esok practically slammed the brakes, bringing the RV to a sudden halt that rattled both the delicate equipment racks and the rest of Brooke's team.

"Here we are," Esok almost sang. "Your 'Point Charlie,' I believe."

And not a moment too soon!

With a more genuine smile, Brooke half turned to the others while her fingers worked to release her four-point harness. Marissa was already out of hers, brushing off the straps and scowling slightly. The younger woman had one hand on her door handle, ready to leap out, and another on the holster of her Nashan Subjugator tranquilizer pistol, as if she half expected to drop into battle.

"All right, kids," Brooke called out. "We'll be camping here tonight, and there's maybe six good hours of daylight left, give or take the next bout of heavy rain. So the sooner we make ourselves at home, the sooner we can start setting up the pods. Lawrence, want to give me a hand with the tent?"

Hearing the veteran spacer's grumbled "yes," Brooke caught Marissa's eyes. The scowl on her face had softened; for the last two days, Brooke had put her to work on pitching the tents, a task she clearly hated.

"Sensor perimeter," Brooke told her. "Esok's going to stand guard."

Marissa nodded silently and hopped out. As the others also climbed out, Brooke closed her eyes and steeled herself. Moving her body—let alone jumping out of a vehicle—had lately become a major chore. Her legs and feet felt like they weighed a half ton each, and had lately started to ache far more than usual. Of course, the normal pains were something she'd naturally grown used to decades ago, but something about the rainforest was really starting to enhance the effect.

That, she told herself, *or it's just the company.*

As soon as her hiking boots hit the soft, green earth, she reached for the communicator hooked to her upper-left cargo-vest pocket. Tied into the antenna she'd mounted on the Ibex, the signal was just strong enough to tap into the local satellite nets and reach Tibor and their DropShuttle.

"*Guten Tag*, Chief!" his voice crackled. "How's it going?"

Brooke closed her eyes and again took in the musty odor of wet soil and alien vegetation. The aromas felt somehow soothing but also chilling—despite the sweat-inducing 28 Celsius (and 80 percent humidity) the locals called the "Mesozonian winter." Opening her eyes again, she scanned the small clearing and made sure everyone was busy and out of earshot, pulling equipment from the RV's rear hatch.

"We're at Point Charlie now, Trouble," she reported, then grumbled. "How're things over there?"

"Well," Tibor said, "this may darken your mood some more, but I've been watching the Able and Baker Point sweeps for the last two days, and I have to say, I'm not getting anything beyond the indigenous species. The rat populations seem lower than expected, but not extinct."

"Damn."

"Yup, and no direct sign of our feline friends either. Just the local bugs, bees, rats, and skathas."

Brooke sighed, feeling the surge of unfocused anger again, but pushed it aside. After six days and a mere fifty-seven kilometers from civilization, could she really expect an easy hunt?

"Still wouldn't hurt to at least have a *clue* we're on the right track," she mumbled.

"Say again?" Tibor's voice came back.

"Nothing, Trouble," Brooke told him. "Just grousing is all."

"Marie giving grief again?"

Brooke narrowed her eyes. "I take it Lawrence is still feeding you the inside scoop?"

Tibor chuckled slightly. "He fills me in on whatever the cameras miss," he admitted. "Can't say I didn't try to talk you out of it."

Had to get your digs in again, didn't you?

"Very funny, Trouble," Brooke said flatly. "Listen, we're about to set up camp now, and then we'll start deploying sensors in the area. I'll check in at the usual intervals. Okay?"

"As you say, boss," Tibor came back, serious once more. "Just watch yourselves out there."

"Always do," Brooke said and closed the connection.

Taking another deep breath of heavy, earthy rainforest air, she surveyed her surroundings again. Not really so much a clearing as a patch of lower vegetation compared to the towering rainforest around it, the area was perhaps no more than forty meters across at its widest, and covered in long wild grasses. Blue-green shrubs and several large rocks spattered with a brackish moss broke through the surface in several locations, each one a hiding space for who knew how many insects and small animals. Esok had managed to tear up some of the looser earth with his braking, and—Brooke noticed on closer inspection—had narrowly missed crushing the rotting, slim corpse of a long-dead tree.

Had this been a vacation and not a mission site, Brooke wondered how much she would be able to enjoy the view rather than be wary of it.

She could see Marissa stalking the rim of the pseudo-clearing, driving sensor stakes into the ground while Esok, hefting some locally produced hunting rifle, stood behind her, eyes probing the wilderness. Brooke studied the guide once more, focusing on his body language and—again—finding nothing amiss. Even with his weapon at the ready and his three charges too obviously busy to notice his action, he remained on guard against the natural dangers of the forest, not preparing an attack of his own.

"Doesn't prove anything," Brooke whispered to herself. "Stay on your guard, girl."

Just behind the Ibex, Lawrence had pulled out two of the sleeping tents and started to erect the first on the closest patch of relatively level ground he could find. Swatting away a close-buzzing insect, Brooke headed over to him on legs that already felt heavier than lead.

Lawrence looked up, gracing Brooke with another good look at his face full of days-old gray stubble. The tips of his hair, now exposed to the forest's heat and a few minutes of labor, were already plastered to his forehead. Still, he smiled warmly.

"Hope Trouble's enjoying *his* vacation," he joked.

"Having such a great time, he wishes he were here," Brooke answered. "Once we get these set up, I think we'll break into pairs. Each of us will take a pack and start laying the sensors in opposite directions."

Lawrence nodded as he turned to stake another corner of the field tent into place. His breathing was slightly more labored than Brooke liked, but she also knew he was still having trouble with Shasta's 0.96 gees. For spacers his age, Brooke suspected getting one's "land legs" back could take almost a month—often just in time to go back to the relative comfort of microgravity.

"Fair enough," he said. "We should pack ponchos, too; feels like rain."

Brooke shook her head as she started to stake the second tent beside the first one. "Damn," she muttered. "I knew I forgot to ask Trouble something."

Lawrence sighed as he locked his tent's uprights into place with a loud *click*. The sheet of slate gray waterproof polymer, along with the support, already glistened with the ambient moisture and random drops of rainwater that fell from the leaf canopy above. After six days in the field, none of them even noticed the constant dripping that made everything not covered in plastic sopping wet by the end of the day.

"So, who're the pairs?" he asked. "Or do I even need to guess?"

Brooke smiled. "You know me too well, old man," she said. "I'm giving you Marissa. I want to keep an eye on our guide a bit more."

Lawrence's ice-blue eyes flicked over to where Marissa and Esok were now talking over another sensor stake. Almost thirty meters away, and half hidden by the Ibex, they both knew there was no way the two could hear them. Lawrence still lowered his voice and spoke bluntly. "If he were going to try something, hon, I imagine he'd already have done it. We're over fifty kilometers from nowhere as it is."

"I know," Brooke said with a wink. "But a little paranoia never hurt anyone. We are, after all, ethnic Lyrans in Free Worlds space."

Lawrence's grin returned. "Touché!"

Brooke's legs burned and her mouth watered with the memory of her last cup of coffee. Her skin crawled with the feeling of her own sweat and the rain that had picked up in the last fifteen minutes and found its way through the gaps in her light green poncho. Traversing the broken, uneven rain-forest terrain—in almost twilight-level darkness thanks to the forest canopy and the rain clouds beyond it—while hefting a bulky pack of five sensor shafts made the journey that much more miserable.

But what concerned her most was she felt like she were being watched—and this time not by Esok. In fact, he was sloughing through the forest ahead of her, rifle at the ready as ever. They had encountered no creatures of any kind since leaving the campsite, which Brooke found a welcome surprise, considering the abundance of snakes, rats, and the occasional skatha they had run across at the other sites. But the initial relief soon faded as she started to wonder *why*.

It also occurred to her that Esok's tour-guide banter had tapered off during the last few minutes. When they first set out, he had begun a proud tale about Shasta's first colonists—mainly peoples from Terra's Argentina and Colombia regions—and their efforts to recreate the lost glories of the Amazon region here. Brooke was only half listening then, giving noncommittal or bland replies as Esok went into how, if one looked *really* close, one could almost see the orderly rows to these trees here, a hallmark of their origins as an artificial grove and natural preserve.

But now he was silent, and his eyes were sweeping the woods as he went onward. His pace had also slowed. Instinctively, Brooke tucked one hand under her poncho and released the holster catch of the Sternsnacht Python at her right hip.

"Something wrong?" she finally dared to ask, keeping her voice low.

"Oh," Esok said with a slight start, his tone still light. "Maybe nothing, Doctor. The forest just feels unusual here."

"'Feels' unusual?"

Esok stopped finally and glanced back at her, but kept his rifle pointed away. Then, suddenly, he started sniffing the air.

Brooke did so too, and immediately picked up a stench she was surprised she had not noticed before.

The smell of something dead, something close.

Her eyes darted around as she sniffed the air again, her tongue curling in her mouth as she fought back the nausea. Whatever it was, it was *very* close.

Then she saw it, just as Esok took a few steps toward a clump of rocks. The carcass lay in the opposite direction, and a swarm of red flies scattered as Brooke drew near it. Struggling against her urge to gag, Brooke removed her backpack and knelt.

Whatever the creature was, it didn't look like the agouti rats Marissa had been telling her about. In fact, with its six bony arms partially covered in gray-brown fur, it looked to Brooke like a juvenile skatha ape. Only its head had been ripped off, and what remained of its torso cavity had been obviously scorched by something, with fur and flesh burned almost to blackness.

So close to the carcass, amid the smell of rotting flesh and something else strange and chemical, Brooke struggled against her gag reflex and coughed once.

"You see something?" Esok asked.

Turning slightly away, Brooke nodded and coughed again.

And that was when she saw the claw, lodged in a hunk of fallen bark. It was curled sharply and blood red; she knew it didn't come from the skatha. She picked it up as Esok cautiously drew near. His sharp, hazel eyes kept probing the trees around them, but finally settled on Brooke when she rose.

"Wha—?"

"Skatha, I think," she explained. "Any idea what kind of claw this is?"

Esok stared blankly at the red hook, and finally shook his head. "Maybe a lute shrike," he guessed, naming what Brooke presumed was a local avian, "but they never venture this deep into the forest, and their claws are never quite so red."

He glanced around again, and this time Brooke's gaze also swept the area. *Something* was making the man nervous, and she suspected it was close by. Her right hand once again disappeared beneath her poncho to hover near the Python.

"What about acid?" she asked, her voice low.

Esok turned a questioning look to her.

"The creature looks like it's been burned by some kind of acid," she told him. "Does anything in this forest secrete an acid?"

"Acid?" he sputtered, his rich voice suddenly unsure. He looked over the remains with a slight choking sound. "N-no," he said. "Nothing here. Nothing that burns like that."

Keeping one hand close to her Python, Brooke pocketed the claw and reached for her communicator with the other. A single click put her through to Tibor. "We may have something here."

"And hello to you too, Sunshine," Tibor said. "What've you got?"

"Looks like a baby skatha, dead. Judging by the remains, something with red claws and an acidic venom or spit did the poor thing in."

"You're kidding!"

"Nein," Brooke said. "Here, Esok. Can you get a sensor camera on it?"

Esok looked down sharply, and Brooke realized he'd been watching the surroundings again. Her own eyes darted about and saw nothing.

As Esok reached for the sensor pods tucked into his pack, a sound—something between a growl and a hiss—drew their attention to a dark cluster of trees ten meters away. In the dusk-like shadows, she thought she could make out a shape in motion, and from the corner of her eye she saw Esok sweep his rifle toward the shape.

He waited for a few moments, holding his breath as Brooke's hand tightened around the handle of her Python.

"Brooke?" Tibor's voice came through the communicator.

"Hang on, Troub—!"

The thunderous *crack* that followed startled Brooke so much she stumbled into the thick grass, landing less than a hand's breadth from the skatha carcass. She heard an answering report from Esok's rifle almost immediately, only to realize he held the weapon skyward. With a strangled cough, the guide fell to his knees, the life in his eyes already gone by the time his body hit the jungle floor.

"*Scheiße!*" Brooke yelled, finally drawing her pistol as another loud crack ripped through the trees and blasted apart the dead skatha. A splash of loose earth and rotting meat sprayed across her right side and sent her diving forward.

"*Brooke!*" Tibor shouted from the communicator still in her other hand.

"Call the others, Trouble!" she yelled back.

Even as she forced her legs beneath her, Brooke's eyes tried to track the source of the shots.

There!

She could barely make out the figure in the shadows of the forest, but the raindrops spattered around it suggested a figure draped in a full-body cloak. Brooke didn't need to see their eyes to know they were trained on her, along with whatever weapon that had just blasted a hole straight through Esok.

A flash of metal swung before the figure and she immediately ducked low, scrambling for the nearest outcropping of rocks at a half-crouching run. Her legs screamed in agony but carried her clear of the figure's next earsplitting shot, which punched a fist-sized hole in the earth and scattered grass and soil in all directions.

In her peripheral vision, she caught the slightest hint of an electric-blue muzzle flash and the silvery blur of the passing slug, even as she juked her way to a thick tree. The stones that had spared her life moments before shattered beneath the pulverizing impact of another shot.

It's some kind of Gauss rifle!

"Brooke!" Tibor was screaming again. "Talk to me!"

"I'm taking fire here, you *dummkopf*!" she snapped back. Her ears were ringing and her body ached all over. Another deafening *crack* punctuated her answer, and fragments of bark rained down on the brim of her cap.

Too close!

"Can you see who it is?" Tibor asked.

"A little busy here, Trouble!" she growled as she forced herself to run again. Wheeling around another tree, Brooke's boots slipped on the slick grass, and she nearly tumbled over an exposed root. Twisting back, she fired twice into the darkness. Shooting more by instinct and guesswork, she hardly expected a hit.

"We're coming, Brooke!" chimed in a new voice, female, and filled with worry.

Marie!

Marissa sounded breathless, her voice nearly lost to a low hum somewhere in the background. Brooke suppressed her annoyance that Tibor had somehow found time to turn her firefight into a conference call.

"*Scheiße!*" she snarled. "Whoever this is, they're wearing some kind of electronic camo—!"

Another slug pounded the earth nearby, moments after Brooke spun around to squeeze off another shot. Twisting around the other side of the tree, she fired again, and saw her amorphous attacker breaking for new cover. For just an instant, she caught the flash of a long-barreled rifle and a very distinct—but strangely disembodied—leg, clad in some kind of black armor.

"Where's Lawrence?" she barked.

"With me!" Marissa answered. *"Hang on!"*

With another heart-stopping *crack*, a slug ripped through Brooke's latest cover, but she was already on her feet again, half running and half ducking under a low-hanging branch.

Her legs burned, but she continued to plunge into the woods, leaping over thick jungle roots and darting between trees and rocks.

Keep moving, girl! she told herself. *Force them to chase. They can't shoot you if they're too busy running!*

"Brooke?" Tibor called out again.

"Still alive," she hissed through clenched teeth. "Esok's dead."

"I've got a fix on you." Tibor's voice grew calm and level. "Can't be sure on the thermals, but I think it's only one shooter."

"Great!" Brooke sneered as she hurled herself down an embankment. The now familiar crack of her pursuer's Gauss rifle heralded another shot that sheared vines off a nearby tree.

Turning sharply at the edge of another dip in the forest floor, Brooke allowed her boots to slip on the earth and she tumbled back, facing backward as she dropped a meter or two downward. Holding her pistol out, she fired twice more, aiming wildly.

In the confusion, she barely made out the sight of swirling semi-nothingness coming up over the rise, scarcely ten meters behind her, and caught a distinctive glint off the lenses of her attacker's goggles. The rifle poked out from their cloak, already drawing a steady bead on her, and only then did she notice the faint violet beam of a targeting laser.

Too close!

For a moment, she wanted to know who they were.

Instead, she squeezed her trigger.

The shooter shifted and their rifle swung wide, but whether it was because she'd hit them or because she'd *almost* hit them, Brooke couldn't be sure.

And then suddenly, her attacker was gone.

Cautiously, painfully, she pulled herself halfway back to her feet before Tibor's voice screamed, *"Look out!"*

Instinctively, Brooke dropped to the jungle floor, practically losing herself in the foliage, mere moments before the roar of a laboring engine echoed across the forest. She peeked up at the rise and saw her attacker turn and fire their weapon just as a massive blur of black and muddy tan streaked past, impossibly close to them.

With ears still ringing, Brooke scarcely heard the *thump* of metal on flesh, but her eyes were briefly glued to the sight of the airborne Ibex RV as it screamed off to one side, eventually bouncing down to the ground and crashing its way through several vines and no less than two young, white-barked trees.

"Christ!" she muttered, already looking for her attacker.

She saw the man much more easily now, since the impact had torn his cloak open. Dazed, he hobbled at the peak of the rise while struggling with his rifle. Definitely male, and definitely wounded, he sneered at her and raised his rifle with both hands. But instead of another loud *crack*, Brooke watched the weapon spit out a cloud of sparks.

She didn't give him the chance to try again. Without standing up, she fired her Python three times. The first slug caught the man high in the shoulder, spraying blood and twisting his body to one side. The second pounded his armored vest, nearly toppling him.

The third drove through his right goggle lens and sent a cloud of blood, bone, and bits of brain scattering behind him.

As the man's body pitched forward, Brooke's own body suddenly gave out. "No!" she told herself. *There may be more of them...* "Tibor..."

"I'm still here," her communicator answered.

"He's down." Brooke sighed. "Are you *sure* he was the only one?"

"No," Tibor admitted.

"Damn it!" Brooke mumbled. "Marie? Lawrence?"

No one answered.

"Scheiße."

Forcing herself up again, she worked her way to the Ibex. The vehicle had slammed to a halt against the fallen remains of what might once have been an impressive sample of Shastan hardwood. Steam and faint wisps of smoke rose from the wreckage, but none of that alarmed Brooke as much as seeing Lawrence slumped over the wheel through the half-open driver's side door.

"Lawrence!" she shouted.

The gray-haired man didn't move, but in a few steps, Brooke was on him, her fingers looking for—and finding—a pulse. The gash on his head didn't look life-threatening, and she could see no other open injuries from where she stood.

Then she saw, amid the cracks of the shattered windshield, a frighteningly distinct hole. Blasted through the passenger side...

And Marissa's body, twisted impossibly beside Lawrence.

"*No...*" Brooke whimpered, feeling her own strength fail all at once.

She struggled to force Lawrence back into his seat and reached across him, gave up and scrambled to the vehicle's passenger side. Her hand reached out and found Marissa limp, unresponsive. The woman's eyes faced Brooke, wide open but unblinking, and a trickle of blood ran from one corner of her gaping mouth. Blood stained the front of Marissa's khaki shirt so darkly Brooke couldn't see the wound itself.

Almost reluctantly, she reached higher, searching for Marissa's carotid, holding her breath, praying for a sign...

But finding no pulse. "*No...*"

"Brooke?" Tibor called out again.

"Oh no, oh no, oh no," she chanted. "Trouble, it's Marie…"

"Dear God…"

Then came the sound again, the low mix between a growl and a hiss—coming from right behind her. Despite the pain, exhaustion, and shock, Brooke heard it.

With a final surge of adrenaline and rage, she spun toward the sound, lifted her Python, and fired.

"Brooke!" Tibor shouted, but his call didn't really register.

Instead, she stared dumbly at the creature before her. It was a beautiful animal, graceful in form, surprisingly small. Its coat was scarlet. Its head bore distinctly feline features. Its golden eyes seemed to glow, even in the darkening shadows of the rain forest…

Even as its very life drained away…

With a final, strained death-howl, the Jardinian firecat—a newcomer to these strange lands—collapsed in a heap of alien flesh before Brooke's eyes.

CHAPTER 4

I still can't believe Marie's gone. I just can't.

I've seen my share of dangers in this job. Hell, I've never seen an IE contract without a hazard clause for things like this. I knew—we all knew—there was a particular danger in this one, but I always presumed we could handle it. I always presumed they'd come after me, or maybe T. Why did Marie have to get back in that damned truck? Why?

And damn it, it had to be then that we finally found the malfing firecats, too! Someone had tried to kill us all, killed Marie and Esok, and we suddenly found the stupid beasts causing all this trouble!

We tracked those twice-damned animals for weeks after that, and I felt about half a meter tall through the whole thing. Marie should've been there. I would've given up and told Croft to shove his entire mission, but I just couldn't. Not after the cost. I couldn't even bring myself to tell Tyler right away. How could I?

And it all led back to an IE ship! A stupid, Bast-damned IE DropShip carried those beasties to Shasta before something brought it down. Somehow, enough cats survived and escaped to breed in the rainforest, where they've been wiping out anything small enough for them to kill.

Lawrence and I found the DropShip's recorders, but they're maybe five years old; Trouble doesn't even think he can decipher them now, but at least we're done with Shasta.

Damn it all! Why did I have to be so angry with her that day?

—FROM THE JOURNALS OF BROOKLYN STEVENS

K-1 DROPSHUTTLE *COLUMBUS*
ZENITH JUMP POINT APPROACH VECTOR
SHASTA
FREE WORLDS LEAGUE
13 OCTOBER 3067

Brooke stared at the readouts before her without truly seeing them. Her fingers had paged back and forth through the information—what little Tibor had scrounged from the flight logs—perhaps a hundred times already, and even now she couldn't recall any of it. The numbers, words, and images all looked like a blur.

It took Tibor four attempts to break through the haze.

His jade and emerald eyes were suddenly before her again, and she realized he'd been standing over her for a while. His hand was on her shoulder, but only now was she aware of it.

I'm a mess!

Seeing recognition in her eyes at last, Tibor let out a heavy sigh and finally sat down in the tiny booth doubling as the DropShuttle *Columbus*'s breakfast table and a midday workstation.

Her mind still hazy, Brooke wondered how many days she'd spent at the table, staring blankly at the computer screens, mechanically writing notes in her journal, or just plain brooding.

"You can't let it eat you up like this," Tibor said, softly. "You *know* that!"

I was supposed to take care of her! she wanted to scream, but couldn't find the strength. How long had it been since she'd eaten? Her stomach growled, and her mouth felt pasty.

"Are you even hearing me?" he asked.

She shook her head.

Tibor's voice grew stern. "Brooke—"

"Damn it, Trouble!" she exploded, fighting back the welling tears. "I *know*, damn it!"

All at once, it felt as though she had snapped back into the present. She could now smell the artificially purified air circulating through the ship, feel and hear the ambient rumble of the main drive engines. Before her, still clutched in her hand, was a compad Tibor had handed her probably over an hour ago, before her latest bout of remorse. The screen displayed fragments of an itinerary, visuals of a planet that, from space, looked like just about anywhere, coordinate values that made no rational sense. A flight log corrupted by five years of neglect and exposure to the elements, recovered from a downed ship with an Interstellar Expeditions registry.

For this, she reminded herself, *we left Marie buried on an alien world...*

"Well?" Tibor asked.

"What do you want me to say?" she challenged him. "She was closer to me—closer to *us*—than anyone we ever lost on a mission! And *you* told me not to bring her along, but I didn't list—"

Tibor took one of her hands in his. "No," he said. "You were right. Marie belonged in the field on this one. She knew what to look for. I wouldn't have done any better."

Brooke pulled her hand back and dropped the compad. It hit the polished steel table with a clatter. She fell back in the seat, arms folding across her chest, and avoided Tibor's gaze. The rational part of her knew the proper thing to do would be to stiffen up and get back to the business of command.

She shook her head again. "Maybe," she admitted. "Maybe..."

"If we're going to finish this mission, we need you back in the here and now. Lawrence and I are getting worried."

"I *know* already! But, damn it, how professional do you want me to be here?"

"Well, for starters, you can tell us what we're going to do next."

Brooke sighed. Her eyes dropped back to the compad.

"You know," she said after a moment. "I have half a mind to take this data, go back to Croft, and tell him to screw this whole mission."

Tibor smirked. *"Ja,"* he said. "I thought you might."

"But you also know I can't do that."

"Honestly?" Tibor arched her eyebrows. "I wasn't sure this time."

Brooke shook her head and met his eyes once more.

"Close," she admitted. "Centimeters close, maybe. But no. We do have to go back to IE with this, though. The coordinates are in code, and I don't recognize the key. The flight data's all mucked up on top of it anyway, so even if we did decode the text, the only people who could make sense of the itinerary would be Croft's."

"Perhaps." Tibor nodded cautiously.

Brooke paused for a moment, catching something in his tone suggesting more than a lackluster agreement. All of a sudden, the fog in her mind lifted. *Of course!*

"You're thinking Croft knew of this ship all along?" she asked. "And thus he also knows what her itinerary was?"

A thin smile crawled across Tibor's face. "Something like that."

"Well," she said, drawing out the word as she rolled the thought around. "That's possible. But as I think about it now, I think he *didn't* know. Suspected, maybe. He would've volunteered that kind of thing if he believed it completely. Then he could've simply turned this mission into a recovery op..."

The realization dawned on her like a flash of lightning. She blinked, and felt as though she had finally awoken from a long, deep sleep. *"No,"* she exclaimed. "He wouldn't have even *needed* us if he knew all that..."

Tibor's eyes narrowed.

"I think he wants *us* to find Jardine first, Trouble. This DropShip—the *Clarke*—went missing before she could report which leg of the journey she was on. You know some of the company's captains are sloppy record-keepers. Hell, maybe the *Clarke*'s captain was even the greedy sort, withholding reports in exchange for a higher finder's fee."

"IE internal politics at its most cutthroat," Tibor agreed dryly. "That's certainly possible. Plus, ships go missing during ops all the time, and so many are looking for places like Jardine. The Green Ghosts, maybe?"

The image of the camouflaged man floated before Brooke's eyes for a moment, and she shuddered. His body had had no identification on it. Even his exotic Gauss rifle and the electronic camouflage failed to yield any clues, as if the gear had been custom-made for its user. The Green Ghosts had been known to sport both Clan and Star League technologies in the past. Then again, so could ComStar and just about any Great House.

"Maybe," she mumbled. "Either way, IE lost the *Clarke* and wasn't sure where she went. Or, maybe, the ship *did* report in, and they knew she'd been shot down—"

"Or," Tibor jumped in, "maybe she was too busy running from whoever wanted to keep the secret to radio in."

"Right," Brooke said with a nod. "Whichever way it went down, it means in order to find Jardine, they needed to find the ship, but they still want someone to carry forward, find the planet, confirm it, get back out alive, and report it."

Tibor nodded. "And for that, they'd rather send in a scout who's *not* directly attached to the company, since the mission's now a proven risk. So, we're bait?"

"Of a sort," Brooke replied thoughtfully. "But we suspected as much going in. What this means is we're half done with the mission, though. We found the missing link, and with IE's records, we *should* be able to find a list of possible destinations. I would presume the *Clarke*'s JumpShip also got wasted. But in deep space, debris would've scattered everywhere before anyone picked it up, so by then, finding a flight recorder would be like finding a needle in a planet-sized haystack."

Tibor's smile broadened. "So we cross-reference any JumpShip losses that coincide with DropShip losses—"

"Particularly around the time this little gem went missing," Brooke finished, while waving the compad. "We have a vessel name, a general location, and an estimated time of disappearance. IE should be able to give us a flight plan to work from, and I'd wager we're within thirty light years of the target. More than one jump away, and there's just no excuse beyond bald-faced stupidity why an IE explorer wouldn't check in with something."

"Well, unless they simply didn't trust the local commonets," Tibor said.

Brooke sagged. "I suppose that works, too, but it widens the search area considerably."

"True," Tibor sighed. "It's about a few hundred stars to choose from, but at least it's a start if we look into anything within the one-jump radius of here. I'm sure we can narrow it down with what we know of Jardine's spectral data in the archives. But an itinerary would let us make a chain of such areas to look into, if the captain followed it right..."

With a grunt, Tibor paused, closing his artificial emerald eye for a moment. "You sure Croft won't cut us loose after we ID the ship, if he has her itinerary already?"

"If he does, we can sue him for breach of contract," Brooke said blandly, "but I don't think he will. He wants *us* to go there and come back. He wants *us* to confirm Jardine before he takes credit for its discovery. And he wants *us* to trip any traps along the way so his people can go in safe."

"The crafty old *Arsch*!" Tibor muttered. "So, then, back to the original question: What are we doing now?"

Brooke pondered again. "We can't HPG a message from here," she said finally. "Too dangerous. We could black box it, maybe, but I'd hate to reveal to IE that we still have another of their most expensive toys..."

"Good call, assuming they don't already know."

Brooke frowned at the thought. IE's possession of black boxes was one of the scattered organization's greatest secrets—one she would bet the *Sacajawea* on that the Steiner and Davion families (at least) would be deadly interested in investigating. Black boxes were an ancient alternative to hyperpulse generators, and IE had used the few dozen or so they had uncovered over the years to build their own off-grid communications network, paranoid over possible ComStar eavesdropping.

And two such boxes had just happened to go missing from IE's inventory about the same time a certain Dr. Brooklyn Stevens and the crew of the JumpShip *Sacajawea* left the company.

"Either way," she said, "we should get clear of the area. Maybe make for Alliance space again. Whoever sent that man back there, they should lose our scent for a while after a few jumps, and we can get a broadcast out or something, arrange a meeting but leave out the particulars."

Tibor nodded. "Sounds like a plan."

Brooke frowned again. Already her mind was drifting, and she could feel the tears welling up. *Why...?*

Tibor's hand was on hers. "Hey..."

"Why...?" she whispered. "Why did I have to be so angry with her that day?"

"You can't live every minute like it's going to be your last," Tibor said. "If you did, you'd never leave the ship."

"Maybe." Brooke sniffed. "But that's a damned poor excuse when the moment comes."

"Anything we say at times like this is just going to sound like a platitude, hon. But you have to know, at the end of the day, that we all took risks coming out here. We knew someone was out to keep this secret."

"Yeah, but if I'd been with Marie instead of Lawrence—"

"Then in all probability, Lawrence would be dead instead of Marie?" Tibor guessed, making Brooke wince inwardly. "Or maybe that guy down there was stalking *you* and not the guide, so it *still* would've been Marie. You and I both know it won't do any good to second-guess."

Brooke sighed, the tears once more under control. "Can't help it," she mumbled. "I just—"

A metallic tap on the bulkhead doorway distracted them both. Looking up, she saw Lawrence standing tactfully silent across the room. Although he wore a sheepish expression, his ice-blue eyes were intense.

"We have company at the jump point," he said simply. "And they want to speak with you."

"*Dr.* Stevens," said the leathery face on the monitor, stressing Brooke's title in a way that made Tibor's eyes roll, "I understand your surprise. My own crew was on assignment several jumps away when IE called us to come here. Henry Croft signed the orders personally, and the contract clearly defines our role in this mission as providing military escort for your investigation, with an emphasis on acting as your security advisor. As such, I would strongly advise your team to pay heed to my experience in such matters..."

"Galatean diplomacy at its finest," Lawrence grumbled.

Tibor chuckled as Brooke sighed irritably. With the annoying four-minute "light lag" between sending and receiving messages, and the arrogance obvious in this Captain Anton Hara's voice, her earlier malaise gave way to simmering anger.

Oblivious to her mood, Hara's malachite eyes stared directly into the monitor, as if trying to peer into Brooke's soul across time and space. His skin was darkly tanned—to the point of premature aging—and his short mop of hair was a sandy blond. Brooke imagined the man's homeworld was likely a colder planet than the one he grew up on.

He wore a flat gray jumpsuit with a black turtleneck undershirt—a fashion common among spacer crews. His voice was rich, with a trace of accent she couldn't quite place, and carried over with a confidence of someone not used to being questioned.

"IE considers this expedition dangerous in the extreme," he continued. "So, unless your team is packing a DropShip or two we're unaware of, it would be in our mutual best interests to work together as closely as possible from here on out, with an emphasis on the security needs of the present operations."

The image froze; after four exchanges so far, this time Hara wasn't even bothering with a proper sign-off.

Brooke sighed and propped a fist under her chin as she studied the monitor. "Who the hell does this guy think he's dealing with?"

In the pilot's seat beside Brooke, Tibor grunted, drumming slim fingers on the flight console, a bland smirk on his face. Behind them, occupying the third seat in the DropShuttle *Columbus*'s cramped cockpit, Lawrence kept himself busy with yet another verification that the life support systems were working normally.

"Well," Tibor said, turning his eyes out toward the canopy to take in the tiny points of light dead ahead that could as easily have been stars as ships, "from what we can tell, he came in with his own Jumper, a *Leopard*, and some fighters, right? So

I'm thinking he's thinking the merc with the bigger guns gets to make the rules."

"That guy's only got bigger guns in his mind," Lawrence scoffed.

Brooke allowed herself a smirk. In all likelihood, the enhanced armaments the *Sacajawea* and her shuttles possessed would surprise the likes of Anton Hara and his crew. Thanks to a legacy of years spent venturing into strange and occasionally hostile regions off the beaten path, both the *Sac* and her complement of small craft had undergone heavy modifications to improve their survivability over long-haul missions, often trading minor luxuries for armor and weapons. Together, the vessels boasted enough firepower to make any unsuspecting pirate band think twice before considering them easy prey. While that factor had saved Brooke and her crew on many occasions since they and IE parted ways, it was a surprise hidden from the casual observer.

But whether the extra weaponry would deter Hara didn't matter so much to Brooke as the fact that he seemed to be confusing his alleged role of "mission support" with "mission control."

"I've half a mind to tell this guy to chase a comet," she mumbled. "But that wasn't Galatean diplomacy, Lawrence. Galatean mercs like to yell and curse a lot more. That was almost scripted. Fifty kroner says he's got an IE liaison whispering in his ear."

"Oh, there's a pleasant thought," Lawrence said.

"Maybe," Tibor replied. "But if so, it means we may want to compromise a little bit."

Brooke arched an eyebrow at him.

"Consider this: We were just discussing going back to Croft anyway to see if IE had records on the *Clarke*'s itinerary. Now here's this guy with an IE contract, signed by Croft, and a liaison watching over his shoulder?"

"You're not saying I should let these hired guns claim command rights in exchange for the data, are you?"

"Oh, hell no!" Tibor exclaimed, giving her his most indignant scowl. "Actually, I think Croft's plans—whatever they are—call for lending us these guys as more than just military support."

"So the mercs aren't here to escort us, they *are* the liaison, eh?" Lawrence asked.

"That sounds possible," Brooke said, mulling over the idea. "But IE has played this one close to the vest from the moment they hired us. Hara and his boys may not even know all the details, or they're simply being misled into thinking they have some authority here. Neither of which is conducive to their actually getting it."

"Yeah," Lawrence grunted. "Could also be the liaison's hoping to weasel what we know and—if it's enough—send Hara and his warriors off to secure the objective or maybe even bump us off."

Brooke shook her head. "That's not really Croft's style, but I won't exclude the possibility, either. It *does* bring us back to square one here. Bottom line, I think we're all agreed we can't just trust these guys to take control, but keeping them around may help us get some missing pieces to the puzzle."

"Then I suppose we got us some new partners, *ja*?"

Brooke nodded. "The trick is getting them to do what we want in such a way as to make them think it's what *they* want."

"Well, my dear," Tibor said with a grin, "I imagine that's *your* department."

Brooke sneered at him and shook her head again as she readied herself for another transmission. "The things I do for this team," she grumbled.

CHAPTER 5

I won't dare put this in a letter to Tyler. Not yet. All I can do for now is build up the list of offenses I'll need to apologize for. Between losing Marie and spending the next few weeks traipsing around that jungle while short a guide and a good friend, it's been a living hell. Adding insult to injury is the pressing need to keep the use of the black box to a bare minimum, and that means the letters home have to be the short and sweet, "wish you were here" types.

This Hara guy, though. Haven't seen quite this bad a case of testosterone overload in a while. The merc and his cronies actually thought they would be able to order us about for IE's pleasure, but a short chat with his liaison (a gray-suited snake named Nathan Bellamy), and we managed to set the record straight. We even scored the Clarke's "formal" travel itinerary, hopefully enabling us to retrace her steps (based on the obtuse assumption she actually went where her captain claimed she was going).

It's taken Bellamy a few days to gather the info (or at least a few days to decide to hand it over), but I'm certain that between his records and the collection of ancient maps we have here, we can narrow down the options immensely. Trouble's already on the case.

That is, as long as the Clarke really did visit Jardine just before she got shot down over Shasta...

—From the journals of Brooklyn Stevens

EXPLORER-CLASS JUMPSHIP SACAJAWEA
ZENITH JUMP POINT
SHASTA
FREE WORLDS LEAGUE
16 OCTOBER 3067

In the heyday of the Star League, the *Explorer*-class JumpShip was a favorite for the wealthy elite, interplanetary corporate officers, and—as the name implied—deep-space exploration crews. The dedicated exploration craft thus often boasted science bays, an observatory complete with high-powered radio telescopes, and (for a crowning achievement) a holographic "planetarium" chamber, in which the sensor feeds and computerized maps of the heavens could be studied with almost godlike scrutiny.

The *Sacajawea* was *not* such an *Explorer*, however.

Instead of the radio-scopes and the first-person feel of an oversized walk-in holotank, the *Sac* reserved a single conference room for a bank of computers, a wall-length projection screen, and a dozen chairs. Paneled shelves lined one wall, containing racks of files—both hardcopy and electronic—behind meshed glass doors. These facilities were decidedly low-tech compared to the JumpShip's Golden Age contemporaries, but to Brooke and her crew, they were more than enough to get the job done.

Even so, Brooke idly wondered how much more efficient the dedicated *Explorer*'s facilities might have been in her circumstances as she leaned back in one of the room's black synthleather chairs and sipped at the bag of bitter, lukewarm coffee in her hand. Standing before the main screen, one hand still resting near the keyboard beside him, Tibor glanced back at the sound of her loud slurp. A look of vague disgust crossed his face.

Brooke shrugged; foil-bagged coffee *was* an acquired taste.

Tibor looked back at the abstracted star map projected on the wall. The slate-black field was filled with stars glowing with colors assigned by their affiliation: purple stars represented the Free Worlds League (including Shasta, which currently pulsed for easy identification), while the blue stars along the upper edge of the field were worlds of the nearby Lyran Alliance. The white stars—which covered far more of space than most people ever gave credit for—represented the dead or uninhabited star systems charted in between. Zoomed in for greater clarity, the map represented only a small slice of the Inner Sphere, along the Alliance-League border. A hazy red circle enveloped a region of stars centered on Shasta itself, while a string of straight green lines traced the intended path of the ill-fated *Clarke* expedition.

The line made only one stop in the red circle, one turn before coming to Shasta. And that point glowed white on the map.

"So," he said with a sigh. "That's it."

Lawrence, taking up the chair beside Brooke, matched Tibor's scowl. "*If* our theories are correct, that is," he said.

Tibor shook his head and ran a hand through his dark, oily hair. "Come on, Lawrence; they're reasonable enough. One jump. Any more than that, and the *Clarke*'s captain or at least his JumpShip would've had enough time to check in or submit a report. But Bellamy confirmed it: the ship vanished without checking in. Now we know where."

"And we presume Jardine thus lies within a jump from here," Lawrence added. "But that presupposes the captain of the *Clarke* and her JumpShip didn't traverse a number of dead or uninhabited systems before returning to civilized space. It's not uncommon."

Brooke grimaced as she sipped the last of her coffee. The bag collapsed in her hand with a loud crinkle, and she crushed the remainder, feeling the sharp foil edges yielding to her grip. Over the last few days, she had reconsidered the theories herself. Since the collapse of the original Star League, as technology declined, it became increasingly unheard-of for JumpShip captains to risk travel to any of the thousands of stars between the named, inhabited dots on the map. Every leap through hyperspace, after all, carried the risk of catastrophic drive failure. And with fewer shipyards left in the Inner Sphere, very few JumpShip captains (or their crews and passengers) relished the idea of such a catastrophe leaving them stranded a few dozen light-years away from any possible aid or breathable atmosphere.

But Interstellar Expeditions and other *lostech* prospectors had made a practice of tempting the void for centuries. After all, the dead systems between the dots was where they made their living. These worlds would be isolated from the HPG network, completely incommunicado, and many could be inhabitable if one knew which planets had been settled before the Star League fell. With that realization came the nagging doubt that the captain of the *Clarke*, pursued by forces unknown, could have broken with his itinerary and stuck to dead systems for a few jumps before coming back to civilized lands.

"But you *know* the drill, Lawrence." Tibor sounded exasperated. "IE standard protocol—especially with chartered JumpShips, like the one Bellamy says the *Clarke* used—says every jump to a dead system has to be within reach of a live system or port of call..."

"And that they must alternate such points," Brooke said, finishing the paraphrasing of the "official" IE handbook, "but we both know not all ships do that, especially when traveling through particularly hostile space."

Tibor's expression collapsed even further. "Granted," he said, "but come on. If we're just going to throw out the data we have here, we'll never make progress with this."

Lawrence held up his hands. "I just want to make sure we all realize that we're working off guesswork here."

"As ever," Tibor grumbled. "But let's look a shade closer, shall we?"

Brooke caught the tone and leaned forward. "You found something else?"

Tibor touched the screen where the white dot flared amid the blackness of virtual space. The view magnified again, and shifted the dot aside to allow room for a stream of text.

"The stellar data," he said. "The Herakleion system. Star type G2V. Four rocky planetary bodies in the system—one in the Goldilocks zone—plus two asteroid belts and one gas giant. According to Free Worlds League historical archives, Herakleion was hit by an extremely virulent biowarfare agent sometime around 2815. The plague was so bad the captain-general placed the planet under a full quarantine and wrote off a population numbering somewhere between forty and fifty million Leaguers."

"Okay?" Lawrence prompted.

Tibor reached down and tapped a command into his computer. The partial map vanished from its half of the screen and resolved as a new series of stellar values, now placed side by side with Herakleion's.

"The archives on Jardine are a wreck," Tibor said. "The planet vanished so thoroughly—sometime during the First Succession War, according to every account—that what records survived tend to conflict in most cases...except what's projected here."

Brooke narrowed her eyes and studied the figures.

"G3V star," Lawrence read aloud. "Four rockies, one gas, two belts... Damn, that's close."

Tibor nodded. "Herakleion was a humble agro world according to League records. Minimal industry. Mostly strong enough for self-sufficiency and part of no major military, commercial, or political power blocs. Granted, in those days the nukes and bioweapons flew pretty liberally, so one never knows why half the worlds that got hit were hit. But add the fact that this one lay about two or three jumps into League space at the time, and it seems odd it got hit so badly.

"And Jardine was no major industrial power base either. In fact, their biggest—and only—noteworthy export was the tabiranth, a domestic riding mount favored by the wealthy, but used locally to tend to ranches and such."

"I think you made your point," Brooke said. "So are we saying that, besides the different stellar classifications, Herakleion and Jardine are basically twins? Some kind of clerical error, maybe?"

Tibor folded his arms and leaned back against the bulkhead. "Maybe," he said. "But there *is* a hitch here that bugs me."

"The fact that Jardine shows up on *none* of the maps we have in storage?" Lawrence asked, gesturing toward the shelves.

"Exactly. I pulled them down myself as soon as I saw these comparisons, and in the ComStar maps printed as far back as 2788, there is no mention of Jardine at all. Even the Dobless maps dating back to the Star League show no sign of Jardine. It's like all the legends say: the planet seemingly never existed, yet everyone seems to remember that it once did, and it died in the Succession Wars. A common theory is it was one of those 'local name' things, where the inhabitants use another name than what gets printed on maps. But of course nobody's ever been sure. And then there are the emphatic reports that say Jardine was nuked into oblivion, not plagued. The net result is we get two similar-sounding worlds and systems, but with just enough discrepancies to make one doubt they're really the same."

"What about the system configurations?" Lawrence asked.

"Not quite the same either," Tibor said. "Herakleion's data says the gas giant is in the fourth solar position, while Jardine's puts a rocky planet there. I looked down to the moons level, even. Jardine is supposedly moonless. Herakleion had two moons."

Brooke tapped her fingers on the table. "So you're saying Herakleion—and not Jardine—may be the last world the *Clarke* came from. Does any other point on their itinerary match the stellar data?"

Tibor shook his head.

"So close," Lawrence said, "and yet so far."

"*Too* close, maybe," Brooke said.

Lawrence arched an eyebrow.

"Could it be possible, I wonder, that this really *is* a case of clerical error? We know the Jardine info is fragmentary. It's based on three-hundred-year-old accounts of a world nobody can find on historical maps today, after all. Heck, if one really thinks about it, the very existence of Jardine could be debated as the product of someone's whimsy."

"Maybe," Tibor said. "People on Terra really believed in Lemuria and Shangri-La, after all. Though I doubt it would be just a 'clerical error.' The accounts are too populous. The reports stretch back for centuries. We all did the research."

"Then that leaves us only one other possibility," Brooke said flatly. "Unfortunately, it also explains why someone's been trying to kill everyone who looks into the mystery of this planet."

"Someone deliberately altered the records?" Lawrence asked. "*All* the records? Even retroactively?"

Brooke nodded slowly.

"Do you realize what you're saying?" Lawrence asked, his expression incredulous.

"There's only one way we're going to find out, you know," Tibor said grimly.

"Yes." Brooke narrowed her eyes. "I know."

LEOPARD-CLASS DROPSHIP KAYLIN
ZENITH JUMP POINT
SHASTA

Anton Hara leaned back in his command chair and rested his chin on his hands. He stared out through the *Kaylin*'s forward viewports, at the crisp, stark brightness of the universe, splashed across the cold, dark heavens.

A chill ran along his spine, but he refused to shiver against it. In his youth, the sight of space *from* space had filled him with an almost religious awe. The sheer vastness of the universe, infinite in all directions yet filled to bursting with starlight and star life, had made him feel so small by comparison. In his fantasies, his younger self felt as though God was watching him, that each pinpoint of light out there was one of his divine eyes. Watching over all beings—all worlds—with a gaze of pure light, never blinking.

Back then, the humbling thought made him shiver each and every time he beheld the night sky...

But that feeling had died inside Hara so very long ago. Space, he eventually came to know, was cold, harsh, and uncaring. There was no God out here, no divine will. Now, Hara knew space for what it truly was: a force of nature, a medium of transit no different from air or water—but due no less respect. Space was an element within which mankind could travel and communicate—or fight and die.

No, awe wasn't the feeling Hara got when he looked out on a sea of stars these days. What sent shivers along his spine now was a different kind of certainty he had come to trust; a feeling born of decades spent at the controls of a fusion-powered mass of armor, weapons, and force.

The sense of a coming fight.

Beside him, unbidden, Lenard Bryce cleared his throat.

"Eagle for your thoughts?" he asked, his voice low to avoid attracting too much attention from the *Kaylin*'s late-evening bridge crew. The two men seated at the pilot's station, at least, appeared not to notice.

"I don't trust her," Hara muttered. Bryce was a good exec, if at times an overeager one. After so many years with the younger man on his wing, Hara could not imagine withholding his thoughts.

To his credit, Bryce betrayed no sign of surprise. His arms still clasped behind his back, he stood at ease beside his captain, his gray jumpsuit and tan undershirt presenting a uniform match to Hara's own attire and conveying his authority as one of the *Kaylin*'s crew without wasting money on hollow finery like rank insignia. Bryce's Eastern Indian skin was darker than Hara's, his short hair was jet black and slicked back, and his coal-colored eyes were framed by a pair of wire-rimmed spectacles perched on his sharp nose. His chin was strong, and his mouth maintained a tight, unreadable line that enhanced his officer-style appearance. Hara often wondered if the man practiced this look, or if it simply came naturally to him.

Bryce finally turned away from his forward-looking stare. His eyebrows came up. "Stevens, I presume?" he asked with his distinctive Regulan accent.

Hara nodded and turned back toward the viewports. Stevens's *Explorer* hung in space only a few dozen kilometers away, but with her furled jump sails and a lack of attached DropShips, she appeared as little more than a stubby metal tube suspended in space. At any moment, Hara half expected the ship to vanish, fading into nonexistence with a simple start of her K-F drive. Then *what would we do?*

"Why did that moron have to give her the data?" he muttered.

"IE works in mysterious ways," Bryce answered. "I wouldn't be surprised if Bellamy was simply following some prearranged plan. Hell, maybe they *want* her to try an end run around us."

Hara nodded uncertainly. *That* was definitely plausible; he'd seen and heard of many variations on such a double-blind play throughout his career. But being a pawn in one was never an idea he particularly relished.

"Do you think she'll really find Jardine, though?" Bryce asked after a moment.

"Maybe," Hara admitted. "IE thinks highly of her, even though they want us to watch her, too."

"Maybe *that's* what's bugging you, Cap—guarding the objective while watching her for the first sign of treachery. Have to admit, though, if I were the one about to find Atlantis, I might consider ditching the hired muscle so I could renegotiate my contract with the employer, too."

Hara's eyes narrowed. *Now* there's *a fascinating thought...*

He was about to say as much when a light flashed on the primary sensor station. The tech already there glanced at her board, then turned so sharply that her short blond hair looked like a momentary explosion. Her slate-gray eyes—intense, but far from panicked—found Hara's in an instant and locked on.

"Heat spike!" she called out in a clipped voice. "Bearing seven o'clock low, roughly eight-fifty klicks."

The chill ran down Hara's spine again, forcing him to shiver this time. *Damn!*

"Go to yellow alert," he snapped. "Have the Ready Five stand by for launch."

"Aye," the tech said.

"Pilot," Bryce chimed in, addressing the second crewman, a younger man who only half turned to face him, "stand by for emergency launch."

"Aye," the pilot nodded.

Hara's stern gaze found Bryce next. "Could be anyone," he said in a low voice, "but I have a feelin—"

The lights flickered for less than an instant—so fast only an experienced spacer would notice the effect. Hara knew before the tech even called it out:

"Emergence wave! I have a silhouette...*Scout* JumpShip, one DropShip, *Leopard*-class."

Hara closed his eyes for just a second, and opened them to find Bryce's, expectant. "Get Stevens on the line," he said, "and call the other pilots to stations..."

LEOPARD *CV*-CLASS DROPSHIP *LUMINUS OMEGA*
ZENITH JUMP POINT
SHASTA

Wene Maseo blinked away the final stars swimming before his vision and ground his teeth against the wave of nausea welling up from the pit of his stomach. Almost as soon as he did so, he saw the green light flash on his console.

His heart raced as he quickly scanned the interface. Engine online, targeting systems active and tracking, communications online, weapons charged and loaded. Closing his eyes, he took but a moment to visualize the connection, to send the thruster controls into launch status. At his back, he could feel the metallic caress of the launch catapult. In his mind's eye, the wireframe schematic of his HCT-213B *Hellcat II* appeared, glowing a brilliant green.

"Raptor Flight!" a voice called out into his ear, pure and strong. *"Go!"*

I am the Master's Hand!

"Raptors!" Maseo shouted, activating his mike with but a thought. His eyes remained closed. He could see just fine without them. *"Launch!"*

With a powerful lurch, he felt the kick of the metal catapult against his backside, and pushed back against it with his legs, firing his afterburners for a surge of acceleration approaching 5.5 gravities, and feeling the almost immediate feedback from his cargo, thumping against his hips.

In an instant, he felt the cold rush of blessed vacuum across his arms, and saw through still-sealed eyes the glowing outline of his fellow wingmen, already arranging themselves behind him in a six-pointed star. The *Luminus Omega*, his home and mother, would wait behind him as he soared toward the two JumpShips hanging in the distance ahead, their narrow-spined forms glowing an angry red.

Reluctantly, he opened his eyes again and took in the pale colors of space all around him through his natural vision. Banking slightly to his left, he reduced his swim into the void to a modest two-gravity jaunt.

His true senses fed him the data as he drifted his crosshairs across the targets: one *Explorer*-class JumpShip and one

Scout-class with an attached *Leopard*. Data scrolled across his peripheral vision, supplementing the sensor feeds with statistics he already knew by heart.

"Look lively, Raptors!" he called out. "At best, they may muster up to ten fighters to oppose us, plus the *Leopard*..."

Even as he spoke, Maseo heard the launch signals coming from the enemy *Leopard*, and it brought a feral grin to his face. His mouth filled with the metallic taste of his own saliva, and a warm flush came over him as his sensors tagged a pair of arrow-shaped *Corsairs* separating from their mother ship.

"Try not to pity them overmuch," he told his wingmen. "They are, after all, only Frails..."

FINDING JARDINE

FORGOTTEN WORLDS, BOOK TWO

CHAPTER 1

My beloved Brooke,

If there's one thing I hate more than the notion of space travel, it's the thought that it keeps taking you farther and farther away from home. The scholar in me knows full well that each discovery you make benefits all humanity, and I know you well enough to know the promise of Jardine had to be impossible to resist (if I weren't such a craven coward, you know I'd have leaped at the chance, too!).

But none of that changes the fact that I miss my beautiful angel, and I hope you'll be home with me again soon. These last few months have been an eternity without you.

Please be careful out there, my love. The wars may be over, but I doubt the Leaguers will be happy to see another Elsie sniffing around their backwaters.

And I doubt IE has changed its policies on ransom demands.

Forever in your heart!

—Tyler Stevens

EXPLORER-CLASS JUMPSHIP SACAJAWEA
PIRATE JUMP POINT
HERAKLEION SYSTEM, FREE WORLDS LEAGUE
16 OCTOBER 3067

"Two more bogeys, closing fast!"

"I have a track! Firing! ... No joy! Damn, I never saw a fighter dodge like that in space!"

"Damn it, Lawrence! What's taking so long?"

"Another goddamned minute! Keep your panties on and those bugs off us!"

"Stevens to Hara! We're ready here! Standby to receive..."

"Jesus Mother-Loving Christ, that was close!"

"What are they trying to do? Ram us?"

"Splash One! Splash One!"

"Great shot, Juan! Hara, Sac is transmitting now! Get your fighters clear!"

"Say again, Stevens? Say aga—!"

"I said clear, damn it! We're engaging now—!"

"Shit! Klaw Flight! Disengage! Get away from that jumper! K-F forming! Disenga—"

"Impact! Brooke, impact !"

"Schei—!"

"Jump—!

The universe shrank around Brooklyn Stevens in the blink of an eye. Time, space, and even the events of moments simply ceased to have any meaning as she suddenly felt herself melt into the infinite. Stars and planets spun around her, and she stretched her hands out to grab them.

One in particular tickled her fancy. With a giddy joy, she found it spinning its timeless way around a yellow-white star, a bone-white moon trailing behind. Giggling, she chased after the warm, cozy world. Feeling the cool waters of its deep blue oceans, the bustling life on its three large continents. She smiled as her eyes traced the eternally familiar landscapes, the cities she knew so well.

Honey, her mind sang to the planet, *I'm home!*

But as her fingers reached out to caress the world she knew as Donegal, arcs of golden fire appeared all across its surface. A rumbling cry rose as the fires spread. Cities, one by one, plunged into the seas, swallowed by chasms that formed, grew, and filled with glowing magma and dark salt water. Smoke and steam filled the skies, obscuring what remained.

"No!" Brooke heard herself scream as flames engulfed the world in her hands. *"Tyler—!"*

Then, suddenly, without warning, everything slammed back down. The universe exploded in a rush of light and cold. She shrank to a pinpoint, swallowed in the void.

And the image of Donegal, engulfed in fire, vanished to the inky blackness of eternity...

She opened her eyes to find herself bent over the life-support control station, her hands still clutching the hard plastic yoke of the auxiliary weapons control she had been using mere moments before, as if she might float away if she let go. The displays in front of her flickered back to life as she struggled for breath, her heart pounding. Instead of targeting information, they now supplied a schematic of the *Sacajawea*'s sixty-seven decks, with color-coded climate-control information to indicate temperature, air pressure, and other vital signs. Only a secondary monitor maintained the weapons display.

But the indicators were green. Clear.

No threat detected.

Her stomach was doing somersaults. The taste of bile rose in her throat, and she gagged on it. She felt like months of her life had vanished in the last few seconds.

As if the cramps weren't enough...

"Oh, *Gottverdammte Scheiße!*" a voice swore, verbalizing Brooke's own sentiments. With her neck muscles aching and her skull pounding, she turned to face the rail-thin, sweat-soaked form of Tibor "Trouble" Mitternacht at the sail controls station next to her. Tibor's station also hosted one of the bridge's six auxiliary weapons-control boards, each of which served as a supplement and backup for the main fire-control console in the bridge's outer ring.

Tibor's eyes were still screwed shut, and he gasped for air through clenched teeth between a series of choking coughs. His head tilted to the left and he clutched at his ear with thin fingers; she assumed he heard the same screaming ringing in her head.

Swallowing acid again, Brooke swiveled her chair to take in the rest of the *Sacajawea*'s command center while her senses adjusted. The central deck held only four other crew stations in addition to the stations she and Tibor occupied—plus the unoccupied command chairs in the center—and three of the stations were presently occupied. Juan Lafferty, at the station-keeping drive console to Brooke's left, had already shaken off his post-jump nausea, and ran a hand across his clean-shaven head as he sighed in relief.

Gretchen Morden, at the communications board across from Tibor, looked lost amid the unruly cloud of her own jet-black hair, until she brushed away enough of it to get a look at her console. And Lawrence Pohl, captain of the JumpShip, sat at the jump-control station opposite Juan, strong arms still braced against the console's emergency handles.

"For Bast's sake, Lawrence," Brooke finally gasped, "a little more warning would've been nice!"

Lawrence shot her an ice-blue glare, a snarl contorting the peppered-gray stubble surrounding his chin. "Did you not hear me scream 'Jump!' woman?" he snarled. "Blake's blood! You tell Hara to lead pirates right up to us, and then have the nerve to complain about my jumping?"

"They didn't need Hara's aerojocks to lead them our way," Tibor grumbled, still cupping his ear. "Those guys were on a bombing run, and *we* were the primary."

Brooke blinked. *Impact! Someone said "impact!" back there!* "Lawrence," she said, "what's our status?"

Lawrence threw his gaze over to Gretchen, who nodded sagely—her hair once more contained in a bun to reveal plain, makeup-free features. As she turned cool brown eyes back to her station and went to work, Lawrence looked over his own monitors, assessing the data in seconds.

"No significant hull damage. We took some light weapons fire, but between our guns, their range, and our out-jump, we likely knocked them out of play before they could do too much."

Brooke nodded, imagining for a moment the drifting hulls of wrecked pirate fighters now light-years away, torn asunder by the sheer power of the *Sacajawea*'s hyperspace field. At least four of the enemy craft had been screaming perilously close to the JumpShip when the Kearny-Fuchida fields engaged, warping Einsteinian space beyond all recognition and punching the *Sac* through the resulting breach.

Very few vessels within twenty or so kilometers of a jumping ship survived the intense release of energies and gravitational effects. For Hara's sake, Brooke hoped every one of the enemy ships had gotten at least that close.

Across the bridge, Gretchen cleared her throat, drawing Lawrence's attention again.

"We're on position," she said in a matter-of-fact voice. "Visual triangulation confirms we are now on the solar equatorial plane of the Herakleion system. Close passive radar shows no contacts. And we're receiving a signal—"

"Signal?" Tibor blurted. Brooke turned and saw him rubbing his temple. "That explains the ringing..."

"You're picking it up, too?" she asked.

Tibor shrugged. While he didn't often talk about them, the bionic implants that had replaced his left eye and his left inner ear—a legacy of his former career—were an open secret among the *Sacajawea*'s crew. Both were well-disguised as the genuine article, but close inspection revealed the color difference between his eyes that some took to indicate a glass cosmetic, and the faint scarring just below his left earlobe.

In truth, one of the features that elevated Tibor to Brooke's best sensor operator and field scout was that he could see in infrared and even hear radio signals unaugmented by external equipment. Once upon a time, these capabilities made him an expert intelligence operative; even now, they enabled him to warn of possible pitfalls such as ambushes.

Or pick up stray transmissions.

"It's weak," he muttered, squinting as he focused on pinpointing the signal. "Sounds like an automated warning sat."

"That's the one," Gretchen said with a nod. "It's coming from what looks like a buoy closer in-system. I can amplify."

Tibor nodded, then shook his head, as if clearing the last cobwebs from his jump-addled mind. Gretchen's fingers flew across her console, and suddenly the command center filled with the crackling noise of radio static.

And a tinny voice, laced with a thick—and, to her mind, old—Terran-English accent:

"—thority of the Free Worlds League and Captain-General Thaddeus Marik, the ComStar Safe Transit and Astrogation Project has identified the Herakleion system as a Class Ten Extreme Biological Hazard Site, highly contagious and unsafe for travelers and settlers.

Until further notice, no vessels are to approach or land on the planet below. Any vessels determined to have done so will be prosecuted to the full extent of interstellar quarantine law, up to and including the seizure and destruction of the offending vessels.

"Once again, to all ships receiving this open-channel transmission, know that you have entered quarantined space. By the authority of the Free Worlds League and Captain-General Thaddeus Marik, the ComStar Safe Transit and Astrogation Project has identified the Herakleion system as a Class Ten—"

Brooke nodded slightly, which Lawrence relayed to Gretchen. With a chirp, the ancient voice was gone, leaving a moment of tense silence in its wake.

"Well," Tibor sighed, "here we are."

"Herakleion," Brooke said. "Just like the old star maps said."

"Thaddeus Marik ruled the Free Worlds from 2804 until his death in 2821," Tibor muttered. "My records put Herakleion's demise around 2815."

"Hoping for another 'clerical error,' perhaps?" Lawrence offered.

Tibor shrugged. "It's a proven fact that even ComStar can't keep a story straight," he replied. "Doesn't prove anything, but I was hoping for something more revealing."

"I doubt a hint would've been *that* obvious, Trouble," Brooke said with a small smirk.

"Either way, we'll have to check out—"

A shrill alarm sounded across the bridge, cutting her off as Lawrence practically jumped out of his seat. His eyes swept the panels in front of him, and an angry hiss escaped his clenched teeth.

"Hull breach!" he snapped before Brooke could even ask. "Missile pod, Deck Sixteen."

"What?"

"Airlocks are partitioning the deck now," Lawrence said. "Air loss minimal, but it looks like— *Jesus, Mary, and Joseph!*"

Brooke felt unfocused anger surging through her again even as she snapped, "A little actual info would be ni—!"

"That wasn't a bomb, Brooke!" Lawrence cut her off. "I'm looking at the vid; that breach was torn right through the mount!"

"Confirming movement on sixteen!" Gretchen called out.

Brooke blinked. "We've been *boarded*?"

"Any idea how many?" Tibor asked.

Lawrence and Gretchen shared a quick glance. Gretchen's eyes swept her monitors again. "Just the one, I think."

"There's only one way a fighter could deliver a boarding party in vacuum," Tibor muttered.

Brooke nodded. "Battle armor." *So those* weren't *bombs back there after all!*

"They'd have to be insane to try," Lawrence said with a frown.

"Or *good*," Tibor replied.

"Over twenty decks between him and anything vital astern," Brooke said, considering.

"And fifteen to us—"

"He could go for the hangar," Tibor offered. "Two decks aft. It'd be risky considering our firepower, but our shuttles will take him dirtside for sure."

"Only *after* he's done with us," Brooke said. "Lawrence, lock down the lifts and seal all ladder hatches between there and engineering—"

"Already done," Lawrence said. "But he could just as easily go for any point in the drive core and screw us all."

Brooke scowled. The most devastating challenge to defending a JumpShip against a boarding attempt was the potential for an attacker to target the drive core. The long shaft making up the core of every needle-like JumpShip in existence—in essence, a combined power capacitor for the drive and an antenna for the jump field—typically lay a mere twenty meters or less from the outer hull. Though generally surrounded by bulkheads, framework, and conduits, this narrow component was vulnerable to damage by anyone sporting heavy enough weaponry or the knowledge to locate and breach the right service panels. A damaged drive core would render a JumpShip incapable of extending its Kearny-Fuchida field along the vessel's entire length, making it impossible to jump. Only the taboo against destroying JumpShips—treated as a crime against humanity ever since the Great Houses realized such vessels were all that held together their stellar empires—had prevented boarding parties from targeting the main K-F drive components, including the antennas.

But that taboo had eroded in the last few decades.

"He's in the lift shaft," Gretchen called. "I have a seal breach on fifteen!"

"He's moving up," Brooke said. "Not going for engineering *or* the core. Put the rest of the ship in lockdown, Lawrence. Signal intruder alert and tell the crew to arm for Toads. Trouble and I will go down and try to meet our 'friend' before he reaches the bridge."

"The hell you say!" Lawrence snapped midway through entering the commands into the panel on his armrest. "I'm coming with you."

"Christ!" Gretchen hissed. "He's in the grav-deck shafts; bypassing thirteen now."

"Come on, Lawrence," Brooke said with an irritated sigh. "You know the standard drill here. The captain holds the bridge; we'll need you three to back us up in case he outmaneuvers us or something."

Lawrence opened his mouth again, but Brooke's hand was already up. "We can argue procedures again later," she said, "assuming we get out of this. For now, let's just get everyone in vac suits and armed for kirians. Trouble, come on."

Despite the muffling effect of her thick, armored helmet and the echoes of her own heavy breathing, Brooklyn Stevens could hear—and feel—the shuddering blast that shook the bulkheads beneath her magnetized boots. The lift shaft fluorescents—strategically aligned to provide clear illumination of the service rungs and hatches—flickered and died, plunging her and her vac-suited companion into total blackness.

"Shit!" a voice snarled in her earpiece. "He's through the Deck Four hatch! He just keeps coming!"

Despite Lawrence Pohl's decades of experience, Brooke could hear the edge of fear in the man's voice, and her own mouth went dry. The intruder had plowed through the starboard lift shaft's air seals on every deck with brute force. Now here he was. One deck below the *Sac*'s habitat section—and a mere two decks from the bridge.

Brooke's toes flexed. Her legs still felt that dull, yet all-too-familiar ache, but the worst had passed days ago, and only the building adrenaline of the last hours reminded her it was even there. To the side of each big toe, she could feel the nub that would disengage her boot magnets with a simple twist of the foot, allowing her to kick free of the bulkhead once the shooting began. But as she raised her TK Industries HG-90 gyrojet rifle and bit her bottom lip, she resisted the urge.

Just ahead of her, and almost ninety degrees to her left, Tibor held his HG-90 at the ready and trained on the hatch ahead.

There would be only one shot, one chance to stop this armored trooper—or at least knock him back down the shaft. Brooke and Tibor had toyed with the idea of opening the lift hatches and driving the starboard lift—now locked down on the bridge—into the intruder, but they knew better. The lift was hardly an adequate bullet against a battlesuit; its velocity would be too low, and would accomplish little against a suit capable of ripping through armored seals.

Especially since the intruder could just as easily tear through any lift doorway and climb out onto any deck.

No, this one would need to go down the hard way. And the intruder's obvious haste put the battleground on Deck Three, where she and Tibor now clung to the lift shaft walls, waiting for their guest to burst through the floor hatch.

Brooke felt her right eye twitch. Suddenly, it was taking too long.

"This can't be good," Tibor's voice carried over the tactical channel.

"He's just sitting out there!" Lawrence's voice chimed in. "Just sitting in the shaft!"

He knows we're here?

"That entire deck is electronics, and he knows it," Tibor said. "Or he knows we're right here, waiting on his ass."

"Either way," Brooke said. "We can't leave him there. Move!"

Twisting her feet inside her boots, Brooke disengaged the magnets and kicked away from the rung on the wall. Keeping her gyrojet rifle at the ready with her right hand, she used her left to guide herself along a lift rail.

Tibor—already on the move—touched down on the deck floor a second ahead of her, his HG-90 still trained on the hatch. "Lawrence," he breathed. "We're in position."

"Alright," Lawrence's voice came back, "but be careful; that guy is just waiting for you. Hatch open in three... "

Brooke tapped the magnets on again, anchoring herself to the narrow outer frame of the hatch iris, and heard Tibor follow suit.

"...Two... "

She sighted down the length of the cone-shaped rifle, bracing herself for the recoil.

Across from the circular hatch plate, she felt Tibor pull himself into a crouch.

"...One!"

With a *clack* and a hiss, the lift's air hatch turned and dilated. In the darkness below, Brooke saw a flash of movement and pulled her trigger half a heartbeat after Tibor.

With a flash of fire and a roar that made her cringe despite the automatic cutouts of her combat envirosuit's external pickups, the self-propelled mini-rockets from both HG-90s screamed into the dark void and exploded.

Smoke filled the lift shaft, and Brooke pressed herself against the wall, half afraid to peer through the hatch.

Tibor's rifle remained at the ready, as did hers, slamming another rocket into the chamber.

Then came the distant explosion—a rocket impacting part of the lift shaft much farther aft.

"Did we get him?" she whispered.

"Guys!" Lawrence exploded on the channel, "We have movement on Four! He's still live! Your boy is still live!"

"*Scheiße!*" Tibor growled. "I'm going through!"

"Bast's sake!" Brooke hissed, launching herself after Tibor as he dropped through the wisps of lingering smoke.

"Careful!" Lawrence barked. "He's in the main corridor, and those bazookas of yours are a disaster waiting to happen in there!"

"Damn it, Lawrence! Don't you think our intruder knows that too?"

Brooke knew the danger: only a madman fought for control of a JumpShip using anti-armor weapons like her HG-90, and then only when he could afford the risk. A misfired rocket or shell could easily rupture major conduits, life support lines, or even—in the right places—set off a helium leak or disrupt a hatch sealed against vacuum.

On this deck, however, the major concern was the sheer volume of computer nodes, storage devices, and switchboxes making up the *Sacajawea's* electronic heart *and* central nervous system. A misfired rocket here could kill a vital computer system, perhaps even disabling life support, jump controls, or the station-keeping drive that made the ship stable in the gravitational eddies of space.

But the alternative to using these heavy weapons against an armored trooper capable of clawing his way through bulkheads and causing such damage *on purpose* was far worse.

Ahead lay a short corridor to one of the ladders running along the *Sac's* hull, parallel to the lift shafts. Too small for battle armor, and with a spiral arrangement between some decks specifically designed to impede "speeding," Brooke and her crew knew the intruder would pass on those.

Beyond the ladder access, scarcely five meters ahead, the corridor ended and branched out in a "T" intersection.

"I'll take left," she whispered into her comm.

"I have right," Tibor replied.

With the mag boots disengaged, their movement was swift. Tibor bounded past the ladder access, thumping to a stop against the right side corner of the corridor's end, while Brooke did the same on the left. Peering over the muzzle of her ten-kilo gyrojet gun, she swung around cautiously, scanning the left-ward corridor, while Tibor scanned right.

In the short length of curved hallway before her, Brooke saw only a sealed, armored bulkhead, less than two meters away; Lawrence had put the entire deck under full lockdown.

"Clear this way!" she called out.

Which could only mean—

"Christ!" Tibor shouted.

Brooke swung around and saw it: the figure of a man transformed into a techno-bear of red armor and ballistic-black joints. It was slender, suggesting a lighter suit design, but before she could recognize the type, she saw the glossy black void of the faceplate flash her way, and the armored gauntlets flashed forward, seizing Tibor's rifle barrel in one hand—and Tibor himself in the other.

Separating the two with a low, speakers-filtered growl, the armored intruder tossed the rifle against the bulkhead behind him, and hurled Tibor backward, into Brooke.

Unable to react in time, she took the brunt of Tibor's impact in her chest, and the air was driven out of her lungs. Her rifle swung wide, a spasm in her hand triggering another shot.

In the close confines of the hall, the micro-rocket's blast shocked everyone. Conduits severed by the explosion showered the hall with sparks and smoke, forcing Tibor to cover his face while Brooke winced behind him.

A half second later, Tibor grunted as the intruder emerged from the haze and seized him again. Flung like an unwanted toy into the hallway bulkhead behind Brooke, his enviro-suited body struck with a sickly *thud*, then tumbled upward from his unexpended inertia. An ominous hum—punctuated by the muted clang of metal on metal—locked the intruder's power armor onto the deck in front of Brooke, and metal-clad hands formed into fists as he hovered over her.

Brooke had enough time to register the mangled plates across the intruder's chest and the bloody hand insignia on his left shoulder before an armored glove shot out once again to slap the HG-90 from her grip and into a clattering tumble behind her.

A laser muzzle suddenly appeared below the suit's left forearm, and now trained a scarlet targeting beam straight at her vac suit's helmet.

"*Frail!*" boomed a strange, masculine voice that echoed in Brooke's ears and rang from her external speakers. "Identify yourself! *Who sent you?*"

Brooke's eyes darted about as she backed up against the wall. In her peripheral vision, she thought she saw Tibor stirring in his corner of the corridor, with her rifle tumbling in the microgravity nearby. But both were too far from her reach, too far away to be any help.

Need to stall him!

"I don't know what you're—" she began, but her words were cut off by a feral, inhuman growl and an armored hand seizing her by the throat Steel-clad fingers dug into her vac-suit's neck, and breathing became painful, each labored exhalation fogging her faceplate.

Instinctively, she clutched at the intruder's wrist, but his metal-shod arm didn't budge. With her back pressed against the wall, she tried a desperate kick, but again, the monster scarcely moved.

"*Answer the question, Frail!*" he bellowed. "I'll not ask again!"

Brooke felt the gauntlet squeezing tighter, but only for a second before she gagged on her tongue. As the hand relaxed—ever so slightly—she coughed up a backwash of acid.

The black faceplate loomed closer, until she felt she could almost make out a faint red glow within. Still gasping for air, she struggled to speak, to say...*anything*...

The deafening booms of two gyrojet explosions drowned out all sound before she could talk, and the sudden pressure of the intruder's jagged chest against hers drove out what little air she managed to suck into her lungs. Only the fact that the monster's feet remained rooted to the deck plates kept him from crushing her completely, though it had been a near thing.

Through the ringing in her ears, Brooke heard an inhuman roar of pain and rage as she whirled through the air and landed back in the hall.

Missing Lawrence Pohl by less than half a meter.

"Wha—?"

"Son of a bitch!" Lawrence's voice snarled over the tac channel. Clad in his own combat vac-suit, he lugged two HG-90s—one in each of his thick-gloved hands. "Two shells in the back and he's still coming!"

"*Trouble!*" Brooke blinked, adrenaline overriding the haze and shock of being hurled against the hallway's unyielding metal framework.

The armored trooper now filled the hallway in front of them, blocking her view of Tibor. Smoke and sparks from the ruptured conduits mixed with gray smoke pouring from the intruder's back and a blotchy cloud of red.

"He's bleeding!" she gasped.

The suit stabbed its left arm forward and fired. Through the haze, a lance of scarlet energy flashed across Lawrence's chest, painting a red dot, followed an instant later by an emerald beam. Caught dead center, the vac-suit's outer layers of ballistic metal-weave fabric exploded in a puff of white smoke, and the JumpShip captain yelped in pain.

"*Lawrence!*" Brooke cried, prying herself off the hallway supports.

"Down, Brooke!" Tibor's voice suddenly rang in her ears.

Brooke kicked herself away from the wall, powering herself into Lawrence's now-limp form and bringing both of them down to the deck. An instant later, the *whoosh-boom* of another gyrojet rocket punished her ears and she looked up to see the armored trooper tumbling toward her, his magnetic grip on the deck torn free by a blast that had mangled his right leg.

More of the intruder's blood clouded the hall in a red mist. Still his armored visor looked up, and one armored glove reached out to seize a rung in the ceiling, arresting his momentum. His laser arm tracked backward, firing a pulse into the smoke beyond.

Desperately, Brooke reached for one of the HG-90s still clutched in Lawrence's hands, and wrestled the bulky weapon upward. The intruder swung back toward her, laser at the ready.

She pulled the trigger, sending one more micro-rocket screaming forward. The intruder took the blast directly to his faceplate and immediately lost his grip on the overhead rung.

As his suit twisted and tumbled backward, his laser fired, its pulse scoring a short line in the wall just above Brooke's head.

The suit tumbled back, lifeless, through the smoky hallway, leaving behind a complex trail of crimson bubbles that shifted and spun in all directions.

"Trouble?" Brooke called out.

"Oh, shit!" came Tibor's reply, his voice filled with alarm and despair.

The explosion came so suddenly, she didn't even have time to blink. The force of the blast rippled through the hall, hurling Tibor through the smoke, sparks, and blood. The curved deck was filled with blinding light that registered for less than an instant before the pressure wave swept Brooke and Lawrence away.

As her helmet crashed against another deck beam, stars swam before her eyes, and she again lost her breath in a strained cough.

Dimly, Brooke realized she'd dropped her rifle.

And then she blacked out...

CHAPTER 2

My dearest Tyler,

If you're reading this, then everything I'm describing here has already happened and the Sac (at least) has gotten clear. I can only hope everyone survived the outcome—including myself, of course.

I'm sorry it's been a while since my last message. We were forced to make an emergency jump, and now find ourselves in decidedly hostile territory, where even transmitting this message will have to wait until we're sure it's safe.

But Tyler, my love, this could be it: We found Jardine!

I won't bore you with the details, but the bottom line is the planet was "hidden" through some kind of elaborate bait-and-switch centuries ago. What star maps now call Herakleion is, in fact, Jardine. We're sure of that now, even without setting foot on the surface.

I just hope it was all worth it.

The Sac was damaged. Lawrence nearly bought it, as did Trouble. Whoever that armored psycho was who boarded us, he was packing a suicide bomb powerful enough to damage several of the ship's operating systems. Fortunately, all of them can be bypassed, but Lawrence says it'll take time, and a number of secondary functions have to be taken offline in the bargain.

So, while his people try to fix the ship (and he recovers in the med bay), T and I are checking out the primary, the world our archives call Herakleion.

And this time, we're taking the 'Mech. Whatever's down there, someone found it important enough to kill Marie for, and I'll be damned if I let that pass.

I love you, Tyler. Always remember that.

Yours forever,

—Brooke

SENTRYSAT J-1098
HIGH ORBIT, HERAKLEION/JARDINE
FREE WORLDS LEAGUE
30 OCTOBER 3067

Drifting high above the darkened world, the centuries-old satellite continued to sing its timeless song. Its bland warning—first voiced at the dawn of the Succession Wars—called out to all within radio distance, warning that the world below was poisoned. Blindly, the ancient orbiter, pockmarked by centuries of particle damage, spun through its latest, uncounted orbit, as if oblivious to the universe beyond.

Oblivious, that was, until it caught the dying flare from an object falling ever closer, looming ever larger.

Alerted at once by the momentary glimpse on its passive scopes, systems inert for decades sprang to life. Electronic eyes narrowed on the heavens, switching from photonic to infrared and electromagnetic. At this range, and with the satellite's grainy resolution, the echo was small—almost too small to discern.

But the watcher was patient and thorough. Though it took nearly a full, eternal minute to verify, the sensors finally confirmed the data: single craft, coasting on near-total emissions control.

And it was getting closer fast. No mere rock tumbling through space, this; the spectral analysis fixed the hull as refined metals, analyzed the thermal trace of the braking thrusters. A work of human hands.

Though the satellite had seen many such vessels come and go through its long, cold night, this one triggered an alert as it drifted closer still. The satellite needed no IFF codes to know the foreign "scent" of the craft's hull; this one lacked the agreed-upon spectral telltales all friendly craft gave off in their final approach to avoid signal transmission.

In less than three microseconds, in the absence of that passive IFF, the satellite's protocols responded. Ancient navigational thrusters fired, subtly reorienting the satellite for the first time in centuries. Bay doors, dented and flecked by space-borne debris, slowly began to part over apertures barely large enough for their occupants. Separate engines—cold for an epoch—thrummed to life.

Lacking launch catapults and arresting gear, the bays were mere tubes for the craft within. Theirs would be a one-way flight, and their launch would kick the aging mother craft into a death spiral from which no number of maneuvering jets could save it.

But even as the three wedge-shaped hunters shot forth into the void, the satellite's ancient song continued, faithful to the last—with but one addition, transmitted on a second carrier frequency: INTRUDER ALERT!

K-1 DROPSHUTTLE *MAGELLAN*
FINAL APPROACH VECTOR
HERAKLEION/JARDINE

The banshee wail of the sensor alarms shocked Brooke out of her deep sleep so abruptly she couldn't even recall the dream she'd been having. Disoriented, she blinked wide-eyed at the half-dark consoles in front of her for a few seconds, unable to comprehend anything they told her. Nor could she entirely rationalize what it was that held her bolt upright in her chair despite the freefall that allowed several stray locks of her hair to swirl aimlessly around her. Or when she had changed from her normal tank top-and-shorts sleepwear into a pressure suit.

In fact, several heartbeats passed before Brooke could even recall where she *was*.

But as she blinked, the shrill, electronic echo repeated itself, and her brain finally shifted into gear. The monitor caught her attention at last, dominated by three flashing red icons, beside which numbers spun and scrolled, describing heading and distance relative to her shuttle.

"Bast damn it!" she hissed.

At that moment, the cabin hatch cycled open and Tibor, black hair in a tangle, still rubbing one eye, stepped through. Like Brooke, he had slept in a pressure suit, leaving the gloves strapped back and the helmet hanging forward by its secondary air tube.

"Interceptors," Brooke told him sharply.

Tibor propelled himself toward the empty seat beside her, suddenly alert as he strapped himself into the pilot's station. The bulk of the suit made the effort a little more difficult, but in the last several days—as the distant world loomed larger on the ship's scopes—they had agreed to the inconvenience of being ready for an imminent attack.

"Had to happen sooner or later, I guess," he mumbled, eyes flashing across the console.

Brooke nodded as she watched the icons form up, while another icon appeared on the long-range passive sweep, immobile by comparison. The computers backtracked the incoming hostiles to the tiny object, floating in high planetary orbit.

"Satellite launched," she said.

"Drones, maybe?"

The image of robotic fighters flashed in Brooke's mind. In their time with Interstellar Expeditions—and afterward—she and Tibor had encountered only a few of the Star League era's long-forgotten unmanned fighters. Though fast and potentially lethal, centuries of neglect and narrow, out-of-date programming had made them a relatively easy obstacle to overcome.

Such drones were often satellite-based, where they could weather the ages better and act as viable early warning systems. Star League-era technology had proved remarkably good at such longevity, reliably supporting traps that still sprung after centuries, even if the tech was no longer up to current standards.

But then again, Brooke reminded herself, *those* machines didn't have living, unseen masters behind them, eager to keep their world hidden.

And if that *were* true…

"These will only be the first wave," she muttered.

"We figured as much," Tibor replied. Two weeks of transit time on the tiny, ovoid DropShuttle *Magellan*—traveling away from the *Sacajawea*'s distant pirate point—had left them plenty of time to discuss the possibilities. "We're oriented for deceleration and still coming in hot. We'll blow right by them if I don't fire the engines now, but they're still going to get at least one shot in."

"We'd hit the atmosphere awful hard," Brooke said. The red icons were closing fast, she noticed, likely accelerating toward the *Magellan*. "Can we orient to spiral in? Bleed off speed in a couple of orbits?"

"We *could*, but we'd alert every aerodrome that may be down there."

"I don't think we have stealth on our side any more, Trouble."

"There's still Plan C," he offered.

Brooke scowled. Isolated from the universe in their long trip, with the *Magellan* running under EMCON—Emissions Control—protocols, Brooke and Tibor had spent hundreds of hours forming, refining and discarding the options for this landing in the likely event of hostile patrols and interceptions. Yet no matter how elaborate the tactics, they always boiled down to three main plans: fight, go for broke, or run.

Fighting was really only viable if the shuttle held a distinct advantage over its opposition—and as dumb as drones could be, Brooke seriously doubted these three would be the only interceptors.

Going for broke—literally powering through any opposition without slowing—would be equally dangerous. Though some drones lacked the ability to follow them into the atmosphere, others definitely would have that capability. And once the shuttle landed after so much interference, it would be short work for any hostiles to track down the grounded *Magellan* and close off any hope of escape or rescue.

The landing would be rough, as well. While the shuttle had already decelerated—through random and spaced-out burns—to a mere 32.4-thousand-kilometers-per-hour coast, that speed was simply too high for an atmospheric insertion. The craft would still need to either fire her engines soon to brake for entry—a five-minute blast at three gravities' thrust—or angle for a more gradual deceleration using an inward-spiraling orbit.

Either way, they now faced an unknown world on high alert, with unknown aerospace assets likely capable of tracking down the *Magellan*'s position wherever she landed.

If they eliminated the other two options, they were left with "Plan C" (as Tibor liked to call it). Under the circumstances, that involved changing the shuttle's angle even more, using the planet's shadow to throw off pursuers and powering away, hoping the accumulated acceleration would keep any hostiles in the shuttle's proverbial dust—at least until she was safely back on the *Sacajawea*.

But even as Brooke watched the red icons closing in, she narrowed her eyes and shook her head. *That* would be admitting defeat.

"No way," she said finally. "We came this far; we're going in."

Tibor gave her a lopsided grin. "Just checking," he said. "Hang on, I have an idea. Better set sensors to max res and warm up the guns."

Brooke nodded and turned to the controls, activating the *Magellan*'s battery of defensive lasers and switching the sensors from EMCON passive to high-resolution active. Seconds later, her secondary monitors sprang to life, and the computer resolved the simple red icons of the incoming fighters into hard data.

"*BlackWasp*s," she muttered.

"Mark-Thirties?" Tibor sighed in relief. "I was half afraid you'd say we were looking at *VoidSeeker*s."

Brooke grimaced. At the peak of the Star League's technology curve, the Mk. 39 *VoidSeeker*-class drone was the pinnacle of fighter-scale unmanned warfare and an integral part of the artificially-intelligent Caspar defense network that had protected many of the Terran Hegemony's core worlds centuries ago. Sleek, blindingly fast, incredibly intelligent, and with the attack precision of a veteran combat fighter pilot, even a single drone of *that* class would likely outperform the *Magellan* in a fight.

The Mk. 30 *BlackWasp*s were, by comparison, the Mk. 39's smaller, slower and dumber cousins. That fact *did* make them easier to deal with, but each Mk. 39 still possessed nearly double the *Magellan*'s thrust potential at full burn and carried a pair of extended-range lasers offering far greater reach and punch than the shuttle's array of Martell mediums.

But *BlackWasp*s were not built for atmospheric combat.

"ETA," Tibor barked. "Fifteen to insertion."

"Got it—!" Brooke started to respond, when suddenly Tibor slammed his control stick forward and sent the *Magellan* into a sharp nose-over-end tumble and poured on the thrust.

On her board, the red icons scrolled wildly, spun around and flashed into the sensors' forward arc panel, cutting across the shuttle's flight angle, even as Brooke felt her stomach doing flip-flops.

A little warning would've been nice!

Slammed back in her seat, she strained to see one of the secondary monitors, taking in the acceleration readings: two gravities of force now pinned her to her seat as the fighters closed in. Not quite the worst Tibor could do to them right now—except for the fact that the glowing green crescent of a planet now swam before her eyes in the forward view monitor.

"Trouble!"

"Hang on!" Tibor said. "And get ready!"

Brooke grunted and reached out to clutch the weapon controls. Flicking the safeties off, she fought the crosshairs to line up with the centermost icon. Even now, nose-to-nose, with both sides burning hot, her targets were little more than electronic blips on which to line up her sights.

But she knew that would change in seconds.

Only a few moments passed before the sensor boards alerted her to the *Magellan*'s acquisition by hostile targeting lasers, replacing the range-finding pings that first alerted her.

A second afterward came the pinpoint flash, computer-enhanced for visibility. An armor sensor bleated a warning—one laser hit out of a half-dozen fired.

The shuttle barely flinched at the blast.

The targeting reticule suddenly flashed gold. Brooke reflexively thumbed her triggers, sending four beams of energy out into the void after the combat computers translated her action and fine-tuned her aim. The shuttle's sensors painted damage to the leading drone's nose and wing, but nothing changed in its profile.

With Tibor pouring on the acceleration, the distance between the *BlackWasp*s and the *Magellan* closed in what felt like an instant to Brooke. Before the forward lasers had even cycled enough for a second firing, three more laser bolts splashed across the shuttle's hull—merely marring the armor plating.

Three iron gray, wedge-shaped craft flashed by the forward viewport monitors, their angle slightly skewed.

"They're turning, Trouble!" Brooke snapped.

"Another second here!" Tibor growled back. "Brace yourself! I'm going to do a hard spin and decel!"

Brooke bit her lower lip and instead tapped the targeting controls over to the rearward guns. Her reticule blinked gold over one drone and she fired, but this time the computers registered no hits.

"*Scheiß—!*"

Suddenly, the *Magellan* was spinning again under *no* thrust, Tibor killing the drive while executing a sharp turn to point her thrusters back toward the planet. Brooke felt herself momentarily weightless again, her body straining the five-point harness even as her chair oriented with the turn. Her stomach lurched, and she coughed at the pasty taste of her saliva.

The drones snapped off laser bolts from their ever-increasing range as their thrusters fought the excess momentum built up to reach the *Magellan* quickly. Once more, the computers sketched out the tracks of six lasers, but the Battle Damage Assessment system reported no hits—the drones clearly did not anticipate the shuttle's sudden reorientation and brief free-fall.

Still dazed, Brooke reached out for the controls just as Tibor fired the engines again—full bore, this time.

Three gravities of force crushed Brooke back into her seat. Though the chair was contoured and cushioned for just such an eventuality, she still felt the bone-snapping pressure all along her back. For a moment, her vision faded and all she could hear were the insistent wails of computer alarms over the roar of the *Magellan*'s engines.

"Brooke!" Tibor was shouting. *"Brooke!"*

"I'm okay," she called out, opening her eyes after suddenly realizing she had screwed them shut. "I'm fine."

"Jesus, girl! I told you to brace for it!"

"Ja, ja," she muttered, squinting at the monitors. The fighters were still out there, but beyond their own weapons' range. Brooke knew that wouldn't last too long.

"Where are we?" she asked.

"Four minutes to entry," Tibor said through gritted teeth. "Maybe five."

Brooke reached for the weapons controls again.

"It's going to be a rough one," Tibor warned her. "We're hitting the atmosphere hot—hopefully hotter than those drones can handle."

"That's great," Brooke said. "Hopefully, that'll buy us some time to find someplace to ground before—"

The new sensor warning shattered her thought mid-sentence. Her eyes immediately noted the two new red icons darting up from the looming green swath of the planet behind them. As their sensor echoes emerged from the planet's far side and resolved into arrows swooping around with deadly grace, the now-active sensors tagged them.

HMR-HD *Hammerhead*s.

Aerospace fighters.

Not drones.

"Son of a bitch," she muttered.

CHAPTER 3

*The Promise foretold of the day when the Light would rise
up to enlighten all of the Lost, back when the Guardians
were new, before the days of the Wayward. But while
our protectors spoke often of the Promise, I never put
much stock in their religious talk, until the coming of the
Master. To me, it was calling enough to live on our Blessed
World, safe from the Lost, under the benevolence of the
Guardians. Even the life of the Wayward was a blessing.*
    *But these last few years, after all I have seen, and all
I have heard...these days, I am not certain what I believe.*

—Administrator Ogima Lunalla,
City of Hope

FOREST OF SHROUDS
JARDINE (HERAKLEION)
FREE WORLDS LEAGUE
30 OCTOBER 3067

The valley below opened to reveal an ancient and majestic sight:
a proud city, awash in the golden rays of pre-dusk sunlight,
stood in ancient splendor, defiant of Mother Nature through the
passing of centuries. Emerald-winged *shino* hawks swept the
skies above, returning to their nests amid the nearly forgotten
spires, preparing for the cool night ahead.

Smaller jungle kites, meanwhile, flocked to the ruins closer to the towering trees of the Forest of Shrouds, many perching atop the ancient, armored sentinels standing vigil in the fields of tall, untamed grass.

Abandoned ages ago, the cracked and worn metal titans now stood as oversized scarecrows to whose presence the wildlife had long ago become immune. Though overgrown with vines and green with moss and algae, three of the four wrecks still rose proudly above the earth, as if to guard the ancient city—and their fallen fourth comrade—against all intruders.

Pausing at the edge of the forest, astride his trusty mount, the hunter surveyed the city and its long-dead guardians, lost in solemn thought.

Until his eyes caught the streak of fire high above, a streak that left a trail of black smoke as it spun in toward the distant hills.

Then his ears heard the thunder of a sonic boom.

K-1 DROPSHUTTLE *MAGELLAN*
FOREST OF SHROUDS
JARDINE (HERAKLEION)
FREE WORLDS LEAGUE
30 OCTOBER 3067

As crash landings went, Brooklyn Stevens had to admit theirs could've been far, far worse. The *Magellan* now looked like a cracked egg. Its broken hull, scorched and blasted in several places, settled awkwardly into the earth. One landing leg—the only one of the four not twisted in the neck-breaking plummet, by the look of it—rested atop the toppled and broken remains of several trees. Fires still licked around the impact site and from several of the shuttle's more grievous injuries, sending a column of dark smoke high into the azure sky.

Brooke silently hoped they hadn't lit a tinderbox.

"Alright, now what?" Tibor Mitternacht's voice sounded strange, coming from the cockpit passenger seat directly behind her as well as through the earpiece of her headset.

Frowning, Brooke glanced back over her shoulder, even though she knew she couldn't see Tibor through the thick, padded crash bar of the pilot seat.

As devastating as the crash was, Brooke counted them both lucky that not only had they survived, so had their modified Alliance Motors *Rock Possum* IndustrialMech. Stowed on its back in the shuttle's expanded cargo bay and strapped down to prevent shifting, the 40-ton prospecting WorkMech amazingly powered up without a hitch as soon as Brooke and Tibor—crawling through the *Magellan*'s twisted interior—found their way inside.

Within minutes of the shuttle crashing into the expansive woodlands, Brooke had managed to snap the 'Mech free of its restraints and crawl it out through the shuttle's door, which of course was stuck shut. A systems check—and her successful efforts to tear free of the *Magellan*'s armored womb—revealed the *Possum*'s right-arm mining drill still functioned, as did its centerline searchlight. Out of commission, however, was its left-arm lift hoist—and while her diagnostics panel gave the left-shoulder short-range missile rack a green light, Brooke wasn't sure she wanted to test the weapon after she noticed a nasty dent in its housing.

At the moment, she was relieved the old WorkMech still walked. She'd brought the machine "just in case," considering it an excellent source of extra armor and reliable transportation on an unknown world; now, it was practically the only thing salvageable in this entire mission.

"Are you picking up anything at all?" she asked.

Tibor offered a noncommittal grunt. "Nothing I can make out," he said. "But Maggie's throwing off a lot of thermals and EM."

Brooke looked again at the *Magellan*. The customized K-1 DropShuttle had made its last flight, she was sure, but the ship's electronic systems and fusion plant were still running when she and Tibor scrambled to abandon ship. Moreover, the sensors were on full active, and Brooke had decided to switch on the communications systems to send just the kind of distress beacon anyone who shot down an interloping shuttle might expect to hear.

It would also, incidentally, inform the *Sacajawea* that Brooke and Tibor had survived at least long enough to make it dirtside, and that Jardine was protected by hostile aerospace assets.

The extra bonus of this effort was that anyone sweeping the woods for them would first have to contend with the electronic noise generated by the crashed shuttle.

"Good," she said with finality. "Then let's get moving."

As Brooke set the *Possum* in motion, turning the lumbering machine deeper into the woods, she planned to put as many kilometers as possible between her and Tibor and the wreck of the *Magellan*.

It was a crude plan, but for the moment, it would have to do.

LEOPARD-CLASS DROPSHIP *KAYLIN*
PIRATE JUMP POINT
JARDINE (HERAKLEION) SYSTEM
FREE WORLDS LEAGUE
30 OCTOBER 3067

Anton Hara forced his eyes open and found himself staring at his own balled fists. Sweat beaded on his forehead, and his mouth was filled with the taste and feel of wet cardboard.

The harness kept him strapped into the captain's chair of the *Kaylin*. But in the microgravity, it hardly mattered.

Hyperspace jumps didn't come with momentum, after all.

Shaking his head as his mind quickly came to grips with the return to rational space, he turned his stark, malachite-colored eyes on the man who sat in the executive officer's chair beside him.

Overweight to the point where his slate-gray "businessman's jumpsuit" seemed ready to burst at its catches, the man convulsed in the chair. His eyes remained screwed shut, and his ordinarily pasty-white face had turned an almost amusing shade of purple as he choked on his own tongue. He coughed once, desperately trying to clear the blockage that wasn't there, all the while struggling to wipe away the sweat pouring off his short, spiky red hair.

The spectacle drew the attention of every man on the *Kaylin*'s bridge, including Hara's exec, Lenard Bryce, who stared blankly at the man from the navigation station. Even through Bryce religiously maintained a practiced emotionless expression, Hara could read the man's coal-black eyes even through the glare of his spectacles, and knew their thoughts matched exactly in that moment .

This man doesn't belong out here.

To be sure, Nathan Bellamy had a fairly mild case of Transit Disorientation Syndrome—as evidenced by the fact he hadn't already redecorated the bridge with his last three meals. But between the psychosomatic choking and the epileptic twitching, he clearly demonstrated the signs of a man whose hubris was the only claim he could lay to the exec's chair during a jump.

The Interstellar Expeditions liaison eventually brought himself under control, but by that time—as with the last jump—any shred of dignity he'd managed to build up had evaporated.

By then, however, Hara had already turned his attention to Bryce, his question asked with the simple arch of an eyebrow.

Bryce caught the look and refocused his gaze on the navigation panel. It took a few moments, but eventually he nodded, allowing himself a small smile.

"The JumpShip's triangulation confirms," he said, almost unnecessarily. "This is Herakleion."

"Any sign of Stevens?" Bellamy suddenly interjected, his voice cracking.

Hara shot the liaison a cold glare, which the man did a great job of ignoring.

Bryce, meanwhile, flicked his gaze over to the sensor watchman, named Jacoby, another of Hara's veteran officers. The officer checked his instruments and looked up, but did not speak until Hara gave him the nod—which came just a moment after Bellamy began to ask again.

"I'm not reading the *Sacajawea*'s beacon within our sensor range, and I haven't found any sign of her sail or EM signature yet."

Hara narrowed his eyes. "But?"

"I *am* picking up signals from in-system," Jacoby added. "From some Free Worlds warning beacons in mid-system orbit. They claim the planet below is a toxic wasteland."

"Fits the profile Stevens fed us," Bryce said.

"But where is *she*?" Hara asked.

"I'll tell you where!" Bellamy blurted. "Two weeks ahead of us! And possibly in a different system, no less!"

"*Mister* Bellamy," Hara snapped, his voice so sharp it almost made the liaison jump. "I'm getting tired of having to remind you that hyperspace travel is an *exact* science. After you handed over those IE records, Stevens' crew sorted out that *this* star was likely your Atlantis, but given the inconsistencies, we needed to be certain we wouldn't be jumping to an unstable pirate point."

Bellamy's cheeks flushed. "Why then, *Captain*," he said with a snort as he began to unfasten his harness, "did your 'exact science' fail to materialize us right next to the *Sacajawea* when we jumped immediately after her?"

Hara felt his jaw tighten. Though Bellamy screwed up his effort to be condescending by stressing Hara's rank, the fact he had lost two good men fighting those raiders over Shasta only to have his objective leap out in the middle of the fight made his blood boil.

And all *this* suit cared about was that Stevens' broken coordinates had forced their own JumpShip to make a blind jump into interstellar space. It took a trickle charge directly from the JumpShip's fusion core to repower her K-F drive for another attempt, and by that time Hara's people on both the *Kaylin* and her *Scout*-class transport had been able to compute a "reasonable" set of coordinates to this system.

"Stevens' jump wave came right in the middle of her coordinates transmission, as you may recall. And as you may also recall, we were under fire at that moment. Our computers had time to make a best guess from the coordinates, but in this line of work, a best guess almost always means you'll need a second jump to correct the result."

Bellamy opened his mouth to reply, but before he could utter a sound Hara had expertly snapped off his own harness and pushed himself out of his seat. The sudden move took the larger man by surprise, and he struggled to retreat as he found himself face-to-face with the mercenary commander.

"Or would you have preferred we stay back there at Shasta, re-plotting jump points while those fighters and their DropShip hammered us into space dust? It was, after all, *your* idea to give Stevens the data, *your* idea that we use 'whatever coordinates Stevens gives us.'"

Bellamy bristled and tried to draw himself up, but in the weightlessness of the bridge, all he managed was to drift up toward the overhead monitors.

Hara closed his eyes and waved dismissively at the man, once more cutting Bellamy off before he could respond. "Never mind," he said. "We could recriminate over this for a week. And in that time we could find your Stevens and the *Sacajawea*, and even your precious lost world. Or we could jump back to League space, and you can tell your IE masters we failed.

"Either way, I see no reason for you to come to my bridge again and amuse yourself by talking down to me and my crew. Do I make myself clear, Mister Bellamy?"

Bellamy's cheeks flushed even redder, and his eyes narrowed to slits, but whatever he was about to say at that moment remained unspoken as a rational part of his brain apparently kicked in and wiped the expression from his face. The change came on so abruptly it surprised even Hara, and once again he found himself wondering just what kind of man IE had assigned him as a liaison.

For his part, Bellamy simply nodded and presented Hara with a forced smile. "Very well then, Captain," he said. "One week. I'll be in my stateroom if you need me."

With that, Nathan Bellamy twisted and propelled himself gently toward the bridge's aft exit. He was gone for less than ten seconds before Bryce appeared, floating, at Hara's side.

"He does have a point," Bryce offered quietly. "What if Stevens deliberately fed us bad coordinates? She could be light years away by now."

"It's possible," Hara muttered. "If so, she'd better pray I never find her or her ship again."

FOREST OF SHROUDS
JARDINE (HERAKLEION)
FREE WORLDS LEAGUE

Adept Errol held his laser rifle ready and focused his true sight along its barrel as his true hearing sorted through the white noise the ruined ship was broadcasting. To him, the field was aglow with a dazzling spectrum of yellows, golds, and reds as fire licked around the still-superheated hull of the tiny craft.

The wreckage was a thing of beauty, a 200-ton egg torn from the sky and cracked on the unyielding ground. The hull, pockmarked by his aerial brethren's Imperator Zeta-20s, had been blasted open with the savage precision wielded by a true artist. Each burst had killed one of the shuttle's major flight systems, forcing the craft into its final plummet.

As he stepped through the flames, scarcely feeling the heat through his ballistic armor, Errol pulled his gaze away from his rifle and glanced back at his squad. Five of the Master's finest—some with eyes aglow with righteous fire, and others displaying the gleaming hints of their transformation from mere Frails to the Master's Hands—swept through the edge of the newly scorched clearing, with rifles braced and ready.

With a quick gesture using his true hand, Errol signaled Adepts Long, Sutton, and Unagi—his fastest Ghosts—to circle the perimeter. In a flash, their true legs sped them away, each choosing a separate route without a word among them. Charred and smoldering wood crackled around them, but their own movements made no sound.

Alone with Adepts Kimiko and Yanara, Errol gestured again. Yanara nodded his clean-shaven head, the wraparound visor for his true eyes gleaming in the firelight, and took the lead. Errol followed him in, leaving Kimiko to trail behind, where her enhanced true hearing—complete with radio-sensitive antennae jutting out from her long, dark hair—would give them early warning of anyone trying to flank their position. Errol's gesture communicated one additional command: *strike to disable only.*

Errol followed Yanara through the crashed vessel's huge bay door, now broken away from the craft.

The hatch, ordinarily designed to swing down as a ramp, had been jammed shut by the shuttle's crash, so it did not surprise Errol that it had been ripped open and outward. The Adept quickly identified the telltale marks at the edges of the tear and the other gouges around the mangled opening.

Single 'Mech. Armed with a mining drill.

Stepping through the hatch, he saw the reinforced strapping and braces that once held the metal monstrosity flat on the expanded cargo bay of the DropShuttle's lower deck—all twisted and shattered either by the crash, the 'Mech's escape, or both.

A quaint innovation, he assessed, but one impractical for military operations; the interlopers clearly had no idea who they now faced.

He clicked his tongue, activating the communications system grafted to his jaw. "Long, Sutton, Unagi," he subvocalized. "Scan for tracks; single intruder 'Mech at large."

The acknowledgements—little more than whispers in Errol's consciousness—came back as one as he continued to work his way behind Yanara, sweeping every opening and cabin in the wrecked ship for signs of life, even fading ones.

It took less than a minute to confirm Errol's suspicions: Two occupants only. Both currently absent.

Unagi's voice—strong, yet lyrical—whispered to Errol as he, Yanara, and Kimiko regrouped in the shattered cargo bay. "Trail sensed," she said. "Invader moving west of crash site, heading two-eight-five degrees."

Errol narrowed his frail, simple eye and shared looks with Kimiko and Yanara. Yanara cocked his head to one side and frowned, holding his rifle muzzle-up. Kimiko's mouth remained a thin line, her black eyes and facial expression completely passive, her rifle held at the ready.

They had heard and understood.

West. Away from the City.

Errol flashed his fellow Ghosts a predatory grin and turned to face the ruined bay door and the smoking forest beyond. His true eye and his true ears filtered out the ruined shuttle's electronic noise, and the sensory input streaming in from

Unagi's channel supported his expectations. Low-level EM field: non-fusion vehicle.

With a click of his tongue, Ghost Adept Omega Errol switched frequencies, sending the signal to *all* of his people—including those in the distant Sanctum.

"Intruders heading for Wayward territory," he reported. "We are pursuing."

FOREST OF SHROUDS
JARDINE (HERAKLEION)
FREE WORLDS LEAGUE

Brooklyn Stevens chewed on her lower lip, tasting nervous sweat, and tried not to think about how colossally messed up the entire mission had become. The thrum of the IndustrialMech's fuel-cell pumps, scarcely audible over the thundering footfalls of its metal-shod feet, drowned out the sound of snapping trees and underbrush, but still she could hear her own nagging thoughts.

In her time with Interstellar Expeditions—and afterward— she had explored worlds forgotten for centuries. In most cases, the missions were simple treasure hunts, picking over the remains of a dead planet already scoured by pirates and prospectors generations before her careful research brought her to their scarred surfaces. In a few cases, there had even been people still living there, castaways of a lost era, or survivors of a mis-jump.

But this was different.

This time, she'd hit a world that knew she was coming.

And for what?

Ego? The chance to be the first to land on Jardine and make it back alive?

Or was it vengeance? The opportunity to expose the secrets that killed Marie back on Shasta?

"Why didn't you talk me out of this, Trouble?" she whispered.

"Would you have listened?" His voice came back, strong in her ears.

"Probably not." She sighed. It didn't surprise her that Tibor, jammed into the cramped passenger seat behind her, had caught her rhetorical question. "But maybe if I did, we wouldn't be in this mess."

"Oh, *definitely*!" Tibor shot back with a chuckle. "But what makes this so different from jumping to uninhabited systems on a regular basis to pick through toxic ruins to find an artifact for which any number of pirates and more than a few government agents might kill you?"

"Thanks for *that* vote of confidence!"

"Hey, *mein Freund*, listen. We knew coming in we could get shot down. But being shot down also means the occupants have working aerospace assets and a communications network. And you know *that* means there's a way off this rock."

Brooke nodded, even though she knew Tibor wouldn't be able to see her movement. In the dozens of scenarios they'd anticipated during the shuttle ride in, what he was reminding her of now had become clear. Even if the planet only had aerospace-fighter defense, there were ways to work around that and journey back to the *Sacajawea*—which would receive their distress signal maybe four hours after the *Magellan*'s crash landing, but would send no reply. The *Sac*, knowing their plight, could send out a second shuttle, but they would wait until a second signal came from Brooke or Tibor to request it, a signal that would include precise instructions for a safe extraction.

It wasn't the first time one of their plans had hinged on escaping aboard a stolen ship, Brooke noted with wry amusement.

But it *was* one of the first she could recall actually needing to.

Of course, that contingency hinged on a lot of factors, among them not the least of which was locating where the fighters had come from to start with.

"Verdammter Mist!"

Tibor's curse made Brooke's heart sink, but also snapped her away from her drifting thoughts.

"What? What is it?"

"We have company!"

CHAPTER 4

...Another potential hazard an IE crew may encounter on uncharted worlds is local inhabitants. It cannot be stressed strongly enough that, while invaluable, official Explorer Corps charts and other published sources detail only worlds with high population densities, major industries, and HPG coverage. However, centuries of human migration has led to numerous instances where human settlements have been established or discovered on worlds that are on no current chart, perhaps as a result of overlooked survivors, pirate activity, mis-jumps, or more reclusive colonial activities.

It is important for IE personnel to establish the degree of danger local inhabitants may represent and protect themselves accordingly, but without resorting to violent means unless no other option is available. Remember, even a people dismissed as "mostly harmless" can present a lethal risk to personnel, equipment, and excavation sites.

— *Interstellar Expeditions Explorer's Field Guide*
(Fifteenth Edition),
IE Publications Unlimited, circa 0

FOREST OF SHROUDS
JARDINE (HERAKLEION)
FREE WORLDS LEAGUE

The woods weren't the thickest Brooke had ever torn her way through—hell, even Shasta rainforests were thicker—but as she thundered her 40-ton WorkMech through the branches and brush, it may as well have been an endless sea of continuous foliage. The trees—mostly conifers, from what she could guess—rose so high above her canopy they reduced the sun to a flicker of light half-seen with every stride. Though their branches bent and snapped easily with every swing of her *Possum*'s massive arms, they were dense enough to slow her progress.

A glance at her WorkMech's dashboard told the tale in unrelenting numbers and glaring white sensor blips: her 'Mech was making nine-point-six kilometers per hour.

Whoever was chasing them was doing close to twenty.

"It's not a 'Mech," Tibor reported, his voice filled with ominous calm. "The EM is way too low."

"Battlesuits, maybe?" Brooke asked, her voice cracking. Her mouth had gone bone dry minutes ago. She felt like she hadn't spoken in days.

"Possibly," Tibor came back, his voice coming at her both in the cockpit and through her helmet speakers.

The image of the monster that had boarded the *Sacajawea* and battled them in the corridor flashed through Brooke's mind. That one's suit had been lightweight, meant for boarding actions, where the onboard opposition would normally consist of some vac-suited marines or a few technicians in space gear—and he had served up a lot of hurt despite having three gyrojet guns fired on him.

How much heavier and tougher would these suits be?

Without breaking the WorkMech's stride, Brooke continued to sweep her control panels. The *Rock Possum* was part of a series of IndustrialMechs that the Outworlds Alliance manufactured with modern scavengers in mind. The centuries of the Succession Wars virtually ensured anyone scouring the forgotten Periphery worlds for salvage would be a prime target for pirates and fellow "prospectors." As a result, the entire AM-

PRM-RH7 *Rock Hound* series featured military-grade sensors and armor, both to spot potential trouble and to protect itself against the likelihood of hostile fire.

Along with these capabilities, the *Rock Hound* series incorporated the theory that a good offense equals a solid defense, as all of these avatars of human scavenging also sported at least one weapons system to make a would-be pirate think twice. In Brooke's case, that was her 'Mech's Shannon Fore four-tube short-range missile rack. On her diagnostics panel, the computer still showed a green light for that weapon, indicating it was functioning normally, but Brooke remembered the larger dent and the slight twist to the launcher's housing she'd seen when she visually inspected the machine during her and Tibor's escape from the shuttle. That memory now warred with the tempting green light on her panel.

At the same time, the sensors sketched a topographic image of the nearby terrain—an endless expanse of trees sprouting from a rolling valley of hills, running along a river's edge nearly two kilometers to her right. And there, trailing behind—a mere half kilometer away and closing—was the indistinct white icon of an EM source the targeting systems couldn't identify.

Nowhere to hide; no way to run.

Brooke swallowed hard against a pasty lump of saliva in her throat and chewed on her lip in thought before she finally turned to the controls.

Tibor noticed. "You have a plan." It was not a question.

"If we can make the river," she said. "I'll at least have a clearer shot when they get to us…"

Ghost Adept Omega Errol sensed the IndustrialMech's course change even though he could not see it through the forest. With a predatory grin, he motioned to his fellow Ghosts and gestured.

As one, the six warriors moved, never slowing. In virtual silence they negotiated the terrain, leaping over fallen trees, stray rocks and scrub brush, ducking under low-hanging branches and leaves. Their boots barely made a sound as they scraped through the loose soil, and though they could all sense their quarry's location, every pair of eyes—every true sense available—swept the wilderness for signs of motion, signs of danger.

Errol, in the lead, leveled his laser rifle for a moment when his true sight caught a red-black blur to his left. For an instant, he tracked it with his laser rifle, but held his fire. In silence that rivaled his own team's, a firecat bounded past, ducking into a shadowy ditch.

So, which is it to be, Frail? Errol wondered. *Are you merely racing for the river, or for the Sanctum? Do you realize where you are, or are you as blind as the others who've come and died here?*

His grin widened as his true vision measured the distance between them. Already, he could sense the heat, the electromagnetic signature. An image resolved of an armored titan that mocked everything that was true about a BattleMech, right down to the white noise of its active targeting array.

"Errol," Unagi's voice whispered at the edge of his consciousness, "I sense Waywards. Possibly two, to the south."

"They know enough to stay clear," Errol subvocalized back without breaking his stride.

"They avoid the hunt."

Unagi clicked an affirmative, her warning delivered. The Master's Hands did not require reminders. The Master's Hands knew their duties.

Ahead lay today's enemy. There would be time for Waywards later.

Errol sensed the intruder more clearly than ever. *Less than two hundred meters to go*, he measured, even as the machine lurched through the sparse tree line that followed the edge of Hope River.

Let's see what these Frails are made of!

Brooklyn Stevens had barely swung the *Possum* around and planted its feet by the edge of the narrow river when the first of them burst from the tree line. Four more emerged by the time her eyes even processed what she was seeing, and by the time her weapon crosshairs lined up on the first, there were six in all.

Those aren't battlesuits!

They wore jungle camouflage and carried rifles, but no helmets covered their heads. In the blur of their movement—far faster than Brooke could imagine possible for human beings— she saw what appeared to be elaborate headgear on at least two of them, a gleam of metal and the glow of some kind of visor. One even seemed to clutch his rifle with a hand made of polished metal.

She was so stunned by what she saw and their amazing speed that Brooke nearly forgot to open fire.

Nearly.

With a loud *whoosh*, the torso-mounted SRM rack opened up, faithfully belching a quartet of missiles into the lead soldier's path. Explosions rippled the earth, sending up soil and loose tufts of grass. One of the troopers tumbled backward, but the one she had aimed at merely surged through the cloud of smoke and fire, unharmed.

A half-dozen lasers answered, peppering the *Possum* with pinprick beams that set off the 'Mech's diagnostic sensors, but scored no real armor damage.

Throwing the throttle into reverse, Brooke moved back a step, angling the machine's torso to keep the soldiers in her line of sight. One leg shifted slightly as the soft soil beneath gave way, but Brooke ignored the resulting lurch as she lightly thumbed her right-hand control stick.

With a nasty roar, the three-headed mining drill that replaced the WorkMech's right hand came to life. Powerful enough to bore a hole five meters in diameter through solid bedrock, the drill was a menace even to the armor of a real BattleMech.

But if the approaching soldiers were concerned for even an instant, they didn't show it. The missile tubes were still cycling as they ate up the meters between the tree line and the *Possum*, fanning out to close from all sides simultaneously.

Brooke snarled and swung the 'Mech's right arm toward the nearest trooper, throwing the machine into a violent twist. The camouflaged trooper simply ducked under the ponderous arm and—much to her surprise—reached up to catch the limb with his free hand. Hauling himself up even as she swung the arm back, the soldier maneuvered with the creepy grace of a spider, never losing his grip on the rifle in his other hand.

"Bast damn it!" she gasped.

"Christ!" Tibor whispered back in her ears. "They're all over us! *Run, Brooke!*"

Slamming the throttle forward, Brooke lurched the *Possum* into a flat run and swung the machine around as fast as possible to follow the river's edge. With fewer trees to impede her progress, she quickly brought the 'Mech to a thunderous sixty-kilometer-per-hour run, all the while swinging its arms wildly and sweeping the torso back and forth. Catching a glimpse of the soldier still clinging to the right arm, she swung the left arm around to brush him off. The limbs connected with a shuddering *clang* that threw the 'Mech off balance for a step or two, and Brooke almost grinned when she saw something fall to the forest floor—until she realized she'd only knocked the rifle from the trooper's hand.

The trooper himself now scuttled further up the arm, and for an instant, Brooke saw a scarred and misshapen face beneath the hood of his camouflage.

Her diagnostics board buzzed a warning: armor damage in the right arm and left leg.

They're gonna rip me apart!

Suddenly, a dark shape flashed over the *Possum*'s broad canopy, drawing startled yelps from Brooke and Tibor.

Clad in forest camouflage, the trooper was female—but only in the vaguest sense of the word. Her face, leering at them through the transplas canopy, was a monstrous mixture of flesh and technology. Metal plates covered most of her skull, disappearing beneath a mask of dark, scarred flesh. Her right eye looked like a pitch-black monocle or steel-rimmed eyepatch, but Brooke suspected it saw her more clearly than the natural, pale-blue half of the pair. Clinging to the edge of the canopy with a hand seemingly forged from cold steel, the trooper used the other to aim a laser rifle straight at Brooke.

"Son of a—!" Brooke heard Tibor curse—

—Just as she slammed her arm controls forward, yanked back on the throttle and pulled her feet off the steering pedals. The actions—so sudden and forceful Brooke had no time to yell a warning—sent the *Possum* pitching forward. In less than a second, forty tons of industrial metal and military-grade armor went from a loping, sixty-kilometer run to a steel-rending sprawl in the lush forest soil.

Brooke squeezed her eyes shut more from instinct than anything else. She felt her harness dig into her flesh through the coveralls she wore. Her pilot's helmet—the WorkMech equivalent of a BattleMech neurohelmet—flew off her head and banged against the console before her.

In the chaos of the moment, she heard Tibor cry out in pain, felt his body slam against the back of her seat despite the restraint of his own harness. Something tumbled forward from behind her, clattering in the confines of the forward cockpit.

She also heard the ominous cracking sound that meant damage to the transplas canopy.

Opening her eyes, she breathed a sigh of relief to discover the canopy cracked, but holding. The monster that had climbed on it was gone, but the diagnostics monitors communicated serious damage.

The smell of wet, rich earth leaked into the cockpit as Brooke quickly reached out to snatch back her helmet. Even as she resettled it, her hands were already working the controls to stand the machine up again.

"Some warning next time, damn it!" Tibor growled behind her, his complaint ending with a soft moan.

From somewhere outside there came a bang, followed by a series of shrieking noises. The diagnostics panel flashed from yellow to red on the *Possum*'s aft torso.

Damn it! These guys just won't give up!

"Hang on!" Brooke snapped back.

The *Possum* was halfway to a crouch when she slammed the machine to its side, rolling the vaguely humanoid titan sideways, away from the river. The maneuver—used for millennia by unfortunate souls who found themselves on fire—was also one of the oldest in combating anti-'Mech infantry.

Somewhere in the middle of the roll there was a powerful *thump*. The diagnostics panel painted more of her armor schematic yellow, but reported nothing crippling—yet.

As soon as the 'Mech returned to its face-down position, Brooke worked it back to its feet and throttled forward once more, plunging into the woods just past the tree line. Branches whipped across the armor, smacked against the cracked canopy, and set off the external sensors over and over.

Brooke suddenly noticed she was breathing heavily, her heart racing. *Are they gone?*

"You okay, Trouble?" she finally asked, once more feeling the dusty dryness in her throat.

"I dropped my gun," Tibor muttered. "But I'm fine."

Brooke glanced down, catching sight of Tibor's Gunther MP-20 machine pistol in the shadows by her left foot pedal. Reaching down as much as her harness allowed, her fingers had barely grazed the weapon when she felt another hard impact against the canopy.

Ghost Adept Omega Errol burned with humiliation and pure, unadulterated rage.

Adepts Sutton and Yanara were dead, their bodies mashed into pulp and ash. Adept Unagi was crippled, her true legs shattered beneath the weight of the machine's fall.

Kimiko had fallen behind, but signaled that she remained in pursuit, scarcely ninety meters away.

That left himself and Adept Long to take down the filthy Frail who dared to profane the Master's haven.

As he crawled across the back of the ponderous WorkMech, ignoring the lashes of a hundred branches, Errol reminded himself with some irony that—under different circumstances— he might have admired the woman who piloted this machine. Indeed, any MechWarrior skilled enough to shake off the Master's Hands, to kill his brethren in battle, would be an opponent worthy of his prowess.

But what rankled Errol most right now was that *this* Frail was no MechWarrior. Her piloting style lacked skill, lacked focus. Even now, she charged blindly into the woods, her course aimless and erratic. She fought recklessly, like a common cadet, with actions that reeked of fear and panic.

Which meant Sutton and Unagi had died from mere chance, fortune favoring an incompetent!

As he seethed, Errol hauled himself forward over the WorkMech's broad, flat head and found the canopy's upper lip with his true fingers. A wide branch struck him hard across the face, distorting his true vision for a moment, but Errol was past caring about such inconveniences.

Hauling himself over the edge, he subvocalized to Adept Long, who clung to the machine's waist below: "This Frail is *mine!*"

It was with a strange sense of déjà vu that Brooke looked at the creature hanging across her canopy, his boots having already widened the cracks inflicted when she fell. Though this one was definitely not the same trooper as before, his appearance was no less bizarre, blending technology and mangled flesh.

He carried no weapon she could see, but as she watched, horrified, he pulled back a metal fist that suddenly sprouted a thick blade and punched it straight through the transplas. Cracked and strained, the reinforced panel shifted, then caved inward. Instinctively, Brooke shielded her face as the canopy collapsed over her, showering her with stinging fragments.

Tibor's curse was barely audible over the noise of the *Possum*'s continued run and the constant, rapid-fire slapping of tree branches. Native air flooded the cockpit with a strangely refreshing, earthy smell. But Brooke had no time to enjoy it as the trooper's left boot crashed down on her right armrest, narrowly missing her.

Half-inside, half-outside, the soldier clung to the canopy with one arm while his bladed, mechanical claw scraped away shards of transplas for better access. His face, lashed and bleeding, sneered menacingly, and Brooke thought she saw his lips move; if he said something, she couldn't hear it any better than she could Tibor's desperate cries.

It was then Brooke remembered the Gunther. She strained against her harness, snagged the weapon by its muzzle, and quickly turned. Keeping her body well away from the soldier's leg, she lifted her foot off one of the steering pedals, throwing the *Possum* into a sharp left turn, heading deeper into the woods. The soldier's balance was thrown off for just a moment.

That moment was all she needed to flip the machine pistol over, aim it, and fire.

Despite the outside din, the MP-20 roared with deafening fury in the confined cockpit space. At point-blank range, Brooke thumped five rounds into the soldier's chest, blasting apart his camouflage tunic and spraying the cockpit with his blood. The man snarled, clutching at the wound with his metal hand, but keeping his grip on the canopy.

"Son of a—!" Brooke hissed, and fired again—this time straight into the leg beside her.

With the pistol essentially pressed against the flesh, the burst tore away the man's calf and showered the right side of the cockpit with blood and gore. Brooke heard one slug ricochet off the cockpit interior, and caught the sparks of a secondary panel blowing out, but the real victory came when the man's foot slid off the armrest and he tumbled backward, roaring in pain.

But instead of falling, the trooper simply swung his other foot into the cockpit, jamming it into Brooke's chest. She coughed out her breath, dimly aware she'd lost her grip on the Gunther. Her vision faded to red.

In fuzzy outlines, she saw the soldier still hanging onto the outside of the canopy, one hand clinging to the upper edge of the forward viewport while his metal hand clutched at his wounded chest. His right leg dangled uselessly outside, while his left felt like it pushed against her with all his weight. What little defense the padded pilot's harness offered Brooke was now a liability, digging into her sternum as she gasped for air.

Meanwhile, the *Possum* charged onward, thundering through the woods, crashing into trees without moving its arms to protect it.

Tibor was screaming something, but Brooke couldn't make out the words.

Another dark shape crept into her field of vision, someone else crawling toward the shattered canopy from below.

A detached part of Brooke's mind wondered if she'd ever stood a chance here.

Suddenly, the world exploded around her. A brilliant flare—almost soundless, yet powerful enough to send a jolt through her—overwhelmed her vision. She squeezed her eyes shut and cringed as a harsh, electronic shriek sounded in her ears. Without warning, she felt herself spinning, her stomach leaping into her constricted throat as the *Possum* seemed to pitch violently forward.

Somewhere, Tibor was howling in pain, and so was her attacker.

In the fraction of a second before she felt the impact of 40 tons on the forest floor, Brooke realized her tormentor was no longer there...

She had no idea how long she lost consciousness. In fact, she wondered for a moment if she even had, when she opened her eyes to see the forest before her. It took a few moments to even remember where she was, but she quickly added up the visuals and concluded the *Possum* was now lying sideways on the forest floor.

Loose soil, shattered transplas and random shards of tree branches spilled into the right side of the cockpit, collected during the machine's uncontrolled plunge. The diagnostic panels—no, *all* of her panels—were now dark, and her experimental efforts to restart the machine, or even fire up a secondary system, met with dark silence.

The *Possum* was dead.

"Trouble?" Brooke called out, nervously. With shaking hands, she snapped free of her harness, tossing her helmet to the floor. *"Trouble?"*

After a long moment, a low, pain-filled moan answered.

She looked behind her and gasped. Though the shadows of the darkened cockpit partially obscured him, Brooke could see blood flowing from Tibor's ear. He hung limp in his harness, pinned between his passenger seat and the back of the pilot's seat. Only his moaning told Brooke he was still alive. She reached out to touch him, and was rewarded by a flinch.

"*Gottverdammte Scheiße*, woman!" he groaned. "Don't!"

"Can you move?" she whispered.

"The hell," he growled back, twisting his head slowly from side to side. "Say that again? I can't hea—wait. *Scheiße!* I can't see, either."

"Look at me, Trouble!" Brooke commanded, gently grabbing his chin. "I'm right here."

Tibor turned toward her, but in the partial darkness, she saw that only one of his eyes seemed to focus on her.

"My implants," he moaned. "My ear and my eye—what happened?"

"I don't know," Brooke said, forcing herself to speak louder. "Can you move?"

"Get me out of this chair. We'll see."

Brooke reached out and unsnapped Tibor's harness. Suddenly free of their grip, he sagged for a moment, then reached out with a trembling hand to lever himself up. "Where are our guests?"

"No idea," Brooke said. "Two of them were on the cockpit when we went down."

"Gun," Tibor gasped, fumbling in the dark around Brooke's chair. He came up with the forgotten MP-20.

"You *sure* you can't see?" Brooke asked.

"Not as well as I used to," he said distractedly.

"Come on," she said, crawling toward the shattered canopy.

The missing transplas made exiting the fallen 'Mech easy enough, but as she crawled through the opening, Brooke's hand touched hot metal. Jerking her hand away, she looked down and saw what looked like the remains of a hand, a sinister-looking blade protruding from its palm.

Charred and twisted, the hand looked as though it had been blown off its parent arm.

Another suicide bomb?

She came to her feet as Tibor clambered into the open. Painfully, he stood up and immediately slumped back again, leaning against the shattered cockpit with a moan.

"Christ!" he sighed. "The universe is spinning."

Brooke glanced at the *Possum* and frowned. The machine appeared to be intact—for the most part—but now was lying in a tangled heap. Scars from hand-weapon fire and what looked like ugly red and black paint smears speckled its body. The left arm, with its ruined lift hoist, lay twisted at an odd angle, but the right drilling arm lay outstretched, as if the machine had simply decided to take a nap in the woods.

The legs, too, seemed fine, and though some scrub brush sprang from the forest floor around them, she could see nothing at a glance that looked remotely like a 'Mech-tripping hazard. *So what in Bast's name brought us down?*

A twig snapped behind Brooke, and she spun around, catching Tibor's reaction only in the briefest of instants as she also swung her arm up.

In that same instant, the unmistakable *snap* of a laser rifle left a bright blue afterimage burned on Brooke's retinas. She heard Tibor yelp as his weapon caught the blast, but she couldn't look away from the shooter.

The woman stood less than five meters away, her laser rifle loosely cradled in her hand. She wore the same forest camouflage as her fellow troopers, but her hood hung down, allowing her long, dark hair to flow freely. Tiny, wing-like antennae protruded from where Brooke figured her ears ought be, but otherwise the woman seemed normal, even attractive. Her almond-shaped eyes, however, were black pools, and her expression was so completely blank that Brooke wondered if it was just a synthflesh prosthetic.

Until the woman spoke.

"You have one chance to identify yourselves and state your business here," she said, her accent a strange mix of Asian and something else Brooke couldn't place.

Stunned speechless for a second, Brooke finally opened her mouth to speak only after the woman's unreadable eyes focused on her, and her rifle came up with deadly purpose.

But before she could utter a sound, a loud report echoed. The soldier flew back, stumbling several steps as a cloud of blood and flesh blossomed over her chest.

The woman didn't fall right away, but her laser rifle dipped as she haltingly turned to face her attacker. Brooke's eyes followed hers, and she was startled to see a man in dark fatigues, riding a powerful feline beast, hunting rifle raised toward the soldier.

"Get down, Lost One!" he bellowed as he fired again.

This time, the shot took the soldier in the stomach and blasted clear through her body.

Brooke threw herself backward, falling against the hull of the collapsed WorkMech. Though the soldier raised her rifle to return fire, Brooke could see her strength was fading fast.

The laser rifle flashed too low, striking the man's mount, rather than his body. The animal roared in pain and pitched to one side, but its rider remained tall in his saddle and managed to get his beast under control.

The soldier stumbled forward one step and bared her teeth as she forced her rifle up again.

Another blast struck her in the head before she could fire, and her body fell sideways.

Before it hit the ground the corpse exploded, showering the forest with fragments of bone, blood, and flesh. Brooke and Tibor ducked a moment too late, and she felt something hard and sharp lance into her side.

Falling to one knee, Brooke reached back and desperately dug out the fragment, coming away with her hand bloodied and what looked like a piece of bone for her troubles. She and Tibor were still staring at it when the rider and his wounded mount stalked over to them in near-perfect silence.

The man was dark-skinned and stocky, with slightly Asiatic features, a broad nose and almond-shaped eyes. His hair and eyes were jet black, and Brooke would have described his expression as brooding. His clothes were plain and dark, but as he moved closer, Brooke could make out thick leather stitching, and his boots seemed handmade, if well-worn. His rifle, its large muzzle pointed cautiously earthward, looked like a custom job as well, with a dark wood stock, a handcrafted sighting scope, and a curiously oversized magazine.

He pinned Brooke and Tibor with an expression that grew darker as he regarded Tibor directly. As they silently considered each other, two more riders seemed to melt out of the forest, rifles held at the ready.

When the first hunter spoke, it was with the same curious accent of the woman soldier, but in a deeper, richer baritone.

"Welcome to the Blessed World of Jardine, Lost Ones," he said. "Peace of Blake be with you."

CHAPTER 5

For generations uncounted, ComStar's guardians preserved the safety and sanctity of our blessed world against the ravages of the wars beyond it, and for that our forefathers were grateful. But despite the Promise, there have always been those who resented our endless solitude, those whom the fear of invasion by the Lost Ones drove underground on our native soil. Unable to flee our world, they instead wandered the lands, straying from the safe haven of Hope to look upon the forgotten frontiers where those who came long before us once lived.

It is important to remember that the Guardians never turned us away, never counted us among the Lost. We are merely the Wayward, children of the Guardians' benevolence, and driven into exile by choices of our own making.

—ALAHNI, KEEPER OF TALES
SHROUDED FOREST TRIBE, CA. 3067

FOREST OF SHROUDS
JARDINE (HERAKLEION)
FREE WORLDS LEAGUE
30 OCTOBER 3067

Brooklyn Stevens shifted uncomfortably on the back of the *tabiranth*, but if the animal took any notice of her action, she didn't feel any change in its casual gait. But since her wrists were bound to a short nub at the back of the rider's saddle, her struggle to adjust her position definitely was noticed by the man sitting there.

The crude blindfold tied over her eyes prevented her from seeing the beast's rider, so she could only guess whether the man turned toward her when he spoke.

"Being dragged along behind a *tabi* will hardly help your situation," he said, his tone somehow simultaneously light and menacing.

"Trying to avoid saddle sores," she muttered. "Or rather, lack of saddle sores."

"Yes, well—we rarely take on *living* passengers after a good hunt."

Thank Bast for small favors! Brooke mused. Though these "hunters" *had* rescued her and Tibor from the last of the cyborgs that had attacked them, she was not really surprised when their rescuers had bound them and hoisted them uncomfortably atop their large, pseudo-feline riding beasts.

To be sure, she'd though about fighting them, but their superior numbers and the half-empty magazine in Tibor's Gunther machine pistol promised an unpleasant outcome.

What did surprise Brooke was that these men had taken great pains to scavenge a half-crushed corpse and certain body parts from the bionic freak-shows she and Tibor had battled. Between that, the size of the weapons they carried, and the electromagnetic burst that had disabled her *Possum* and several of the monsters swarming it, Brooke wondered what these men actually hunted.

But even that curiosity paled beside the primary concern gnawing at her stomach. Just before the blindfolds came down, she had watched in horror as Tibor slumped forward on his mount. She'd yelled his name but gotten no reply. A few moments later, one of the other hunters—in a rich voice filled with hate—announced that Tibor still lived.

"EMP mines, heavy rifles," Brooke observed at length. "Do you actually hunt these cyborgs?"

"The machine men are no one's prey," the hateful-sounding hunter spat, his voice sounding distantly from one of the other *tabis*. "We fight them only in self-defense."

"Then why scavenge them?" she pressed. "If you're concerned about revealing your location, you have to realize their implants must be trackable."

"We can use the tech," her rider answered flatly. "And we have ways of making sure the signals stay inert and nothing goes 'boom' until we're ready for it."

Brooke scowled. For a moment, almost against her will, her senses absorbed the scent of a forest in rich, full bloom, and the sounds of rustling foliage, *tabi* growls, and the squawking of some other local fauna. For a moment, she had a hard time hanging on to her anger.

"What about my friend?" she finally asked.

"He's a machine man, too," said the one she had christened Hateful Hunter. "Right now, he's lucky to be alive...kind of like you."

Charming!

They rode for a long time in silence. Were it not for the *tabis'* occasional growls and the heat of her rider's body, she felt she could almost forget there was anyone else around.

They made several turns in the woods, and every so often she felt the brush of a branch along her arms and legs, and even the occasional stomach-lurching sensation of a sudden drop in the forest floor.

When the *tabiranth* she was riding abruptly slowed, then stopped, and she lurched forward into her rider, Brooke realized she had very nearly fallen asleep from the sheer tranquility of the moment.

Voices broke the silence, accented the same as those of her rider and the other hunters, but more heavily so. They spoke in low, urgent tones.

"Welcome back, Ravid," the first voice said. "I gather there were complications?"

"You could say that, Moze," Brooke's rider answered.

"Likeke won't be pleased," a second voice said.

"Tell me about it!" Hateful Hunter shot back.

"Who are they?" asked the voice she now identified as Moze.

"Lost, it seems," said her rider—Ravid. "They were fighting Guardians down by the river."

"That one doesn't look well," Moze said. Brooke turned to catch the words. *Tibor?*

"He's implanted," Ravid said. "Caught some of the EMP and fainted a bit after that."

"A machine man?" the second voice asked, his tone shocked.

"Doesn't seem so."

"Oh, Likeke *really* won't be pleased!" Moze said.

"Maybe not," Ravid sighed. "But we'll see what he says, won't we?"

"Alright then," Moze's voice said after a moment. "Move along."

The *tabis* began to move again, and Brooke waited in silence. In her mind's eye, she imagined moving deeper into the forest, past an unseen perimeter. She envisioned tents and rocks, or maybe caves in the hollows of the hills. In less than a minute, she became aware of the sound of other voices, perhaps a dozen or so, all speaking quietly, words impossible to make out—many not even in English, she guessed. Gasps followed her as they moved, questions whispered too low to make out clearly.

And she smelled...was that beef roasting? Her mouth began to water.

The *tabis* continued walking at a casual gait for another few moments. The smell of roasted meat lingered in her nostrils, reminding Brooke just how long it had been since she last ate anything with *flavor.* She thought she heard Tibor moan in the background, but before she could speak, the ride came to a sudden stop, and she felt Ravid twist around in his harness.

"Right," he said. "Here we are, Lost One."

Brooke felt his hand against her face and flinched as he firmly yanked the blindfold away.

She blinked in the sudden light—though it was not as bright as she'd feared. Before her eyes had fully adjusted, Ravid dismounted, his feet hitting the soft earth almost soundlessly. He reached up to the ropes securing her to his harness, and deftly freed her from the anchor without unbinding her wrists.

Brooke scowled as he then helped her down, and winced at the rough landing.

She looked around. The clearing was barely fifteen meters across, almost completely shaded by a think canopy of leaves. Along one side, the *tabis* were being led to a fallen tree by three young boys dressed in the same mix of hide and synthetics as the hunters. With thick brush and tall grass around the perimeter, only one avenue looked clear enough to be a traveled path, and in that direction she could see a few curious men and women peering back at her. Brooke decided this led back to the main camp.

The hunters had retained their rifles, and Ravid nudged her toward the spot where another hunter had placed—or dropped—Tibor on the ground, his blindfold still in place. An angry glare from a second hunter—probably good 'ol Hateful—settled briefly on her before regarding Tibor's limp form.

Tibor moaned just then, and Brooke felt a wave of relief.

Ravid looked at the angry hunter. "What are you waiting for, Dimka? Help the man up!"

Dimka sneered at Ravid, then reached down to roughly yank Tibor up off the forest floor. Brooke felt her rage swell suddenly out of control and stepped forward, but the third hunter swung his rifle around and fixed her with a wide-eyed stare. Without blinking or looking away, the third hunter shook his head, his meaning clear.

In a flash, Ravid smacked Dimka hard across the temple. Dimka blinked and shot a deadly look back at him, but Ravid had turned away to pull off Tibor's blindfold. Brooke winced at the sight of the black-and-blue ring around Tibor's eye.

"What the—?" Dimka growled.

"We're not savages here, miss," Ravid said coolly, looking at Brooke. "Even though some of us try real hard to be."

"Where are we?" Brooke finally asked, almost immediately realizing how inane the question truly was. *What does that matter?* she asked herself. *No matter where we are, it may as well be the middle of nowhere.*

"The exact location is not important," Ravid said. "Except, perhaps, for the fact that it exists at all. There are so few of us left, you understand."

"So few of who?"

"*Us*, of course!" Dimka snapped.

Ravid let out an exasperated sigh. "This can all be explained better by Likeke. For now, we have to tend to your friend, and see about salvaging those Manei Domini parts."

Brooke blinked. "The what?"

"Manei Domini," Ravid repeated. "The machine men who attacked you and your strange BattleMech."

"BattleM—?" Brooke began, then stopped. "You mean the machine I was driving? That was no BattleMech."

"A WorkMech, then?" Dimka scoffed. "Strange weapon for fighting the Guardians with."

Ravid sighed again and gestured toward the third hunter. Brooke followed the direction of his arm and saw a gathering throng. Many bore distinct ethnic features—a mix of AmerIndian and Polynesian, she guessed—and their clothing matched the hunters' styles to greater or lesser degree, mixing hide and synthetic fibers. A few, she noticed, were armed; she spotted sheathed knives and holstered pistols at their hips, even on a girl who couldn't have been older than thirteen.

The third hunter walked toward the gathered crowd, slinging a sack over his shoulder Brooke noticed was stained with blood. Holding his rifle casually in the other hand, he used it as a staff to clear a path through the others as Ravid nudged her forward with the butt of his weapon.

The path out of the clearing was short, and led to a second clearing scarcely any bigger. But instead of simple foliage around the perimeter, Brooke noticed earthen hillocks and rocks, creating harder barriers all around—a naturally defended clearing. As she walked ahead of Ravid, she spied a couple of natives along one edge of the clearing using "flameless campfires" to cook some kind of animal carcass. Again her mouth watered at the smell of the meat, and she flushed slightly when her stomach growled noisily.

"Brooke...?" she heard, Tibor's voice weak.

Glancing back, she saw him stumbling ahead of Dimka, who managed to look indignant as he prodded his gaunt prisoner forward with one hand and helped him keep to his feet with the other. Tibor's natural eye was open only slightly, and his other eye seemed swollen shut.

"It's okay, Trouble," she assured him.

Sure it's okay, she thought. *We're just tied up and being dragged around a strange camp full of armed people in the middle of nowhere!*

Brooke counted maybe two-dozen or so pairs of eyes following their progress through two more clearings similar to the first before they came to the entrance of a natural cave in an earthen hill. The third hunter stopped at the entrance, but Ravid urged her into the darkness. Behind them, Dimka helped Tibor enter the cave—nearly tripping, if Tibor's soft Teutonic curse was any indication.

Brooke breathed deep, focusing to settle her nerves. The smell of earth and moisture filled her nostrils, along with something else, curious and metallic. The thought of throwing her weight into Ravid to throw him off balance and try to escape crossed her mind for perhaps the hundredth time, but once more she dismissed it. For one thing, the cave tunnel was too narrow for good maneuvering. For another, Tibor's condition made it clear he would not be able to fend for himself once they started running—if he could even run.

But most of all, she realized that even if they could escape, a central problem remained. *Where would we go?*

The tunnel's darkness didn't last long. After a dip in the ground and a short hook to the left, she saw a steady glow straight ahead, beyond a thin, tattered curtain.

As Ravid led them through it, she found herself in an earthen chamber, its roof supported by a clever arrangement of wooden frameworks, with a thick hide canopy holding back the loose soil above and a woven "carpet" keeping the floor clean. But more surprising to her—beyond the curious engineering that made such a chamber possible—were the tubes of light that ringed the chamber, providing a degree of ambient light.

"Fiber-optic sunlight channels?" she whispered. "Ingenious!"

"Centuries-old technology, really," said a man seated at a crude desk on the far side of the room. Brooke took in his appearance: middle-aged yet well-built, with short graying hair, stubbly chin, and clothes as plain as those worn by the hunters.

He looked up from the pages of a worn-looking paper book, which he had been reading in the light of a small oil lamp beside him. Rising smoothly from a handcrafted folding chair, he maintained an expression that was at once unrevealing and curious.

"I realize we may appear as savages to you, Lost One," he said in accented English, "but I can assure you we are—mostly, at least—anything but."

The man crossed the small chamber to stand before Brooke, half a head taller than she was. She could smell his sweat and a faint whiff of some kind of alcohol she couldn't place.

He met her eyes for a second, then looked over at Tibor. An eyebrow arched.

"Dimka—?" he began.

"He didn't strike him, Likeke," Ravid quickly jumped in. "The man was injured when he and his companion set off a trip-mine. He has...modifications."

Likeke's brow furrowed. He glanced once again at Brooke, and then stepped closer to look at Tibor. Somewhat more coherent now, Tibor blinked back at him through his good eye and gave the man a feeble smile.

"How're ya doin'?" he drawled.

Likeke frowned and turned back to Ravid. "A *modified* Lost?"

"Yes," Ravid said. "The Manei Domini were all over their shuttle when they landed. They attempted to escape in some kind of WorkMech, but both the machine and the Domini were destroyed by one of our EMP mines."

"A WorkMech against Domini and a modified Lost One?" Likeke snorted, his focus returning to Brooke. "Did you people not realize who you were dealing with here?"

"Perhaps not," Brooke admitted, finally breaking her silence. "But, in a pinch, any tool may save one's life. Wouldn't you agree?"

As if stunned by her ability to speak, Likeke blinked. A smile crept slowly over his face as he nodded. "More than you know," he said. "Who are you, then? What has brought you to Jardine?"

Brooke frowned. *Lie or truth?* she debated. "My name is Brooklyn Stevens," she began. "This man is my partner, Tibor.

We're explorers. We were contracted to find the lost world of Jardine."

Likeke grinned, and stifled a laugh. "Lost world, you say?"

Dimka barked his derision, and Ravid chuckled.

Brooke raised her eyebrows. "It's the truth," she said. "Jardine has been off the maps for centuries."

"Of course it has," Likeke said. "So. Is it true, after all? Have the wars finally ended?"

Brooke tilted her head. "Which wars?"

"Why, the Succession Wars, of course!"

"Then you know," Tibor said, the slight slur in his speech sending a chill down Brooke's spine. "You've been lost since the fall of the Star League. It's been three hundred years since—"

"We *know* how much time has passed, Lost One," Likeke said, briefly shooting him an intense glare. "But have the Houses truly awakened from their chaos, as the Guardians' machine men claim? Is the Third Transfer truly upon us?"

"Third Transfer?" Brooke repeated. "I don't understand."

Likeke opened his mouth to speak, hesitated, then snapped it shut. His gaze turned to Dimka, whose scowl remained etched on his face.

"Fetch Alahni," he said. "She can explain."

Dimka looked as if he'd been struck. "Likeke," he started, "we do not know these people. This could be a Guardian trick."

"If it were," Likeke scolded, "I would already be dead, and Domini would already be descending upon us. Fetch. Alahni."

As Dimka retreated, Likeke's eyes returned to Brooke. His gaze dropped low and came back up, a response she was used to seeing accompanied by a lecherous grin. But from this man, it felt more like being scanned by an X-ray machine.

"Dimka is right, you know," he said at last. "I could be taking a great risk here, but you do not have the look of Guardians, nor the blackened soul of the Domini. My instincts tell me you are definitely of the Lost."

"That depends," Brooke finally said. "Am I rightly guessing the Lost are what you call anyone from beyond this world?"

"Yes," Ravid answered. "Other-worlders. Not of the Five."

"Five *what*?" Tibor asked.

Brooke frowned. *That didn't explain a damned thing!*

"Alahni is our Keeper of Tales," Likeke explained. Ignoring her bewildered look, he gestured to Ravid, who produced a hunting knife and—before Brooke could react—seized her wrists and cut their bonds. "She can explain more eloquently than any of us, while we get your friend here some medical attention."

As Ravid freed Tibor, he added, "The Keeper of Tales is the teacher for our young."

Likeke nodded. "Yes, though we fled the city to live apart from the Guardians, we know better than to forget our past, or the wisdom of Blake. In that way, we avoid becoming savages, like the Lost."

"Now, what's that supposed to me—?" Tibor started to ask, but his words abruptly cut off when the curtain opened and Dimka returned, accompanied by a young woman.

Her exotic beauty took Brooke by surprise. Though she looked similar to her kin, her appearance was somehow regal. Rich, raven-black hair, straight and thick, cascaded over her shoulders. Her wide brown eyes swept over Tibor and Brooke with a sparkle of curiosity tinged with caution. Her face was delicately heart-shaped, her complexion flawless, so she looked radiant even with a complete absence of makeup. Even her posture and manner were alluring, somehow demure and confident at the same time—especially impressive as Brooke guessed her age to be no more than nineteen or twenty.

For a moment, Brooke felt a pang of jealousy; at her best, she probably never looked *that* good.

"Brooklyn Stevens," Likeke said. "This is Alahni."

Alahni nodded, and Brooke did the same, her eyes locking onto the girl's as she favored her with a small smile.

"Alahni," Likeke continued, "Brooklyn and her companion are of the Lost."

The young woman's's eyes widened. "Truly?"

"Yes," Likeke said. "She and her companion crashed on our world from one beyond. While our healers see to her friend, I hope you will explain the history of our people. Ravid will accompany you."

Tibor scowled and looked at Brooke, concern written all over his bruised face.

"It's okay, Trouble," she said softly. "Get some rest. I'll be fine."

"What makes you so sure?"

"Because considering the alternatives," she said slowly, once again meeting Alahni's gaze, "things could get a whole lot worse."

THE SANCTORUM
CITY OF HOPE
JARDINE (HERAKLEION)
FREE WORLDS LEAGUE

Specter Precentor Omicron Apollyon towered over his desk on legs of polished metal, his toe-claws digging into the soft carpet.

The chamber was spacious enough for its three occupants, but the pale gray of the stucco walls, the single bay window of tinted, bulletproof ferro-glass, its furnishings and decorations all created a sense of cold functionality. There were only a few chairs in the office, including the pseudo-hide "captain's chair" standing unoccupied behind Apollyon; where pictures and framed documents might have hung on the walls of a similar office anywhere else in the Inner Sphere, only flat-screen monitors hung here. Apollyon needed no distractions of beauty or vanity; the vista overlooking Jardine's Forest of Shrouds and the beautiful ruins of the City of Hope were all he needed to touch his humanity, to remember why he had become the Master's Hand.

His body was massive. He stood with his arms crossed, the bulky, scarred flesh-and-blood arm resting atop the hard metal and polymer construction of his true arm. Though another might consider the flesh and blood to be frail, the dark skin reminded Apollyon of the humanity he had willfully sacrificed a lifetime ago for his Master. Beneath the flesh lay bundles of true muscle, augmenting the arm's strength to that of its counterpart. His red robes covered the expanse of his chest and most of his arms, but even as he inhaled deeply—the better to focus his feelings of disappointment—he could feel the enhanced musculature beneath his chest, sliding over his true ribs and the frail heart they protected.

His scalp, laid bare now with his red hood drawn back, stretched taut as he frowned deeply at his guest, and he closed his dark-brown left eye, keeping his focus on the other man through the thermal vision of his true eye. The faint red glow his vision gave off was little more than an affectation, but it underscored one simple fact in burning crimson.

That Apollyon, Prince of Scars, Thrice-Blessed of the Master, was not happy.

With an ominous finality, Apollyon exhaled and opened his frail eye. The man before him looked up, his jet-black eyes wary as they peeked out from beneath the hood of his robe; he was anxious, but not afraid.

Precentor Sigma Damien Lucille, Poltergeist-class, remaining kneeling before the desk, the metal of his right arm revealed by the sleeve of his red robe as it rested on his bent right leg. His left leg and arm remained hidden by the robe, but Apollyon did not need to see them to sense their enhancements.

In many ways, Lucille was almost as heavily enhanced as Apollyon himself. His true vision—replacing both frail eyes, despite enhancements that made them appear otherwise—could sense heat and radiation almost as well as Apollyon's own. His true hearing—also cosmetically hidden from prying eyes—could sense radio transmissions and ultrasonic frequencies. His scalp, unseen beneath his hood, was covered in a fine stubble of black hair that failed to hide the narrow channels of subcutaneous tattoos converging at the base of his neck in a round port. Apollyon knew these features and more with a single blink, as he knew the specifics of all his "charges."

Yet for all the upgrades, the gifts of the Master, the training, the strength of Blake in his heart, this man brought news of failure against mere Frails.

"Explain," Apollyon's voice rumbled at last.

Lucille did not rise. He spoke from his kneeling position, locking his eyes onto those of his master.

"Adept Errol's team was specifically instructed to ignore Wayward activities while pursuing the intruders," he said. "Given the proximity to the river and the city, it was presumed—

erroneously—that the Waywards would have a minimal presence there. In the race to capture the invaders, the team grew careless."

"Electromagnetic pulse mines." Apollyon nodded grimly. "Inside the patrol zone. Careless is a term I would apply to others, in addition to Adept Errol and his team."

The statement was no mere accusation. Lucille's face flushed only slightly, but enough for Apollyon to catch the rising heat with his true vision. Lucille had every reason to feel shame; so promising, so close to the Ascension, and he had just lost a squad of the Master's Hands to a booby trap laid by refugee hunters. Some of that same shame burned within Apollyon's own heart; Lucille was his to mold, and this failure stung him deeply.

Lucille did not beg forgiveness. He knew better than that.

"The fault is mine alone, Precentor," he said. "Hunting the Waywards was a practice we indulged in at our leisure; since our brothers and sisters have deployed, I have allowed our remaining troops to lapse in anticipation of the Transfer. I offer no excuses beyond my own Frail failings, and would ask only for the chance to rectify both matters once and for all."

"Would you?" Apollyon asked, his tone cold.

"Yes, sir," Lucille responded. "The Wayward nuisance and the intruders are easily contained. Both lack the mobility to escape the general vicinity, and pose no significant threat to our world or our operations. We could destroy them at our leisure, as ever sending a message to the other Waywards in the bargain."

"Failsafe Epsilon?" Apollyon asked, raising his hairless eyebrows. "Bombing the woods around our enclave will waste resources and imperil the security of our enclave from orbital observers.

"Besides," he added, his voice softening as he looked out the bay window. "I *like* those woods, Precentor. I will not have such a vista of untouched beauty ruined for something that you assure me is 'no significant threat.'"

Lucille bowed his head in agreement. "Understood, sir. I shall assign additional squads to the hunt, and we will triangulate the Waywards' location based on the EMP mines detected to date."

"Add a Two of 'Mechs to your hunt, Precentor," Apollyon commanded. "Let our Phantoms test themselves as well."

"As you command, sir," Lucille agreed. "What of the intruders' JumpShip?"

"Our passive sensor net has yet to detect it's point of origin, but we know it's out there. I have ordered the outer-ring satellites to activate for a better look, but they are also running passive to avoid alerting our interlopers.

"The shuttle's distress signal will serve as a beacon to them. But they would surely have recharged their drives by now. An interception by any of our patrols before they can confirm their comrades' survival could inspire them to jump away again, and perhaps tell others what limited information they have acquired."

"Understood, sir. So we wait?"

"We wait," Apollyon said with a grim nod, "until you have brought me their comrades, alive."

EXPLORER-CLASS JUMPSHIP SACAJAWEA
PIRATE JUMP POINT
JARDINE (HERAKLEION) SYSTEM
FREE WORLDS LEAGUE

Lawrence Pohl reclined in his command chair, trying not to let the worry show on his face. A part of him desperately wanted to replay the message his JumpShip's receivers had picked up less than an hour ago (the message *not* sent by ancient drones, that was).

But he knew better; the new message was just as automated, unchanging, and simple—hearing it again would reveal nothing further.

"Mayday! Mayday!" Brooke's voice—pre-recorded for the occasion, Lawrence guessed—called out. *"DropShuttle Magellan taking fire from hostile aerospace fighters! Unable to break orbit! Attempting to land—"*

The message was as much a relief as it was an omen of doom. The relief, of course, came from knowing that Brooke and Tibor had, in fact, survived their long flight toward the planet below.

The ill-omen, equally obviously, came from how he knew that.

Any doubts that the world below him was Jardine disappeared as he absorbed the simple facts Brooke's last words gave him. It seemed someone had gone to great lengths to keep the world seen by many as a modern-day Atlantis hidden from prying eyes. Whoever was keeping this secret had killed a xenobiologist to do it, and later had claimed one of the *Sac*'s own crew—Marissa Borefijn—on Shasta. These same protectors of Jardine's secret had seen fit to assault the *Sacajawea* and another JumpShip-load of Interstellar Expeditions' mercenaries in the depths of space.

A part of Lawrence had hoped his team was wrong, that this world was another wild goose chase. If they were wrong, it would have meant Marissa had died for nothing—but at least the message received would be more along the lines of "Landed safely; nothing to see here!" than the distress call they'd received.

Hell, at this moment, Lawrence would have accepted a mayday for engine trouble, something he could send one of the *Sac*'s other DropShuttles out to address.

At least then, he thought, *the clock wouldn't be ticking.*

Looking up across the *Sacajawea*'s half-lit bridge, Lawrence caught Gretchen Morden's cool brown eyes. She was watching him from the communications station, the only other post manned on this shift. Her headset remained in place, likely still receiving the signal sent from Brooke's crashed shuttle, counting the time and adjusting for light-lag.

The signal's duration more than anything else told them the *Magellan* had survived its landing—another hopeful sign—but now, Lawrence and Gretchen both knew, it would become a waiting game.

"They're alive," Lawrence said, his tone reassuring.

"Of course," Gretchen said, her expression guarded.

She knew the score too. Brooke and Tibor now had seven days to send a signal calling for extraction, seven days to give the *Sacajawea* instructions before the mission would be considered a bust, and its commanders lost in the field. For Lawrence, this was always the most nerve-wracking part of the job; the waiting, never knowing for sure, unable to even send a reply. He thanked his stars when Brooke waived these radio-silence protocols, but she only made that concession when the target world was believed to be uninhabited.

After Shasta, any hope Jardine would be lifeless had gone straight out the airlock.

And so the *Sacajawea* would wait one week for instructions, with only the assurance that Brooke and Tibor were alive as of eight hours ago, and the knowledge the system was home to hostile aerospace forces of unknown strength and numbers.

Lawrence frowned deeply.

A sudden alarm from the sensors console shattered his thoughts. Gretchen flinched at the sound, but recovered quickly and tapped her controls, snatching the feed from the secondary station.

Lawrence was bolt upright, his ice-blue eyes watching her intently.

"Jump wave," she said. "It's rather weak, maybe eight AUs out..."

Lawrence felt his mouth go dry. "Can you track it?"

"On it," Gretchen said without looking up. Seconds dragged into minutes as she worked in silence. Lawrence rubbed at his chin, mulling the options. At eight Astronomical Units' distance, any new arrival was too far out to take the *Sacajawea* by surprise. Still, it was a fact that few JumpShip captains simply "passed through" a system via non-standard proximity points on the elliptical plane. Those who did so usually were pirates—and others, like the *Sac* herself—who suspected trouble and did not want to be easily found...

Or they were ship captains who knew the system's non-standard points intimately, and knew *exactly* where to go to catch an intruding ship.

"Hmmm," Gretchen said at last.

"What do you see?"

"Could be something," she said after another moment. "Our sensors got enough data for a basic triangulation. It's a little above the solar plane, around heading seventy by twenty..."

Lawrence narrowed his eyes. "Any indicators?"

Gretchen threw him a crooked scowl and Lawrence shrugged. *Right,* he thought. *As if anyone jumping into an unfamiliar system along a non-standard point would run with an active IFF or open communications, but it never hurts to check for stupidity ...*

Lawrence slipped out of his chair and floated over to Gretchen's console. Maneuvering around her with an expert twist of his body, he grabbed an overhead handle to keep his inertia from carrying him too far. Peering over Gretchen's shoulder, he followed her finger when she pointed.

The sensor screen was in passive mode, and the triangulation was an estimate based on a one-shot, momentary detection, so it displayed the "contact" as little more than a series of concentric, colored circles. The computers nevertheless framed this vague reading with red brackets, and numbers scrolled estimating its distance and probable orientation. As sophisticated as the *Sac*'s instruments were, her telescopes and sensors remained capable of only rudimentary detection and analysis when it came to spotting and identifying distant JumpShips on passive sensors only.

"Think someone's spotted us?" Gretchen asked.

"We're under EMCON, with our sails stowed," Lawrence said. "If they tagged us when we came in, why show up way the hell out there, and why wait two weeks after we got here to do it?"

"Pirates?"

"Maybe," Lawrence said, but even then, the insight struck him. "Or maybe someone who got lost along the way..."

Gretchen's eyebrows rose in mild surprise, and Lawrence nodded.

"Keep an eye on them," he said finally. "If they send a signal, let me know, but do not respond until I give the word."

Captain Hara, Lawrence thought, *welcome to Jardine!*

CHAPTER 6

My Dearest Tyler,

I write this in the hope you will one day read it. This may not be the first time Trouble and I have found ourselves marooned on a forgotten world, but rarely has the situation looked so dire—or so incredibly fascinating!

In all those years with IE and since, I've seen many worlds that "vanished" in the early Succession Wars, cut off from the rest of the Inner Sphere and written off as dead. I have even seen several where populations persisted despite the holocausts, some unaware the Star League had fallen, or barely even able to remember what came before their worlds were smashed to pieces.

But not Jardine. These people not only know the Star League is dead and gone, but almost everything that's transpired since. Their "Keeper of Tales," Alahni, says their "Guardians"—ComStar itself—kept them (mostly) in the loop ever since their first arrival centuries ago.

But why they sheltered this world (and others?) from the horrors of the Succession Wars?

That's the trillion-kroner question!

Oh, Tyler, when next we meet, there will be so much to tell!

—From the journals of Brooklyn Stevens

**TRIBE ENCAMPMENT
FOREST OF SHADOWS
JARDINE (HERAKLEION)
FREE WORLDS LEAGUE
31 OCTOBER 3067**

The sun had set and risen again, but Brooklyn Stevens hardly noticed. Although she suspected it had been more than twenty hours since she last slept, her mind and nerves still felt energized, ever since yesterday's dogfight high above Jardine's atmosphere.

She had to admit a lot of that energy came from the young woman who had been her guide through the tiny enclave dug into the thriving woods around her. Seemingly so innocent, and at the same time so amazingly intelligent, Alahni's ability to explain the history of her people—and of Jardine itself— left Brooke once more wondering if she were truly the girl she appeared to be.

As they talked, Alahni's "grand tour" of the camp brought them back through the tunnels hollowed out beneath a large hill and back onto the surface. The early morning sun, far to the east, left many of the camp's natural glades deep in shadow, but not so deep Brooke couldn't make out Alahni's fellow Waywards harvesting berries along the fringes, which Alahni told her were used for both a simple juice and a healing balm. Others were tending to one of the camp's two neatly concealed wells (the other one was located underground), and the camp cook was already preparing a morning meal of dried jungle-kite meat and salted firecat soup.

Brooke licked her lips as she passed the fire, remembering the brief taste of the succulent leftovers she'd been treated to the night before. "The Domini don't appear to hunt your people too actively."

Alahni frowned. It was her most common expression, Brooke noticed, second only to the intense, animated look she had when relaying one of her "tales." "The Master's machine men have only been among us for the last twelve summers," she replied. "Many come from Hope—the city where most of our own tribe was born—but others hail from the rest of the Five.

"Most times, their encounters with our kin come only through unfortunate circumstance—like when our hunters stray too close to the patrols out of Hope, or when their 'exercises' run too close to our camps. But once—a few summers ago— they did hunt us actively, when they discovered the Malu Tribe farming the open plains to the south. After the Malu were gone, they returned to Hope, and their forays into the forests were few.

"We know their Master—and his steward here, Apollyon— see us as no threat. So long as we remain invisible, and do not interfere with their Third Transfer, there is an unspoken truce between those of Hope and we who wander."

Brooke arched an eyebrow. For all the hours spent covering the history of Jardine and its centuries of survival off the interstellar grid, this was only the third or fourth time Alahni had mentioned "the Five" and "the Master" without explanation. Her references gave Brooke only the impression that "the Five" were places far away, and "the Master" was a leader of some kind. Hope, she already knew, was the nearest city to them—a mere forty kilometers or so to the east, from which most of the Wanderer tribes in these parts seemed to spread outward. But these repeated, scant details had finally worn down Brooke's willingness to let Alahni tell her tales at her own pace.

"This 'Master' you speak of..." she began, allowing the question to hang.

"He came here long ago," Alahni said, her quick reply catching Brooke off guard. "Well before my time, in fact—even before our tribe. He was one of the Order, who came to our world badly injured. In the years since we were isolated and the Inner Sphere became Lost, the Guardians had come to see our world as a place of research, particularly in the fields of medicine and cybernetics. Given the nature of his injuries, it was only natural for the Guardians to bring him here."

"He must have been important," Brooke said, "if they found it necessary to bring him to a hidden enclave like this."

Alahni nodded. "He was unique, they said. Brilliant, and filled with potential..."

"An indispensable asset?" Brooke asked. "A scientist, or Primus?"

Alahni looked confused for a moment and shook her head. "No," she said. "He was Lost. He had never been to our havens, never seen the Five."

"He came from beyond? The Successor States?"

Alahni nodded and abruptly slowed. Brooke looked around and saw they were near the camp's makeshift stable, where six *tabiranths* now stood or lay about. The tallest of these, she realized, was the one Ravid had ridden when he had picked her up the day before. Now, the creature sat before her, resting on its haunches as it groomed its right forepaw. In the gloomy shadows, its rust-colored hide appeared almost black, but as it sensed her gaze, the animal looked back, fixing her with a golden-eyed stare—but only for a moment.

Alahni walked to another of the beasts and gently stroked its shaggy mane, a casual gesture that reminded Brooke of something a seasoned lion tamer might do. The *tabi* gave a rumbling purr and twisted its head into her touch, then silently yawned to display a wide mouthful of jagged teeth.

"He was a House Lord," Alahni continued. "But one the Order had somehow reclaimed. His arrival led many to question at least part of what we'd been told. If the Houses had truly lost control and fallen into the chaos of war, how could the House Lords still claim their titles?"

"Many of us 'Lost' have asked that very same question through the centuries," Brooke said with a wry smile.

Alahni looked for a moment as though she would smile, but simply shrugged instead.

"It's important to understand," she continued. "For centuries, ComStar's Guardians here told us of the Promise—the day when the Lost would collapse into final ruin, unable to wage war on an interstellar scale. Our own world suffered nuclear strikes that left two continents uninhabitable and led the Guardians to centralize the survivors around Hope. We were told the destruction was even more widespread beyond us, with whole worlds erased from existence."

Brooke nodded. "That was true," she said. "The First and Second Succession Wars were devastating—"

"Yes," Alahni cut in. "And so the Guardians sealed the Five off from the rest of the universe. As the Inner Sphere fell, our havens would play dead until the time when the Promise unfolded."

"And the arrival of this 'Master' changed that?"

"To the contrary, Brooklyn Stevens," Alahni said, her face and tone suddenly hard. "To many, it seemed as though Blake's prophesies had become all too real, and it scared us."

"How do you mean?"

Alahni's expression softened again, and with another stroke along the *tabi's* mane, she began to walk. Brooke realized that pacing somehow made it easier for the young woman to tell her tale, and followed her through another tour of the camp's surface glades.

"Blake's words—handed down to us for generations, since the collapse of the Inner Sphere—told us that, when the Inner Sphere suffered its final collapse, it would be ComStar's time to rise. Then, it was said, the children of the Five would join in spreading the Word of Blake to the Lost. A new order would be born, a second coming of the Star League."

"There are many among Blake's followers who preach those same words throughout the Inner Sphere," Brooke said. "Even today. In fact, the Star League—"

"Is reborn," Alahni finished. "Yes, we know."

"I'm sorry."

Alahni surrendered half a smile in reply. "I realize we appear to live a primitive existence here, Brooklyn Stevens, but we were never ignorant of the universe beyond."

"You'd be surprised by how refreshing I find that," Brooke told her. "I have visited many worlds lost to our maps, forgotten to everyone, where people who live much as you do have never heard of the Succession Wars, or the Clans, or—"

"The Clans!" Alahni hissed, her eyes narrowed.

Brooke blinked.

Alahni shook her head again, regaining her focus. "To cut short the story of the Master," she began, "the man who came to us, broken, *was* extraordinary. His mind was keen, despite the injuries to his body. His knowledge and understanding of the Word was far beyond the grasp of many—especially remarkable for a House Lord. He could see the future, they said, predict the currents of history. While he healed on our world, hidden away from the Lost, he spoke to many, telling them the time of the Promise was coming, but a great upheaval would take place first—a catalyst. It would not only shatter the Inner Sphere, he said, but the impact would even divide the Order itself, separating the faithful from the faithless. That catalyst was the Clans."

"You're saying the Master predicted the Clan invasion?"

"Yes, though he was not the first to foretell their coming. In past ages, our ancestors have warned of the returning children of Kerensky; most claimed these warnings as visions or religious epiphanies. As devoted to the Word as he was, the Master offered his prediction as based on the currents of history itself, a science only he seemed able to grasp."

"Predicting the future through examining history isn't a very exact science," Brooke cautioned.

"Yet he was correct. Even ComStar had grown stagnant as your Succession Wars raged. The creation of the Federated Commonwealth and the Fourth War represented a sudden shift in the balance, and when that happened, rifts formed within ComStar as it seemed the Promise would be denied us. But the Master said this shift was necessary, a change that would prepare society for something larger, something big enough to sunder the Order."

"The Schism."

"Is that what they call it?" Alahni asked.

"The separation between ComStar and the Word of Blake? Yes."

"Separation?" Alahni's eyes narrowed. "The Word and ComStar are *inseparable*, Brooklyn Stevens. But the Master's predictions—and what came to pass with the coming of the Clans—turned those who lost faith in the Promise against those who feared its coming and saw Blake's legacy wholly unprepared for it.

"The Master changed all that. The Master turned to the Five, to *us*."

Brooke hesitated for a moment. "What did he do?"

"The advances achieved by Kerensky's children exceeded even the Star League technologies the Order managed to secure and preserve for all those centuries. The contents of the warehouses here would help to stem the slaughter the Clans could unleash, but with so many in the Order disillusioned, it was manpower the Master saw a need for—an army of warriors who could take on even the genetically enhanced Clans without fear for their lives or ever once questioning the Promise."

"Those cyborgs?"

Alahni nodded gravely.

"Apollyon was the first," she said. "Although that was not his original name, it is the one he now answers to."

"Apollyon..." Brooke repeated.

"Created in the Master's image," Alahni said. "His name is taken from mythology. It means—"

"The Destroyer. I know."

"Apollyon was one of us," Alahni said. "A warrior-citizen of Hope. He was the first to embrace the Master's vision, his promise of the Third Transfer, when the new Star League would embrace the Word and re-forge the universe by destroying the common enemy."

"Then you're saying these machine men, as you call them, are—"

"An army, yes. An army that only recently left our home to prepare for the Third Transfer."

Brooke paused. The sun had risen far enough to illuminate the camp's glades through the thick foliage above. She saw two men astride brown-furred *tabiranths*, trotting out of the stable clearing toward the camp's southern outskirts. Their high-powered rifles—age-worn, yet powerful enough, she knew, to take down one of the cyborgs in a single shot—were holstered by their sides, while straps and saddlebags lay against their flanks to harvest any kills.

An army of cybernetically enhanced soldiers, she thought. *Intended to fight the Clans, raised in secret for a dozen years.*

"How many of them are there?" she asked softly.

Alahni shrugged. "Thousands have come and gone through Hope," she said, "but we are just one of the Five. The others, we have heard, produce more materiel for the Master and Apollyon."

Brooke fixed her with an intense gaze. "What are the 'Five,' Alahni? Cities like Hope?"

Alahni's eyes widened slightly. "No, Brooklyn Stevens," she said. "Like Jardine, all of the Five are lost to your people, spared the horrors of your wars by Blake's Guardians.

"They are *worlds*."

THE SANCTORUM
CITY OF HOPE
JARDINE (HERAKLEION)
FREE WORLDS LEAGUE
1 NOVEMBER 3067

The hunter's name was Pilipo. Like all of the Waywards, he claimed no last name. His physique was excellent, and his skin—the color of caramel—bore only light scars from years of rough living. He was missing the pinky finger from his right hand, the flesh long since healed around the old injury.

His eyes were a startling blue—unusual for his ethnic background—and his hair was jet black, long and straight. His goatee was well trimmed, immaculate, the sign of a man concerned with his appearance. His age was somewhere in the neighborhood of twenty-three, but even he could not be certain of the exact number.

Pilipo belonged to the Shrouded Forest Tribe, but as he lay naked, strapped spread-eagle to the stainless-steel table in the gloomy chamber, he was far from of his natural element. Indeed, since his capture in the Forest of Shrouds less than a day previous, his home had been this cold, lonely cell, within which there had been no mercy, no compassion.

Only pain.

His hair, soaked with sweat, adhered to his forehead and the table. His eyes remained wide, the rims red and prickling with tears. A thin trickle of blood flowed from the corner of his gaping mouth, through his well-trimmed goatee, and pooled on the table.

So frail, thought the man who stood over him in robes of crimson and gold, a man who was more machine than flesh.

Both of Apollyon's eyes—frail and true alike—turned their focus to the robed precentor who stood over Pilipo. Her true metal-and-polymer hand extended from beneath the folds in her white robe, pressed against the Wayward's chest. She rested her hand there for only a moment, then met her master's gaze with silvery eyes and nodded.

Apollyon's true eye remained in thermal-scan mode, but with a virtual wink, he reactivated its red glow, casting a blush across Pilipo's corpse, the precentor's robes—and the face of Precentor Sigma Lucille.

Neither Lucille nor the precentor flinched against the glow; cowering before Apollyon was neither expected nor required. Instead, Lucille nodded with an almost imperceptible smile toward the body.

"Twenty-three hours," he said. "An impressive feat for one without training."

"He is a child of Blake," Apollyon whispered in a bone-chilling tone. "Even as a Wayward, his will is iron."

The reprimand evoked a blink from Lucille, followed by a short, grim-faced nod. Apollyon kept his own expression frozen and severe. It was tempting, he knew, to see the Waywards as "mere Frails," but he fought constantly against this perception. The Master's Hands needed to remember their origins, needed to remember those of the Five who sacrificed for the sainted Blake and his vision.

The children of the Five should *never* be seen as Frail, and the Master's Hands could *never* afford to forget that, no matter how close the Promise was to its final fulfillment.

And for the Master's Hand to strike down the children in such a way as this...the frail parts of Apollyon cringed inwardly at the thought.

"Nevertheless, Precentor," the third precentor finally said, breaking the moment's silence, "his vitals betrayed him. He spoke the truth."

Apollyon tossed her a glance and nodded before turning his eyes back to Lucille.

"Then stating my orders should be unnecessary," Apollyon said.

Lucille nodded solemnly, his eyes briefly closing. "Tragic as they may be, sir—I know my duty."

"Then form your Two and await my final authorization. The danger is too great to spend resources on reclamation. Excise the Waywards and bring me the intruders—alive, if possible."

"Understood, sir."

Apollyon turned to the third precentor and tipped her chin upward, seizing her attention.

"Summon Ogima to my office, Lamashti," he said. "I must explain to our kin what must be done."

LEOPARD-CLASS DROPSHIP *KAYLIN*
PIRATE JUMP POINT
JARDINE (HERAKLEION) SYSTEM
FREE WORLDS LEAGUE
1 NOVEMBER 3067

Anton Hara arched an eyebrow as he tried to decide when, exactly, Nathan Bellamy had gone mad. But more to the point— as he watched the portly, gray-suited man's face across the tiny table in his stateroom—Hara began to wonder when *he* had gone mad enough to take a liaison officer like Bellamy seriously.

Mere hours after the *Kaylin*'s JumpShip carried them through hyperspace to this system, a tight-beam signal had come in from a JumpShip dangling in space eight astronomical units away. Understandably cautious, the transmitting JumpShip didn't identify itself, but instead sent a general hail—adding some slightly out-of-date Interstellar Expeditions code phrases. That immediately told Hara not only the identity of the other JumpShip, but that they were bold enough to suspect the vessel materializing nearby as the one hauling Hara's crew.

It also told Hara this system was not safe.

All of which told Bellamy that they had, indeed, located Jardine.

All of which brought Bellamy to Hara's stateroom after his bridge watch with the suggestion that had left both men staring at each other in icy silence for the last several seconds.

The IE liaison surprised Hara with the unwavering gaze of his slate-gray eyes. Though his bulky physique, pasty complexion—and inability to handle hyperspace jumps without retching—spoke to a multitude of obvious flaws, Hara had to give Bellamy credit: he had hidden reserves, to show such intensity now. It took more than guts to ask one mercenary commander to play an active part in an effort to double-cross another.

Everything about the situation told Hara the world below him was *that* important to Interstellar Expeditions.

Or that Stevens' history with IE was every bit as stormy as he had come to suspect.

Hara sighed at last, suddenly aware that his mouth was parched. "You realize what you're suggesting, Bellamy?"

Bellamy frowned. "Stevens is still down there," he said, "or they'd be gone already. Their drive is charged and ready to go, but they're afraid to send signals in the clear. A common protocol for IE scouts and their JumpShips is for the scouts to send the first signal in the clear."

Hara nodded. He was familiar with the procedure IE used when traveling to a system it suspected would be hostile. The scouts would go in, ascertain the situation, and send word back to indicate the threat level. Certain code phrases in these transmissions would tell the mother ship whether it was safe to relocate further in-system, whether they should wait for another signal from the scouts, or whether the scouts were done for and the world was too "hot" to approach.

If anything, the *Sacajawea*'s tentative transmission demonstrated that Stevens' people still flew by the book, and from that Bellamy quickly concluded Stevens was still dirtside, and her crew was awaiting her next contact.

Presumably, such a signal—broadcast in the clear—would herald her return journey. And Bellamy was now proposing a slight change in plans for that eventuality.

A bold move, to be sure.

"The minute we do this—" Hara began.

"Unless Captain Pohl has gone senile," Bellamy cut in, "he'll jump before the threat becomes significant. For all her tweaks, the *Sacajawea* can't fend off your DropShip and its fighters. And once she jumps, it'll be a week before that ship can come back."

"Unless Pohl's daring enough to charge his drive from the fusion core instead and cut that time down," Hara cautioned.

It was common knowledge that a hyperspace jump took an average of a week's worth of recharge time using a JumpShip's solar collector sail, but an alternative favored by the desperate (or the over-confident) allowed jump drives to recharge directly from the vessel's fusion reactor in a fraction of the time. The delicate nature of a K-F drive usually meant direct-from-fusion charging was safest when done at sail-charging rates, but that didn't stop some captains from pushing their luck when circumstances demanded it.

"Risk a blow-out?" Bellamy asked, demonstrating that he, too, knew the risks of such a measure. A crooked smile snaked across his face. "At a reasonable best, he could try it and be back in three days, maybe. But by *that* point, we'll have Stevens and anything she's gathered on the world below."

Hara fell silent. It was a neat enough plan, and one that—played right—wouldn't cost Stevens or her crew any lives. That made it infinitely better than many other backstabs he'd seen by employers in his career.

But Hara wondered if he really wanted to see Stevens' face when the *Kaylin*—and not her *Sacajawea*—was the vessel picking her up after her odyssey on the planet below...

TRIBE ENCAMPMENT
FOREST OF SHROUDS
JARDINE (HERAKLEION)
FREE WORLDS LEAGUE
2 NOVEMBER 3067

The "grand tour" lasted until Brooke felt she could no longer stand, let alone walk, at which point Alahni led her to a small chamber off what seemed to be the tribe's underground common room. Despite the slightly clammy chill in the air and the hard, uneven feel of the earth beneath the hand-woven mat she laid on, Brooke managed to fall into a deep sleep almost immediately. Even so, she felt like she'd barely closed her eyes when the heavenly aroma of something resembling steak and eggs woke her the next day.

"*Aufgewacht, Schlafmütze!*" said a familiar voice.

Brooke slowly opened her eyes to see Tibor crouching over her, a grin on his thin, bruised face.

"Hey there," she said weakly. "You okay?"

"The eye and ear are killing me, actually," Tibor said matter-of-factly, "but these guys really know their painkillers."

Brooke blinked as the world came into focus again, and realized Tibor's left eye no longer had the same focus it once had. In fact, the way the artificial eye now floated, apparently aimlessly, she wondered if he saw anything through it at all.

But before she could ask, she realized Alahni was there as well, hovering right behind him, a small bowl in her hands. "How long did I—?"

"A good five hours, maybe," Tibor said. "Long enough for the tribe to register a half-dozen complaints about the noise."

Brooke rolled her eyes. "Surely," she said, "even the blessed children of Blake have been known to *snore.*"

Alahni's eyes widened, and Brooke immediately found herself biting her lower lip.

Damn it! These people owe their existence to whatever game Jerome Blake was playing when he hid them away in his day, and here I go making jokes in his name!

"My apologies," she said, sheepishly.

"You are Lost," Alahni said after a moment's hesitation. "Some things are to be expected."

Tibor frowned as Alahni knelt down and handed the bowl to Brooke. It was not a gesture of deference, but merely the act of a hostess tending to a guest.

The rough-hewn bowl was filled with slices of some sort of local meat that smelled so much like beef it set Brooke's mouth to watering, with clumps of an equally unusual (yet still recognizable) form of scrambled eggs mixed in. The fork-tined spoon provided with the bowl invited Brooke to dig in at once, but instead she gave Alahni her most respectful bow and a humble smile. "Nevertheless," she said, "I *do* mean it. I intended no disrespect."

"Obsequiousness does not become you, Brooklyn Stevens," Alahni said. "Eat, please. I have been asked to make sure you are well fed before your journey."

"Journey?" Brooke's gaze flashed over to Tibor, who frowned awkwardly as he sighed.

"Brooke," he began slowly, "I don't need to remind you the *Sac* will be waiting for our signal, and these guys don't have the kind of transmitting power we need to—"

"So you took it upon yourself to ask for a guide to someone who does?" Brooke finished. "Think we could have *conferred* a little on that subject first?"

"You seemed a little preoccupied..." Tibor said, letting his words hang for a moment. Ignoring the quizzical look Alahni threw him, he continued, his tone hardening a little. "Meanwhile, I've gotten my own read on the place. Our hosts aren't universally pleased having us around, especially if the cyber-folks know we're here too."

Brooke narrowed her eyes and fought back the urge to hit Tibor with the first insult that came to mind; snapping at the man would hardly change the fact that he had a point.

"From the sound of things," she said instead, "this city of Hope is the nearest place with anything we'd need—"

"But, of course, it's crawling with these Manei Dominus guys."

"Domini," Alahni quickly corrected.

Tibor shrugged. "Either way, our welcome's almost worn out here, and the clock's ticking. We can't ask the tribe to shield us forever, even if you were keen on taking up housekeeping here."

Brooke rediscovered the bowl in her hands and automatically shoveled a spoonful of egg-and-meat mixture into her mouth, as much to settle the craving that was beginning to make her stomach growl as to think through what Tibor was saying. The food tasted saltier than she expected, and the meat was magnitudes tougher than she'd hoped, but compared to DropShuttle rations, it was heavenly.

"So," she finally said, tilting her head back to face Alahni. "Likeke wants us out?"

"It is not our way to turn our guests over to the Domini," Alahni replied with a deepening frown. "Even if the guests are Lost."

"No," Brooke said sourly. "Instead, you exile us, and hope nature takes its course in due time."

"It's not quite like that, Brooke," Tibor said, "though it is close. Ravid tells me there are many in Hope who are still sympathetic to the tribes. They might be able to help us—to some extent."

"Going to be risky," Brooke said. "With or without help."

"Well, I'm pretty sure we'll pull it off," Tibor said, managing something of a smirk. "We've been in worse scrapes before."

Brooke smiled as she thought about it, but it was only half a smile. *Maybe, my friend*, she thought. *Then again, maybe not.*

"Hey Brooke," Tibor added, "remember that time on Bob?"

Brooke was part-way into her next bite when she started to chuckle at the memory. "Oh, yeah," she said. "That *was* pretty messed up..."

Alahni's head listed to one side for a moment. "Wait," she said. "*On* Bob? This is a planet you are talking about?"

"Sure is," Tibor said, smiling even wider.

"Someone actually named a planet 'Bob'?"

"Well, it's not around anymore," Brooke told her. "Kind of like your Jardine here, it vanished from the maps."

"But who would name a planet 'Bob'?" Alahni asked, incredulous.

"Well," Tibor said, shifting himself forward, "the story goes that it was settled by German or Swiss colonists, and had an authentic Germanic name—the kind that exceeded the syllabic limits of a haiku—so some smart-ass locals started a movement to just rename it planet 'Bob'."

"And they *won*?"

"Oh, the local governor *loved* it," Tibor said. "He wasn't terribly fond of German *or* Drac influence." His real eye practically sparkled with mirth, while its mismatched counterpart looked dull and unfocused.

"At least the name could fit into the haikus," Brooke said with a grin. "Big plus when your world finds itself on Kurita's side of the border."

At this, Alahni finally laughed.

THE SANCTORUM
CITY OF HOPE
JARDINE (HERAKLEION)
FREE WORLDS LEAGUE
2 NOVEMBER 3067

For most warriors of the Inner Sphere, riding into battle in a suit of armor weighing three-quarters of a metric ton might have felt like they were wearing a hard shell insulating them from all sensation. But for Poltergeist Precentor Sigma Damien Lucille, the bulky plates and myomer bundles making up the flesh and muscle of his Achileus battle armor felt as comfortable as his own skin.

As he stalked through the cavernous, subterranean 'Mech bay, he could feel the smooth, cold surface of the ferrocrete floor as though his feet were bare. The humidity in the air gave him goosebumps, and the smell of fresh ozone and machine oils assailed his nose. Flexing his hands, he could feel the weight of the 150-kilogram flamethrower beneath his right forearm, and the Mauser 1200 light support weapon beneath his left. With a simple gesture, Lucille disengaged and then re-engaged both weapons' safeties, ready for battle with a mere flick of his fingers.

Straight ahead, lined up in two neat ranks of three, stood the giant avatars of death that would cleanse the recent taint from Lucille's record and purify the lands around Hope.

Though a mix of lightweights—consisting of two blocky 35-ton *Owens* OmniMechs, two sleek 25-ton *Nexus*es, an insectoid *Raijin* weighing 50 tons, and a 55-ton *Griffin*—their presence dominated the massive bay. Their armor—fading from jet black at the base of their massive feet toward harsh crimson at the head and shoulders—reminded Lucille of smoke rising through a bloody sunset, an image accentuated by the gold trim that brought out each war machine's details.

Milling about at their feet were several techs in gray, hooded coveralls, as well as eleven of his brethren clad in battle armor similar to his own, each sporting the same distinctive colors.

The colors of Apollyon's Chosen, the Master's most blessed.

A swell of pride—mixed with shame for letting down his masters—flushed Lucille's cheeks as he looked upon them, and he was inwardly relieved his shame was hidden by his Achileus' stealth plating. This was no time for emotion; the Master's Hands had work to do.

As he walked closer, the battlesuits, technicians, and even the 'Mechs arched themselves to attention. Lucille smiled and activated his external comm with a click of his tongue.

"Look alive, people," he barked, "this is it. Although it pains us, on this day we must cleanse the corruption near our home. When we reach the Waywards' camp, I want the MechWarriors to surround and contain the area. The rest of us will sweep the grounds and the tunnels, so we may confirm each kill and ensure the intruders are accounted for."

"Any orders specific to the intruders?" came a low rumble from the external speakers of the *Griffin* above him. Lucille turned upward to face the warrior inside the machine's bulbous cockpit.

"Precentor Apollyon wishes them captured *if* possible, Adept," he declared. "If not, termination is acceptable, as long as the bodies can be recovered."

"Understood," the *Griffin*'s pilot responded.

"This is a day of mourning for our people," Lucille said as he moved toward the nearest *Owens*, his squad automatically following his lead to mount up. "Do not take this duty lightly, but with the Master's blessing, the blood we shed today will purify our destiny in the days ahead."

As he reached out and grasped the cold, reinforced grapples and clambered up the *Owens*' side, he frowned and felt his mouth go dry. No sooner had he reached his perch on the OmniMech's shoulder than he felt its massive legs swing into action beneath him.

With a loping gait, the war machine thundered forward, taking the lead as the massive bay door rumbled open.

Lucille closed his eyes for just a moment.

The hunt was on!

ESCAPE FROM JARDINE

FORGOTTEN WORLDS, BOOK THREE

CHAPTER 1

Blake foretold that the day would come when all fighting ends and we—the believers of his Word—would emerge as the saviors of all humankind. The victories would come for us "one world at a time—then one House at a time—until we control everything." Mankind, it was said, will do so willingly, inviting us to rule.

But ruling requires sacrifice, and to end all fighting, we must be prepared for the greatest of sacrifices. On this day—the Third Blessed Transfer—Terra, and the Inner Sphere with it, will see a new dawn in one last, great conflict. The war that will, truly, end all wars. Our victories shall indeed come one world at a time—then one Bloodhouse at a time—until we destroy the greatest threat mankind has ever faced.

Then, and only then, will we prove that we alone have earned the right to lead our people to a new, everlasting, Golden Age...

—Excerpt from *"The Master's Promise"*
(authorship and date unknown)

FOREST OF SHROUDS
JARDINE (HERAKLEION)
FREE WORLDS LEAGUE
2 NOVEMBER 3067

Kona was a magnificent beast, a credit to her species. Weighing in at a mere two hundred and twenty kilos, she was lean, almost wiry, beneath a fine coat of reddish-brown fur. But her muscles were as powerful as myomer, and even with an extra ninety-five kilos of harness, rider, and saddlebags, she could tear across six meters of uneven ground a second at a sustained run and barely make a sound while doing it.

Right now, she was clawing through soil and undergrowth at a frantic nine meters a second, her breath blasting through bared fangs with a savage grunt at every pounding stride. Within her massive chest, her oversized heart hammered away, powered as much by primal fear as it was by the exertion of her mad sprint through the forest.

In the saddle above her—his body crouched forward, one hand clutching the reins for dear life, and the other grasping the handle of a rifle easily five generations older than himself—rode Elike. Like Kona beneath him, his heart raced, and his breath came in ragged, low grunts. Like the *tabiranth* he rode, his eyes scanned the wild forest ahead for threats, obstacles, dead ends, and as one, man and beast plotted their desperate course through the foliage.

Like Kona, Elike knew the terror urging them onward.

Unlike Kona—as he heard and felt the thunderous crashing behind them—Elike realized no amount of speed the animal could provide would save them from their pursuers.

In spite of his own fear, he dared a glance back. Smashing through ancient trees and snapping centuries-old vines like cobwebs, a titan of metal chased them. Fading from scarlet at its bulbous head to black at the broad metallic feet, the lumbering giant stood easily as tall as six men. Upon one shoulder sat a boxy missile launcher, while the right forearm carried a weapon so large it mimicked a heavy rifle in human hands.

Intellectually, Elike knew of these BattleMechs from the ancient wrecks littering the forest and the clearings around the City of Hope.

But facing an operational one—for *real*—was something well beyond the hunter's twenty-two years of living in the wilds of paradise.

Even so, at the first thumping sound of the approaching war machines, his raw instinct had taken over.

Run!

The BattleMech lifted its left arm, bringing a smaller laser weapon to bear. Elike felt the beam's blistering pulse slice the air just overhead and gritted his teeth. A tree ahead exploded into steam and splinters that showered him and Kona, ripping through the flesh of man and mount alike.

Elike shoved his rifle into its saddle sheath—its power would be useless against the armored skin of the monster behind him—and seized the reins with knuckle-whitening tightness.

Other parties had encountered Hope's 'Mech patrols and lived to tell the tales, but to Elike those were just stories for the night lamps. This was no patrol. Somehow, deep down, he just *knew* it.

But others had survived them. *How?*

Another blast, this time directly ahead and into the ground. Elike's eyes registered the blue-white flash, and he felt the prickling sensation that set his and Kona's hair on edge only after the earth erupted in hunks of superheated soil and rock.

Kona's instincts took over, and she darted around the blast. Elike felt the *tabiranth* buckle, almost stumbling as she lost her footing on the underbrush, but before they could go down together, the animal pounded the earth with all four legs and propelled them over a fallen trunk he hadn't even noticed until a millisecond ago.

They were airborne for only a second, leaves whipping across Elike's face as they brushed too close to a tree. Kona let out a low growl as she landed. Her gait faltered, and Elike knew from the stride and the breeze they'd lost speed.

And still the 'Mech thundered after them, shouldering through the trees and sending branches flying.

Suddenly, it occurred to Elike—possibly their only chance! All he needed to do was get his bearings, remember where to go, and guide his wounded beast to the right spot.

...And hope the Guardian now hunting the hunter would continue to enjoy his game of cat-and-'Mech until they got there...

Phantom Adept Tau Iukini Moakay frowned as he tracked the Wayward scurrying through the woods before his *Griffin*. More than once, his crosshairs flashed gold over the mounted rider, begging for the simple caress of the firing studs to unleash enough megajoules of raw energy to slice through the man and his majestic *tabiranth* in less than a heartbeat.

But more than once, Moakay found, he simply could not take the shot.

Deep down, he burned with shame. He was one of Apollyon's Chosen, the Master's most blessed. A lifetime ago, he had sacrificed his frail legs in the name of Blake, and the Master had rewarded him with true legs that never tired and never felt pain. His frail muscles had been enhanced with the true strength of myomer bundles that would never tire and would never flinch. Within his skull, he could hear his true conscience—the clipped chatter of his team, the orders barked quickly by Precentor Sigma Lucille as the rest of the Level II turned toward the Waywards' camp, entrusting Moakay with this straggler's fate.

And yet, he could not kill this Wayward!

There was little question why, he knew; the Waywards were not the enemy he had trained for. Indeed, they were not his enemy *at all*. The man now attempting to flee from him on his magnificent cat could have been part of the Chosen himself but for the act of fate or poor judgment that now sent him fleeing into the woods beyond the City of Hope. And it was with that in mind that Moakay had grown up on Jardine, and trained to be one of the world's guardians, to help fulfill the Promise one day—all so the Wayward might return home and share in Blake's blessings.

This was no sub-human Clansman Moakay now targeted; he was as much one of the Master's children as Moakay himself!

But fate, and cruel necessity, now dictated that this man die for the sins of his tribe.

"And it is my solemn duty to be your executioner..." the adept muttered.

The *click* in his true ear told Moakey his true conscience had heard him. A metallic taste filled his mouth.

"Is there a problem, Adept Moakay?" Lucille asked with just a hint of malice.

Mentally, Moakay stood at attention. His vision cleared before he even realized he had lost his focus. "No, sir," he snapped back, his voice instantly transmitted through his conscience. "The Wayward has simply changed course and is heading further east."

"He is undoubtedly trying to lead you away from the camp," Lucille replied. "Perhaps toward more of their EMP mines. Do *not* play with him, Adept! Take your shot!"

Moakay allowed his eyes to close for only a moment. Lucille was right; this was foolishness. When he opened them again, he felt his resolve returning, and swung the crosshairs around to meet the fleeing Wayward.

At least this way, it will be quick...

"Yes, Precentor," he said to his conscience. To the hunter, he added, "Blake's mercy be with you."

The crosshairs flashed gold, and he fired.

The bright crimson beam sliced through the hunter's body just as he executed a hard turn on his animal, trying to drop behind a fallen tree that sprang up in his path. Meant to carve military armor, the laser found no obstacle in the flesh and bone of the man they struck, and the body all but exploded from the heat.

The beast fared little better as excess energy sliced its body in half. Its hindquarters flashed away, leaving its head, half its torso and two fore paws to tumble forward and vanish into the brush.

But the horrific deaths of the rider and his cat were the last things to register in Moakay's mind, for at that moment—just as he began to slow his *Griffin* to a halt—his entire universe suddenly dissolved into a burst of electric-blue light, and it felt as if the hand of God Himself had suddenly reached out to crush his chest...

TRIBE ENCAMPMENT
FOREST OF SHROUDS
JARDINE (HERAKLEION)
FREE WORLDS LEAGUE

Mikeke had read the pages of this old tome a dozen times before, but for some reason he could not explain, he always found himself drawn back to it time and time again. It was a classic Star League-era piece of science fiction, written long before the Fall, about mankind encountering an alliance of intelligent alien beings that seemed hell-bent on ending all life in the galaxy. The story, he realized, was probably a retelling of any number of even older fantasy tales; even in the centuries before man left Terra's blessed soil, his kind had wondered if they were alone in the universe.

These stories amused the tribal chieftain in a way that tugged at his cynical side. For all of pre-spaceflight Terra's certainty in discovering new civilizations among the stars, humanity's fiction on the subject overwhelmingly presumed any such civilizations would set its sights on genocide. Even in the glorious days of the Star League, it seemed, the storytellers fixated on the possibility that overpowering agents of death lay just beyond the boundaries of explored space.

Mikeke often wondered how many of these creative thinkers would have been surprised to know that man would breed his own genocidal alien menace—with nary a strand of non-human DNA required?

He was just about to start the chapter in which humanity's warring factions put aside their differences to unite against the common foe when the sound of running feet echoed from the outward cave entrance. Without so much as a rap on the threshold beams to grab his attention first and await permission to enter, Ravid burst through the curtain.

The chieftain raised his head to see a look of panic on the young hunter's face. Seeing also that Ravid's age-worn gyroslug rifle was in his hands, rather than slung over his shoulder, sent a foreboding chill down the older man's spine.

"Mikeke!" Ravid said breathlessly. "It's Guardians... Dimke radioed in! He says they're heading this way! 'Mechs and armor!"

The book fell out of Mikeke's suddenly numb fingers, completely forgotten. His mouth went instantly dry, and a second chill shook him. He was out of his chair before he even realized it, reaching for the rifle affixed to the cave wall behind him, and the bandolier of magazines hung beside it. His old hunters' instincts came back to him with a surge of urgency.

"How many?" he snapped. "How close?"

Ravid's eyes remained tense. "Two kilometers at most," he replied. "Dimke counted five 'Mechs, maybe two squads..." He swallowed hard before adding, "They're *his*!"

Mikeke wished that information surprised him, but instead it only made his heart sink further. There was only one complete Domini formation left on Jardine he knew of, but it was the only one that needed to be here. First Pilipo's disappearance on a hunt, and now this!

Any hope left in his mind that this could be just a random patrol vanished like smoke.

"They're coming for the Lost ones," Mikeke said flatly. "But we won't be spared."

"Couldn't we just *give* them to him—?" Ravid started, even though the words clearly pained him. It was the kind of thought Dimke would have uttered.

"That wouldn't stop them now." He closed his eyes and bent his head for a moment. "May Blake have mercy, for his Guardians won't."

He looked up to find Ravid had bowed his head as well, silently praying with him. Mikeke checked his rifle, assuring its magazine was loaded. Ravid's eyes came back up the instant he moved. The men locked gazes.

"Find Alahni, Ravid," Mikeke told him. "Tell her to take the Lost to the city, through the secret pass. I would send you with them, but—"

"My place is with the tribe," Ravid finished for him. It was both an acknowledgment of his duties and a vow not to run in one determined statement.

Mikeke nodded. "Try not to panic her, but tell her to stay with Uku and his people until we call her back; tell her you will catch up, if you must, or she'll try to stay. Moze and I will send as many of our kin through the deep tunnels as we can spare. But you, I, and the rest of our hunters will need to delay the Guardians for as long as possible if they are to have any chance to survive."

Ravid nodded, but said nothing. He knew, as well as Mikeke did, that the Shrouded Forest Tribe had already seen its last sunrise.

Sending Alahni away with the Lost was merely a way to ensure that its memory survived.

THE SANCTORUM
CITY OF HOPE
JARDINE (HERAKLEION)
FREE WORLDS LEAGUE

With the hood of her robe thrown back, the delicate curves of Lamashti's head and face could be seen in all their glory. Not one strand of hair or bit of stubble marred her scalp; even her eyebrows were bare and pristine. Her porcelain skin was absolutely smooth, and free of all but the tiniest wrinkles—save for those forming slight crow's feet around the reddish rims of her eyes. It was as though her entire visage had been sculpted and polished from a single piece of unblemished ivory.

The lighting in the communications chamber had been muted for her benefit. Her true eyes had just received their final upgrades a week before; cosmetic modifications made to give them an *almost* natural appearance—save for the silver discs replacing iris and pupil alike. That personal choice in aesthetic, combined with her flawlessly smooth skin, lent Lamashti an otherworldly appearance. But for now, in the wake of the surgery, she found it better to shield her eyes and reduce any glare in order to avoid too much strain while her frail flesh healed.

These final modifications had come after her Ascension, after she rose from the ranks of the Manei Domini's elite Ghost operatives to the rank of junior Precentor. Now, she possessed the very best in true vision, true hearing, and true speech—abilities so finely tuned even her commander could scarcely compete.

To the mere Frails of the Inner Sphere, Ghost Precentor Sigma Lamashti would seem supernatural, almost telepathic for all intents and purposes. Her true vision could sense electromagnetic wavelengths from gamma rays through infrared as easily as any other human being could see in visible light. Her true ears could not only detect sound waves at greater range and distance than normal people, but could even eavesdrop on radio waves. And her true voice, capable of modulating to the very same ranges as her ears, gave her the means to communicate to others even when she appeared to stand mute.

At this moment, however, Lamashti's eyes were closed, her true voice silent at all frequencies. She focused her mind completely on the sense of true hearing now, studying, memorizing, and assimilating the recordings of radio transmissions sent by the DropShuttle that had brought two misguided Frails to her homeworld. Her mind studied every nuance and inflection in the feminine voice that made those calls to distant, unseen allies. She picked apart the foreigner's accent (Lyran, likely raised in Donegal's Eastern Hinterlands region), assessed her vocal tones (tense, but far from panicked), and mentally mapped her vocal range (contralto, *fascinating*!).

Unfortunately, none of the terms this woman used in her recorded transmissions felt stressed enough to Lamashti's extra-sensitive ears to suggest code phrases or special cues to her colleagues. If there were any special commands hidden in the messages, they were hidden so well, and spoken with such discipline, even one of the Domini's best intelligence operatives would miss them.

Something Lamashti knew to be impossible.

Ergo...

"Nothing, my Precentor," she said, knowing her master still stood nearby (precisely 2.6 meters to her forward right, and facing her).

Her silver eyes opened, but the visual confirmation Apollyon stood nearby was unnecessary. He had not moved a muscle for the past ten minutes. His arms remained folded together, tucked into the sleeves of his red robe. His hood was pulled back as well, leaving his bronzed scalp bare, and allowing the dimmed lighting and blue-green haze from the comm center's nearby vid screens to glimmer upon the metals of his prosthetics.

Apollyon nodded, almost solemnly. He had not truly expected to find codes hidden inside the intruder's mayday, but that was hardly the only reason to have Lamashti analyze the message. "Can you mimic her?"

Lamashti favored him with a crooked smile. It was hardly worth saying, but she immediately re-modulated her true speech, and replied in the foreigner's voice: "Brooklyn Stevens. At your service, *Herr* Precentor."

Scoring the name of the woman, and even that of her crew's JumpShip, came from a careful analysis of her wrecked shuttle, rather than the mayday transmission. It was a wise enough move of this Frail to omit such details in case of hostile eavesdroppers, but clearly she had not thought it all the way through. Or lacked the training of a proper covert operative.

If Apollyon smiled at all in recognition of Lamashti's resourcefulness, it was imperceptible even to her true eyes. He merely nodded again. "It'll have to do," he said. "Perhaps, with some properly timed interference, we can make a call just convincing, yet garbled enough, to make up for any lack of known keywords."

"A challenge," Lamashti replied.

"May Blake reward our efforts, then," he agreed. "I will leave you to compose the message, Ghost Precentor Sigma. Feel free to broadcast when ready, using the same frequencies as her distress call; it would seem unlikely that they would reserve a secondary channel for further such hails. In the meantime, I will be at the 'port, seeing to our shuttles."

CHAPTER 2

My Dearest Tyler,

I don't care what the vid-games tell you—driving an actual BattleMech is even more awesome than it seems! Oh, I know you don't really care for them, but this 'Mech-obsessed culture we live in has all but assured that half of these IE missions will call for us to either retrieve some walking junk-heap dating back to the Camerons or drive one of their armed WorkMechs into a dig site.

The new guy assigned to us, Tibor Mitternacht, apparently has some tech skills and knows the ins and outs of 'Mech operation. He's ex-military, he says, but doesn't go farther than that. His accent tells me he's Lyran-born, though. Anyway, he was so impressed with my handling of the clunky old DiggerMech here that he decided to convince one of the 'Mech jocks in our attached security detail here to let me take the helm of an actual BattleMech!

It was a smaller model. A Commando, *they called it. They make them on Coventry, and I'm told it's one of the lightest machines they still use in the LAAF today. Anyway, I just have to say even though it was described like the runt of the litter, there's a genuine thrill in piloting a walker that moves with such fluidity. I've heard the MechWarriors talk about how much more refined and flexible their rides were compared to the civilian variety, but until I put that* Commie *through its paces, I didn't believe it!*

I tell you, it was like learning to drive on an old farm tractor, and then being handed the keys to a Hurricane Windracer with all the options! Well, except in this case there are also missile launchers and lasers mounted on it to blow your way through the typical Donegal City gridlock!

Tibor says I handled the thing like a natural! And while he may just be saying that just to get in my pants (Men!), the Commando's owner did say I managed a pretty good shots-to-hits ratio for a "dirt digger."

—From the collected writings
of Dr. Brooklyn Stevens (ca. 3060)

FOREST OF SHROUDS
JARDINE (HERAKLEION)
FREE WORLDS LEAGUE
2 NOVEMBER 3067

By Brooke's estimate, they had traveled through at least four kilometers of jungle when the sound of distant thumping reached them. Tibor was the first to hear it, pausing abruptly and raising a fist as his old training kicked in. Brooke, standing just to his left, caught the motion and stopped short herself. She had just begun to ask what was wrong when Tibor put a finger to his lips and made a sharp hissing noise.

It was that noise that told Alahni, walking ahead of them, that her charges had stopped. She turned around, and Brooke caught her gaze. The young Wayward's eyes were wide, showing the same fear as when Ravid had found them back at the encampment and urgently told Alahni to lead "the Lost ones" to the city. Tibor's alert stance registered in Alahni's expression as well, along with his repeated gesture for silence. The girl's face grew whiter as the first *thump* finally resonated across the earth.

Followed by another.

And another.

"'Mechs," Brooke whispered. She turned slowly, trying to get a fix on the direction, until she noticed Tibor had already locked onto that: behind them. "Following us?"

Tibor held his breath and closed his eyes for a moment. "No," he muttered back. "I don't think so. Not yet, anyway. But it's more than one..."

Brooke listened again, and realized she heard it too. The distant pounding was not synchronized; it was irregular, like competing drumbeats. She narrowed her eyes.

"The Domini don't send their 'Mechs into these forests on patrols," Alahni said, her voice low, tense, nearly cracking.

They're looking for us, Brooke thought. She looked back at Alahni, unsure what to say. But before she could speak, a sound like distant thunder interrupted the distant footfalls.

"Scheiße!" Tibor spat.

There was no need to explain that noise, or the other brief rumbles that quickly followed. Alahni's face paled, and Brooke saw true terror and heartache in the young woman's eyes.

"No!" Alahni shrieked, tears welling in her eyes. "For the love of Blake, *why*!?"

The girl had taken two steps forward—back toward the camp—before she even knew it. Instinctively, Brooke reached out and grabbed her by the arm. Alahni strained against her grasp, crying hysterically.

"Alahni, *don't*!" Brooke shouted. "There's nothing you can do for them!"

"Jesus," Tibor hissed. "I figured they knew something was coming when they rushed us out of there, but *'Mechs*?"

"We just wanted to live in peace!" Alahni whimpered, her face now pressed into Brooke's shoulder. Brooke held her awkwardly, and looked over at Tibor. "We were no danger to them!"

"It's..." Tibor started, but his voice trailed off.

"It's us," Brooke finished. "It's our fault, Alahni. I'm so sorry..."

Alahni pushed herself away from Brooke, breaking free with surprising strength. Brooke held her breath, braced for the tirade, but while the look on the Wayward's face showed rage and fear in equal measure, the words that came out were heartbroken.

"Damn you all!" she screamed.

Suddenly, she was gone, darting into the brush before Brooke could stop her.

Tibor blinked. "Crap! There goes our guide—"

"Come *on*!" Brooke snapped back, already breaking into a sprint. As she, too, lunged into the woods, she called Alahni's name.

With Tibor on her heels, Brooke raced almost blindly into the forest. The trees and underbrush were thick in this region, shadowing the landscape, giving her little time to watch her steps. Low-hanging branches raked across her face, and she nearly tripped more than once.

Ahead, she could hear rustling leaves, accompanied by infrequent sobs. Behind her, Tibor's labored grunts reminded her he was in no shape for a foot race like this.

They'd been running for almost a full minute when she heard him fall. Hard.

"Son of a—!" he growled, then abruptly stopped.

Brooke came to a stumbling halt, looking back to find him on his knees. For a moment, she almost didn't see what he was staring at with incredulous eyes, so entangled was it in the undergrowth.

Then she recognized the powerful, clawed forelegs of a reddish-brown *tabiranth*, connected by half a torso to a large feline head that stared at her with sightless eyes, its fanged mouth agape. How Brooke had missed the massive carcass in her charge through the woods defied her imagination, but as Tibor pushed himself up, she noticed he'd actually tripped over the remnants of a riding saddle.

"Poor beast," Tibor muttered, his eyes beginning a sweep even as he gasped for air.

"It's fresh," Brooke said, her own voice low and breathless. "One of them came through here. "How did we miss them?"

Tibor was shaking his head. "Dunno," he answered, "but we better find the girl, before—"

The scream cut off his reply, and his eyes snapped in its direction. Brooke spun around, following the sound as well. With only a moment's glance back at Tibor, she bolted toward it.

Seconds later, they burst out of the undergrowth and into a swath of broken trees and fallen branches. The broken cover and the forest canopy still made it difficult for Brooke to home in on exactly where she'd heard Alahni's cry, and her footsteps faltered as she instinctively slowed to survey the path ahead.

Until Tibor jogged past her, clapping her on the shoulder as he went. "This way!"

Brooke fell in behind him now, quickly beginning to realize what she was seeing. The ruined foliage, the unmistakable scent of freshly split wood and churned soil—all told the tale. But there was something more, a sound, so deep and so faint she almost couldn't sense it over the sound of her own footfalls, ragged breathing, and pounding heartbeat.

Ahead, she saw Tibor clamber over a short hillock, and felt a moment of surprise when Alahni suddenly emerged from beyond it to embrace him.

She's safe! Thank Bast she's safe!

Relieved, Brooke's stride slowed as she reached the hillock and ascended it, her feet slipping a little as she found the soil beneath looser than expected. The deep hum in her ears was rising, but over the distant sound of more gunfire, she'd almost forgotten about it.

Until she saw what lay just beyond the rise.

There, sprawled awkwardly on the forest floor, lay the massive hulk of a BattleMech, painted in foreboding shades of red and black.

TRIBE ENCAMPMENT
FOREST OF SHROUDS
JARDINE (HERAKLEION)
FREE WORLDS LEAGUE

With an ear-shattering pop and a flash of electric blue light, the sleek, humanoid form of a 25-ton *Nexus* came to a sudden, lurching halt. Smoke billowed around its right foot, and its arms tensed to the sides, locking into place as if frozen in shock.

Feeling the ripple of hot air and the tingle of the electromagnetic pulse, Lucille's head snapped around in time not only to see the BattleMech crash-land on the forest floor, scattering brush and earth in all directions, but also the twitching death of at least two more of his own troopers, whose bodies soaked up too much of the pulse themselves.

Adept Jorg, the closer of the two, clutched at the helmet of his power armor and howled in enraged pain. A flash of light inside his visor and the abrupt end of his scream told Lucille the man's true eyes had exploded. A heartbeat later, the suit itself flew apart as the rest of Jorg's body followed, showering the field with shrapnel, bone, and gore—small chunks of which even reached Lucille's battered Achileus.

Adept Sonia's own self-destruction was lost beneath the falling hulk of the *Nexus*. Her true voice, likely destroyed when the EMP struck, never even uttered a sound.

Lucille felt his jaw tighten and released his rage in an incoherent snarl.

These frail Waywards had gotten lucky—*too* damned lucky—since this hunt began. Already, Lucille had lost two BattleMechs and five armored troopers to their EMP trip-mines and salvaged weapons.

That the nomads knew who they faced and had modified their weapons to deal with them was hardly an excuse! That Lucille and his men had already killed over twenty of their misled kind was little consolation! The hunt should *not* have been going this badly!

Another rocket-assisted shell exploded against his armor's flank, tearing through to find the flesh within. The pain barely registered to Lucille; he simply used it to determine where the shot came from.

With a battle cry roared through his external speakers, he lunged toward the shooter. Closing the distance in a fraction of a second, he tore through the brush and the fallen tree the Wayward had used for cover. The hunter was male, with long black locks and a scarred, stubbled face. His dark eyes widened, and his mouth opened to say something even as Lucille punched through his frail chest with an armored gauntlet.

Lifting the gurgling, blood-soaked Wayward high, Lucille flung his corpse into another hunter—this one a woman with flowing brown hair, flimsy flak armor, and an elephant gun.

The body struck the woman dead-on, knocking her to the ground and sending her weapon flying. Still snarling through his speakers, Lucille stomped toward her, incidentally crushing the male Wayward's forgotten gyrojet rifle beneath one of his meta-shod feet.

Though clearly dazed, the huntress struggled to free herself from the weight of her companion's body. She gasped as Lucille towered over her, stabbed the muzzles of his Mauser 1200 toward her, and painted her forehead with the steady beam of the rifle's targeting laser.

"Where are they, Wayward?" he demanded. "Where are the Lost ones?"

She opened her mouth to speak, but by that time, Lucille was already pulling the trigger, unleashing a burst of laser fire that transformed the once-pretty young girl into a smoking mass of exploded flesh and bone.

Answers were unnecessary; this entire camp would burn the moment he could account for the intruders personally.

A voice spoke in Lucille's ears just then; strong, confident, but devoid of any real emotion. "East flank secured, Precentor," the warrior said. "We count a dozen kills here, all Waywards."

"Blessed be," Lucille replied. "A number have fled into the caves below. My troopers will move in to flush them out while you and the other MechWarriors hold the topside perimeter. Maintain thermal scans to track any others, but remember to engage all hostiles with minimal overkill; we'll need something to conduct tests on in the event you should catch the off-worlders."

"Understood, Precentor."

"No obvious damage. And my eye's getting a heat glow from the engine, so it's clearly operational," Tibor said, admitting his implant was working again. "Terrain doesn't seem too rough for 'Mechs here, so I'm guessing he must've triggered one of those EMP mines."

Brooke put a cautionary hand on Tibor's shoulder and looked around. He caught her gaze for a moment and twitched his head toward the fallen *Griffin*'s bubble-shaped head. The transplas armor that gave its MechWarrior an unparalleled field of vision was polarized for glare, but it looked as if the Domini had tinted it as well—with what looked like a highly reflective form of dark, metallic green.

It was also lying sideways against the soft earth, quite intact. The 'Mech had come down on its right shoulder, trapping the right arm beneath it, while its left hung limply across its mid-section. The legs had locked almost perfectly straight, forming a neat V-shape behind its half-twisted torso.

And so far as Brooke could see, not a single hatch was opened.

"The engine's rebooted," Tibor said, "but the thing's still down, and the canopy hasn't blown. I'm betting the pilot's still inside; probably took too much feedback for his implants."

"The Blakists were in a rush to catch the tribe off guard," Brooke mumbled bitterly. "Didn't even bother to pick up their toys."

Then the crazy idea hit. She rolled it around in her head for a few seconds before finally catching Tibor's gaze. "Can you hotwire it?"

"The machine men can merge with their 'Mechs," Alahni muttered. Her voice was still tiny and distant.

Brooke turned to her, perplexed.

"The controls," the Jardinian continued, utter defeat written all over her face as she stared back through puffy, unblinking eyes. "They need special implants to work. No neurohelmets or manual systems are needed, so the Guardians remove them."

"*Scheiße,*" Brooke whispered. *So much for* that *idea, then...*

Tibor leaned against the machine's cockpit until he was practically pressing his nose against it, and cupped his hands over his eyes to block out all daylight. Suddenly, mere seconds later, he burst into a coughing and gagging fit, and stumbled back from the machine, collapsing into an awkward sitting position on a mass of churned up earth and roots. Brooke took a step closer as he covered his mouth for a moment and stood back up, still fighting an obvious urge to retch. When he removed his hand, he revealed an expression that was at once shaken and...*pleased*?

"Well," he said after one last cough, "*this* one must've missed that memo. I'm seeing standard system controls in there. Throttles, panels, and displays, all lit up. I wouldn't even need to hack it. But it looks like the *Arschloch's* cyberware betrayed him all the same."

Curiosity got the better of Brooke, and she also peered through the tinted transplas—only to regret it instantly. Now it was her turn to blanch.

"Thank Bast for small favors," she croaked out between coughs. She clambered to the side of the BattleMech's head and yanked on its emergency latch. There was a hiss of air as the hydraulic release complied, parting the cockpit seal enough for her and Tibor to grab onto and pry open.

The stench that hit them was unholy—a mix of burned metals, ozone, and human waste. Both explorers turned away for a moment to gasp for fresh air. Brooke glanced over to Tibor and nodded, then turned to face Alahni, who now stood behind her. Though still horror-stricken, the look in the Jardinian's eyes also betrayed an eagerness to see what lay within.

"You'll probably want to look away," Brooke told her. "This won't be pretty."

"What do you—?" Alahni started, then her entire body recoiled and her face twisted in a look of revulsion as the odor reached her. "Oh, *Blake's blood*!"

"Close enough," Tibor darkly quipped, as the young woman twisted herself away.

Brooke joined him and suffered a new gagging fit at the sight. In her career, she had seen many corpses, of course, but this may have been the first time she saw one that looked like it had both imploded and exploded at the same time. Blood was everywhere, painting much of the control systems, splashing and pooling along the right side of the canopy and—almost certainly—the lowermost areas, which she could not make out for all the shadows. Bits of bone, shrapnel, meat, and other unidentifiable tissues clung to surfaces all over the chamber, some wetly coming loose even as Brooke and Tibor forced the opening even wider.

At the center, still buckled into its seat, still clad in the tatters of what once had been a pristine cooling suit, was a sagging, skeletal...thing. The pilot's body was twisted as close to a fetal position as its five-point harness allowed, and its limbs looked compressed, as if they began to shrink while they curled inward. More blood dripped slowly from several tears in the suit.

But the most disturbing part was the head. Still attached—but only barely—and still inside a neurohelmet of first Star League design, it was remarkably intact. The MechWarrior had been male, and Brooke guessed by his skin tone that he shared the same ethnic heritage as Alahni's people. But his eyes had sunken completely inside their sockets, vanishing somewhere deep inside the skull, while his jaw hung open crookedly, blood painting the lips, chin, and right cheek a bright crimson. It was a rictus of incredible, soul-crushing agony—one that told her the man had *suffered* in his final moments.

Good, was the first thought that struck Brooke as she realized that, and allowed herself one final shudder of revulsion.

She pressed on the body's harness release, which sank into the chest of its collapsed torso. Something inside the cooling suit made a sound reminding Brooke of the time she once tripped into a steaming mud bath. Thankfully, the release popped before she had pushed her hand all the way through the squishy, spongy remains.

Together, she and Tibor heaved the vaguely humanoid sack of pulp out of its seat and hurled it into some nearby brush. In the process, the head had separated, ensnared by the neurohelmet still wired into the consoles. After pulling the chin strap upward, Brooke gave the helmet a shake; the head slid out like a single hunk of canned meat, thudding against the forest floor. Tibor kicked it into the same brush as its body.

Glancing back in, Brooke sighed in relief. Protected largely by the suit and the head's apparent failure to explode, the cockpit seat and the interior of the neurohelmet were mostly clean. Lacking the suit would be a problem, but not insurmountable. She handed the helmet to Tibor, then set herself to clearing the spattered blood from the cockpit displays and controls, wishing she had a bundle of rags to do this with instead of her bare hands.

Alahni had turned back, but now stood a few extra meters away, staring at the Lost ones in bewilderment. But it wasn't until Brooke began shedding her clothes on the forest floor that the girl found her voice again. "What are you *doing*?"

Brooke froze for a second, her eyes meeting Alahni's. Standing in the open in just her undergarments, she suddenly remembered she had an audience (beyond Tibor, at any rate), and the gooseflesh spread quickly over her arms and legs. A soft snort from him deepened the flush burning her cheeks, but it also shook her out of her momentary pause.

"Y-You two will need to stay put," she stammered. "Trouble, is your radio implant working?"

"Fortunately, yeah," he mumbled as his hands continued working the insides of the helmet. "Both it and the eye are a bit fuzzy, but they're working."

"Then I'll tune a private channel to you," she told him as she put her boots back on.

"Okay," he replied, handing her the helmet. "But I'm with Alahni here. Just what *are* you doing?"

"Something stupid, maybe," she said as she climbed into the cockpit, feeling for all the world like someone who was now modeling one of those tasteless "Sexy MechWarrior" costumes that became so popular every October. Despite the awkward angle, she managed to leverage herself into the seat enough to refasten the harness around her torso.

She kept her eyes focused on the harness, then the control displays, afraid to look at either of her companions—especially the young Jardinian.

"But I'll be damned if I'm letting these monsters get away with this slaughter scot-free," she added. Secured into the command couch, she reached up for the canopy handle, before finally meeting Tibor's judgmental gaze. Any one of a thousand things could go wrong at this point, but she shoved those doubts away.

"If I don't make it back," she told him, "tell Tyler I'm sorry..."

With that, she shut and dogged the hatch, turning her attention to completing the *Griffin*'s restart sequence and recalibrating the neurohelmet to her own neural patterns.

Outside, Tibor gathered up her discarded clothes, then guided Alahni to a safe distance.

A few minutes later, the 55-ton monster rose from the forest floor once more.

LEOPARD-CLASS DROPSHIP *KAYLIN*
PIRATE JUMP POINT
JARDINE (HERAKLEION) SYSTEM
FREE WORLDS LEAGUE
2 NOVEMBER 3067

Lenard Bryce, executive officer of the *Kaylin*, straightened up from the comm station just as Captain Anton Hara floated through the bridge hatch. Hara's malachite eyes caught his within moments, asking their question silently.

Bryce was just about to respond when he noticed the second man trailing behind him. Instead of speaking right away, he flashed his captain a frown. *Why, in the name of all the heavens, does that IE slug have to follow him around like a lost puppy?*

Hara acknowledged Bryce's ire with a sympathetic roll of his eyes, and the subtle shrug that communicated his own non-verbal comment: *What are you gonna do?*

If the exchange of expressions even registered to Nathan Bellamy, the liaison assigned to Hara by Interstellar Expeditions, he was damned good at hiding it. Before either man spoke, he nudged himself sideways with a gentle shove against one of the bridge rails. The maneuver almost made him look graceful, had he not misjudged and began a tumbling spin he was forced to stop by grabbing one of the ceiling rungs.

Not for the first time since they had been saddled with the man did the ancient word "landlubber" flit through Bryce's mind, leading him to favor Hara with a cock-eyed smirk.

Hara didn't even bother looking back to see what Bellamy had done *this* time. Instead, he broke through the white noise of bridge systems and air circulators with a simple question: "This just came in?"

Bryce nodded. "In the clear, sir," he reported. "It's slightly garbled, but it tracks back in-system."

"Let's hear it, then."

Bryce nodded again, and tapped on the panel in front of him. The senior comms officer for the bridge was off-shift at this hour, likely asleep in his cabin. Bryce had been on solo watch when the transmission came in. Though the message from the dark took him by surprise, the monitors had faithfully recorded every word as it came in.

And now, the voice of Doctor Brooklyn Stevens crackled once more from the speakers in playback, faint and distorted by random bursts of static:

"DropShuttle Magellan *to* Sacajawea— *Guys, it's Brook— We're still here— Trying to repair the ship— We think we'll be able to— When we're ready, we'll try to sig— But fuel is limited— We'll need telem— Not send anyone else! I repeat: do not— Still unsafe—"*

The transmission ended with a sharp *chirp.*

Hara's eyes, closed throughout most of the playback as he focused on trying to hear through the signal noise, opened again, and met Bryce's.

"That's all we picked up," Bryce told him. "If there was any more, it's likely something blocked it out; maybe even the planet's rotation."

"The channels used?"

"Standard IE distress frequency. Looks like another case of her crew still using their old employee handbook."

At this, Bellamy sniffed. He now clung to the ceiling rung nearest the comm panels, his wide form casting an imposing shadow. Had anyone actually been seated here, Bryce noted, the poor soul would probably feel claustrophobic with three men surrounding the small, free-standing podium of a station.

"Did the *Sac* respond?" Bellamy asked, pre-empting Hara's next question.

Bryce raised an eyebrow at the man, but directed his answer to both of them. "Not yet, so far as I can tell."

"Are we sure they heard it?"

"It's unlikely we would've heard anything they didn't, Mister Bellamy," Hara said flatly.

"Indeed," Bryce said. "So, judging by the content, Doctor Stevens is reporting she's still alive and well, trying to fix her shuttle, and trying to get telemetry for a return trip."

Hara nodded. "Sounds like low fuel, which would make sense if they'd burned much on the way in, or suffered a leak from whatever damage they took. She doesn't want to make escape velocity only to have to waste whatever's left in the tank on course corrections."

"And yet," Bellamy said, "Captain Pohl hasn't replied. For all Stevens knows right now, the *Sacajawea* might not even be here."

Hara sighed. "Technically speaking, Pohl doesn't have to reply...yet."

"It *does* sound like Stevens plans to signal again when she's ready to launch," Bryce agreed. "Telemetry info sent now would be useless if it takes her several days to make repairs."

"Or her friends are watching what they say around us," Bellamy offered.

"Or just around whoever else may be watching," Bryce countered. "She did warn them not to send anyone else, after all."

"Whatever the case," Hara said, "it lets us know to expect something sooner, rather than later. If Stevens is planning to make her escape, it seems she intends to do it as quickly as possible, and she's telling her crew to get ready for when she starts."

"Then *that* is when we should be ready to strike, Captain," Bellamy said, betraying the hidden edge Hara had warned Bryce about.

TRIBE ENCAMPMENT
FOREST OF SHROUDS
JARDINE (HERAKLEION)
FREE WORLDS LEAGUE
2 NOVEMBER 3067

As he stepped through another *tabiranth*-hide curtain into a chamber that appeared large enough to be a communal barracks, Lucille spared a moment to admire the Waywards' resourcefulness. Fiber-optic light channels, hewn wood structural supports, woven rugs, ancient-yet-well-maintained firearms, EMP mines on triplines, and all manner of portable energy devices (likely scavenged from Hope itself), all worked to provide maximum habitability within their earthen enclave without giving away their presence to the world outside. Just like their brethren in the city, these Waywards valued their invisibility; clearly, the lessons of the Malu Tribe had not been lost on them.

It was a shame they still had to die.

Just because two off-world Frails entered their midst.

As quickly as the warring surges of pride and regret washed over Lucille, they were gone. Mercy was not the way of the Master's Hands. The mission was paramount. Although these Waywards were not the enemy they had been made to fight, the Manei Domini had only one ultimate function. Everything else belonged to those who were *not* monsters.

The shoulder of Lucille's Achileus armor scraped a furrow into a curved, earthen wall as he swung about, scanning a small side chamber for signs of life. Two corpses—still cooling toward ambient temperature in his thermal-augmented view—were all he saw. Each had been penetrated by no less than four shots, and left propped up against the wall.

His HUD flagged them as a navigation point labeled "*Null.*" The flag told him what he already knew from the bodies' hand-made hunters' garb and deeper skin tones. It also told him his troopers were still minding their job and inspecting their kills to confirm these weren't the off-worlders they sought.

"Precentor!" a voice harshly snapped in his ear—Adept Quang, the MechWarrior commanding the *Nexus* he left to hold the perimeter above. "I have a contact approaching."

Lucille's eyes narrowed. Quang's tone hinted at his confusion. He keyed the warrior's channel directly. "And?"

"It appears to be Adept Moakay's *Griffin,* sir."

This time, it was Lucille's turn to sound bewildered. "*Moakay?*"

His mind raced. There had been no time to confirm the *Griffin*'s pilot had survived his fall. Indeed, after the squeal of the warrior's comms going dead amid a roar of unspeakable agony—followed by his machine's IFF winking out while chasing that Wayward hunter—Lucille simply presumed Moakay had suffered a fatal run-in with another of these Waywards' damnable mines. After trying to regain contact several times, it was Lucille himself that ordered the *Griffin*'s last known position flagged for later investigation, certain they would find only a dead husk of both man and machine there when this was all over. The odds certainly did not look good, after all.

It *was* possible he had miscalculated. But that would make Moakay the luckiest Domini in this entire operation.

And Poltergeist Precentor Sigma Damien Lucille did not believe in luck.

"Adept Quang," he barked, "hail that BattleMech at once!"

Though Brooke had recognized and adapted to the main control systems quickly enough, the cockpit of this *Griffin* was much different than any BattleMech she had ever driven before. For starters, it was all so *brand new*; save for the smears and spatters of darkening red and black left by its previous occupant, the various boards and panels looked pristine. Even the smallest retaining screws gleamed amid the cockpit lights, as though they had been machined only yesterday.

For another, it was remarkably cool; where many combustion or cell-powered WorkMechs rarely required cooling vests to operate, and could accommodate a pilot just fine by leaving the windows open, the act of merely walking a fusion-driven BattleMech in springtime conditions tended to require a refrigerant-lined vest to prevent a sudden onset of heat exhaustion when waste heat filled the nominally sealed piloting compartment. And yet, even at a mad run through a rainforest, this cockpit was only a balmy twenty-nine Celsius, according to one of the secondary displays Brooke found no reason to doubt.

Then there were the electronics, some of which she scarcely understood. If the HUD was to be believed, she was getting updates on the positions of all known battlefield units in the area—friend and foe alike—in real time, rather than via periodic sensor sweeps. Hell, it took her several minutes to even realize the targeting sensors were in passive mode to begin with, the changing of which only made the flow of information more dramatic, as she suddenly found all those friendly icons had names and 'Mech designators ready to go. It was only after wracking her brain over memories of Star League-era engineering that she realized what this meant. But since there was no way she could imagine anyone driving a heavy, well-equipped command vehicle into these thick woods, it had to be one of those much more recent C^3 computers she'd only read about before now.

After that came her mental inventory of the 'Mech's capabilities—something she felt she'd "cheated" on a little bit by running the diagnostics. Extended-range particle projector cannon, large LRM launcher, two extended-range medium-size lasers, and a Guardian electronic countermeasures suite—a combined amount of equipment nobody could have crammed into a frame like this during the Succession Wars, but might have in the days of the Camerons (if all of it even existed back then). And all put together perhaps as recently as last month by the self-proclaimed protectors of mankind's knowledge.

So, basically, what Brooke was driving right now was the single most advanced hunk of military hardware she'd ever *seen*, much less commanded.

Inwardly, she knew she would probably feel more impressed by all of that if she wasn't seething with rage right now. That, and possibly the fact she was also struggling to ignore the overwhelming stink of blood, remains, and excrement she probably couldn't have scrubbed out of this thing without a power hose and a dozen liters of bleach.

Opening the few cockpit panels she could to ventilate the foul air accomplished next to nothing, but she'd done it anyway. Because of that, she also heard the snapping of branches and the thunderous footfalls of her captured 'Mech as it plowed through the foliage toward the nearest "friendly" marker on her tactical display.

She was breathing through her mouth, hissing through bared teeth, when that marker blinked, and a click sounded in the left speaker of her neurohelmet (the only speaker that apparently still functioned).

"Inbound *Griffin*, identify at once!" commanded a male voice, his accent nearly identical to that of Alahni's tribe. "Adept Moakay, is that you?"

Brooke bowed her head a little, as every muscle in her body tensed. Ignoring the hail, she lined herself up until the *Griffin*'s targeting reticules projected onto her HUD hovered over the brackets surrounding the still-unseen 'Mech. The battle computer flashed the target's identity as "*2M: NXS-Quang.*" Beside the brackets appeared a range reading: 300 meters... 270... 240...

"Inbound *Griffin*," the target shouted again, but never budged. "Halt and identify yourself! This is your final warning!"

Brooke snarled and shoved the throttle to maximum. The reticules flashed red, then gold, as the distance readout fell past 200 meters.

At about 120 meters, the foliage suddenly gave way to a clearing. Her eyes barely registered the thin wisps of smoke drifting throughout the area, or the bodies—human and *tabiranth* alike—scattered among the grass and rocks. But she knew they were there.

She had come to avenge them.

Her trigger fingers mashed down their studs, and the *Griffin* obliged immediately. A bolt of cerulean lightning shrieked forth from her particle cannon, stabbing into her enemy's left flank. At the same time, twin beams of crimson light flashed out, each aimed for the same spot. Superheated armor panels burst open, exploding away from the spindly-looking machine and exposing equally ravaged chassis supports beneath.

Its own weapons, arm-mounted lasers triggered a heartbeat after Brooke's salvo, found their aim spoiled as the wounded 'Mech twisted under the *Griffin*'s punishing fire. One—the right—managed to hit, burning a thin trench across the bigger 'Mech's left thigh, but the other shot harmlessly skyward as the arm it came from suddenly broke free of its mount.

With its balance completely lost, the BattleMech designated "*NXS-Quang*" crashed down onto its side even before Brooke had managed to close the distance. But she still wasn't done with it; growling, she slammed the left foot pedal hard. Once again, her captured *Griffin* complied with incredible ease, swinging a broad-based foot forward and into the enemy's "abdomen" with enough force to nearly fold the flimsy-looking thing in half. The Manei Domini 'Mech flipped over and onto its back, sparks and smoke pouring from a tangle of ruined armor and engine shielding.

Despite the stench, and the surge of heat now finding its way into her cockpit, Brooke almost managed to smile. In all the times she ever found herself using the firepower of a 'Mech—*any* 'Mech—in anger, she had never enjoyed a victory as swift or decisive as this one.

But where vid games, serial dramas, and even actual wartime holo footage agreed an enemy would stay down after an assault like that, the *NXS* defied them all. With twists and turns that seemed almost organic in nature, the one-armed machine rolled itself over, tucked its feet in, and levered itself back up.

"No goddamned way!" Brooke hissed.

As BattleMechs go, the *NXS* already looked like the image of warmed-over death to her. Half its body was gone, and the smoke flowing from its core was already giving way to open flames. And yet it stood up, faced her *Griffin*, and stabbed its right arm gun muzzles forward—both now caked in grassy hunks of soft earth. The lasers pulsed, instantly vaporizing the debris, and sent scarlet darts of energy into her chassis. The *Griffin*'s damage readout registered no hits to critical systems, but the armor wireframe went from green to yellow.

Meanwhile, her sensors tracked two more "friendly" 'Mechs incoming.

The *Griffin*'s PPC had not finished its recharge cycle yet, but her lasers were ready—as was the missile launcher (though she knew it would be useless at this range). Wincing in anticipation of the heat, she ground her teeth together and fired.

This time, only one beam found its mark, but it was enough. Lancing into the machine's burning heart, the laser finished off whatever high-tech components allowed the *NXS* to hang on as long as it had. Its support structures collapsed, and its head fell into the gap, vanishing amid a thick plume of smoke and flames as the rest of the chassis swayed awkwardly. Then the right arm fell limp, and the rest of the 'Mech soon followed suit.

As she drew in a lungful of hot, near-toxic air, waiting desperately for her *Griffin*'s heat sinks to do something about it, Brooke spared the wreckage one final glance before turning her attention toward the new contacts.

"And *stay* down this time, *Saftsack*!"

CHAPTER 3

"Even the 'social generals' of the LAAF would tell you fighting a force three times your number (or more) is a losing proposition. Hell, that magic number may be why the Clans tend to run their Trials of Position with three opponents per trainee, for surely only the best warriors could even prevail in the face of such 'impossible' odds.

"And yet, how many battles in history have shown us overwhelming numbers alone don't always determine the victor? Marathon, in 490 BC; Agincourt, in 1415; Samar Island, 1944; Longewala, 1971; or the Vale of Tears, in 1973—battles from Terran antiquity that easily match far more recent examples, like the Wolf's Dragoons on Crossing in 3028, or Kai Allard-Liao at Twycross' Great Gash in 3050. These rare instances stand as proof numbers alone don't win the battle. Even an "underdog" may triumph, despite being massively outnumbered or outclassed.

"In the end, it's guile that can make all the difference. With enough guile, a clever warrior can change the victory equation, even the odds, and defeat any enemy who might otherwise be too overwhelming, too overpowering, and too overconfident to understand the value of subtlety.

"It also helps, of course, to be lucky, cat-shit crazy, or best of all: both!"

—Tibor Mitternacht
as quoted in "*Changing the Objectives*"
(Warrior Digital Productions, Solaris VII, May 3061)

TRIBE ENCAMPMENT
FOREST OF SHROUDS
JARDINE (HERAKLEION)
FREE WORLDS LEAGUE
2 NOVEMBER 3067

Poltergeist Precentor Sigma Damien Lucille could not remember a time when he had been filled with as much rage as he felt now—and he'd been among the blessed warriors who had fought, bled, and sacrificed so much against the traitorous heretics of Focht's ComStar!

The rumbles of a 'Mech battle above shook the earthen walls around him, threatening to entomb him and the rest of his squad even as they rallied back toward his position in what may once have been the office of the tribal leader. Numerous fiber-optic light channels abruptly darkened, their surface connections somehow severed in the chaos, and at least one of the chamber's supporting beams tore loose, spilling boulders and large clumps of hard-packed soil as it fell.

As he had feared when Adept Quang first alerted him to the return of a MechWarrior they'd all presumed lost, the *Griffin* that closed in was not piloted by Adept Moakay. And there were no Jardinians Lucille ever heard of who had been trained in BattleMech combat and counted themselves among the Wayward.

That meant whoever just charged Quang's *Nexus* was one of the two Lost ones he'd been slaughtering some of his own misguided people to capture! At the very moment that realization hit home, Quang's IFF and comm channel suddenly vanished from the heads-up display on Lucille's Achileus battle armor.

And *that* was what had him seeing nothing but red right now.

"All units," he shouted into the tactical channel, "abandon pursuit! The Lost are here! Converge on primary site at once! Our target has commandeered Adept Moakay's *Griffin*! Repeat, the enemy has captured—!"

A new voice—feminine, with an unmistakably Lyran accent, and filled with nearly as much seething hatred as Lucille's own—suddenly cut into the channel. *"Verdammte Missgeburt!"* it spat. "Call for all the help you like! I'll see all of your kind *burn*!"

"Defiler!" Lucille hissed back at her. "Identify yourself!"

The channel went dead before he even finished his demand. In its place came a horrific shriek of incoherent static that overwhelmed Lucille's helmet speakers and drilled into his very skull through his true hearing.

For a brief moment, Brooke felt rather proud of herself. Until that Word of Blake Guardian—or *whatever* the hell they called themselves—started spouting off orders in her speakers, it never even occurred to her that her new ride would be tuned to the same receiving frequency. It made perfect sense, though, and it also reminded her of the fancy communications and targeting suite she had at her command.

The same one they were *all* probably using, right this minute, to coordinate with!

After sparing a few seconds to indulge her need to verbally spit in that monster's face, she reached over to the *Griffin*'s fancy comm panel and dialed its transceiver to a specific frequency she knew by heart. After tuning the secondary dials to the same frequency, she then snapped the toggles controlling her Guardian ECM suite.

Star League-era push-button technology did the rest.

But the sense of accomplishment she got from all of that melted as her sensors noted not only the two 'Mechs approaching from the west, but now a *third* coming in from the north. And then the woods in front of her exploded as a short, blocky machine surged out and unleashed a quartet of missiles at her as she threw the *Griffin* into a reverse walk.

Oh, this might hurt a little!

Explosions shook her BattleMech, but not enough for her to miss the stuttering bursts of scarlet laser darts and machine-gun fire that followed when the newcomer continued bearing down on her. The *Griffin*'s wireframe damage display showed its right arm was now a cautionary yellow, along with the 'Mech's "heart" zone. Its armor was holding, but starting to thin.

On Brooke's HUD, the targeting brackets now only gave her the enemy's range and a simple model designator *"OW1."*

Her crosshairs never flashed gold—the universal standard for a solid weapons track—but she couldn't imagine why against an enemy running so close to her.

Instead, she simply fired another volley from her particle cannon and lasers.

And spat a curse as only a single laser found its mark.

The *"OW1"* didn't even flinch from the hit. It simply pivoted on one foot, tearing up the battle-scarred earth beneath its foot as it changed course to maneuver behind her, its machine guns still rattling away. Brooke tried to turn with it, but the smaller 'Mech was moving too fast.

And that's when the other one of the damnable machines showed up to add its own missiles to the melee.

"Verdammt!" she spat as the *Griffin* rocked under the new assault. The damage wireframe now put her left flank in the yellow.

Her mind raced, even as she rotated her 'Mech's torso around enough to confirm that the new attacker...looked just like the last one. On the sensor display, attacker number three was still coming. *Outnumbered* and *outmaneuvered! Damn it!*

"Scheiß drauf!" she hissed, and slammed the throttle forward again.

The *Griffin* responded instantly, its next step propelling it forward just as the new *OW1* tried to skirt past. Brooke heard a *crunch* of metal on metal accompanying the collision that was so satisfying she hardly minded the sudden struggle to keep her 'Mech upright.

The smaller machine, probably unbalanced more by the surprise than the actual hit, careened away, slipped on some ground clutter, and crashed to the forest floor in an ungraceful heap.

Brooke almost wished she had meant to do that.

Adding a spin of her own to the maneuver, she aimed her 'Mech southward, and twisted its torso far to the left—enough to catch the first *OW1* in her sights again. With only her lasers and missiles ready to fire, she triggered the lasers. Armor flashed away as one beam struck, but the boxy little thing kept moving as though nothing had happened.

Instead, the 'Mech unleashed another quartet of missiles from the sideways turrets it had in place of arms. Brooke felt each blast as they hit, tearing away more of her *Griffin's* armor.

The damage wireframe now painted her entire rear torso in yellow.

Bracing herself, Brooke pushed her 'Mech into a full run, charging toward the southern end of the clearing. Behind her, the two *OW1s* appeared to hesitate. But not nearly long enough as two more missiles slammed into the back of the *Griffin's* right shoulder.

Her mind continued to race, rummaging through years of scattered, on-the-job training for any more pointers Tibor and other career MechWarriors had given her. 'Mechs could theoretically handle just about any terrain one could have any reason to fight in, but woods, she knew, cut the range and mobility options down a lot.

To deal with that, some 'Mechs had jump jets—integral thrusters powerful enough to launch their mass into the air and rocket forward dozens—even hundreds—of meters at a clip. In her recollections, Brooke knew most *Griffins* had jump jets...including this one, according to those pre-fight diagnostics she'd run.

Okay, she mused, *so how* do *I make this damn thing jump?*

Even with his battlesuit's communications system shut down, Lucille's audio implants could hear the continuous screech of incoherent noise blasting from the intruder's stolen 'Mech. Although it was a simple matter of will to switch his hearing modes and shut out the electronic countermeasures, he could already sense the static was clearing. The enemy was moving away.

The burning rage that overtook him moments ago was gone, contained by a renewed focus on regrouping his team amid all this chaos. To that end, he welcomed the off-world woman's decision to flee the scene, and held onto his confidence the MechWarriors piloting his faster-moving machines would be able to maintain contact and run her down.

In the meantime, he continued digging at the hard-packed dirt, rocks, roots, and other debris that currently blocked his exit.

The tunnel collapse had happened just as he and two of his fellow troopers rounded the last bend. Triggered, no doubt, by the fighting above, the last meter or so of the passage gave out as its wooden beams buckled. What little sunlight passed through the foliage above died as a sheet of earthen debris cascaded down to block the entryway. Only the faint glow from fiber-optic light channels in a few of the chambers behind him remained.

To be sure, this latest obstacle was nothing the enhanced muscles and armored gauntlets of Lucille's Achileus battle armor could not handle. Between himself and Adepts Rumiko and Assad, they would clear it in less than a minute.

But a lot could happen in a minute!

"Precentor!" a voice abruptly called into his true ears, breaking through the static with a welcome chirp. It was Adept Halua, the MechWarrior piloting his group's 50-ton *Raijin*.

"Halua," he responded without pause. "Report!"

"The target is presently moving south-southwest," Halua replied. "Adepts Evans and Laori are pursuing. I have no reading on Adept Quang or his BattleMech. My 'Mech has suffered minor actuator damage from a Wayward mine, but I am still able to pursue. Do you require assistance?"

Pride nearly compelled Lucille to refuse. Even as he listened to Halua, he could feel the last of the earth crumble away under the force of his armored gauntlets. But he thought better of it. "We may," he said. "Bring your 'Mech into the main camp clearing and stand by."

Switching his suit's communicator back on with a click of his tongue, Lucille felt a twinge of relief that the ECM screech was now completely gone. "Able and Baker squads," he called out, "sound off!"

A flurry of radio clicks and acknowledgments followed. Lucille tallied them up and frowned. Of the two six-man squads of battle armored Domini he had led to this Blake-forsaken camp, he only had seven troopers remaining—counting himself. Meanwhile, he had also lost three good MechWarriors, and a

Frail off-worlder had somehow managed to steal one of the Chosen's own BattleMechs.

There will be time enough for shame later, he reminded himself before dialing back to his command channel.

Dragging its narrow, backward-canted right leg just a little bit, Halua's red and black *Raijin* thumped to a stop just as Lucille led Adepts Assad and Rumiko back into the clearing. On the battlesuit's proximity sensors, he could see the other troopers either gathering ahead of them or just coming around from other tunnel entrances.

Looking at the nearest troopers, Lucille did a quick appraisal of their armor, and singled out two who looked the worst for wear.

"Adepts Rumiko and Warren," he snapped, "you two stay here. Secure this site and get me an accurate casualty count. All remaining troopers form up on me. Adept Halua...?"

The *Raijin*'s body twisted slightly until its canopy faced him.

"...prepare to be boarded."

FOREST OF SHROUDS
JARDINE (HERAKLEION)
FREE WORLDS LEAGUE

It was hard for Tibor Mitternacht to believe it when the call came buzzing into his ear implant, but less than twenty minutes had passed since Brooke hauled off in that captured *Griffin* of hers.

Dealing with Alahni's mood swings had made the time seem more like an eternity by now. In the relative silence following the BattleMech's departure, the reality of her situation—*their* situation—continued to sink in; the realization that her home, her family, everything and every*one* she ever knew or loved, were gone. Worse, they had been killed by those she had been raised to see as their guardians and protectors. Rage, aimed alternately at her "Guardians" and at the "Lost," seasoned with the pain and tears of immeasurable loss, all washed over the poor girl as Tibor stood by, helpless to soothe her. She'd screamed at him, cried on his shoulder, and even struck him once or twice—and in all of that, the best he could do was to just be there to endure it.

Be there and, of course, make sure they stayed out of sight in case any of those Manei Domini cyborgs came back.

Her agitations had finally waned only a minute or two ago, as Alahni withered from the emotional exhaustion. Her head now rested on his shoulder, her face invisible beneath her long and disheveled hair, while he leaned against a tree and kept watch. His eyes kept drifting westward, toward the battle he could only hear as thunderous rumbles that felt as if they were receding further into the distance.

In the comparative silence, the faint *chirp* inside his own skull, followed by the weak and scratchy sound of Brooke's voice calling his name, nearly made Tibor jump. As it was, his body tensed enough to rouse Alahni, who pulled away from him and brushed her hair back, revealing eyes that were puffy and red, but still alert.

Tibor caught her attention and held a finger to his lips before answering. "Brooke?"

"Trouble," Brooke came back, the distracted tension in her voice still detectable, despite the weakness of the transmission. "So, I got their attention…"

Tibor blinked. "Um, was that something you *wanted*?"

"Yes, believe it or not. Bast, this thing is an *oven*!"

"Well, you *did* leave the cooling suit behind," he deadpanned, then shuddered at the thought. "So, what's the plan?"

"Gah!" Brooke yelped, for reasons Tibor could only guess at. "How do I…? Okay. Listen, I looked over the maps in this thing, and I think I've got my bearings. You guys keep heading east—the way we were going before we stumbled on the 'Mech. When you find the river, head south. And keep your eye peeled."

"My *eye*?"

"You'll know what you're looking for when you find it…"

Tibor turned back to Alahni, catching the look of confusion on her face. With a silent *"Oh!"* he pointed at his ear, then mimicked the act of holding a device against it. Whether or not the girl fully understood, he couldn't tell.

"East, then south along the river, then," he said, which only made Alahni's eyes widen. She opened her mouth to speak, but Tibor held up a hand first.

"Yes," Brooke said in his ear, her voice nearly vanishing in a momentary burst of static. "Hopefully, I'll catch up to you before long. If not…"

Tibor felt the tension in his own jaw, and saw Alahni's reaction in the form of an urgent tilt to her head. "Understood," he said. "Luck!"

"Thanks!" Brooke said. With another *chirp* in his skull, the line went dead.

Alahni was still staring at him.

"She wants us to get to the river, then follow it south."

"South?" Alahni repeated. "But Hope is *north* along the river."

Tibor blinked. "Then why—? Oh! *Of course!*"

"What?"

"C'mon," he told her. "I'll explain on the way…"

When the damage monitor began to paint her aft torso armor red to the staccato rhythm of sustained machine-gun fire, Brooke realized the *Owl*s (the name she'd settled on for the "OW1s" chasing her, anyway) still had her at a distinct disadvantage in a leg race. They hadn't overtaken her yet, but machine guns had a notoriously short range of effectiveness against modern heavy armor—which meant that, by now, they were probably close enough behind her to count any surface rivets on the *Griffin*'s rearward hull.

Knowing *that*, she finally felt bold enough to bet they didn't have jump jets, or she'd have trouble coming at her from both sides.

"Oh, I hope I got this right," she muttered as she slammed her feet down on both foot pedals at once.

Her 'Mech's computers instantly translated the command to its entire 55-ton frame. Its speed dropped for a second. Its legs braced, then bent a little. Its arms pulled inward as its upper body leaned forward. Finally, an almost deafening hiss blasted in from the cockpit's still-open air panels. Brooke felt herself pressed deeper into her sweat-slickened command seat as the five half-ton thrusters in the *Griffin*'s legs and back fired in unison to blast a machine twenty-two times their own mass into the sky.

She suddenly felt very sick.

The *Griffin* vaulted high enough to clear the forest canopy, affording her a brief—but breathtaking—view of the woods around her. She squinted a little against the dazzling yellow sunlight, but not enough to miss what looked like a sea of greenery rolling off toward a hilly horizon. She glimpsed a few breaks here and there, but the biggest of these was far off to the left, where she could almost make out a single, coherent line snaking its way through the foliage.

The river!

At the apex of its jump, the *Griffin* abruptly cut its jets and realigned its posture, its complex computer systems preparing the 'Mech to brake its jump and land upright. From a technical aspect, thanks to years of working with gearheads and explorers alike, Brooke understood this was an effect of its limited stores of self-replenishing reaction mass. BattleMechs simply weren't built for sustained flight, and so few of them could leap farther than thirty meters or so (per properly-sized thruster) at a time. She also understood most jump-capable 'Mechs incorporated software to handle the entire process from beginning to end—freeing the pilot for other functions, like shooting.

Still, there were so many variables that could affect a 'Mech's jump, ranging from terrain and weather to battle damage and the sheer lack of aerodynamics one can only expect from multi-ton machines built in a blocky parody of the human form. For those reasons, good MechWarriors preferred to take a more direct hand in navigating their jumps—lest their entire triumph of brute force and technology over physics end in a landing that could be equal parts embarrassing and deadly.

All of these things went through Brooke's mind at once as her *Griffin* crashed through the treetops nearly a hundred and fifty meters away from where it used to be.

The jets gave one last, momentary blast to cushion the landing, but even so, Brooke felt the shock through her spine. Her top teeth bit deep into the flesh behind her lower lip, leaving her in eye-watering pain. The coppery taste of blood filled her mouth. She saw stars before her eyes, and imagined a tiny, sarcastic voice somewhere in the back of her head reminding her *why* she'd forgotten how to jump.

Almost instantly, she felt her 'Mech pitching forward, losing its footing on whatever uneven ground its feet had struck. For a few panicked heartbeats, she struggled with the controls and angled her head, hoping the *Griffin*'s computers could make sense of those efforts to restore its balance.

Then, as suddenly as it all began, it was over. The 'Mech and its warrior remained alive and upright. On one of the secondary boards, indicators for the jump jets flashed yellow as the fusion reactor and jet intakes began rapidly processing the ambient atmosphere for reaction mass...

Meanwhile, the *Owl*s continued rushing toward them from behind.

"Bast help me," Brooke mumbled as she slammed the throttle forward again. "There's no way I can keep this up!"

CHAPTER 4

AEROSPACE HANGAR 104
CITY OF HOPE
JARDINE (HERAKLEION)
FREE WORLDS LEAGUE
2 NOVEMBER 3067

From the air, the City of Hope's spaceport looked about the way one would expect of a centuries-old ruin. Trees and vines overgrew the decrepit hulls of rusted hangar buildings, wild grasses covered the rubble of fallen towers, and massive, ferrocrete blast barriers formed well-weathered rings around former landing pads now little more than crack-filled craters in the ancient tarmac. Here and there, one could even spot the remains of ancient, forgotten vehicles and LoaderMechs— rusted and disintegrating hulks now decaying in mute testament to what had once been a central hub of interplanetary commerce.

Of course, it was all just an illusion—a balanced mixture of pure artistry, Star League-era engineering, and meticulous landscaping. Had anyone managed to land amid the spaceport— or simply traveled there on the ground—they would soon see through the ruse. The hangar buildings stood very much intact, their rooftops covered in a masterful camouflage that was equal parts clever paintwork and carefully cultivated foliage. The fallen buildings were actually quite stable and upright, their rooftops merely painted and cluttered with enough irregular masonry and overgrowth to appear ruined. Even their actual windows and doorways were deliberately skewed, arranged to appear properly aligned with their "collapsed" orientation.

The tarmacs were smooth, level, and largely unblemished, save for elaborate paint work that perfectly mimicked the few actual cracks and clumps of wild grass that existed in only the most infrequently used areas. Within the rings of blast panels, the "craters" were actually the surface lids of ultra-massive DropShip-sized elevators, artfully disguised to blend with the surrounding ferrocrete surface. Beneath them lay cavernous bays large enough to contain most spheroid DropShips, accessible through a multitude of reinforced tunnels.

In fact, the only authentic things throughout the entire affair were the wrecked vehicles and WorkMechs. Keeping a few around, strategically placed throughout the spaceport hundreds of years before, and simply letting them decay was an easy enough thing to do—providing excellent places to hide sensors and traps rigged to detect and discourage any unwelcome intruders.

Inside one of the not-truly-wrecked hangars, within a space large enough to stow a pair of *Leopard*-class DropShips end to end, stood Specter Precentor Omicron Apollyon.

Impassively, he watched the technical crews as they busied themselves with dozens of tasks about the floor. On the far end of the hangar, maintenance teams installed weapon pods into six of the division's newest aerospace fighters—85-ton, ultra-sleek SHV-O *Shiva* OmniFighters. Though freshly built in Free Worlds League factories on distant Lopez, these six specimens already bore the distinctive, red-to-black colors of the Fifty-Second Shadow Division. Four were even further modified from factory specs, their cockpit and control systems upgraded to accommodate their assigned pilots' direct-neural implants.

Closer to where Apollyon stood, a dozen suits of battle armor were the subject of similar maintenance and armament work. Like the fighters, half of these suits—Longinus models, which looked for all the universe like thick-bodied, overteched versions of ancient knights—bore the colors and insignia of the Fifty-Second. The other six, set up ten meters away, lacked these colors—but only because the digital mimetics of the sleeker Purifier adaptive suits required no painting. With their camouflage programs deactivated, they stood in simple, gunmetal gray, their chest plates open as the tech crews worked on their interior interfaces.

Finally, and closest to the most powerful man on Jardine, there stood a K-1 class DropShuttle—a humble, lightly armed, 200-ton, civilian spacecraft. Bearing no distinct markings or livery to differentiate it from thousands of identical craft across the Inner Sphere, its only real "colors" were bare metal and the permanent scorching that blackened the entire lower half of its squashed-egg form, the inevitable result of repeated launches and landings over its decades-long lifespan.

It was this DropShuttle that held the Precentor's attention now, as well as the young, dark-skinned brunette, clad in plain light-gray overalls, who approached him with a noteputer in hand. Technical Adept Kaulana Tin showed little of the awe or fear many of her fellow civilians did when in the presence of the Manei Domini—a trait Apollyon found refreshing. Though he himself was born of this world, raised as a citizen of Hope, and as a follower of the Blessed Blake, his transformation in the years after Tukayyid, and his Ascension to the leadership of the Master's Hands had rattled many of his kindred. But Tin— all of seven years old when the first Domini Ascended—saw nothing to fear in the Guardians' new forms.

A true child of Jardine, this one!

"Precentor, sir," she said as she stopped before him, just far enough away to avoid any undue neck strain when she looked up to meet his eyes. "The shuttle is fueled and stocked as you requested. And the suits are undergoing final systems checks for vacuum ops, as you can see. We will be able to load as soon as you're ready, and the DropShip is on the platform."

"Excellent, Adept Tin," Apollyon said with a sincere nod. "And the transponder codes?"

"Already set, sir," she said without hesitation. "I verified them myself."

"Your dedication honors us, Adept."

Without switching his true sight to thermal vision, Apollyon could not be certain, but he imagined from the way the young woman beamed at him that she was blushing. Her brilliant teeth flashed as she handed over her noteputer. "The honor is to serve the Blessed Blake's Promise."

Apollyon accepted the device, quickly scanned its contents, and signed his name, using the index finger of his true hand instead of the stylus. With a short bow, he handed the 'puter back to Tin. "Blessed be those who walk the Sainted Blake's path, Adept."

"Blessed be, Precentor," she replied, her composure already reclaimed.

She had moved no more than two steps away when Apollyon's true hearing received a familiar chime. Turning away from the technicians, he opened the channel, and spoke without waiting for the voice on the other end. "How fares your hunt, Precentor Lucille?"

"Precentor," Lucille replied tersely, "the target camp has been located and destroyed. I have a present estimate of thirty-two kills made on site—all Wayward. A few stragglers may have slipped away through the tunnels, but given the level of resistance we faced, I posit any such survivors are would-be non-combatants of negligible consequence..."

Apollyon closed his frail eye and sighed. *Such loss!*

"Unfortunately, we have suffered casualties of our own. Wayward mines have disabled or destroyed two of our 'Mechs and damaged a third. We have also lost five troopers to mines and weapons fire. A chance encounter with a hunting party, several kilometers from the main objective, undoubtedly alerted them."

Apollyon resisted the impulse to grimace as the part of him that mourned the loss of Wayward lives warred with the part that admired their ability to still cause damage to the Master's Hands. "And the invaders?"

Lucille's voice took on a much more guarded tone. "One is currently engaging us."

"Currently *engaging* you?"

"The female Lost we were told of somehow managed to salvage and reactivate Adept Moakay's *Griffin*. She attacked us at the campsite while most of my remaining units were otherwise occupied, and managed to destroy Adept Quang's

BattleMech before the others could support him. She is now headed south. We're pursuing."

"Precentor, you are telling me you have lost half of your force against a lightly armed platoon of our self-exiled kin, and a *single* Frail using one of your own BattleMechs."

It wasn't a question.

"As you say, Precentor," Lucille came back after the briefest hesitation. "I accept full responsibility; once again, I underestimated the resourcefulness of our Wayward cousins."

"Your responsibility is noted," Apollyon said darkly. In his mind, he envisioned the regional map and considered the only landmarks south of Hope holding any potential value to an invader at this point.

"Continue your pursuit, Precentor," he commanded. "But remember: I want these intruders *alive*. If this Frail is moving south, she may be trying to return to her shuttle for some reason. I will dispatch another team to that location; between them and your group, she should have nowhere else of consequence to run."

"Understood, sir. Lucille out."

As the line went dead, Apollyon finally opened his frail eye and took in his surroundings once more. Adept Tin and her techs were beginning to load the Longinus battlesuits onto the DropShuttle, aided by powered dollies specially built for the task. Nobody else stood close by the Precentor; nobody was even paying any attention to his presence.

Without a word, he strode out of the hangar.

On the plus side, Brooke thought as she reached up to dab the sweat from her eyebrows, *I hardly even notice the stink anymore!*

Despite executing a series of jumps, draining the *Griffin*'s reaction mass as quickly as the BattleMech could replenish it, the *Owl*s continued pacing her, plowing through forest and underbrush as quickly as their tiny, blocky forms could manage. Too far away now to reliably cause any real damage with their machine guns, they both were forced to rely on their SRM launchers, their missiles tearing away more and more armor with each concussive blast.

In an increasingly frustrating effort to slow them down, Brooke had been zig-zagging her jumps, and twisting her 'Mech's torso side to side in a desperate effort to send at least some firepower back at them. Between her jumps and the occasional blast from her particle cannon, the cockpit had quickly become a sauna. She now regretted—in spite of herself—not taking the time to pour the *Griffin's* last pilot out of his cooling suit before she started this foolish charge.

For that matter, a snarky voice from one corner of her mind reminded her, *you could have avoided this entire mess by never taking on these cyborgs in the first place!*

Right now, Brooke wished that part of her brain would just shut up already.

Slamming the pedals down once again, she sent the *Griffin* into yet another jump, sailing over a particularly thick group of trees she could not imagine driving a jeep through, much less a BattleMech. The leap carried her forward over a hundred meters, but not before one of her pursuers managed to pump two more missiles into the *Griffin's* rear armor panels.

Sparks and fire flashed out from the large canister perched on the 'Mech's right shoulder. The small explosion startled her for a moment, but an internal alarm and the winking out of one of her weapon status lights quickly identified the extent of the damage.

A relieved sigh escaped her lips. *Not dead yet.*

"You can have that launcher," she muttered to no one in particular. "I wasn't using it anyway."

Despite the damage, the *Griffin* managed another (relatively) smooth landing—in so much as it kept to its feet with only a little extra coaxing. Brooke rotated the 'Mech's torso left and extended its arm to snap-fire a laser into the general vicinity of one of the *Owl*s. The shot flashed into the trees dead-center of the brackets her HUD placed around her target, but whether or not she actually hit the thing was beyond her.

Sweat stung her eyes, but she dared not blink. Instead, she pushed the *Griffin* back into a run, shifting course yet again, but continuing to keep going vaguely southward.

On the sensor board, Brooke noticed the third 'Mech remained off the scope. Only the two *Owl*s appeared to be within sensor range. But years of experience had long since taught her better than to trust what *appeared* to be, especially when gunplay was involved. ComStar and the Word of Blake were known for having the best tech outside of Clan space, and that included Star League-quality ECM and stealth gear most folks only saw in holovid action thrillers. Hell, even something as mundane as ground clutter could be preventing her radar from picking up the third 'Mech's electromagnetic signature.

That happened in some environments, right?

A furtive glance at the map display put her close to five kilometers south of the Waywards' camp, now. The wireframe now colored both arms, her forward left flank, and one leg yellow, while the rear armor and other leg glowed red. Only her machine's head and the rest of its forward torso armor showed green. And her unfired LRM launcher was now dead.

Not that it had a prayer of hitting these bastards anyway, she mused.

The time to end this play was coming up fast, and suddenly she knew just how to do it.

Glancing up, she sought another thick cluster of trees in the forest, about a hundred meters ahead and to the right. The branches there spread out so thick their leaves seemed to blot the sun out almost entirely.

Perfect!

With a hard jerk on the steering controls, Brooke swung the *Griffin* toward that dark grove. As she did, a keening wail from her sensor board gave her a second's warning about the pair of missiles one of the *Owl*s just lobbed at her. Both warheads struck the 'Mech's exaggerated right shoulder pauldron; already, her shadows were closing the gap.

Another double blast shook her a heartbeat later. A new alarm screamed for attention, but the new wave of heat that seemed to come from the floor beneath her told her all she needed to know: reactor damage.

Now or never!

The *Griffin*'s run continued, shattering branches and undergrowth with each step as it neared her objective. With only one hand on the steering controls, Brooke scanned her weapons panels. It took a few seconds to find what she wanted.

"Here goes nothing," she warned herself.

Releasing the controls, she allowed the *Griffin* to plod onward at full throttle, while she reached for the straps that kept her neurohelmet in place. Cringing in anticipation, she then reached out to the weapon panel, opened the black and yellow plastic cover marked "dump", and pushed the button beneath.

The grinding noise that followed sounded horrifically loud in Brooke's ears as she tore off the helmet and pitched it behind her seat. Bereft of balancing input from her temples, the *Griffin*'s gait became a drunken stumble on the uneven ground. The 'Mech slammed into one tree after another, each threatening to topple it while Brooke flailed to reach the ejection handles over her head.

The explosion she'd expected came just as she finally managed to grab one of them. Squeezing her eyes shut and yelling into the cockpit, she quickly grasped the other and yanked both handles down hard.

Between the ammunition explosion, the *Griffin*'s wild bucking, and the ejection itself, Brooke felt almost like she was being torn in several directions at once. Her eyes remained closed, and every muscle in her body stiffened. Wind and leaves whipped past her as the pilot's seat blasted clear of its dying host with a deafening roar. She felt herself soaring skyward, and bent her head down while her hands clutched at the straps of her five-point harness for dear life.

She felt her ascent slow as gravity began to take over, and her seat shuddered a little to the sound of its parachute deploying. Only then did she open her eyes again, looking up to make sure the damned thing opened properly.

What struck her most about the first few moments of freefall was the cool and wonderful smell and feel of fresh, Jardinian forest air. Her arms and legs crawled with gooseflesh. Compared to the rancid hothouse the *Griffin*'s cockpit had become, she was now in heaven, even as she cast her gaze downward in time to see the 'Mech's fiery death.

Momentum, combined with the forward pitch the *Griffin*'s head had been at when she pulled the ejection handles, had launched her dozens of meters forward and slightly left of where the 'Mech died. As the chair began its lazy decent, she watched for the telltale shaking of trees to see where the *Owl*s were moving, and used that to recover her bearings.

Only then, as she watched the forest canopy rising to meet her, did she draw in a breath, mentally declare herself insane, slap the release on her seat harness, and kick herself into the sky.

The next few moments were a whirl of green leaves and shadow, a symphony of snapping branches and pain-wracked grunts, and a desperate fight between blind panic and intense concentration. Falling was almost as familiar to Brooke as running, but in most of her previous jobs, falls tended to happen when she had the gear and protection to better weather the bumps along the way, and when she could be reasonably sure certain death wasn't waiting for her below.

Dropping into an uncharted jungle-turned-war zone while practically naked and unarmed was another experience entirely!

The branch that finally stopped her fall was almost as thick as her body and stretched out over a clump of leafy underbrush some eight meters below. Dazed, but thankfully conscious, Brooke clung to the rough branch for several seconds, taking stock of her condition. A lot of places hurt, but miraculously, nothing felt broken. Still, she felt a bit woozy, and a part of her wanted to stay in this tree and rest a while.

The part that told her to keep moving, on the other hand, recognized that the burning wreck of her 'Mech and her empty ejection seat wouldn't keep the cyborgs distracted nearly long enough for a shock-induced nap.

Shimmying down the tree punished her mostly bare flesh, adding scrapes to the bruises she'd surely find all over her body when this was all over. When she reached the forest floor, she was glad she'd at least had the presence of mind to keep her boots; the underbrush was far rougher than it looked.

East and north, she reminded herself as she half-crawled, half-ran through the underbrush, doing her best to keep to the heavier undergrowth while putting the thickest trees between her and the flickering light of the burning *Griffin*.

East and north!

Oh, Tibor better *have my clothes ready when I get there!*

Scarcely five minutes had passed since Adept Laori reported the downing of Moakay's stolen *Griffin* to Precentor Lucille. In that time, he could do little more than wait tensely and refresh his grip on the large muzzle of the ER PPC currently serving as his saddle on Adept Halua's *Raijin*. The regular lurching motions of the 50-ton 'Mech and the random blows of passing branches hardly fazed him. But the fact that this machine was not properly built or balanced to carry an extra eight to ten percent of its weight in battlesuits meant the only effective handholds were those a swarming infantry squad would normally be trying to destroy.

Halua was also complaining that the squad's presence made him itchy. While that initially amused Lucille, the occasionally violent hitch in the *Raijin*'s stride and the awkward, random swings of its turret-like arms betrayed the MechWarrior's efforts to scratch at the psychosomatic feeling his neural implants clearly kept feeding him. The result was an annoyingly unpredictable ride in which Lucille and his squadmates had nearly been thrown off several times.

Lucille grunted as another such lurch took the form of a torso spasm, and he once again focused on the mission. The Frail had fallen a little more than five kilometers south of the Wayward camp, apparently while trying to move for thicker cover. In her flight, she inflicted only minimal damage to the pursuing *Owens*es; the worst damage reported was the destruction of Adept Evans' TAG system. When Laori reported the kill, Lucille instructed Evans to secure the wreck and tasked Laori with searching for any ejector seat beacons.

"Contain the Frail," he'd ordered, "but do *not* kill her when found; Apollyon wants this one alive."

That was five minutes ago, and since then, there had been silence. On the drop-down map in his armor's HUD, he could see he and his group were still a half-kilometer away; the two OmniMechs were fully resolved on the sensor display, and both read as active units.

Lucille's impatience finally got the better of him. "Report, Adept Laori!"

"Sir!" Laori replied instantly. "I have located the pilot's beacon and 'chute, approximately fifty meters from the crash site. The chair appears empty, but I am seeing a great deal of blood. The seat looks drenched in it. The Frail could be mortally wounded; I have been sweeping for a body."

A body? "Did either of you score any headshots on the target during the pursuit?"

"Uncertain, Precentor," Laori replied. "Visual contact was spotty throughout the engagement, and the ejection left little of the head module to go by. It *is* possible."

"Anything on thermals?"

"Included in my sweep, sir, but ambient heat from Moakay's *Griffin* and resident wildlife has been generating false positives."

Lucille grunted again. "Continue your sweeps, Adept. Evans, assist her, but both of you maintain your proximity to the wreckage. My team will be there shortly to assist."

Even as he closed the line, Lucille realized there were only two possibilities now. The intruder was either dead or alive. If dead, her corpse was probably hidden by some foliage on the forest floor or hanging from a tree, and growing too cold for sensors to differentiate from the ambient environment. If alive, she was somehow stealthy enough to have eluded the Master's Hands in broad daylight.

Lucille now knew better than to underestimate this Frail again.

And with that decision came the sobering certainty his team would find nothing there when they finally arrived.

After more than an hour of walking through the crowded forest, Tibor and Alahni finally found the river and began their trek southward, keeping well inside the tree line just to be safe. Tibor struggled to keep his mind focused on searching for what he knew Brooke wanted him to find, but it wasn't easy. Between Alahni's ongoing shock that her people were being ruthlessly gunned down by their "Guardians," and the realization he'd simply *allowed* Brooke to take an unfamiliar 'Mech back there specifically to avenge them, his own dismay grew with each passing minute.

Now here he was: trapped on a world whose masters were so determined to hide it that no amount of murder was beyond them and running around a forest filled with God-knew-how-many natural hazards. His partner was effectively missing in action, and he had a native tagging along who now had no obligation to help him whatsoever—and *every* right to blame his very presence for the loss of her friends and family!

"This is *way* worse than Bob ever was..."

"What?" Alahni asked, her nervous voice coming from several steps behind.

The question surprised Tibor. He glanced back at her, and offered a sheepish smile. "Sorry," he said. "Didn't know I said that out loud."

The Jardinian tale-keeper made a noncommittal sound and lapsed back into silence for several seconds. Tibor was retreating back into his own thoughts when she suddenly spoke again. "Why do you do this?"

"Wh—?"

"Traveling to forgotten places," she added. "Is it just for money? Or did some House Lord send you?"

Her tone was hard to read. Behind her words, Tibor felt both genuine curiosity and scornful accusation in equal measure. He didn't dare glance back at her this time, preferring instead to keep moving, his gaze continuing to sweep the nearby foliage.

She wants to know why her people had to die, he warned himself.

"Sometimes," he admitted with a sigh. "Sometimes both. But that's never all of it."

"What do you mean?"

"How can I explain this?" he muttered. "I mean, the money can be nice, but only because it pays our bills, keeps us fed, helps us maintain our lifestyle. Basically all the reasons most folk in the Inner Sphere get jobs, you know? Yeah, sometimes the job offers come from a House or some other government, but a lot of times it doesn't."

"That sounds rather mundane for a 'job' that entails trespassing on worlds that may not wish to be found."

Tibor grunted at that. "I suppose that's one way of seeing it," he told her. "But most of the places we've seen didn't exactly hide on their own terms, if you follow me. Remember that planet Brooke and I talked about before? Bob?"

"The one that changed its name?" Alahni asked, her tone softening just a little.

"*Ja*. That one. Well, as funny as the story about *why* it changed its name was, the results of that choice were tragic."

"How so?"

"From what we could work out," Tibor began, "the people chose to make that name change at the very worst possible moment in history. The Star League had just collapsed, and their realm—the Draconis Combine—was in the middle of a full-scale invasion of the Federated Suns. 'Bob,' meanwhile, was a low-resource world way out near the Periphery. The name change, from…*Dunkelwalden*-something? *Dunkel…schatten…*? Well, believe me, it was a very *long* word, put together by some colony founder with a shaky grasp of the German language at best.

"Anyway, the local leaders chose to make the whole name change as a way to take their people's minds off the war. It seemed like a great idea at the time, especially for a world that looks gloomy all year round, and has a biosphere that's generally hostile to human life. So it was supposed to be a big morale booster. They took votes from kids as young as twelve years old, held big parties, ran silly advertisements on their local networks, and just had fun with the whole affair…"

Tibor trailed off for a moment as he found himself climbing over an old, fallen tree trunk. As he did so, he spotted a length of bark that appeared to have been dug out of the trunk by something with claws as big as his head. *Tabiranth claws?*

"So, what happened?" Alahni asked. The accusatory edge in her voice was gone now, at least for the moment.

Tibor shook himself out of his distraction. He turned back toward the young woman, prepared to offer his hand to help her over the trunk, but she waved him off. Her eyes, like his, seemed to fixate on the shredded bark for a moment, but if those gouges concerned her much at all, she didn't show it. Instead, she simply hopped over the fallen tree and threw him an inquisitive look.

"Well," he continued with a shrug, "when the votes were tallied, and the new name was all picked out, they sent word to the local district ministers, who evidently got as far as reporting the name change to the right people to get it recorded on some of the local star maps. But they apparently missed a few key people in the bureaucratic chain. Whole shipments of food, equipment, and other vital necessities sat in Combine warehouses light-years away because they were earmarked for a planet that *wasn't* named Bob."

"Truly?" Alahni asked, bewildered. "Didn't anyone think to check up on them? Didn't the people of Bob think to send a message when the shipments didn't show?"

Tibor frowned. "The First Succession War, as you seem to know, was really bad. The strategy at the time, for pretty much every side, was to capture or destroy factories and shipping wherever and whenever possible. This extended even to civilian ships, which could always be used to carry troops in a pinch.

"And the Combine was moving a *lot* of troops into Davion space at that point. As more of their ships got lost in action, or were otherwise tied up on their front lines, the Kuritans started pressing more and more merchants into military service. Worlds considered lower priority—including pretty much anything near the Periphery—were generally stripped of their support first..."

"So there just weren't any ships to send to Bob? House Kurita simply abandoned them?"

"Yes," Tibor answered slowly, "and no. The war left the Combine with fewer ships to cover the local transit routes, but they still had enough for periodic supply runs. But between the planet's name change, and the confusion caused when the wrong people were left out of the loop, House Kurita was stockpiling supplies for that world under Bob's old name. So, they didn't really abandon the planet so much as they effectively just *misplaced* it."

"Surely the people of Bob would have noticed the lack of supplies soon enough, though, right? Couldn't they call for help?"

Tibor winced. "ComStar was still repairing the hyperpulse network at that point," he said after a moment's hesitation, wary of her reaction. "And even Jerome Blake had to prioritize which worlds to get back online first as his organization spread outward from Terra. Bob's HPG had apparently gone down some time during the Amaris years—"

"Wait," Alahni interrupted, just as Tibor feared she would. "The Blessed Blake was still restoring HPGs in the Inner Sphere? I thought the House Lords rejected him in their rush to destroy one another."

Tibor drew in a breath before finally turning around to meet the woman's gaze. "Not exactly..."

Alahni's voice regained its edge, and her eyes narrowed. "What's *that* supposed to mean?"

Tibor felt his jaw go slack. *Oh*, this *is going to be fun*, he told himself.

"Um," he stumbled. "Alahni, I can see Blake means a lot to your people, but it's becoming clear to me that not all of the history you've been told matches what really happened out in the Inner Sphere."

Alahni's expression darkened, and her hands twitched. For a real moment there, Tibor expected her to strike him, and he found himself unsure whether he should try to block it or simply take the hit.

To his surprise, she blinked instead, and suddenly seemed to reclaim some manner of control. Though her eyes still bored angry holes into his own, he could practically feel her reflexive rage subsiding.

"I'm sorry," he lamely offered. "Brooke's always so much better with this stuff; I thought she would have told you some of this when you two were talking the other day..."

Mentioning Brooke's name appeared to help soften Alahni just a bit more. The young woman blinked again, and tension bled out of her posture. "She mentioned ComStar, and the division that followed its temporary victory against the Clans... something she called a 'schism'. She mentioned how bad the first two Succession Wars were as well, but nothing about ComStar being active among the Lost in that time."

"Well, that was when they came to this world in the first place, wasn't it?"

Alahni now seemed less certain of herself. "Yes..." she began slowly, "but that was to save us from oblivion, after the Steiners bombed us..."

Tibor grimaced at that one, but decided to barrel through it. There was no point in making apologies for the inexcusable. "Didn't it ever seem odd to you that they would only pick your world to save at that time?"

"The Order was new back then," she said. "We were told they could only save a few..."

"That's likely true. Jerome Blake's primary mission, though— at least, the one given to him by the House Lords just before the Star League's collapse—was to rebuild the hyperpulse network across the entire Inner Sphere. After taking Terra, and convincing the various Houses to honor ComStar's neutrality, he *did* just that..."

"Then, he *did* try to save the Inner Sphere?"

Tibor shrugged. "I suppose you could see it that, way, yes."

"But we were taught the Inner Sphere rejected him," Alahni countered, "that they'd all but destroyed themselves in less than two generations."

"You could say that, too, I guess," Tibor admitted with a sigh. "By the end of the First War, a lot of worlds began to die off, like Bob did. Like we all believed *this* world did. You told Brooke there were five worlds like Jardine, didn't you?"

"The Five, yes."

"Well, maybe that was all Blake could save at the time, at least after taking over Terra."

Alahni stood mute for several moments, her expression almost blank. Tibor decided to continue. "What I guess I'm saying is your knowledge of history beyond your world has a few gaps. Either that, or—for whatever reason—Jerome Blake exaggerated when he told your people the Inner Sphere had completely collapsed, and he'd been rejected by all."

Anger flashed again in the young woman's eyes. "Are you suggesting the Blessed Blake *lied* to us?"

"*If* he did," Tibor said cautiously, feeling for all the world like a man trapped in a minefield, "it was most likely for your own protection. By convincing your people the Inner Sphere at large was ruined, he would have discouraged anyone who wanted to leave Jardine at that time."

Alahni scoffed. "And now you make it sound like he wanted to imprison us! That's too f—!"

"Alahni! Please understand me; I'm not *trying* to offend you here! You see Blake as your savior and protector. I get that. But Brooke and I have come upon several worlds where the local leaders used deception on their own people to keep them complacent and allowed future generations to live on in blissful—" *Don't say "ignorance"!*"—um, un-awareness. Most of the time, it's less about control and more a part of the bigger plan to keep those people safe and hidden from pirates and other enemies.

"Think about it: Jerome Blake wants to save your world from the war. His Order changes the maps, fudges some data, and passes it around throughout the hyperpulse network as a free navigational update to all parties interested in avoiding planets destroyed or infected during the most horrifying war since before the Star League. But what happens if someone from one of these now-hidden worlds just shows up one day because they realize the neighbors are fine, and decides to open trade with them?"

Alahni continued glowering at Tibor. For a long time, she said nothing, but he could practically hear the gears turning in her mind. He found himself half-surprised she was even willing to entertain the idea; in most of their past encounters with isolated peoples, he and Brooke had found the locals so entrenched in their own dogma they couldn't accept any other truth at all.

"Is this why you and Doctor Stevens do this, then?" she asked at last, a slight catch in her tone. "To shatter the illusions of people who did you no harm?"

"Oh, for Christ's sake!" Tibor spat. "No! We do it to *learn*! We do it to find all that was lost since the Star League fell! We do it because we can practically *feel* what humanity has lost every time we set foot on an abandoned world, or find some city, or some priceless artifact, that was once part of our collective history! We do it for probably the same reasons you and your people left your Guardians' city, maybe even the same reasons that *you*, personally, chose to become the story-keeper you are! At least, I *assume* it was a choice!"

At that, Alahni flinched as if he'd just struck her. Suddenly realizing he'd begun shouting, Tibor clamped up, and instinctively glanced around as he remembered where they were. Finally, he sighed, turned away from her, and continued on into the woods, resuming the search for what he knew Brooke expected them to find. But one more thought slipped into his mind, begging for release.

"Like I said," he grumbled, "it's not really about money, or fame, or any of that. And it's not about the Houses—Lord knows I did my bit for one of *those* long enough in my day! And it sure as *hell* isn't about spite! Brooke and I, we do this because it gives our lives some kind of meaning beyond mere existence."

Although Alahni remained silent, Tibor could hear her footsteps behind him. He didn't know if anything he'd just said made any sense to her, or if it did anything to help her cope with what had happened in the last few hours.

Hell, he wasn't even sure it did anything to make *him* feel any better about the situation as it now stood. After all of that, the doubt still nagged at him.

That was, until, barely five minutes later, he heard the woman freeze in her tracks and suck in her breath with an audible hiss.

Tibor spun around to check on her. Alahni's eyes, wide but not panicked, were locked onto something else. She gestured toward it with her chin, directing his gaze further to their right.

Instantly on his guard, Tibor turned slowly that way until he spotted the graceful, feline form of a gray and brown-striped *tabiranth*, lurking among the brush barely fifteen meters away. At his movement, the animal's green eyes, originally focused on Alahni, flashed around to meet his own.

A low growl rumbled from somewhere within the beast's throat, but instead of baring teeth, it hunched down and stepped backward.

"Lower your hands," Alahni whispered, "hold your eye contact, but blink—*slowly*—at him."

Tibor wasn't about to ask how she knew the thing was a male. He forced his hands, which he'd automatically raised to chest level in anticipation of an attack, to ease their way back down. The giant felinoid took another step back, but kept its gaze locked onto his.

Exhaling through his nostrils as quietly as possible, Tibor closed his eyes slowly, like a young child fighting sleep. When he opened them again a moment later, the animal appeared to have taken yet another step back. He could see the tip of its tail twitching nervously behind it, and its gaze remained fixed on him, but it was now rising back to its full height.

"No sudden moves," Alahni whispered, her voice now recapturing the beast's attention. "Let it move away first..."

The *tabiranth* blinked at Alahni, raised its chin, and sniffed the air a few times. With a sound somewhere between a snort and a sneeze, it abruptly shook its head and whipped its tail. Without another noise, it turned away from them both, and strode off, meandering deeper into the woods.

Alahni let out a relieved sigh.

"Good," she whispered. "Wild *tabis* are not normally aggressive toward humans, but the males tend to interpret direct eye contact as a dominance challenge, and they panic easily at sudden moves."

Tibor felt like he needed to unlock his jaw before he could respond. "Thanks," he mumbled, his gaze still hovering over the brush.

And that was when he saw it, about twenty meters past where the *tabiranth* had stood just seconds before. Shaded behind a thick cluster of tree trunks and broad-leaved bushes, it was almost invisible at a glance.

"*Unglaublich!*" he blurted.

Alahni started to speak, but stopped short as she followed his line of sight and spotted it as well.

There, on the forest floor—sprawled on its side, with its broad, dull-green back jutting up above the lower foliage— lay the abandoned remains of a dull-green *Rock Possum* ProspectorMech.

CHAPTER 5

"Brothers and Sisters of the Master's Hand, hearken to these words!

"The day of the Promise fast approaches; the hour of the Third Transfer looms ever nearer. Soon, it will fall to us to strike from our Shadows at the enemies of all of Terra's Blessed Children!

"To the last, all of us have given ourselves to the Blessed Blake's cause! With no thought of reward, no promise of compensation, no expectation of survival, we have sacrificed our own blood, flesh, and bone. And, in becoming the Master's Hands, we have given our very souls to this cause!

"We have become the instruments of history, the greatest hope for Humanity's survival. When we fulfill our part of the Master's Promise, we will commit horrors that will damn us for Eternity! Future generations will see us as the monsters we became, as any rational being should...

"But, thanks to us—the Manei Domini—there will be future generations left alive to judge us!"

—PRECENTOR MANEI DOMINI APOLLYON
JARDINE, 3067

THE SANCTORUM
CITY OF HOPE
JARDINE (HERAKLEION)
FREE WORLDS LEAGUE
3 NOVEMBER 3067

"Don't you think this plan of yours is needlessly...overcomplicated?"

Those were the first words to tumble from the mouth of Precentor Damien Lucille since providing Apollyon with his report on yesterday's operation in the Forest of Shrouds.

The sun had barely risen over the horizon when he, his team, and the extra squad sent to the intruders' crash site finally received orders to return to Hope for further instruction. As soon as he had shucked his damaged Longinus battlesuit in the recovery bays of the city's southern staging grounds, Lucille donned his robes and headed for the tunnels leading to the Sanctorum entrance.

Through the window behind Precentor Apollyon's seat, Lucille could see the early morning mists were already dispersing over the western forests, their evaporation surrendering the endless greens to the golden glory of Jardine's day star. Having spent the better part of the last twenty hours in those woods, rummaging through the thick foliage and shadows for any sign of his prey, Lucille felt strangely impressed at how they still seemed so untouched from afar.

Assuming his customary descent to one knee, Lucille had recited the full report to his commander as bidden. The Shrouded Forest Wayward Tribe's camp was destroyed. Thirty-five Wayward men, women, and children had been killed during the main assault. Another six Waywards were encountered and dispatched during the mop-op, mostly by the two warriors Lucille left behind to secure the site. An additional ten to twelve survivors—all presumed to be non-combatants—were believed to have escaped, and may still be in flight at this time, with signs they were proceeding further westward, away from the city.

Of the twelve battle-armored troops and six BattleMechs taken for the operation, Lucille's force lost a total of six troopers, along with three 'Mechs and two of their MechWarriors. Adept Moakay's *Griffin* was recovered and could be restored (barely!), as was Adept Basset's EMP-shocked *Nexus*, but Adept Quang's *Nexus* had been a complete loss. And while all of the remaining units in Lucille's force remained functional, each one had suffered varying degrees of damage by the time they'd returned to base.

Worst of all, of course, was the fact that the two known interlopers—who he now knew to be one Doctor Brooklyn Stevens and one Tibor Mitternacht—had escaped. As Lucille had feared, the blood soaking the *Griffin*'s recovered ejection seat turned out to be Moakay's after all, debunking the initial theories of Stevens' demise. Thanks to the heat and electromagnetic clutter created by the 'Mech's collapse and the thick forest, the clever Frail had managed to slip past his warriors' sensors before Lucille's battle armor could reach the scene and begin their search.

Lucille found only miniscule relief in the fact that Apollyon's own presumptions about the woman going for her wrecked DropShuttle also proved to be false. Wherever the intruder was headed, it was either toward an objective they knew nothing about, like a heretofore undiscovered Wayward camp somewhere past the Open Plains...or it was a feint, in which case, Blake only knew where they might be right now.

Either way, it meant she had outmaneuvered *both* of them for the time being.

Naturally, Precentor Apollyon decided to apply some lateral thinking to the matter. Wherever Stevens and Mitternacht went, the only way to truly escape Jardine was to get to their JumpShip—something that was supremely difficult, given the fact that all of the planet's functional spacecraft were currently stored in the hangar bays beneath Hope's thoroughly secured spaceport. Combined with the orbiting sensors and drone launchers, Stevens would need divine intervention if she and her companion were to leave Jardine's atmosphere alive, let alone undetected.

And even then, Apollyon noted, she'd need a JumpShip to leave the system entirely. Given the broadcast Stevens had made when she crashed, the leader of the Master's Hands knew said JumpShip was somewhere in the system, but it was clearly running silent and likely positioned far enough away to be missed by passive sensors.

Capturing or destroying that ship before it could leap out-system was the best way to guarantee Jardine's secrecy and ensure Stevens could neither escape nor receive any outside help. The biggest problem there was the certainty that Stevens' JumpShip had already been tipped off to a hostile presence in the system, and so would almost certainly bolt or relocate if Jardine's elaborate, system-wide sensor network suddenly pinged them after switching from passive to active detection mode.

And so the plan was hatched—and initiated—while Lucille was still in the field. After taking in the junior Precentor's report, Apollyon bade him to rise and presented the basics to him. Using a DropShuttle of the same mundane make and colors, with IFF codes copied from those found in Stevens' wreck, Lucille and a boarding team would "escape" Jardine and call for help from Stevens' JumpShip. Voice-modification software, expertly configured by Ghost Precentor Lamashti, would allow Lucille to communicate with the intruders' vessel, and answer any questions necessary to bring their Trojan Horse into striking range.

That much of the plan was basic.

The complexities that now concerned Lucille were in the extra details Apollyon had added to make the whole mission "more convincing."

Apollyon stood behind his desk, peering over the translucent pane upon which a schematic map of Jardine's solar system had been projected in a clever mimicry of three-dimensional space. His hood was back, leaving the brown flesh of his scalp exposed. The mechanical orb of his true eye was dimmed, while the brow above his frail, natural eye arched with interest. His arms were crossed, but uncharacteristically exposed; he'd pushed the broad sleeves of his red and gold robe back to the elbows. Lucille could thus plainly see the contrast between the unnaturally bulky flesh of Apollyon's left forearm and the noticeably sleeker collection of metal, plastic, and myomer comprising his right.

"In this day and age," Apollyon said, "there's no longer a guarantee of what resources the frail heathens of the Inner

Sphere might have. A charged and ready lithium-fusion battery could nix this entire operation before our people even get into firing range."

"But doesn't having my shuttle barreling in—with a hostile DropShip hot on its tail—risk overplaying the hand? They could see through the ruse, perhaps even open fire upon my shuttle before we draw near enough, and then jump out before the bigger guns can reach them."

Apollyon's frail eye narrowed slightly. "Do I detect a hint of *fear*, Precentor?"

Lucille felt as though he'd just been slapped. Fear was the very first conquest all Domini made before beginning their path toward Ascension; those who yielded to fear could never make the first sacrifice of the flesh—the one that came without promise of reward! To fear was to value personal well-being over the greater good. It was selfishness in its most primal form.

Fear was the *ultimate* Frailty!

Lucille absorbed the insult without allowing its sting to pierce his soul.

As it was, Apollyon held up a hand to forestall any possible retort. "The pursuit ship will add to the immediacy of the threat and help reduce the chances of the target suspecting your ruse. The intruders' JumpShip is aware that Stevens crashed while under fire, and Ghost Precentor Lamashti has already set the stage for you to explain any oddities in your flight path and communications as lingering damage. That would, naturally, include why you will be 'unable' to transmit video or send and reply using laser tight-beam methods.

"Meanwhile, your voice masker will even send intermittent bursts of static to maintain consistency with the earlier transmissions. If they try to get you to reveal any pertinent information on this system and our presence here, you will, of course, refuse this, because there is a hostile craft close enough to eavesdrop. This will encourage them to stay put at least long enough to collect you, as the alternative is fleeing this system completely empty handed. This gives your 'pursuit' ship an incentive to spend as little time as possible debating the options, while their colleagues' lives are on the line."

Lucille's gaze returned to the projected map again, and he studied the flight plans. Based on the sensor contact data of the intruders' original arrival, he noticed his shuttle's "return trip" was plotted to begin by moving back along that same general heading from a lift-off point near the original crash zone. That was a sensible enough choice, which would likely raise no red flags among the target's crew, should they be able to perceive it somehow. "Stevens" would then radio to her unseen cohorts for current telemetry as soon as she clears the planet's ionosphere. This will be the first such transmission in which "she" requests a response, while continuing along her initial course (roughly along Jardine's main orbital plane, heading outward) until corrective data comes in. The timing of the response would help narrow down just how far out the target JumpShip lay, which would naturally be fed back to Hope along a secure frequency to aid in triangulation and any potential avenues for alternate interceptions.

The pursuit DropShip—a *Union*-class—would then launch roughly one hour or so later, burning hot. This chaser would be running with active sensors and a Free Worlds League IFF, which should make perfect sense to a JumpShip lurking in League space. With both Lucille's shuttle and its pursuer roughly matched for acceleration, they could pace themselves and manage their separation naturally enough to be convincing. Since the shuttle should be damaged and low on fuel, this would easily excuse the DropShip's gradual gain as they flee across the system, adding to the "incentive" Apollyon talked about... maybe even enough to convince the outworlders to make an in-system jump in an effort to close the gap and rescue "Stevens" sooner.

It was those details, Lucille realized, that would all need to be played by ear, since so much relied on the JumpShip's reactions.

"My concern, Precentor," he finally said, "is not for myself, but for the mission."

Apollyon nodded slightly, but said nothing.

"The success of this operation relies entirely on the reactions of people who have already managed to surprise us several times," Lucille continued. "Should they do so again..."

"Then you improvise," Apollyon said gravely. "These people must *not* be allowed to reveal our existence before the Third Transfer. The lives of everyone left on this world—and perhaps all of the Inner Sphere—depend on it."

FOREST OF SHROUDS
JARDINE (HERAKLEION)
FREE WORLDS LEAGUE
3 NOVEMBER 3067

"*Digger One*" was the name stenciled just below the lower-most transplas panel of the *Rock Possum*'s cockpit. The canopy window itself was largely missing, with only a few shards in the corners to indicate it ever existed at all. Indeed, of the seven distinct openings reserved for the control module's polarized windowpanes, only three of the smallest remained intact; the rest were shattered, exposing the seats and controls within to the elements.

When Tibor Mitternacht led Alahni back to the wreck, he explained to the young Jardinian woman it was what Brooke meant for them to find. Having driven the machine to this point only days ago—before falling to a combination of Manei Domini cyborgs and a Wayward EMP mine—she would have been most familiar with its route and general position relative to the surrounding terrain features. By her estimates, Tibor realized, the fallen WorkMech would make a decent "midpoint" between wherever she was driving her stolen BattleMech, and where she'd originally left Tibor and Alahni to wait for her.

Although part of Tibor silently hoped to find something worth salvaging at the wreck site, he told Alahni that Brooke was using it as a rendezvous point.

What struck him first when they arrived was how thoroughly "cleaned up" the site was. He could easily make out several tracks in the area. Most were made by human footwear, but there was no shortage of *tabiranth* paw prints either; telltales from the Wanderer hunting party that had saved—then captured—him and Brooke. But gone were any Manei Domini bodies he half expected to find there.

"Our hunters would take any weapons, electronics, and other technological equipment they could carry," Alahni explained, "but a whole 'Mech would be rather conspicuous."

"Would they have taken the cyborgs' bodies?" Tibor asked, incredulously.

"No," she answered after a few moments' thought. "Some of their modifications can be useful, but the Guardians always recover their own."

"Yet they left Digger One..."

"Your WorkMech?"

"Yes."

"They likely felt it was useless. The Guardians have left many old machines out to decay, most in open areas, like Sentinel Valley and the Open Plains..."

"The Word of Blake *abandoning* tech?" Tibor chewed on that thought for a few moments, ignoring the scowl flashing across Alahni's face.

"*Useless* tech," she stressed. "Like your 'Digger One'. They have far superior equipment in Hope, and in storehouses elsewhere, both here and among the others of The Five."

"Makes sense enough, I suppose," Tibor conceded as he gave the 'Mech another cursory examination. "Leave the junk out to rust in the open, and any curious prospectors who get close enough will naturally see it as forgotten wreckage. Exactly the kind of stuff you'd expect to see on a world bombed to death in the First War..."

With that, he began to climb up into the *Rock Possum*'s cockpit. But no sooner had he reached out to grab part of the bent canopy supports and started to hoist himself up a step, when a high-pitched chittering pierced the air, and he suddenly found himself swarmed by a flock of tiny, winged creatures. The storm of blue and green alien feathers passed quickly, but not before he'd lost his grip and fallen back-first onto the forest floor.

He was halfway into a curse when he heard something he genuinely did not expect...

Alahni's laughter.

EXPLORER-CLASS JUMPSHIP *SACAJAWEA*
PIRATE JUMP POINT
JARDINE (HERAKLEION) SYSTEM
FREE WORLDS LEAGUE

"DropShuttle Magellan *to* Sacajawea... *Guys, it's Brook... We're still here... Trying to repair the ship... We think we'll be able to... When we're ready, we'll try to sig... But fuel is limited... We'll need telem...* Not *send anyone else! I repeat: do* not... *Still unsafe..."*

The message ended with a *chirp* just as Lawrence Pohl, captain of the independent JumpShip *Sacajawea*, heard the bridge hatch close behind him. He half-turned away from the communications station to see its normal occupant, Gretchen Morden, floating toward him. In her left hand was a squeeze thermos undoubtedly filled with almost as much dissolved sugar and cream as hot coffee.

Gretchen's cool brown eyes met the older man's ice-blue gaze, and she nodded to him. Lawrence was already pushing himself out of her way, allowing her to reclaim what had become her favorite chair over all these years. Still, he hung onto one of the crash rails along the console's right side, anchoring himself to the station for the time being.

"How long have you been reviewing that same message now?" Gretchen asked while she reached for the chair. As she settled herself in, she locked her thermos into its usual cradle—a worn (and somewhat stained) adjustable cup-holder along the console's left side.

"A while," Lawrence admitted. "It's just nagging at me."

"Yeah, me too. But I don't think listening to it again and again is really going to help get that out of your head."

"Maybe," Lawrence agreed. "Just wish I could put my finger on whatever it is that makes the message sound so odd."

"Well," Gretchen began. "There's the fact she broadcast that in the clear after saying she was attacked by hostile aerospace..."

"Which could just be a calculated risk."

"Or the fact she named our JumpShip on the same open frequency..."

"Hmmm..."

"Or that she added 'Guys, it's Brooke,' like we could somehow could have forgotten..."

"You've been thinking about this a lot, haven't you?"

Gretchen shrugged. "That was really all I had. But it's not like these are things we'd *never* seen her do when she was rattled."

"And getting shot down over a supposedly dead world *is* a bit rattling," Lawrence conceded.

"I almost wonder what would happen if we answered her, really."

"You mean, apart from possibly giving our position away to whoever else might be listening—besides Hara, that is?"

"Sure," Gretchen said as a sly, knowing grin suddenly spread across her face, "if we broadcast on open channels." Without breaking eye contact, she leaned back in her chair, grabbed her thermos, and squirted a shot of coffee into her mouth.

"We're a good fifteen Units out from the primary here, Gretch," he told her. "There's no way we can laser-beam at this range."

Gretchen's smile faded into a look of disappointment. "Of course not! But, we can send messages on channels *other* than those approved by the merchants' playbook and IE, you know."

Lawrence stared at her for a moment more before the final pieces locked into place in his mind. It was *still* risky, especially if the bad guys really *were* the folks everyone now suspected them to be.

But it was *something*.

"Alright," Lawrence said, finally. "That gets a message *to* them, presuming nothing's happened to Trouble. But that comm implant of his just isn't strong enough to get a signal this far."

"True," Gretchen said with a nod, "*but* it's strong enough for us to detect that he's *sending* a signal."

"How so? You mean like a ping?"

Gretchen nodded again. "Just about everything in this system aside from those ancient buoys seems to be running under EMCON conditions, so any spike on Tibor's channel— however small—should show up if we're focused enough to hear it. We'll need to rig up a better detector for the job, though. If this tug of ours hadn't been modified by someone's grand-folks, we'd have a radio telescope or three handy and ready to go, but I think we can whip something up using some parts and gear we have around the ship. There's some reflective parachutes and tarps in storage, which can be used to make a receiver dish. And a few of those portable radar sensors we have could be put together as a focal point. With a little liquid helium drawn from the core—"

"You really *have* been thinking this through!"

"It's either this or rely on prayer that they have reliable access to a radio. But since we're *both* uneasy with the message we already received that way, that's a bridge too far for my tastes."

Lawrence let out a heavy sigh. It was a long shot, but it was better than just...waiting.

"Okay," he said at last. "Let's do this. How long do you think it'll take to set up?"

"I'll grab some of the others to help out. Figure we should have something together in...maybe an hour or so?"

"Alright, then. If nothing else, it gives us something to do."

"Think *positive*, Cap!" Gretchen chided, offering a thin smile.

"Didn't you just say you weren't prepared to rely on prayer?"

"That's why I'm relying on myself," she answered with a wink and another swig from her thermos. "But I do have one more question for you: Do you think we should tell our shadows about any of this?"

Lawrence looked up and stared into the space beyond one of the armored viewports ringing the *Sacajawea*'s bridge module. Somewhere out there—eight standard astronomical units away—lurked the JumpShip and DropShip that carried Anton Hara and the liaison Interstellar Expeditions had assigned to watch over him. Hara was the blustering type, who rubbed everyone the wrong way from the moment he and his ship inserted themselves into this mission.

But Hara's fighter jocks *had* helped cover the escape from Shasta, at no small risk to themselves. And, of course, were it not for the information Brooke managed to get from his IE liaison, they wouldn't have been able to get this far to begin with. Lawrence harbored little doubt Hara and his crew had picked up the same signal now giving him and Gretchen such pause, but he was absolutely *positive* they were having none of the same gut reactions.

It would be common courtesy to let Hara's team know the *Sacajawea* was now working on a plan to try and verify the call's legitimacy...

And yet, he could not bring himself to fully trust them.

His decision made, Lawrence looked back to Gretchen and shook his head.

She smirked. "Yeah, I didn't think so, either."

FOREST OF SHROUDS
JARDINE (HERAKLEION) SYSTEM
FREE WORLDS LEAGUE

Digger One was most definitely dead.

As the sun moved across the Jardinian sky, casting beams that lazily swept across the forest floor through gaps in the canopy above, Tibor had focused most of his attention on the fallen *Rock Possum*. Although its structure was completely intact, and much of the military-grade armor remained in place, its left leg actuators appeared to have been almost completely fused. Partially melted strands of myomer peeked out from blown joint housings, and sprung tension governors jammed awkwardly into the gaps, locking the knee, ankle, and hip joints in place. Tibor recognized a replacements-only job when he saw one; even if the ProspectorMech could have been restarted, it would be so terribly hobbled that foot travel would be far safer.

Of course, the leg damage was just one of many issues that had killed Digger One. After quickly realizing Alahni also had some degree of technical knowledge—she'd found the hip joint failure before he even noticed it—Tibor had her check several other systems while he tried to diagnose the fuel cell engine. Given the lack of proper tools to open the maintenance housings, it took some doing, but he eventually managed to get a good enough look to see the main hydrogen cells had ruptured. If the power plant had any juice left at all, it was stored in the engine's limited back-up capacitors—which would only be good enough to turn on its searchlight (were it not already shattered), or run the cockpit life-support systems for half an hour (at best).

Meanwhile, Alahni had nudged aside the bird nest Tibor accidentally disturbed in the cockpit so she could get a look at the control panels. (She refused to toss the nest out entirely as he'd suggested, saying there were several unhatched "turqueet" eggs in it, and she didn't want to see them abandoned by their "flock litter.") She confirmed that several panels were completely dead or fried, including the sensor board and the all-important DI monitor.

"The comm panel looks good!" she exclaimed at one point, while the two of them were resting in the hulk's shadow.

"Great," Tibor responded sarcastically. "No engine, minimal control systems, and a busted leg...but there ain't nothin' wrong with the radio."

"Perhaps you could call your friends in space?" she asked. "That's where you're trying to go, isn't it?"

Tibor shook his head. There were so many things wrong with that suggestion, but he decided on humoring rather than humiliating her; he didn't want to risk upsetting her all over again.

"They're so far out-system it would be hours before they heard it," he said, "if they heard it at all. Then, it'd take about two weeks for a shuttle to reach us if they sent one. At which point your Guardians would undoubtedly shoot them down just like they did us. That, of course, would be long after they also detected our outgoing signal and came for us here."

"Then what was *your* plan to leave this place?"

Tibor sighed. There weren't many *good* options, under the circumstances. "Well," he began, "the long and the short of it is basically sneaking aboard one of the Guardians' outbound DropShips. The stowaway approach."

Alahni seemed intrigued. "And hope you don't get caught? How would that take you where you need to go?"

"That's always risky. See, out in the Inner Sphere, where merchant traffic is common, and a lot of JumpShips pull double-duty as military and civilian transport, a stowaway can potentially climb aboard an outbound ship and stay hidden for the ride in some cargo bay or maintenance area—give or take some rather bumpy moments and enough food, drink, and erm, waste disposal to pull it all off undetected. Then, when the DropShip links up with a Jumper, they slip through the dock whenever they can, and either ride that JumpShip to its next destination, or get to another DropShip that's headed toward a safe port.

"A lot of refugees and outlaws do it. Many get caught, especially when boarding military ships, but you'd be surprised how many don't."

"That sounds...*incredibly* dangerous!"

"It is," Tibor conceded. "But when the alternative is staying on a world where you're marked for death, with no ride of your own that can run an armed blockade, it's about the best anyone can do. The alternative is to live out one's days in the wilderness."

Alahni's voice became sad again. "Like my people did..."

Tibor looked at her and frowned. He put a hand on her shoulder in as reassuring a way as he could, but steeled himself for another grief-stricken outburst. "Alahni," he said softly, "to your people, Jardine was—*is* home. You clearly love this world. You didn't seek to escape it..."

"No," she agreed sadly. "We just sought a life outside of the city."

Tibor found nothing he could say he hadn't repeated several times before. He squeezed her shoulder, then let go, turning away for her to stare off into the darkening woods. How long had they been there now? It felt like the better half of a day had passed, with still no sign of Brooke.

And he really didn't like that.

Tibor closed his eyes and inhaled deeply, drawing in a mix of natural, earthy air and the lingering scent of spilled coolant and burned electronics. At the sound of a flutter, he looked up to find one of those "*turqueets*" returning to the broken cockpit. The strange bird, which seemed to have two sets of tail feathers almost as large as its wings, was a striking shade of blue-green he imagined lent to its native name, but its eyes—or perhaps just the flesh and feathers immediately around its eyes—looked bright red. The tiny creature perched on the cockpit frame, and blinked at him repeatedly as it continuously tilted its head from side to side.

He released a soft sigh, trying not to startle the bird. After a few moments, the animal evidently decided the two humans below were no threat and hopped into the cockpit, disappearing from sight.

"What will *you* do now?" he asked, softly.

The question seemed to snap Alahni out of whatever deep thoughts had gripped her. She refused to meet his gaze, or even look in his direction. Instead, she stared out into the forest. "I don't know..."

"Would the city be safe for you?"

Alahni shook her head.

"Are there any more Wayward settlements around here?"

"Maybe..."

Tibor paused. Not sure if he wanted to suggest what now came to his mind.

"I don't know," Alahni weakly repeated.

"Do you want to..." Tibor began, but trailed off. Leaves were rustling somewhere nearby. He looked around quickly, closing his real eye and focusing his attention on what his implant saw. A blurry image of reality, painted mostly in dark greens and blues, appeared against a mostly-black backdrop. Heat sources—most of them tiny—appeared among the trees, and some small forms appeared to be crawling among the brush in the distance.

But nothing that appeared to be human. Not from where Tibor was sitting anyway.

"Want to what?" Alahni asked, her voice still weak.

"Um..." he answered uncertainly. "I mean, have you considered, maybe, leaving *with* us?"

Alahni blinked. Suddenly, she was looking back at him, her expression confused. "Wha—?" she began.

But then they both heard it: the snap of a dry tree branch, from somewhere behind the dead 'Mech's outstretched leg...

...Accompanied by a curse, muttered by a female voice. In German.

Tibor bolted to his feet. Alahni rose quickly behind him. The turqueet inside the cockpit bolted into the sky with a high-pitched twittering.

"Brooke...?" Tibor called out in a low voice.

Limping around Digger One's foot, her athletic figure covered in scratches and smears of dirt, her long, auburn hair a tangled mess, Brooklyn Stevens came into view. Her underwear, stained a deep red with blood Tibor hoped came from someone else, covered her modesty, and her hiking boots were intact, but her arms crossed over her chest, holding in place what seemed to be the tattered remnants of her sports bra.

She looked up at both of them and smiled weakly before fixing her gaze on Tibor. "*Please* tell me you still have my clothes..."

BENEATH LAUNCH PLATFORM A7
CITY OF HOPE
JARDINE (HERAKLEION)
FREE WORLDS LEAGUE

The reinforced chambers beneath the City of Hope's spaceport were designed and built using the same techniques Star League engineers had used to construct their infamous Castles Brian. As such, they were—at least theoretically—immune to the detonation of all but the heaviest strategic nuclear weapons widely available in their day. This was a particularly wise choice, given that Hope was established perilously close to an immense, but largely dormant, super-volcano.

The subterranean magma chamber closest to the surface was identified early in the planet's colonial period, but was initially classified as stable. Stable, that was, until a low-grade earthquake in the area spontaneously transformed a 3,000-square kilometer expanse of forest into a desolate geyser field a mere fifty years later.

Rather than relocate the settlements already established in the area, the colonists opted to harness the hotspot, and built the planet's first large-scale geothermal power plant. The centuries since saw many of the earlier enclaves damaged by periodic earthquakes, until—by the mid-2600s—the locals ultimately undertook a massive project to consolidate most of the regional towns and cities into the high-tech metropolis now known as Hope. Benefiting from the latest in Star League mega-engineering techniques, every building, road, and bridge in Hope was safe, clean, and tremor-resistant.

The abandoned cities, located mostly to the north and east of Hope, eventually vanished as the forest rapidly reclaimed the land. This not only left Hope free to harness virtually all output from the nearby geothermal power plants, but also established the city as the *only* major population center within a hundred kilometers of the sleeping caldera.

These factors made the city a natural focus for ComStar's eventual stewardship over Jardine after the Star League's demise. Built with the integrity of a fortress, powered by non-nuclear means so close to a natural heat source, with an ample water supply amid fertile lands, surrounded by other ruins, and isolated from the more densely populated areas that always became targets on so many worlds in their day—it was contained, defensible, and easily overlooked.

And so, when Jardine was excised from the maps of history, the city that would become Hope arose as the only settlement on the planet worth saving. As the First Succession War raged, secret teams of engineers, scientists, and troops—all sent by the Sainted Jerome Blake himself!—built on the work started generations before, adding hidden facilities, defensive bunkers, and even an entire subterranean spaceport.

It was in the vast underground chambers of this spaceport that Poltergeist Precentor Sigma Damien Lucille now stood, surveying the final preparations for his latest mission.

The hood of his white robe was drawn back, exposing his face and black-stubbled scalp. The subcutaneous filaments of his direct neural interface implants etched symmetrical rows that mimicked the furrows of a freshly planted cornfield, sketching an almost stylized mimicry of a hairline that began in a neat line from his forehead to his temples, then streaked backward, over his ears, before uniting at a circular metal nexus at the back of his skull. To an untrained eye, they looked almost like faded tattoos, but in fact they were the very latest in vehicular control implants, the likes of which the Clans dabbled in, and which the Federated Suns had once tried—and failed—to develop fully.

Also exposed, by virtue of his pulled-back sleeves, were the metal and plastic prosthetics that replaced his original, frail arms. These too were state of the art, even though they eschewed the cosmetic modeling and synthflesh that could make them pass for the real thing. Built for the battlefield, Lucille's true hands each featured retractable claws that could rend flesh and scale the armored skin of a BattleMech with equal efficiency, while his true forearms each concealed extending vibroblades—for what he occasionally liked to call "extra emphasis."

Blake willing, he would be able to *use* them soon enough.

As Lucille watched in silence, the launch bay techs and acolytes guided a high-capacity lifting hoist to the K-1 DropShuttle that would soon be his ride into space unknown. The small craft had already been loaded with two complete six-man sets of battlesuits—one for each of the boarding teams he was to command in this operation. To conserve its limited fuel, it was now being placed on board the *Union*-class DropShip *Hera's Shield*, a 3,600-ton assault vessel that looked like a stubby, iron-skinned, age-worn techno-mushroom. He and his team would launch the shuttle from the *Shield*'s bay as soon as they cleared the atmosphere, after which the DropShip would make a few "frantic" orbits around Jardine before rushing off to "pursue" them. This little modification to the original plan would give his shuttle more of a "realistic" head start, he felt.

His gaze drifted to the distance beyond the large underground bay, where shadows enveloped the gigantic cubicles reserved for other large DropShips. From his vantage point so close to *Hera's Shield*, where banks of bright, wall-mounted spotlights bathed him, the work crews, and the ship in a blue-white glow, the rest of the underground complex was all but invisible. Yet he could still make out the ovoid hulls of at least three more *Union*-class DropShips, each stowed in its own open-framed hangar of reinforced ferrocrete pylons and heavy, multi-level gantries. Beyond those, however, he noticed one more bay was lit; another DropShip—this one a newer *Merlin*—was being serviced or prepped for launch.

He was distracted from his thoughts by the approach of a young, dark-skinned brunette in plain light-gray overalls.

Technical Adept Tin carried her noteputer as if it was some kind of prize, but presented it to Lucille with a curt—almost banal—remark: "Your final inventory, Precentor."

Lucille took the device and tapped the side to light its screen. His eyes scanned the display without expression, taking in the manifest. Most of it was mundane; field rations, fuel cell-powered recharger units, emergency back-up batteries, tool kits, med kits, and so forth—all the basics for operating a twelve-man team in the field for up to three weeks. Then, of course, there were the battlesuits: all twelve certified for vacuum operations, including optional equipment that could swap out the Longinus suits' short-range missiles for extra maneuvering fuel.

But Lucille's jet-black eyes narrowed on the last line item, one he simply did not expect to see here at all: *"Type 1-Alpha 0.5 Kt Infantry-Portable Tactical Device – Qty: 6"*

Allowing himself no further reaction, Lucille took the notepad's stylus and signed on the indicated line, recognizing the payload was now his to command. He managed to maintain his stoic façade just long enough to thank Adept Tin, send her on her way, and make sure nobody else was within earshot, an effort that only grew more maddening as the seconds ticked by.

Only when he was reasonably certain none were left to hear him did he finally key the communicator socketed over his left wrist...

...so he could ask Precentor Apollyon exactly *why* he needed to carry six nuclear warheads into this battle!

FOREST OF SHROUDS
JARDINE (HERAKLEION) SYSTEM
FREE WORLDS LEAGUE

While being fully clothed again was a relief in and of itself—one at least half as pleasant as finding Tibor and Alahni again— Brooke now felt as though her skin was crawling. Dozens of scratches and bruises vied for her attention, but Tibor's quick inspection assured her nothing was "too broken." Still, her run through the forest had done her no real favors. Her legs ached, and she felt as though her body was covered in an oily grunge that was a mix of sweat, dirt, and Bast-only-knew *what* else. Combined with the occasional twig, leaf, or unidentifiable bug still tumbling from her hair—even after she'd finally managed to tame it into a simple ponytail—she found herself longing for a scalding hot shower.

Preferably delivered by a power washer.

The awkward looks she was getting from Alahni and Tibor, combined with their apparent determination to stay at least three meters away from her at all times, told her she undoubtedly looked—and *smelled*—just as bad as she felt.

They remained in the shadow of Digger One for the moment. Tibor had already explained the old WorkMech was dead. At best, he could maybe broadcast a signal from its radio, but that would accomplish little more than drawing the cyborgs' attention. They'd found no weapons among the wreckage, either. Brooke would have been lying to herself if she said she hadn't hoped for *something* more when she'd sent them here.

"So, what's the plan?" Tibor finally asked. "I know the city's our best—and maybe *only*—hope for a ride out of here, but I seriously doubt we can convince the locals to let us in by pretending to be a pizza delivery service."

Alahni threw him a quizzical look. "'Pizza' delivery?"

Tibor responded with an expression that was a mix of mild surprise and pity. "I mean," he said, "it's not like we can just stroll into town and not expect to be shot, right?"

"These Manei Domini don't seem the type to skimp on security," Brooke agreed with a sigh. "Alahni, do you have any ideas?"

Alahni frowned and looked away. Brooke caught the concerned glance from Tibor that swung first from the girl and then back her way. During his earlier poke-and-prod inspection for broken bones and other trauma, Tibor had explained what happened between them after Brooke decided to play "Immortal Warrior" (as he put it). She knew about his struggle to try and keep Alahni from a complete breakdown at the realization that her entire tribe was most likely dead, "thanks to us" (again, as he put it). Brooke understood all this, and sympathized with the poor girl. Her blood *still* boiled with rage toward those Bast-damned "Guardians" and their needless cruelty.

But, as much as it pained her to admit the girl's people would *certainly* still be alive had she and Tibor not come along, Brooke couldn't escape the fact that Alahni now represented perhaps their only real hope of getting off this planet in one piece.

Or her relief that, after everything else so far, she was *still* here.

Tibor might have his doubts about the young Jardinian's willingness to help them any further, but something inside Brooke told her the girl was—and remained—a friend.

"The water lines," Alahni said quietly.

Brooke arched an eyebrow.

"Hope relies on the river," she went on without prompting. "For drinking water, irrigation, sanitation. Blake's Guardians improved the system over the years, maximized the flow-through to work as clean and efficiently as possible with no surface pumps or obvious signs of active technology. Like everything else, they wanted to make the city self-sufficient, while still looking abandoned to outsiders."

Alahni turned toward Brooke, finally meeting her gaze with those brown eyes she found so alluring. "Those newer lines are well maintained and well secured by the Guardians. Lots of filters and gates, and passages too small for people. But there remain a few older lines dating back to the times before the coming of Blake. Many were collapsed or shut off during the reconstruction, but a few remain intact. Mostly."

"Mostly?" Tibor repeated.

"Through the years, we Waywards have used these lines to sneak out of the city...or back in. But they're not maintained like the active lines. Most have a lot of debris in them. They're still big enough for people to swim through, but it can be tricky, especially with no light down there."

"Swim through?" Brooke felt her stomach tighten a little at the thought.

Alahni nodded. "Water from the river still fills these passages. There are air pockets here and there, I think, but it's the only way in or out of the city that the Guardians don't really seem to care about."

Brooke frowned and looked to Tibor.

Tibor matched her expression and added a shrug.

"Beggars can't be choosers," he said. "Alahni, do any of these passages lead to the spaceport? Or maybe an armory?"

The story keeper shook her head. "The only one I truly know about leads to the Overseers' Quarter. It's the part of the city where the most privileged of our people reside. The ones who work closest with the Guardians."

"That sounds...less than ideal."

"The Overseers are highly entrusted by the Guardians," Alahni explained. "They work as administrators for most of the city functions, and lead work teams when needed. They have access keys and pass codes that can let them travel more freely among restricted sections—"

"But they also sound like the types who'd turn us over to your Guardians the moment we showed up."

"Trouble's got a good point there, Alahni," Brooke cut in. "It sounds too risky."

Alahni's voice took on a slight edge as she focused on Brooke again. "Try to remember, Doctor Stevens, that for years—*generations*—before you two came along, the Guardians tolerated the existence of Wayward communities. Many of us were allowed to simply walk openly into the forests, so long as we all lived as secretly as do the people of Hope. It was a humane policy; we were *never* slaves to the Guardians, but we couldn't leave the system for fear of revealing our kin to the Lost. So, they allowed those of us who chafed under the more restricted rules of the city to simply leave, and—as *you* put it, Mister Tibor—'let nature take its course.'"

Brooke saw Tibor open his mouth, but whatever retort he had in mind was silenced when Alahni quickly held a quieting hand. "My *point*," she continued, "is that we of the Wayward tribes were never seen as enemies of our city-dwelling kin. Truly, it was actually the Overseers who helped us leave the city most of the time, getting us out with the least amount of disturbance, even giving directions to nearby camps. Some even trade with the tribes."

"All without their Guardians' knowledge?" Brooke asked.

Alahni shrugged. "If the Guardians know, they never did anything about it."

"Meaning this *could* be an 'open secret,'" Tibor muttered. "They could know and just allow it to happen as long as it doesn't pose an actual threat."

Alahni's impatient sigh oddly reminded Brooke of how Marie used to act whenever she and Tibor got into their periodic spats.

We could second guess ourselves about this forever!

"Unless you have a better plan, Trouble," she said. "Like you said, 'beggars...'"

Brooke suddenly noticed Tibor's head was tilting awkwardly, his real eye appearing as glazed as its artificial companion. He held a hand up toward her absently, then raised a finger to his lips. Picking up on the abrupt silence, Alahni's gaze alternated between the two off-worlders, her expression growing increasingly concerned by the second.

"Why, that clever little minx!" Tibor finally exclaimed.

"Who—?" Brooke started, but Tibor was still holding a hand up for silence, his expression still blank, listening to something she now suspected was in his own head.

But who could be signaling him on his implant frequency?

After a few more seconds, Tibor shook his head, blinked, and looked back at Brooke as if he'd just awakened from a particularly interesting dream. "You're not going to believe this," he said, "but I just got a call...from the *Sac*!"

CHAPTER 6

"When you get down to it, it's pretty much impossible to sneak around in space these days. Most DropShips, JumpShips, and even shuttles have the means to intercept and identify any type of radio signal and track it back to its source. And sensors can detect the plasma exhaust of your ship from hours—even days—away at best speeds. Sure, your chances are better if everyone's trying to run silent and you're coasting more than you're burning, but even then, you're still just gambling that nobody is paying attention when you do something.

"At greater distances, it can get even more ridiculous. With so many cues to go on, your ship class and acceleration profiles can be pegged from so far away that some pretty simple math can guess where you're going, and when you'll get there long before you do. At that point, intercept strategies can be formed, reinforcements can be called to action, and what started as a stealth job can end up as a sorrowful note home to your next of kin (if you're lucky)!

"All of this is why a lot of covert missions rely on indirect travel or long-range pre-ops. Sleepers can spend months, or even years, living among the populace of a planet that might never be targeted for spies, but just happens to lie along a routine trade route to someplace of more importance. When time's not on your side, stowing away on ships is another option, but comes with its own obvious risks. And sometimes, another is to basically toss

something juicy at the enemy guards in the hope they'll take the bait and be too busy looking another way when you do whatever it is you came to do.

"That last option in particular is a bit of a dick move, of course, especially if your "decoy" happens to be an innocent bystander—or worse, a friend."

—TIBOR MITTERNACHT
AS QUOTED IN "*CHANGING THE OBJECTIVES* (PART 2)"
(WARRIOR DIGITAL PRODUCTIONS, SOLARIS VII, JUNE 3061)

**THE SANCTORUM
CITY OF HOPE
JARDINE (HERAKLEION)
FREE WORLDS LEAGUE
3 NOVEMBER 3067**

The rumble of the DropShip's engines could be felt in the floor and walls of the Sanctorum, even though its launch platform was more than half a kilometer distant.

From his vantage point, by the north window, Precentor Apollyon could see the bone white *Union* rising majestically toward the heavens on a column of yellow-gold plasma. His eyes—true and frail alike—tracked the great vessel's skyward journey for close to a minute.

Enough time for him to utter a quick prayer.

"May the spirit of Blake smile upon those warriors, and may Fate favor them with victory in his name," he intoned. *For if they fail*, he mentally added, *our very home may pay the price.*

"Blessed be those who walk in Blake's Divine Light," came the solemn reply, spoken by the man behind him.

"Blessed be," Apollyon acknowledged.

Turning away from the window, he found Ogima Lunalla had not moved since his arrival. The chief administrator for the City of Hope was not one of the Master's Hands. He was not even a soldier. But, to Apollyon, he was still a brother, a fellow son of Jardine.

They stood in Ogima's office, rather than his own. Apollyon felt the news he had to convey was best delivered in person, and he was not going to add insult to their injury by making this innocent soul come to him.

Compared to Apollyon's personal chamber, Ogima's was luxurious, with blackwood paneling covering its ferrocrete walls, a textured ceiling, and two tinted glass windows compared to Apollyon's one. Paintings, all produced by local artists, adorned three of its four walls—the largest, of course, being a rendition of the sainted Jerome Blake so reverent the ComStar founder looked positively messianic. Native broadleaf ferns, kept in tall planters of polished marble, occupied the corners behind the administrator's handmade blackwood desk. Three black, synthleather chairs were present in the office, but all of them—including Ogima's own—stood unoccupied at present. Ogima's personal workstation was also disengaged at the moment, its flat-projection monitor blacked out, since the man had switched it off as he rose to greet his unexpected visitor.

Ogima wore a simple, light brown robe over a set of khaki coveralls, unadorned with any form of decoration or insignia. Here on Jardine, formal attire outside of the military was rare; the locals prided themselves more on their works than their appearance, and Ogima himself rose from among the ranks of the Technical Guild. He was no stranger to getting his hands dirty—just not in the same manner as those of the Guardians and the Manei Domini.

In his hand was a slate gray compad. Though the device's screen was lit brightly enough to cast a slight white glow across his face, Ogima's eyes appeared to have glazed over. The moment did not last; sensing somehow that Apollyon's attention had turned his way, the city administrator blinked and turned to meet his gaze, his posture stiffening at the same time.

Apollyon favored him with a slight nod. "I feel as you do," he admitted, in tones as sympathetic as they were foreboding. "They were still kin to us, even if they *were* Wayward. It pained me greatly to order their destruction."

"But the Lost," Ogima said, sadly. "They escaped?"

"Precentor Lucille and his team were unable to locate the invaders. Presuming them killed in the fighting would be unforgivable in the absence of evidence. Reclamation teams will be sent into the woods shortly, to comb for stragglers; until then, our secret—and the Promise—remain in danger."

Ogima hesitated a few long moments before he finally placed the compad down and nodded. "I understand."

"Then you must also understand what I must say next," Apollyon told him. "These invaders have forced us to take extreme measures. We cannot risk allowing the Lost to taint our world, not even now, with the Third Transfer so near at hand. Not while the Clan corruption lies so close to their hearts.

"And so, while Lucille attempts to neutralize their compatriots in space, I must ask you to prepare for the cleansing of our own house..."

Ogima's eyes again seemed to glaze over again for a time, only to snap back into focus as the realization dawned on him. "The city?" he whispered. "You believe the Lost will come *here*?"

"Almost certainly. And it is imperative they do not, or that they are captured and surrendered to my soldiers if they somehow manage to do so."

Ogima bowed his head solemnly. "I understand, my Precentor."

As the words hung in the air, Apollyon considered blinking his true eye into infrared mode without activating its usual crimson glow. That way, he could study Ogima's thermal reactions, gauge whatever emotional struggle the man might have as the implications set in.

But he held himself back. It was one thing to peek at the hidden emotions of a captured Wayward whose tribe had already broken the Promise. It was quite another to presume guilt from a child of the City of Hope.

"Do you, my friend?" he asked instead. "I am aware, as you are, that some of Hope's children sympathize with the Waywards. Like you, I was willing to overlook it; they are, after all, kin to both of us. But the Wayward have always been more susceptible to the influence of the Lost.

"Ogima, we stand now on the eve of the Third Transfer— the time of our Great Promise—and we have been infiltrated from without. At this critical juncture, I fear what decisions the Master might be forced to make, if word of our work here reaches the wrong ears."

Ogima's eyes rose to meet those of Jardine's most powerful resident, the first of those rebuilt in the Master's image, for a crusade meant to save mankind itself from madness by fighting its savagery with even greater savagery. In years gone by, he had felt perfectly at ease with this man, his brother and countryman. But now, he felt only an unresolved mixture of dread, sorrow, and desperate hope.

Shoving aside the sorrow, and driven by the dread, Ogima clung to that hope as he held Apollyon's gaze.

"I promise you, Great Guardian of Blake," he said firmly. "I promise you I shall personally relay your orders to the people, and make them understand this grave danger. If the intruders come here, we will find them, and they will pay for the pain they have caused our world."

BENEATH THE CITY OF HOPE
JARDINE (HERAKLEION)
FREE WORLDS LEAGUE

The water was dark and cold, but the thermal sensor replacing Tibor Mitternacht's left eye kept him more or less glued to Brooke's tail. Well, that and the improvised lifeline made from former WorkMech power cables, which now tied the three fugitives together. Still, in the silence and shadows, he felt alone and isolated just enough to notice the accumulated pain from all the injuries and exertion he'd sustained over the last few days on Jardine. These combined aches tortured him with every move through the narrow confines of Hope's ancient water mains, adding painful difficulty to the already arduous task of avoiding the wreckage and false turns created by centuries of neglect and the incidental damage of later renovations.

Holding his breath against every impulse to cry out, of course, was just the final insult on top of it all. How Brooke was handling all this in her condition—while completely blind to boot—Tibor could only guess.

It had been a long swim, but fortunately one with enough breathing points to avoid drowning. Alahni seemed a little unsure of their course, reminding them at each pause that it had been some time since she had navigated these tunnels. Twice now, she had promised they were "almost there," or they had "one more to go." At the last pocket of air, though, she warned them: "This will be a long dive; get as much air as you can."

She was definitely right this time. By Tibor's estimate, they'd already been under for close to a minute.

It now felt like they were inside a broad sewage line, but one that was particularly compromised. In the inky blackness, Tibor's hands had struck large hunks of what felt like stone or collapsed masonry. But the real trouble began when his body brushed against something sharp.

Whatever it was, it raked him all along his left side, starting just below his shoulder blade, then tearing along his rib cage as he tried to twist away from it. The pain was intense, and he gasped through grinding teeth.

And that was when the choking began. Losing what little air was left in his lungs, Tibor struggled—and failed—to keep himself from coughing underwater. As panic and adrenaline took over, he began to thrash; there wasn't even time to think about what was happening.

Suddenly, a hand slashed down and seized him by the collar of his shirt, yanking him upward.

He broke the surface in a frenzy, desperately flailing in the darkness while trying to cough, inhale, and vomit water all at the same time. The rational part of his brain quickly recognized he was out of danger, but his body still had a multitude of involuntary actions to work through as it caught up. Someone— Brooke—was talking to him, her voice low and intense, worried. He didn't get the words, but knew the intent.

Through all the coughing and gagging, he managed to croak out a reply. "—I'm okay."

Eventually regaining control, Tibor managed to take stock of the situation. Whatever had caught him underwater, it left little more than a deep scratch. He now found himself with the others in what seemed to be a narrow, horizontal tunnel of formed cement, its walls slick with mildew and God-knew-what-else. The air here was dank, reeking of stale, tainted water.

"It'll be a miracle if we don't catch something from all this, though," he grumbled.

He felt a gentle tug on his lifeline; Brooke, silently urging him to follow her as they started moving again.

"It's here someplace," Alahni whispered. "Hold on... There!"

Tibor saw Alahni's heat aura begin to rise, reaching up for something he could not make out on thermals. His line tugged again as Brooke moved to follow.

"Going up, Trouble," she muttered.

"Thank Christ!" he hissed. "Don't think my lungs can take much more of this!"

They were following a set of metal rungs that felt cold and rusty to Tibor's hands, ascending through a vertical shaft. Idly, he pondered its function; a sewer line would have a grate of some kind to let fluids, small debris, and light through. But he saw no light above them. Just the thermal images of Brooke and Alahni—all legs and butts, covered in soaking wet clothes.

And that was the moment some embarrassingly primal part of Tibor's brain *really* wished there was some actual damned light in here.

Then he saw a small hand moving about in the distance; Alahni was searching again. He saw her fingers grasping, then heard the sound of metal grinding on metal. The Jardinian grunted, fighting the mechanism with as much strength as she could manage one-handed. More metal on metal. Flecks of something—corroded metals and bits of concrete, perhaps—dropped past, bouncing off his shoulders like a shower of pebbles.

And suddenly, there *was* light—precious little of it, but definitely light!—as Alahni won her battle with the hatch above and shoved it away. A shiver ran through Tibor that could have been caused as much by the chill of fresh air flowing past him as it could the elation of knowing their journey back to the surface was finally near its end.

Either way, he embraced it, and let that sensation power him on for the last few rungs of their climb.

They emerged in a cell-like chamber stinking of age, mildew, and rot—but at least it was relatively free from stagnant water. An ancient LED lamp in the ceiling, its diffuser painted a deep, brownish-yellow by stains likely older than the three of them put together, provided the weak source of light that made anything visible. Tibor saw two old metal hatches on opposite sides of the room.

"Where are we now?" Brooke asked in a low voice.

"Almost there," Alahni told her as she fumbled at the knots to her lifeline. She then reached out for Brooke's end of line and began tugging at its knots for a moment before Brooke seemed to figure out what was happening and began to work with her.

As he finally began to undo his own knots, Tibor felt the line go slack. Glancing up at Brooke, he cleared his throat loudly when he noticed she'd somehow forgotten to let go of the girl's hand.

If Alahni was at all embarrassed, she hid it well as her attention bounced between the room's two door hatches. Still, it took her a few moments to decide which one to open. After all the twists and turns of their swim through the ancient drainage lines, Tibor had given up trying to figure out which way was north, and he doubted their guide was any better off by this point.

The latch Alahni grabbed was ancient and heavily corroded. She grunted as she tried to force it, the muscles in her arms and back clearly straining through the drenched fabric of her top. Brooke took a step toward her, but Tibor moved more quickly. Together, they managed to break open the rusty seal, but it still took extra effort to force the door itself to open, its hinges loudly protesting as only decaying metal on decaying metal could.

Dim light streaked into the chamber beyond, partially illuminating what looked like a service access no wider than a child's closet. Scattered about the floor, Tibor could just make out bits of ancient, unidentifiable debris, and the decayed remains of what he could only presume were Jardinian vermin.

"Oh, this is promising," he muttered.

Alahni shrugged weakly as she stepped into the passage. Tibor followed, leaving Brooke behind for a change. He could almost feel her glare on the back of his head.

"I think this is an old service line," Alahni whispered as they walked into a narrow corridor of ancient pipes and power conduits, all badly corroded, bent by age, and covered in dead roots and other decay. "It runs parallel to the old city water mains, under what is now the Overseers' Quarter. Some of the lines here are still active, used for city communications, residential power and such, but the main power grid, the one the factories, administration centers, and hospital facilities use, is completely separate and better maintained."

"Fusion?" Tibor asked.

"No," Alahni said. "Geothermal. Hope stands near the outskirts of a truly large volcanic zone. It's mostly stable, but a lot of the land north and east of the city is covered in active geysers and hot springs. The early settlers decided to draw power from the subterranean magma chambers, and it's been that way since. Hope was reinforced in the early days of the Star League, and was one of the few cities left in this valley area when the others were abandoned during the Fall. The rest were in the eastern side of the zone, where the Menehune now rule."

"The Menehune?" Brooke asked. "Another Wayward Tribe?"

"No," Alahni told her with only a glance backward. In the near-complete darkness of the corridor, Tibor noticed, she was carefully guiding herself forward by lightly dragging her fingertips along the corridor's walls. "The Menehune aren't people. Just truly smart creatures who live on this world. Tricky little monkey-cats, you might say."

"Sounds cute," Brooke said.

"Interesting that we never saw any of those around here," Tibor said.

"Not precisely," Alahni said. "Most see them as pests these days, especially in Hope. Even Wayward hunters usually shoot them on sight, so they've learned to stay far from humans."

Suddenly, Alahni stopped and let out a huge sigh. In the minuscule light, Tibor almost couldn't see why, even as he peeked over her shoulder. Then he noticed the jagged darkness that turned the entire path ahead into pitch black.

"What is it?" Brooke asked.

"Cave in," he told her.

"Have I mentioned lately I haven't been here since I was fifteen?" Alahni muttered to no one in particular. She then excused herself as she squeezed past Tibor and Brooke so she could lead them back the other way...

LEOPARD-CLASS DROPSHIP *KAYLIN*
PIRATE JUMP POINT
JARDINE (HERAKLEION) SYSTEM
FREE WORLDS LEAGUE

Jacoby was once again the man at the sensor console when the signal came in. A veteran of countless missions with Anton Hara, he knew his job well, and flew through the verification procedures without any unnecessary prompting. So, when he finally did turn his attention back to the captain, there was no question of what his nod meant.

Brooklyn Stevens' shuttlecraft, the *Magellan*, had just boosted from the atmosphere of Herakleion.

No, Hara reminded himself. *Not "Herakleion." Jardine!*

With its emergence came a desperate, somewhat broken, audio-only transmission from Stevens herself, requesting telemetry for the return flight. It was everything they'd been hoping for—although it *was* odd that the *Sacajawea* remained silent.

Hara had asked Jacoby to double-check the back logs, just to be sure. After all, given the sheer distances involved, it was at least vaguely possible for the *Sac*'s reply to have reached them at the same instant they picked up Stevens' initial plea.

But there had been nothing Jacoby could detect on any of the frequencies IE or Stevens had been known to use.

Meanwhile, Hara knew Stevens' shuttle had only so much fuel capacity for its return trip, especially if things were as desperate as the good doctor sounded. So, she couldn't just idle in orbit and wait for her JumpShip to acknowledge. She'd have to have boosted for deeper space, starting with a best guess on her out-system course to start with—something to refine when the *Sac* responded. For her jump skipper to maintain EMCON even now made little sense.

Could they have simply missed the call, or were they just *that* paranoid?

In either case, Hara made his decision with a simple nod to Jacoby. With a single finger tap on the man's console, a pre-recorded signal went out in a condensed, electronic burst—one that, Hara hoped, would light up whatever receivers in the solar system were even casually turned their way, from the *Sacajawea* to Jardine itself.

Settling back in his seat, Hara steepled his fingers and stared into the emptiness of space for a few silent moments.

"Jump charge?" he requested at last.

Jacoby checked his instruments. "Twenty-four-point-three percent."

Hara closed his eyes and did the rough calculations, rounding for simplicity. When he opened them again, he turned to his exec.

Lenard Bryce, for his part, was leaned forward in his chair, assuming the classic "Thinker's pose," complete with one hand supporting his chin. With only the barest of turns, the dark-skinned officer met his captain's stare, and arched an eyebrow.

"I come up with about thirty-six hours," Hara told him. "Half, if we redline it."

Bryce nodded, confirming the estimates. "But do we really want to push the redline?"

"Knowing Bellamy, he'd want the jump skipper to go past even that, but it gives us a window."

"Alright," Bryce sighed at the mention of IE's liaison, and pushed back in his seat. "Jacoby, give us two clocks. Eighteen hundred and thirty-six hundred."

"Aye," Jacoby responded. Swiveling his chair back around, he turned his attention to one of the substations beside his main console. On its attendant screen, two digital stopwatches popped up and began counting down. The first, in glowing yellow, began its count at *36:00:00*, while the second started at *18:00:00* in searing red.

The same readouts appeared on multiple displays throughout the *Kaylin*'s bridge, including the small flip-down monitor anchored above the navigation table near the chamber's heart. Moments later, a chime accompanied text alerts flashing on both Hara's and Bryce's armchair displays.

Neither man needed to review the alerts. At this stage, acknowledgment from the skipper of their *Scout*-class JumpShip, *Broken Knee*, was little more than a formality.

"Speaking of Bellamy," Bryce said, "should we let him know yet?"

"He'll figure it out soon enough," Hara replied. "Either way, the decision's out of our hands right now."

"And what about the *Sac?*"

Hara stared blankly into the space beyond the *Kaylin*'s thick, armored windows. Somewhere out there hung Stevens' JumpShip—due for a rude surprise in about twenty minutes or so. "Fortunately for them, that decision's even out of Bellamy's hands now. Shooting up Jumpers is bad business, anyway."

UNION-CLASS DROPSHIP *HERA'S SHIELD*
HIGH ORBIT
JARDINE (HERAKLEION)
FREE WORLDS LEAGUE

"Doctor Stevens, this is DropShip Kaylin. We and Sacajawea have received your message and are sending telemetry now. We are on station and able to scramble for advance intercept at your request. Please advise."

Poltergeist Precentor Sigma Damien Lucille was still fascinated, in spite of himself, as the playback concluded for a second time. Although he was still awaiting confirmation from passive listening buoys spread across the system's asteroid belts, the preliminary data and the telemetry included with the audio-datapack message looked authentic. The sender—this DropShip *Kaylin*—was apparently floating eighteen AUs out-system, and perhaps only ten to twelve degrees above the solar plane.

As pirate points go, it wasn't really the kind of choice for a quick raid or even a full-on assault mission, but the position and distance was sufficient for the incoming jump pulse to escape easy detection. In that respect, it was kind of clever. But it also meant the intruders who came here likely had to coast for more than two weeks on their inbound flight, as much to conserve fuel for a return trip as to keep up their stealthy approach.

Of course, that didn't exactly work out so well for them, did it?

But what truly amazed Lucille was that *Kaylin* identified as a *Drop*Ship. If Stevens had a DropShip at her disposal, why did she take the riskier option of a shuttle? The difference in ship sizes and thrust plumes would not have lowered their detection profile enough to offset the relative security of a vessel with greater armor, fuel stores, and onboard support. The intruders had been nearly obliterated by the drones on approach, for Blake's sake; a DropShip would have been able to either weather that storm and land or immediately burn away for the safety of its crew at a fraction of the risk.

Perhaps the DropShip was used as a midway point, giving her a boost in velocity before launch and acting as a rendezvous point or fast reaction option just in case? That was possible, Lucille admitted, but if so, what was it doing transmitting from eighteen Units away, rather than holding station much closer to the planet, to better support its landing teams? If anything went wrong in planetary orbit, a distance so far away would put any type of rescue over a week away at best.

And if the telemetry matched what Lucille was beginning to suspect, that meant...

Lucille turned to the *Hera's Shield*'s comm officer, a short, pale-skinned, black-haired Acolyte who had yet to earn his first augmentations. The crewman responded to Lucille's attention with an arched eyebrow.

"Acknowledge that signal with text only," Lucille told him. "And give me a direct line to Precentor Apollyon. Our targets have multiplied."

BENEATH THE CITY OF HOPE
JARDINE (HERAKLEION)
FREE WORLDS LEAGUE

Brooke sensed they had doubled back at least one more time before taking the route they were now following. Although there were dim lights working here and there—powered, she presumed, by some bit of long-forgotten wiring still somehow connected to the city grid—most of this time was spent in darkness so complete even Tibor's thermal vision was barely useful. And so, they had all banged into, tripped over, or brushed against more mysterious obstructions than she cared to count.

Because of all this, Brooke knew they had entered a new area at last when they found themselves in a passage where the walls and floors of jutting debris became suddenly, conspicuously clear. Her hands—stretched out cautiously to either side—quickly discovered smooth surfaces, which her fingers lightly explored further. She felt seams, and differences in material from cool metal to dull plastics. In her mind, she pictured storage crates, stacked neatly along the walls.

"Supplies?" she asked in a whisper.

Ahead, she felt Alahni pause for a moment, perhaps long enough to discover the stacks for herself. When the younger woman finally answered, it came after what sounded like a small sigh of relief.

"Yes," she said in a low voice. "A secret stash, you could probably say. Even before there were Waywards, our ancestors stored food, medicines, equipment, and even some weapons down here. Things the Guardians preferred to ration otherwise. Some of these were found, but others were used by Waywards. Entire tribes were born, or survived, thanks to these caches. But when the Guardians began building strength about ten years ago, it was said that they rooted out most of what remained."

"Looks like they missed one," Tibor quipped from the shadows behind Brooke.

"No," Alahni said. "This one's newer. This means we're close. Come along."

Blindly, they continued further, following the wall of crates mostly by touch. Until, with little more than a *thump* and a muffled grunt, Brooke heard Alahni come to a hard stop.

But before she could say anything to the girl, she heard the scrape of what sounded like a metal latch being worked. Moments later, a seam of feeble light appeared, widening to reveal a passageway that cast an eerie glow through what Brooke could now see was a narrow corridor lined with floor-to-ceiling stacks of assorted containers. Ahead, Alahni's silhouette peeked through the opening, and something approaching a smile appeared on what little of her face reflected the light.

"This is it," the Jardinian whispered. "Keep silent."

They entered what appeared to be little more than a storage closet smelling of dust and mildew. An ancient but clearly abandoned sink was anchored to one wall by rusting fixtures, its control knobs and faucet removed, leaving behind only a basin of stained enamel now good for nothing more than a place where old rags and other debris accumulated. Metal shelves, built along the wall opposite the door they'd come through, buckled with the weight of cleaning supplies and other random junk so faded and dust-covered their purpose could only be guessed at on a quick glance. The light in the room came from an old, uncovered fixture in the center of a cracked and flaking ceiling.

Looking back at the door, Brooke noticed it was set behind a break in the wall's normal contour, and was painted and stained to match the rest of the scenery when closed. Cracks she could make out along the surrounding wall suggested the secret passage had probably been made using crude tools, but she imagined the result was good enough to fool a quick inspection.

Alahni headed toward the other door in the room, a heavy metal hatch that looked dented and corroded, and lacked any obvious handle or features beyond a panel of blackened glass. The young woman hesitated for a few seconds, her head turned just enough for Brooke to see her closed eyes and pensive expression. Her lips moved silently for a moment, when suddenly, whatever it was she was trying to recall must have come through. Nodding once, she glanced back at Brooke and Tibor with the shadow of a smile before finally confronting the hatch with her full attention.

It was easy enough for Brooke to guess the strange, irregular rhythm Alahni used when she rapped on the age-worn metal was some kind of code knock. But if it came from any kind of song or cadence, it wasn't any she had learned or heard before. She glanced back at Tibor and was met with little more than a blank expression and a weary shrug.

In fact, under this light, he looked gaunt and sickly. His clothes hung awkwardly on his frame, clinging in some places, and drooping in others. His short, dark hair looked equally soaked and disheveled. But it was the play of shadows on his wiry physique, combined with the sallowness of his ever-pale skin, that made him look only slightly better than a reanimated corpse.

All the same, Brooke imagined she would probably say the same about her own appearance right now, had there been a mirror around to confirm it.

Alahni repeated her knock twice more over the next five minutes, and was midway into her third repetition when the blackened glass panel suddenly snapped open, and a pair of dark eyes flashed their intense gaze at her and the others.

"*E imi i ka malamalama,*" Alahni said to the eyes.

"*Ka malamalama imi oe,*" a gruff, masculine voice answered.

With those words, the panel snapped shut and a series of loud clanks sounded from the other side of the hatch. The door opened to another room shrouded in shadow—but not nearly so darkened that Brooke failed to notice the three rifle muzzles leveled in her direction.

Nor did she miss the broadsword insignia of the Word of Blake on the tunic of one of the weapons' holders.

As Alahni did before her, Brooke raised her hands slowly. From behind, Tibor let out a low, frustrated groan.

"Who are you?" a deep voice growled from the darkness. "Why have you come here?"

"I am Alahni," Alahni said with no trace of hesitation or fear, "of the Shrouded Forest. We've come for help."

"And *them*?"

"Friends. From far away."

"Step through the door," the man said as the three rifles moved back, deeper into the shadows. "Slowly."

Alahni never lowered her hands, but made a gesture with one for the others to follow her as she walked through the hatch and moved slightly to the left. As Brooke joined her, she noticed they were in another storage room of some kind, albeit one that currently stored very little beyond its current occupants.

Like the last room, it smelled of dust and neglect, and felt as cool and damp as an abandoned basement.

As her eyes quickly adjusted to the weak lighting, Brooke took stock of the rifle-holders. Of the three who greeted them, two were young men whose complexions and facial structures, like Alahni's, suggested their descent from Terrans of the Pacific Islands. The third was a girl—younger even than Alahni—whose skin was lighter and whose features were much more Asian. Another armed woman stood by the far door, her weapon also raised and ready. All four wore loose, open jackets over what seemed to be simple coveralls, but only one displayed any kind of insignia, in the form of the Word of Blake broadsword, set upon a green disc on the left side of his jacket front.

The man wearing that symbol stood nearest to Brooke right now, squinting as he studied them. "They look foreign."

"They are Lost," Alahni admitted.

"*Tabi* shit!" the other man snapped, hovering dangerously close to Tibor. "This one has a false eye! This has to be a Guardian trick!"

"Jerome Blake was Satan incarnate!" Tibor snarled before anyone else could answer.

In a flash, the second man swung his rifle around until the blackened carbon steel of its butt smashed into Tibor's face. The blow sent him tumbling back onto the hard, musty concrete with an agonized grunt. Instinctively, Brooke moved toward his attacker, only to find two guns in her face, their owners one twitch away from firing.

"*No!*" Alahni cried out.

Tibor's assailant stood over him now, his weapon trained on the fallen man's head as he hissed, "Filthy savage! Never take the name of the Blessed Blake in vain! *Never!*"

With one hand covering half of his battered face, Tibor fixed him with a defiant glare. "For a man who seemed worried about whether or not I'm a Guardian," he growled, "you certainly seem eager to do their dirty work for them."

The man sneered at him for just a few moments longer before the words registered. Within the blink of an eye, his tension bled away, and the faintest approximation of a smile appeared on his face. "Heh," he grunted. "You have a point there, little barbarian!"

Leaning back a bit, the man lowered his weapon, and twisted to offer Tibor his free hand. Tibor hesitated at first, but finally accepted the help in getting back to his feet. At the same time, Brooke noticed the other Jardinians were relaxing as well. The rifles in front of her moved back and away, and she saw the man with the Blakist insignia now wore a lopsided grin as he once again ran his gaze over her and Tibor both.

"So," he said at last. "You are the invaders Apollyon and his soldiers turned the woods upside down for, are you? You don't look like much to me."

"Thanks," Brooke muttered back as she slowly—and, to her annoyance, somewhat painfully—lowered her hands.

"I'm Uku," the man explained. "Tech Overseer Epsilon. I should probably tell you that coming to the city was foolish—" his eyes settled on Alahni, "—for *all* of you. Ogima has already sent out orders calling for any who see your like to report you to the Guardians immediately. You're fortunate my friends and I here put little stock in Ogima's demands these days."

"Well, thanks again," Tibor dryly said.

Uku's glare immediately speared him. "You can thank us by leaving, Housespawn!" he snapped. "Your being here is disruptive enough. Just because we chose not to end your lives doesn't mean we wish to risk ours to help you with whatever treachery you came to do."

"We're not spies or House agents," Brooke said. "We're just explorers. We didn't come here with treachery of any sort in mind. We just need to get aboard one of the Blakist DropShips, and—"

"Are you deaf?" the other Jardinian man snarled. "Uku just said we will *not* help you!"

"Please, Uku," Alahni said, her voice soft and pleading. "These people are not our enemies—"

"They are *Lost*," Uku reminded her. "Off-worlders. They and their kind have never been friends to us. Maybe they don't look as monstrous as those machine-men *things* the Guardians have made, but at least the Domini *protect* us."

Alahni stood her ground. "The Guardians 'saved' our world by keeping us prisoner upon it, Uku," she said. "And the Domini were made to keep it that way."

"That was the price for our salvation, little one. Even a Wayward should know this. Barbarians like these two destroyed the Inner Sphere in their lust for power. And now that the wretched Clans have come to finish them off, they look for the last havens we have left—!"

"The people you call barbarians have hardly destroyed the entire Inner Sphere," Brooke interrupted, resisting the impulse to flinch when Uku's eyes and rifle turned her way again. "Yes, there were wars, and yes, many worlds were lost in the process, much as we thought yours was, but hundreds of worlds still thrive, and the Houses still stand. They even restored the Star League to oppose the Clans, defeating them on their own home worlds. This Wayward knows this, so I'm certain you do, as well.

"In the meantime, your Guardians—the Word of Blake— contributed *nothing* to that effort. They've been keeping you from the universe, and making these cyborg monsters of theirs, for wars that are already over. Why do you imagine that is? What possible good can come from this?"

"Deceptions," hissed the other male.

"My companion and I are living proof," Brooke said without looking away from Uku. "We had wars, and some were pretty savage, but more worlds survived than died in them. And when the Word broke from ComStar, we soon learned some of our troubles were sparked by the very people who faked your planet's death in the name of this 'protection' you now enjoy."

"The new Star League you talk about is a sham," Uku said. "Yes, we've heard of it. We know your Houses still stand, and of their desperate alliance to stop the Clans, led by House Lords terrified of Kerensky's vengeance. We also know it didn't end the fighting between them. But true peace, they say, is coming, with the Great Promise..."

"A 'Great Promise?'" Brooke echoed. "Can you hear yourself, Uku? A part of you—all of you—*knows* there's something wrong here, or you'd have shot us already, or turned us over to these Domini of yours. You know the Houses still live, and that they effectively united to defeat a common enemy, but you call it a sham and a lie when *we* say it. You talk about true peace coming with this 'Promise,' while your Guardians make an army of monster soldiers out of whom? Your own people? Where do you think such things fit in with this vision of true peace?"

"Meanwhile," Tibor added, briefly capturing Uku's attention, "they've started using the Waywards for target practice."

In the corner of her eye, Brooke saw Alahni wince at those words. Uku turned to the young woman with questioning eyes.

Her nod was shaky, reluctant, and her voice dropped to a near whisper. "They sent Domini soldiers and BattleMechs into the woods," she said, "to kill us all. There was no call for surrender. No warning at all. They just started shooting..."

"They... They killed *everyone*?" Uku asked, his face growing pale.

Alahni was fighting tears, but she still met his gaze and nodded grimly. "As far as we know now," she said, "I'm all that's left of the Shrouded Forest."

"Just to get at these Lost...?" one of the Jardinian women asked, incredulously.

"They didn't say *anything* about the Lost," Alahni told her. "I heard no demand that we turn them over. I'm not sure they even knew whether or not we'd seen them. Likeke, our tribe leader, sent me out of the camp with these two before the Domini got close. He stayed behind. We saw dead hunters as we came this way..."

"There would have been children there... They even killed the children?"

Alahni looked helpless. Brooke reached out to put a comforting hand on her shoulder.

"I went back," she told Uku, but her gaze eventually settled on the poor young tale-keeper. "They left a 'Mech down in the field when it hit a mine, didn't even try to recover it on their way to the camp. I had some experience with 'Mechs, so I took it, and tried to stop them. I tried so hard... But there were too many, and I was too late... I saw no survivors. I'm so sorry, Alahni."

Alahni didn't—and, perhaps, *couldn't*—look at Brooke. With tears still pooling in her eyes, she spoke to Uku instead. "They didn't do anything to us," she said. "All they want to do now is leave."

For a long time, Uku was silent, but Brooke could sense a tremble in his expression even in the dim lighting. He lowered his rifle entirely, allowing it to hang limp at his side, while his comrades turned uneasy glances his way. Brooke felt a fleeting, survivalist's urge to take advantage of the tactical situation and seize the man's weapon, but she held herself back.

Uku's gaze fell to the floor. "We knew the Guardians were clashing with the Waywards since they put down the Malu," he said. "But after that, Apollyon promised they would never make war on a tribe again. He swore to Ogima they would only fight if provoked..."

"Seems to me your Destroyer had a change of heart," Tibor grumbled, earning himself another savage glare from the man looming near him.

"If that's true, Uku," the other man said, "maybe we *should* take them to the Guardians?"

Uku put his hand on the other man's shoulder, and it looked to Brooke as if that act alone bled out all the tension left in the darkened room. "No," he said. "Stand down, Lani. Everyone, stand down."

Slowly, the other Jardinians—including the one named Lani—lowered their rifles. With a dismissive gesture, Uku ushered his people toward the far door. Only after they were out of earshot did he turn his focus fully toward Brooke.

"Understand this, Lost One," he said. "Your words would have meant nothing to me if this Wayward sister hadn't backed you up. We know the monsters the Guardians have made here. We have witnessed their creation, and the rise of their master, and we know why they have come. We know how and why we were hidden from your kind for generations. It was *your* ancestors— the Great Houses who destroyed the Star League—who made all of this necessary, and I feel no sympathy for you, even now."

"Oh, don't hold back," Tibor scoffed. "Tell us how you *really* feel."

"Trouble!" Brooke growled at him.

Uku's free hand clenched and relaxed as his eyes shot daggers at Tibor. "What I *really* feel," he hissed, "isn't your concern, Housespawn scum. But what I'm *not* feeling right now is any particular desire to kill for the Domini. So, if you want to commit your suicide on one of their DropShips, I'll oblige you. A *Merlin* is preparing for liftoff as we speak, taking on supplies in the underground bays for some kind of support mission or other. I can slip you on board in a crate if you do exactly as I say and keep your filthy mouths shut. But after that, you off-worlders are on your own."

Brooke nodded stoically. "Fair enough," she said. Sensing Alahni's gaze, she turned to the young Wayward and offered her a brief smile that she hoped was reassuring somehow. "I suppose this is it, Alahni. It only gets more dangerous from here. But one way or the other, once Trouble and I hit space, we won't be coming back."

Alahni, her eyes strangely unreadable, stared at Brooke for a long, uncomfortable moment, and nodded.

CHAPTER 7

My Dearest Tyler,

I know we've had this discussion before. I know where you stand, and I know why you stand there. Truth be told, if our positions were reversed, I'd probably be every bit as upset with you as you get with me. The risks we take out here, no matter why we take them, can get pretty insane. So the fact that we do them for trinkets and historical footnotes the rest of mankind has forgotten about makes it all the more questionable. Perhaps as questionable as any other mercenary job, really.

But, of course, if I hadn't chosen this line of work, we'd probably never have met in the first place. You have to give me that, at least!

With that said, I think I must finally admit that there are limits, even for me. I've seen savage locals, noble intrigue, and beasts of all sizes scarier than the works of humanity's greatest horror writers. I've visited worlds and shipwrecks from the Axumite Providence to the Outworlds Wastes. I've been sued, shot, stabbed, assaulted, arrested, poisoned, plagued, and propositioned more times than I care to remember.

But after Jardine, I don't think I can do this anymore.

There's just a point where the thrill of discovery pales in comparison to its costs, and after what I saw here... Well, maybe it's just time I listened to you for a change.

Just promise me you won't gloat too much about it when I get home, alright?

—FROM THE JOURNALS OF BROOKLYN STEVENS

LEOPARD-CLASS DROPSHIP *KAYLIN*
PIRATE JUMP POINT
JARDINE (HERAKLEION) SYSTEM
FREE WORLDS LEAGUE
7 NOVEMBER 3067

Maybe it was the short distance, or the uncommon, mid-system destination they'd plotted, but something about this last jump felt even more disturbing than usual to Captain Anton Hara. He felt a strange vibration to the air, in his nerves, or both. Sounds and silence echoed and reverberated through his consciousness, and ghosts of the people around him blurred ahead of their every move. Even his mind felt like it was out of synch, processing past, present, and future at different and overlapping rates. It was both just like, and a distortion of, the sensation of déjà vu he normally experienced only in his dreams.

Though it felt much longer this time, the experience truly took only one or two seconds to subside.

As usual, Hara felt himself return to normal space with all his muscles locked up, and his jaw aching, but aside from the psychedelic strangeness of this leap, everything appeared normal when his eyes, ears, and other senses finally caught up. Slowly, he relaxed himself, slowing his breathing and reclaiming his faculties by sheer force of will. He briefly closed his eyes again while the soothing sounds of his ship's bridge systems filtered through the last of his jump-induced haze.

An unexpected gasp for breath snapped Hara out of this inward focus. Turning toward the source of the sound, he found his exec, Lenard Bryce, gripping his own console so tightly his knuckles appeared stark white. Bryce's face was twisted in a way that suggested pain at first, but as he drew in another breath, Hara recognized it was more like shock. The black-haired, dark-skinned, and bespectacled officer wrestled with this state for only a few more seconds before he finally shook his head with purpose and reclaimed his normal, self-commanding composure.

Glancing suddenly to Hara, Bryce let out a heavy sigh filled with relief, and his lips formed a thin, sheepish smile. Hara nodded reassuringly to him; the jump clearly affected them both in much the same way.

Bryce turned back to his displays. "Jump complete," he croaked. "Showing us seven-point-one-eight units further in-system, position-aligned with target's last-known trajectory."

"Good," Hara said with a crisp nod. "JumpShip status?"

"No report yet," Jacoby called out from the sensor station. His voice was calm and firm; if the jump had affected him any differently than usual, it certainly wasn't showing now. "But umbilical power and data feeds show green and stable."

"They're fine, then," Hara declared. "Their skipper knows we have a four-day window now. They're probably resetting the reactor feed to the drive."

"Assuming nothing blew out from the last quick-charge," Bryce cautioned.

"We'd know by now, I think," Hara told him. "I'm more worried about Stevens' crew pulling the same stunt, and why they didn't do it already after we gave away their position."

Bryce merely shrugged. For the last several hours leading up to their mid-system jump, he and Hara spent much of their time debating possible reasons for the *Sacajawea*'s apparent lack of any reaction at all to recent events. Even when *Kaylin* broadcast a message and telemetry to Stevens' shuttlecraft, revealing both of their JumpShips' presence together for anyone to hear, they picked up nothing from the rogue *Explorer*.

In Hara's mind, there was no way the *Sac* couldn't have built up a full jump charge by now, especially not after having a two-week head start over *Kaylin*'s JumpShip. Yet they just... sat there. It made no immediate sense to him, and Bryce had few ideas to offer. Perhaps their KF drive was damaged during the attack back at Shasta? If so, they requested no help when they saw the *Kaylin* and her JumpShip arrive. Well, they *did* have little reason to trust them, but at the risk of simply stranding themselves in hostile territory? And not even talking to their own mission leader? What could that have been about? Did they really think Stevens could make a fifteen-AU journey in a shuttlecraft with a hostile DropShip on her tail?

Whatever was going on with the *Sac*, though, it didn't seem to faze the liaison officer IE assigned to Hara. Nathan Bellamy insisted there was no point puzzling out the inscrutable when the real prize was busy racing across the solar system. Pointing out—and rightly so, much to Hara's eternal disgust—that any hope of rescue now hinged on them jumping ahead with painfully narrow transit and recharge windows, in hopes of catching the good doctor before her friends could try and do the same. And since there was little practicality in simply obliterating the *Sacajawea* to take them out of the equation (as Hara explained to him just before the jump), Bellamy decided their open-channel broadcast was enough to give those ex-IE runaways pause while the *Kaylin* claimed the best intercept point first.

Thus began a race that, maddeningly enough, the *Sac* did not seem to even care about, and so Hara and Bryce alike were left on their bridge, trying to imagine what they might have missed.

Meanwhile, somewhere out there, on a course that should take her straight to them, was a shuttlecraft carrying one Doctor Brooklyn Stevens, and whatever evidence she had to prove this system truly was home to the lost world of Jardine.

**EXPLORER-CLASS JUMPSHIP *SACAJAWEA*
PIRATE JUMP POINT
JARDINE (HERAKLEION) SYSTEM
FREE WORLDS LEAGUE**

"—And there they go," Gretchen Morden said as an indicator flashed on the sensor board before her. The electromagnetic pulse from the JumpShip carrying IE's other mercenaries washed over them just a few moments ago, but the infrared surge had been picked up a few seconds earlier—the telltale signs of a hyperspace jump.

"I thought they'd never leave," Lawrence Pohl dryly replied. Seated as he was at his regular command chair, he caught

Gretchen's sidelong smirk only in profile before turning to the only other occupant in the *Sacajawea*'s command center at the moment.

Juan Lafferty was only half-seated at the jump station, dividing his attention between two displays filled with scrolling data. A few indicators on his panel flashed in lights of cool green. But for all those distractions, the man immediately sensed his captain's attention and looked up.

"Well, Cap," Juan said with a crooked smile, "No pulse close by, so I guess you win this round."

"You're the one who picked the long odds," Lawrence told him. "Hara and his crew might have gone for Crazy Jane-ing us, and getting some digs in, but he's no jump skipper, and I doubt that blood limpet, Bellamy, would risk his own hide that way even if he was."

"Never bet against good old-fashioned IE spinelessness, eh?" Juan asked.

"Maybe they just ran, then," Gretchen suggested. Swiveling her chair enough to face them both, she favored Juan with a wink and a smile fueled by the knowledge that *her* bet was still in play. "What with all the radio chatter and other signs we've seen here, they have to know we've found their Atlantis by now—if not something just as juicy. They could just as easily toddle off to Croft and the others, claim mission accomplished, and write us off."

"Oh, sure," Lawrence agreed, "but I'm sticking with my theory. They moved in-system; they want Brooke."

"Wish I could see the look on Hara's face when he finds out it's not her," Juan said.

"After blurting our position to those guys on open channels, he deserves it," Gretchen said. "I just hope they were smart enough to give themselves some escape time."

"Which brings us back to us," Lawrence said. "Juan?"

Juan glanced at his panels again before returning his attention to Lawrence and nodding. "Calcs are done, and the window's open. It's close, though; we're not leaving ourselves a lot of time if they have ships that can pull more than three gees."

"I don't think we can afford to push the drive too hard with the quick charge this time," Lawrence said. "We still have some minor damage from that freak show that boarded us, after all. Five days is our best."

"Then, we're ready on this end, Cap."

"Gretch?"

"Nothing since Trouble's last ping," Gretchen said.

"Then pray for them and for us," Lawrence said as he pushed himself back in his chair and reached for its straps. "Juan, start jump procedures."

As his crew settled in and got busy, Lawrence closed his eyes and drew in a deep breath, wishing he was as confident about all of this as he tried to sound. There were at least a hundred ways he could think of that this could all end badly. He knew it, and so did they.

But sooner or later, everyone had to take a chance and just throw the damned dice...

MERLIN-CLASS DROPSHIP *AGRAVAIN*
HIGH ORBIT
JARDINE (HERAKLEION)
FREE WORLDS LEAGUE

"Captain on the bridge!"

Adept Petra Inagi, captain of the *Agravain*, had barely stepped onto the bridge when she heard an alarm sound from the sensor station. The crewman already seated there, Acolyte Ru Yuen, an olive-skinned Jardine native with black hair and eyes, immediately turned his fleeting attention away from Inagi to inspect the readings on his displays.

Inagi met her first officer's gaze and arched an eyebrow. Adept Jakab Lantos, a pale-faced, green-eyed man with short, brown hair and a goatee, stood at ease beside the captain's chair, and shrugged. Whatever was going on right now, it was also news to him.

"Jump pulse, Captain," Yuen said after a moment. "Three AUs out, by the look of it."

Inagi made it to her chair, but instead of claiming the seat, she took an extra step forward and engaged the small holotank occupying the nearby tactical station.

Instantly, a map of the immediate vicinity flashed up, projecting Jardine—and the arc of its orbital path—in the center, with the *Agravain*'s position as a speck of white slowly circling the planet well beyond the exosphere. Dialing out the zoom, Inagi widened the view field, past the orbits of Jardine's two moons, until the path of the next-nearest celestial object came into frame. "Position?"

"Getting listening sat data now, sir," Yuen answered. A silent moment passed, when suddenly a series of red, concentric rings appeared on the tactical display, their focus shifting slightly and narrowing swiftly, until they settled on a position... "Approximately four degrees above the solar plane, retrograde of Jardine."

"No IFF signal," Lantos added, as he leaned over the unoccupied communications station. "But no random pirate could make a jump like that."

"Not unless they've been here all along," Inagi added, "quietly mapping the place."

"Precentor Lucille's second JumpShip?"

Inagi nodded and approached the comms station, gesturing for Lantos to take the helm. "I'll call this in," she said. "Take us off auto and get ready to plot a high-V intercept. We'll need to get to her before she can recharge."

Brooke Stevens awoke to the sensation of being carried upward by an elevator run amok. She heard the creaking of metal, the irregular thumping of something heavy, and a dull but persistent rumble that sounded like it came from everywhere. The darkness around her was total, and when she moved, she felt as though she was trapped in a web. Disoriented by her sudden rousing, a panic welled up in the pit of her stomach, and instinct drove her to convulse against her restraints.

Somewhere in the darkness to her side, a feminine voice groaned, then gasped.

"Easy," came a reassuring male voice from just a bit farther away. "We're okay."

"Trouble?" Brooke called into the darkness.

"Good morning, Sunshine," said Tibor Mitternacht. "And may I say again how wonderfully *quiet* you sleep when strapped to a wall?"

Brooke's mind was already clear enough to disperse her initial terror. For three days now, she guessed, they had made their home in an empty crawlspace between the outer and inner hulls of this Blakist ship.

After being smuggled into one of the cargo bays with the final batch of supplies—courtesy of the one or two citizens of Hope Alahni and Uku managed to persuade enough to help— they'd endured the initial burn into orbit within the confines of a single, slotted storage bin. Escaping the bin with the aid of a vibroblade dropped in with them, they pillaged additional survival supplies—mostly rations, weapons, and four bundles of cargo webbing—before Brooke and Tibor managed to find and pry open an access panel both secluded and innocuous enough to let them into the space between decks and hull supports.

It was a time-honored approach favored by smugglers and stowaways since the early days of spaceflight, but Brooke had to admit she'd never snuck into a hull gap nearly as clean and fresh as the one they'd found. Even the insulation pads appeared to be pristine, as they shoved them aside to build their makeshift nest.

"This ship's brand new," Tibor observed when they rigged up the harnesses serving as their safety beds during the long flight. For a day or so—long enough to be sure they weren't detected, they figured—the plan was to remain in silent hiding before deciding on their next steps. In the meantime, they'd eaten little and spoken to one another only in low tones and whispers.

"We're under thrust," Brooke said now, even as she felt the netting tighten around her body. "Hard acceleration."

"They made a reorientation burn a few seconds ago," Tibor said. "A sharp turn, definitely not routine. There was a brief yellow alert sound at the time."

"Think they smell something?"

"If so, it's not us. They'd have us already. And this certainly doesn't feel like the kind of acceleration they'd use for reentry. It feels like maybe two gees. Probably an intercept."

This DropShip—"*Agravain*" according to the Jardinians who slipped them on board—was being deployed on an orbital patrol, a sweep the Blakist Guardians occasionally (if rarely) performed when there was concern of intruders lurking in the system. In addition to scanning the immediate space around Jardine and checking on the various "ancient" satellites serving as the planet's normal, passive-defense network, it would also perform sensor sweeps over Jardine's two small moons, just in case.

While the ship was equipped and supplied with the means to service those satellites—including those that could deploy ancient drone fighters, like the ones that had attacked Brooke and Tibor's shuttlecraft—its primary mission was simple reconnaissance. For that reason, the locals claimed, the crew should be pretty light, perhaps barely more than a half-dozen men and women in all. Admitting the hull design was new to him, Tibor could neither confirm nor deny that advice, but most military DropShips could be flown by only a handful of souls these days, so it seemed a good enough estimate. The crew would be necessarily spread out to various sections, so the main worry would be less about numbers and more about how competent (and how deadly) such crewmen could be in the inevitable close-quarters combat sure to come.

After all, it was one thing to stowaway on a ship one knew was already leaving the system; but sneaking aboard a ship one knew was just going to return a few days or so later necessitated a far more *proactive* strategy.

"Intercepting what, though?" Brooke asked. "I thought they already sent a ship for the *Sac*?"

"Or for Hara," Tibor hastily reminded her.

"Right," Brooke said, recalling the message Tibor received through whatever sorcery Gretchen and Lawrence had rigged up to call him. IE's other mercs apparently managed to find their way to the system well after the *Sacajawea*'s arrival, but maintained radio silence ever since. That was, until *someone* claiming to be Brooke had called out into the void for return telemetry. Then, not only did Hara respond, betraying his own presence to the Blakists, but he also fed them telemetry leading straight back to the *Sac* herself.

Foolish, opportunistic bastard! Brooke thought when she heard the news, but she couldn't be sure if she was thinking of Captain Hara or Nathan Bellamy, the IE liaison who had probably put him up to such a stunt.

Regardless, Tibor received another of Gretchen's "secret messages" at about the same time, asking if Brooke really was asking for telemetry. For whatever reason, it seemed, neither she nor Lawrence believed it entirely. With a "ping" he managed to somehow send back, Tibor confirmed their suspicions, so at least the *Sacajawea* knew the message was false.

But that still left them in the path of the DropShip the Word of Blake already launched—a DropShip that, if the locals could be trusted, possibly included a team of those Manei Domini cyborgs specifically equipped for boarding and capturing operations. Tibor's math assured Brooke there was no way the *Sacajawea* could be in any immediate danger from such a mission. Not yet, anyway—especially since they now had a full drive charge and complete awareness of the Blakist ruse. The *Sac* would be safe, but they were now waiting on a "ping" from Tibor to tell them when they could move to pick up their actual crewmates.

A "ping" Tibor had been sending at semi-regular intervals as best as he could, while hoping the *Agravain*'s hull didn't completely mute him. At this stage, there simply was no way to know one way or the other.

But there was one last concern still lingering on Brooke's mind as she once more tumbled the thoughts of how and when they should move through her head...

Beside her, Alahni moaned again. "Ooooh," she said, groggily, "I think I'm going to be sick again."

Brooke looked in the girl's direction. Even at less than half a meter's distance, she still couldn't make out any of her features in the blackness. Whatever had possessed Alahni to come along, Brooke couldn't be certain, but the part of her that feared for the young Jardinian's safety was glad she came anyway.

In theory, Alahni *could* have stayed behind, *could* have melted into Hope's native populace, or perhaps even sought out another Wayward settlement, where she *might* have been safe from reprisals. But the loss of her tribe—to the very Guardians they'd admired, even as they hid from them—had severed all her connections to the world below. She'd insisted on boarding the DropShip with them, even though it was clear she didn't know a thing about what it would be like to fly into space. Nor did she seem to even consider that they would all need to seize the ship by force if they were to secure any real hope of escape. It occurred to Brooke that Alahni might have learned to use small arms and such to protect herself or hunt with her tribemates in the wilds of Jardine's forests, but could she possibly be ready to fire upon another human being, especially one she'd been raised to see as one of her people's saviors?

"Breathe," Tibor told Alahni. "Don't think about your stomach. Just breathe deep."

"This air still smells like metal," she complained. "And I feel so heavy."

"Yes," Tibor said. "The ship's speeding up."

"Is it always like this?"

"Well, not *always*. But it's common enough."

"Only this time," Brooke added, "we think they may have spotted something, which could be our friends."

"Your JumpShip?" Alahni asked.

"The *Sacajawea*, yes," Brooke said. "I think we're going to have to get out of here and get to work."

"You won't hear me complain," Tibor said. "If this ship's on an intercept alert, they're probably not watching the cargo bays right now. We can slip out, get our bearings. I think I saw a crate marked 'Boarding Ordnance' during our last gear search..."

"*Boarding* ordnance," Brooke repeated. "Probably nothing too destructive."

"Right. I'm imagining smoke bombs, flash-bangs, maybe tear gas. Whatever it is, should make our work a bit easier... maybe."

"What should I do?" Alahna asked, nervously.

"Keep your head down," Tibor told her before Brooke could. "From here, things can turn ugly really fast."

LEOPARD-CLASS DROPSHIP *KAYLIN*
PIRATE JUMP POINT
JARDINE (HERAKLEION) SYSTEM
FREE WORLDS LEAGUE

"Jump pulse confirmed," Bryce reported from the navigation console. "Looks like a pirate point on the solar plane, five days or so trailing the primary."

Hara sat in his command chair and processed this news. In his mind, there was no doubt whatsoever that the pulse came from any ship other than the *Sacajawea*. After spending days just floating out there, seemingly oblivious to the signals shooting back and forth between the outbound shuttlecraft and the *Kaylin*, IE's rogue *Explorer* must have decided to make its move less than an hour after they last saw her.

He felt no surprise that the *Sac*'s crew had merely waited him out, but their destination concerned him. It was nowhere *near* close enough to intercept Stevens' shuttlecraft; in fact, it was entirely in the opposite direction.

What was he missing?

"Have they contacted her yet?" He asked, directing his attention to Jacoby at the communications station.

"I'm not seeing anything," Jacoby said.

"The shuttle's course hasn't changed," Bryce volunteered, "so, my guess is no. That, or she has no choice."

Hara nodded absently, though he remained unconvinced. Whatever modifications Stevens and her people might have made, her shuttle was still based on a standard, old-model, K-1 class craft. That meant it burned at least two tons of reaction mass for every day spent under thrust, and probably couldn't carry much more than thirty tons of fuel in all. Of that reserve, the craft heading toward *Kaylin* had already spent about eight to ten tons Hara could be sure of. Turning about and accelerating to the *Sac*'s new position would force the shuttle to use up almost all its remaining fuel, even on a full tank.

Meanwhile, there was apparently a heavily armed *Union* DropShip lagging behind—a combat vessel with a much greater operational range. Though slower than the shuttle in a short race, it would still eventually run Stevens down even if she held her course. Turning back would only end the chase faster once the DropShip adapted to the course change. And even if they couldn't match the shuttle's new speed for long in passing, a *Union* boasted more than enough firepower to take out a K-1 in a single volley.

These immutable factors gave Stevens few options if she hoped to survive.

But something about it all was still off, and Hara sensed it the moment *Sacajawea*'s jump had registered on their sensors. Could Stevens' crew have truly miscalculated *that* badly? Or was this perhaps an attempt at some kind of diversion, hoping to distract whoever wanted to keep this planet hidden long enough for *Kaylin* to make the pickup? Were they desperate—or merely naïve—enough to entrust their commander's fate to *him*?

...Or did they know something he didn't?

Hara frowned as that thought finally hit him, and his eyes narrowed at the space beyond the *Kaylin*'s forward viewports. "Something's wrong," he said. "Call the launch deck, Len. Tell the techs I want our planes loaded and ready to fly ASAP."

"We lost two during that shootout under Shasta," Bryce cautioned.

"That's why *we're* going with them," Hara said, turning to meet Bryce's gaze.

K-1-CLASS DROPSHUTTLE *STILETTO*-7
OUTWARD INTERCEPT COURSE
JARDINE (HERAKLEION)
FREE WORLDS LEAGUE

"Flash from *Shield*: Target is separating from its Jumper."

Precentor Damien Lucille nodded gravely to the square-jawed woman seated beside him. Adept Talia Rumiko wore her raven hair in a queue that sprang from the top center of her head and split just above the circular interface jack mounted at the lower backside of her skull. From there, twin braids curved forward over her taut shoulders and ended just below her collarbone. The rest of her tanned scalp was shaved bare, exposing the thin scars along her temples that hinted at the procedures used to enhance her hearing and vision.

Her all-black eyes, set in almond-shaped lids that never blinked, met Lucille's for just a moment before returning to their instruments. Lucille did the same, noting the data now scrolling onto his navigational displays.

"About time," he said. "Coming to 'rescue' us before we run out of fuel. We'll give it a few more hours before 'Doctor Stevens' asks for a sitrep. For now, let's push the engines a bit."

"Understood. Any idea what that other Jumper's doing?"

Lucille scowled. The news of the JumpShip arrival closer to Jardine had come in hours before. It was an unwelcome confirmation of his suspicion about just how many ships now lurked in-system, but there was no way to go back now; their course was locked. And it didn't really change his mission all that much, anyway. *All* invaders to this system would need to be dealt with, no matter who they were and what games they were playing.

But what truly bothered Lucille now was the dark certainty he'd never get the chance to kill that Stevens Frail personally. Once again, the universe seemed to deny him his chance for redemption.

That this DropShip ahead of him, *Kaylin*, was now moving to speed up their rendezvous could have something to do with the other JumpShip, or it couldn't. Either way, it was now his primary target, and its JumpShip was the immediate secondary. Like the second vessel, it also had just executed an in-system jump deeper from wherever it had lurked, which meant its crew was now desperately recharging its drives directly from its fusion plants—if they were smart. That gave Lucille's team perhaps four days, at best, to splash both of the ships ahead of them to the uncaring void.

That *other* JumpShip—probably Stevens' *Sacajawea*—had effectively become someone else's problem.

"Whatever that's about," he finally told Rumiko, "Precentor Apollyon will see to *them*. Our targets lie ahead of us."

Rumiko nodded, this time acknowledging his words without glancing away from her boards. Her hand reached out for the thrust controls and paused there. Lucille switched open the tactical intercom linking both his shuttle crew and that of the *Hera's Shield* behind them.

"Manei Domini!" he declared. "The enemies of the Promise lie ahead, and our time grows short! But the legacy of Blessed Blake is with us, and we shall not allow them to escape! Brace for acceleration!"

MERLIN-CLASS DROPSHIP *AGRAVAIN*
RETROGRADE INTERCEPT COURSE
JARDINE (HERAKLEION) SYSTEM
FREE WORLDS LEAGUE

Agravain's main engineering chamber was so factory-fresh, one could still smell the paint, polish, and metalwork. Brightly lit, and efficiently laid out, its main deck encircled the bulkheads protecting the ship's fusion reactor housing. The deck grating was finer than the old Succession Wars standards, designed for comfortable travel whether one was wearing magnetic engineer's boots or simple slippers. The computer panels and keyboards were clean and shone with equal intensity. Fire suppression kits and tool lockers—all with crisp, new paint—lined the outer bulkheads, fully stocked and well secured. All of it was a marvel of engineering and ergonomics, brought to life by the fine folks at Brigadier Corporation of Gibson.

Three crewmen in spotless, light-gray coveralls were on duty at the moment, strapped into their station seats and monitoring their systems while idly chatting with each other in soft voices. Even with the DropShip pouring out a constant acceleration slightly past one-gee, the chamber was oddly serene. The sound baffles lining the under-floor kept the roar of the engines to a dull hum that practically harmonized with the soft buzz the reactor constantly gave off, if only to remind the crew that, yes, it was still active.

And so it was, in that well-lit, library-calm chamber—until a side hatch, reserved for outer structure maintenance purposes only—suddenly unlatched and swung inward, startling all three of its occupants. Slapping their restraint releases, two of them were nearly out of their seats when a pair of small, green, cylindrical canisters clanged onto the floor nearby, and exploded.

In seconds, the clouds of noxious vapor and smoke engulfed them, racing to fill the entire chamber.

The two standing engineers gasped and choked on the gas, struggling to keep their feet, while the third one fell into a coughing fit and turned his wild eyes to the panels in front of him. In their distraction, none saw the two filter-masked figures poking their heads and arms out from the hatch with weapons in hand.

Firing first at the Blakist standing to her left, Brooke caught him once in the chest, and sent another slug his way for good measure. Tibor also put two rounds in his target, one slamming into the woman's abdomen, and the second to her neck. Blood sprayed across computer panels and bulkheads as both crewmen dropped in the haze, and the chamber rang with the echoes of gunfire and short, alarmed cries.

Ducking back in unison, they waited a few tense seconds for explosions that never came. Instead, they heard the loud, whirring hum of the chamber's air filtration system ramping up to overdrive, sucking away the gases and clearing the haze that crept after them.

Then came the alert klaxons, blaring over the din with shocking power. It was only then that they peeked around again and saw the third crewman.

"*Scheiße!*" Brooke spat as she fired her pistol again. The blast caught the remaining Blakist in the head just as his mouth opened to say something. Once again, no explosion followed.

Tibor raced through the opening, toward the third man's panel. He arrived just in time to make out an angry voice coming through the speakers.

"Engineering!" a male voice shouted. "What in Blake's name is going on down there?"

Tibor blinked and swept his eyes across the blood-splashed panel, but didn't find the mic until he dared to look back at the operator's corpse. Snatching it from the ghastly remains of the engineer's head, he brought the device toward his lips while trying to ignore just how warm and slick it was.

"Ah, sorry, sir," he stammered. Finding the panic switch the engineer struck, he slapped it again. Mercifully, the alarms stopped, but his ears still rang painfully. "We've had a slight...

coolant breach down here, but we've managed to lock it down. Everything's fine now, sorry."

Brooke was at his side now, her focus divided between watching the other ingress hatches around them and scanning the controls for anything useful. Tibor's spidery fingers were already working at them, poking and fumbling across buttons and switches half-obscured by her handiwork.

"Who is this?" the voice from the console demanded.

"Crap, crap, *crap*!" Tibor hissed as he tossed the mic away. His hands moved faster, slapping overrides and throwing switches. The monitor above his panels flashed up a schematic of the DropShip, with various decks and sectors blinking from green to red, but only for a moment. Finally, the engine room lights flickered, and Brooke could hear a brief change in the reactor's buzz, a momentary hum that reminded her of several times when the *Sac* suffered a power surge.

It all passed in a heartbeat, and the alarms began anew.

"Trouble?" Brooke asked.

"They didn't buy it, obviously!" he snapped back. "I tried to kill life support on the bridge, but of course they've already cut me out."

"Scheiße!"

Tibor studied the displays one last time before glancing back at the dead engineers. A grim, uneasy smile appeared on his face as he bent down to snatch a set of small, colored cards from the belt loop of the corpse at his feet.

"It's not all bad," he said. "Well, okay. They slaved control through the bridge directly, and their effort to stop me from voiding everything else above us has locked the ship into anti-breach mode. Emergency bulkheads are down all over the place; should slow down anyone left between here and the bridge. There's two fighters of some kind in a bay above the cargo hold. And these engineering keys should allow us to override the locks at will, though a portable E-console would be better, if we can find one. If we move fast enough, we may have a clear path to either place."

Brooke stared at the screens for a moment, tracing the routes in her mind.

"Alright," she said. "Try to find a console, in case they remote-kill those keys. I'll get Alahni."

Petra Inagi pounded a fist on the edge of the tactical station holotank. The state-of-the-art device barely flickered at the disturbance, which only magnified her frustration.

"What do you mean we have intruders on board?" she demanded as her eyes speared those of her first officer.

Adept Jakab Lantos was still leaning over the communications station, holding one half of a headset to his ear. Though his pale cheeks flushed in the face of his captain's rage, he nevertheless met and held her gaze. "Someone in engineering tried to void the bridge," he said quickly. "Half the airlocks in the gunnery stations, crew quarters, engineering, and flight decks have blown. We've locked them out and initiated breach control, but I can't raise anyone down there now."

"How the hell—?"

"Must've triggered an emergency containm—!"

"I know *that*!" Inagi snapped. "Override engineering control and repressurize the main decks. Sound ship-wide alert and get someone down there. I don't care if you have to go yourself; I want these bastards *found*!"

"On it!" Lantos said.

"And get me a direct line to the Sanctorum; Precentor Apollyon must be informed!"

CHAPTER 8

Forgive me, Master, for I have sinned.

With all my heart, flesh, and soul, I have embraced the wisdom of the Blessed Blake, and your Promise for the days ahead. Though I freely admit I gave in to despair in the wake of the traitor Focht's heresy, and the failures of our fallen Saints Waterly and Aziz, it was by your grace and that of your Thrice-Blessed that I was saved. It is through your inspired will and the glories of the Great Architect that I was made whole again, that I was reborn in your image. That I became one of your Hands.

Your faith in me, in my devotion, was as a gift from the Heavenly Father himself! I could not have asked for a greater honor than becoming one of Apollyon's Chosen, even without my final Ascension!

Yet, in my zeal to prove myself worthy of your gifts, I have found myself tempted by the sins of Pride, of Arrogance, of Ambition. It is for this, I seek your forgiveness and redemption!

Apollyon, my Pater, *I can see his disappointment in my frailty of late, and I am shamed. It is not for the Hands to defy the Will. Flesh, blood, and steel must do as they are told, without question, without hesitation, without desire for glory. Yet, for moments—mere moments!—I have weakened to these petty impulses, these frailties of the mind.*

And so I venture to the void, incomplete, to save my home, my people, and my soul, knowing my life is forfeit without redemption.

Mea maxima culpa, *Master! Forgive me, for I have sinned!*

—From the journal of Damien Lucille
(final entry), 3067

**THE SANCTORUM
CITY OF HOPE
JARDINE (HERAKLEION)
FREE WORLDS LEAGUE
7 NOVEMBER 3067**

Had she been flesh and blood, rather than a mere projection on a flatscreen monitor, the *Agravain*'s captain would've died under Apollyon's metal shod fist. But this fact offered the Precentor Domini no comfort. As he stared at the shattered glass and circuit boards, his first impulse was instant regret. Such blind rage was a frailty, not an expression befitting one of the Master's Hands—let alone the Master's personal champion! As the last wisps of smoke from the broken screen dissipated, he closed his eyes—both true and frail—and chastised himself for this moment of petty weakness.

Inwardly, Apollyon sought the cause of this lapse. Was it the disappointing failures of his *own* chosen to catch these two frail mercenaries? Was Lucille's disappointing tendency toward immaturity and hubris soaking into his own psyche after all these years? Could it be his own sense of ego at the heart of this, for that matter? That part of him which was enraged that the possibility of Jardine's three-hundred-year bliss now stood just days away from being ruined on *his* watch?

Or could it be the frailest and most primal of all human emotions driving him: *fear?* Fear of the contingencies the Master Himself would ask of him, should news of this world reach the Inner Sphere at large?

Apollyon opened his eyes again and turned them solemnly to the windows of his nearly featureless office. Beyond the boundaries of Hope's faux ruins, the lush, thriving jungles spread across the hilly landscape as far as he could see, so beautifully green beneath the clear, azure skies of his homeworld. Protecting this splendor had already claimed so many lives, and more sacrifice would be necessary if it was to continue.

Already, his orders had gone out to the hangars. Every vessel possible was preparing for launch, the usual concealment protocols suspended for expediency. But these invaders had half a day's head start on one of the fastest ships in his fleet, itself racing to kill their JumpShip. Though he knew Adept Inagi would heed a self-destruct command from him to ensure Doctor Stevens' death, it would also buy Stevens' compatriots more time to fast-charge their drives before any other ship from Jardine could reach them.

And so now, all Apollyon could do was pray.

Pray, and prepare for the worst.

MERLIN-CLASS DROPSHIP *AGRAVAIN*
RETROGRADE INTERCEPT COURSE
JARDINE (HERAKLEION) SYSTEM
FREE WORLDS LEAGUE

"I *knew* we should've taken the bridge first!" Brooke groused as she climbed up the maintenance ladder. Behind her by a few rungs was Tibor, followed by Alahni, both already gasping and grunting for breath.

The shaft they were in ran alongside the DropShip's main starboard personnel lift, and was roomy enough for techs to traverse, even while burdened with oxygen tanks and tool satchels. There were ample handholds and overhead rails for climbing in either normal gravity, or the complete absence thereof. But the fact that the ship was still pouring out enough thrust for something past two gees of acceleration—by Brooke's estimate, anyway—made what should have been a "quick and easy" ascent a test of herculean endurance.

Now her limbs ached at every joint, with even her fingers and toes screaming in agony at every step. She'd tried to distract herself by counting the steps, but every time she'd glanced up along the shaft, her goal just looked that much farther away. Already, they'd paused to take quick breathers, resting their limbs by sitting on the thick ridges that both reinforced the shaft and marked the passage of each deck level.

"If they'd not been so damned fast," Tibor grunted, "we would've taken it with no problem, I tell you!"

"And I'm sure firing off that escape pod to distract them *really* helped," Brooke said between gasps.

"It *might* have—"

"The Guardians," Alahni breathed from behind him, "are hardly fools."

"Well," Tibor grumbled, "*we* clearly are, trying to storm the bridge when we know it's going to be a fortress—"

"Trouble," Brooke snapped, "shut up, will you? We broke orbit all of four hours ago. There's maybe a four-*day* trip ahead of us at a constant burn. Whatever fighters they have in the launch bays, they can't make a haul like that, and you know it."

"*Ja, ja...*" Tibor said, "Still—"

With a loud hiss and a metallic *clang* that nearly deafened her, metal plates inside the ridge just above Brooke's head suddenly emerged and slammed together, blocking the shaft. Behind her, she heard Tibor's yelp of alarm as another set closed beneath them, right under him and Alahni.

"*Scheiße!*" Brooke spat.

"They're onto us!" Tibor growled. "Swing across! Let me at that side hatch next to you; Maybe I can—"

It was at that moment the hatch Tibor was talking about slid open on its own. Instantly, Brooke found herself face-to-face with a pale-faced, goateed man wearing crisp black coveralls under an open red jacket. The Word of Blake logo appeared prominently on his shoulders, and a rank insignia she didn't recognize was pinned to his collar. In his right hand, already leveled at her, was a nasty-looking flechette pistol.

Brooke reacted almost purely by instinct. Reaching out with her right hand while anchoring her left arm to its current rung by the elbow, she seized the man's jacket and pulled him forward with all her might, deliberately twisting her arm back and away from her. The Blakist yelped and fired his pistol, but all she heard was a hail-like rattle of plastic on metal in the tube behind her.

Suddenly unbalanced and teetering into the shaft, the man clutched at the hatchway and might have been able to right himself under normal conditions. But with the ship pulling more than two gees, his efforts amounted to little more than flailing against physics. Losing his footing, he tumbled head-first into the shaft, and slammed against the pressure bulkhead three meters below with a sickening *crunch*.

"He aha lā!?" another voice shouted from further beyond the open doorway.

Brooke looked up and her eyes widened at the sight of a second Blakist in the hall. Though he was dressed just like the man she'd tossed, this one looked far more imposing, with dark skin, stubble-short blond hair, and glowing red, metal-rimmed eyes set beneath a hairless brow.

Lunging forward, he reached out with a leather-gloved hand and grabbed her forearm. As he ripped her off the ladder and flung her into the hall like a rag doll, a sharp new agony radiated out from Brooke's left elbow and shoulder. But before she could even cry out about it, the back of her head banged heavily against the metal bulkheads of the inner corridor. Stars swam before her as her vision dimmed.

"Kaha to Bridge," a deep voice said from somewhere in the haze. "I have them."

Brooke was only partly aware of her surroundings as the large Blakist tore the pistol from her belt and tossed it away. But everything came clear again in a flash, as the monster seized her by the throat and dragged her up against the wall. Over the conflicting noise of her ears ringing and the faint rumble of the ship's thrust, Brooke could hear a sickly popping in her neck, and her vision began to swim and waver once more. She tasted blood and felt her lungs spasming in vain for even a single gasp of breath.

"Frail, feeble, ungrateful *wretch*!" The Blakist roared in her face. "You—*Rah*!"

Brooke suddenly found herself back on the deck, half-upright against the bulkhead, as the brute swung around. A flash of reflected light drew her eyes to the aluminum accents of the otherwise carbon-black metal knife hilt, jutting out from the man's back. It took another moment before she recognized it as a vibroblade Tibor must have claimed from the corpse of a ship's engineer. Tibor himself now stood in the hallway before the Blakist, just inside and to one side of the still-open shaft.

Despite the presence of a humming, twenty-centimeter blade jammed into his back somewhere near where a lung should be, the cyborg moved as though unfazed. If anything, the attack only angered him further. With two steps forward and a vicious backhand, he swatted Tibor across the face, smashing him against the wall with a sickly *thump*. Tibor sagged and dropped to the floor.

"Savages, all of you!" the Blakist seethed as he twisted a hand back and ripped the blade out as casually as one might scratch an itch. The deep red blood spurting from the wound spattered along the corridor wall behind him, but didn't even slow his rant. "You profane our worlds like you would your own!"

Looking away, Brooke found her pistol down the curved hallway, just a few meters away. Though her left arm screamed in a chorus of agony and her entire body shook as though electrified, she forced herself to tumble forward and crawl toward it. But before she could reach the weapon, she felt a large hand grip her leg, and—once again—she was airborne, clanging against another bulkhead.

This time, she didn't strike the walls head-first, but instead managed to twist her body just enough to let her back absorb most of the impact. The impact left her momentarily breathless, but nowhere near as dazed as before. As quickly as she could manage, she began to tuck her feet in, struggling to rise again.

"And, to *think*," the red-eyed monster went on as he stepped closer, the blood-slicked vibroblade now buzzing menacingly in his hand, "we did all of this for the likes of *you!*"

With one more purposeful step, the Blakist towered over her and raised the blade. Automatically, Brooke raised both arms to intercept it, crying out in defiance of the pain that shot through her tortured joints. But before the man's arm came down, she heard a deafening *bang* from somewhere behind her, and felt a warm spray wash over her arms and scalp.

Even with no eyebrows and crimson camera lenses for eyes, the Manei Domini's expression registered a look of complete and utter shock. Blinking away pain-induced haze and tears, Brooke stared in wonder at the gunshot wound that now appeared right where the man's heart should be. He stumbled back one step, then two, before dropping to his knees. The vibroblade clattered to the floor.

The Blakist's head came up, just enough for Brooke to realize he was looking *past* her, when a second shot rang out. This one smashed through the man's left eye, sending fragments of bone, flesh, and electronics exploding through the air.

Only then did Brooke finally find the desperate strength to surge forward, plowing headlong into the man's chest. Knocked back by her bull rush, the dying cyborg tumbled past Tibor's insensate form, and into the service shaft. One fast heartbeat later, his suicide implants went off with an air-sundering *boom*.

Even then, it was not until Brooke felt someone tugging gently on her arm, and looked up into Alahni's worried face, that she realized the danger was over—if only for now.

Even without the sudden wail of warning alarms from several of the monitor stations around them, the three officers within the *Agravain*'s forward command center could tell something—somewhere belowdecks—had gone terribly wrong. Mere minutes before, Adept Kaha had confidently radioed in, reporting he'd found the intruders who had somehow stowed aboard their ship. But whatever relief that news promised was shattered by an explosion in one of the service shafts just two decks down, aft of the bridge. The blast tripped more of *Agravain*'s automated damage control alerts, adding to those already sounded by multiple deck decompressions (and the seemingly random launch of the aft escape pod).

Pressed into her command chair, Adept-Captain Petra Inagi turned a fierce look to the comms station. Adept Lantos, wearing his headset askew to keep one ear free, was already on the case, calling Kaha's name into the microphone. He didn't look up from his screens, but the flush on his face assured Inagi he knew she was watching.

"Kaha," he repeated, louder now. "What is your situation? *Respond!*"

Inagi turned to the sensor station, catching Adept Yuen's attention. With a twitch of her neck, she directed the sensor tech to man the damage control station. "Kill those damned alarms," she snapped.

Yuen nodded curtly and forced himself to rise.

Inagi's eyes were back on Lantos a moment later, only to find him staring back at her. "Tell me," she commanded.

"I can't raise Adept Kaha or Acolyte Senne!" Lantos shouted, his last words echoing as the wailing sirens abruptly fell silent.

Inagi stared at him for a moment, her mind reeling. After first learning the fate of her engineering crew, she recognized the stowaways for the threat they were. So, naturally, within minutes of their failed attempts to vent the ship's atmosphere and Lantos' ship-wide lockdown, she'd asked Adept Modesto Kaha—the sole Guardian on board—to hunt them down personally.

Confident two "frails" would be easier to defeat within the confined spaces of a DropShip, Kaha took only one other crewman with him, junior tech Acolyte Ellick Senne. But Inagi was far from reassured. According to Precentor Apollyon, these invaders had not only proved crafty enough to penetrate Jardine's centuries-old veil of secrecy, they had somehow managed to elude some of the Master's finest warriors, and were responsible for the death of an *entire* Wayward tribe.

"Captain," Yuen called out from his new station, "that last explosion came from Support Shaft Charlie on Hab Deck One!"

Inagi's heart sank. That was right where Kaha and Senne were headed when Kaha radioed in and said he had them.

...Just one deck below the bridge.

"Damn it!" she spat. Between the original Engineering crew, the unfortunate loss of Acolyte Olanu to one of the blown airlocks, and whatever Lost One trickery just took the lives of Kaha and Senne, half of *Agravain's* complement was now dead.

Instantly, Inagi's mind raced to tally who was left. Aside from her three-man bridge team, there were only three other crew left on board, two of whom—Adepts Monro and Sykes—she'd sent down to reclaim Engineering. The third—Adept Lorne—was posted to the launch bay, in case the intruders went there to capture an escape craft. Prior to the intruders' discovery, all three had been strapped into their bunks, having come off-shift less than half an hour before. Positioned as they were now, none of them could possibly move forward in time to be of any help.

Inagi's eyes went to the main hatch at the back of the bridge. Even under lockdown, she knew, it would be only a matter of time before the enemy would breach it. Her own technical expertise could think of at least a half-dozen ways to circumvent a locked hatch (unless they actually welded it shut)—and she could only assume these invaders also knew them, if they'd already made it *this* far.

She turned back to find Lantos and Yuen staring at her, their expressions grim.

"Vac suits and sidearms," she snapped at last, pointing at the storage lockers tucked between the stations ringing the bridge's operations center. "They're not taking *this* ship without a fight!"

Before he even reached out to grab the latch, Tibor knew it wasn't going to move for him. To leave their bridge doors unlocked while known stowaways were running about the DropShip, these Blakists would have to be stupid on levels beyond even the comically bad field agents of the Clan Watch he'd encountered a lifetime ago. Still, he reckoned, he had to try.

Across the door from him, leaning against the door-side bulkhead with a captured pistol at the ready, Brooke smirked for half a second and shrugged slightly. Tibor returned the gesture and stowed his own pistol, freeing his hands to grab the small utility computer hooked on his belt. The device was already lit up and ready for use, but Tibor still needed to fumble along the wall to find the right access panel he needed to pry open and plug into.

Portable engineering consoles were a staple of spacecraft technology since long before the first JumpShips launched mankind into the void beyond the Terran solar system. Part diagnostic tool, part emergency rescue system, they could be used to bypass severed control conduits and open doors auto-locked during a catastrophic hull breach. Like most high technology, they became scarce during the Succession Wars, but even then, it wasn't uncommon for local recharge stations and system patrol craft to carry at least a few for the express purpose of boarding damaged or crippled ships in search of survivors. But while many holovids through the years made them out to be magical ship-hacking devices—capable of overriding everything from the doors and lights to a DropShip's engines and weapon systems—the fact was one could only do such things when the proper conduits and ports were available to patch into, and those things simply didn't exist everywhere.

Tibor had a little more than passing knowledge of such things, but only because of the many times he and Brooke had boarded derelicts in their days with (and after) Interstellar Expeditions. Even then, he didn't consider himself an expert in hacking a DropShip, *especially* on a ship class he'd never seen before. So finding a vital system's control port to patch into was scratched off his list of priorities since before he grabbed his factory-fresh console back in Engineering. Plus, as long as a bridge crew remained active on the ship, it probably wouldn't have done much good anyway.

But doors were another matter. For the same emergency rescue reasons PECs existed to begin with, doors were easy to override. If one had the time.

The door's access panel, barely larger than his palm, was higher on the wall than he anticipated, but its sheet metal cover popped open readily enough under the pressure of his vibroblade. Inside, it took a little bit of blindly feeling about to locate a connection port to plug the console into, and when he found it, it proved remarkably difficult to plug into, thanks to its odd placement and the PEC's short interface cord. These little inconveniences were deliberate, he imagined—just enough to slow someone down who was perhaps not *supposed* to be doing this.

Someone like him.

As he began to work the console, Tibor glanced over to Alahni. Like Brooke, the girl was holding a captured pistol at the ready. Any nervousness he might have felt about allowing her to handle a weapon ended when she had shot one of her world's vaunted "Guardians" to save them. He felt a little guilty about doubting her—and, for that matter, Brooke's judgment in letting her come along on this suicidal escape plan—but he couldn't deny the expectation of a double-cross had lurked in his mind since the moment he'd met her.

It certainly wouldn't have been his first betrayal, after all.

He was nearly finished inputting the hatch's emergency override sequence when the console suddenly flashed a pressure warning.

"Oh, *Scheiße*!" he spat.

"What?" Brooke said.

"The bastards in there just purged the bridge!"

"Bast *damn* it!" Brooke hissed.

"What does that mean?" Alahni asked.

"It means they shunted the airflow systems to space," Tibor said. "We'll be walking into vacuum if we open this door now. If this was an older ship or had an aerodyne setup, we'd probably find ourselves spacediving to boot."

"We're a few meters from outer hull, though," Brooke said quickly, her tone softened just enough to reassure the girl. "So we're safe from getting shot into space."

"But there's still air out here," Alahni said. "Won't it just push in with us?"

"For a few seconds," Tibor said. "But not much longer while the bridge vents stay open. Depending how good the venting is, the pressure shift could even blast us into the chamber the second this hatch pops, leaving us gasping for breath the whole way like fish out of water. Hell, if they just waited another second—or opened the door themselves—that's exactly what *would* have happened—"

"Then we got lucky they didn't open up for us," Brooke cut in.

"I guarantee you that means they're already suited up and waiting for us behind any cover they can find in there."

Brooke looked around quickly. "Plenty of handholds by the door here," she said, pointing out one for Alahni on the far side of the hatch. Wide-eyed, the Jardinian reached for it and pressed her body against the wall. "And you still have the filter masks."

"*We* do," Tibor agreed as Alahni took the hint and pulled hers into place. "But yours was broken by that cyber-brute back there."

"Then we'll need to work fast, won't we?"

"Wait," Alahni started. "What are you—?"

"Tear gas won't do anything to them if they're suited," Brooke explained while Tibor settled his own mask in place, "but the smoke they create will give us a brief bit of cover. We'll just need to deploy it creatively."

"Flash-bangs and spike-bombs would be better," Tibor said through his filters. "Especially if we also had needlers."

"We'll make do," Brooke said, "but maybe we can add a little more chaos to the mix..." Her eyes darted quickly about before settling on a large, scarlet metal box anchored to the wall just across the corridor from them.

Tibor followed her gaze and snorted out half a chuckle. "Well, thank the gods of the interstellar safety code."

As Brooke stepped across the deck to crack the seal on the firebox, Tibor tucked his console under one arm and reached into his hip pouch with the other. His hand came up with a pair of green-striped mini-grenades, the last of the ordnance they'd used to take Engineering. He passed them both to Alahni.

"Keep your mask on, grab on to something, and stay close," he told her as he made a show of hooking his arm through one of the handholds by the doorway. "And get ready to pop those when I say. Brooke and I will handle the rest..."

A subtle change in the deck's vibration warned Adept-Captain Inagi that the main hatch was cycling open seconds before it did so. Buttoned up in a light-duty vac suit that fit easily over her duty uniform, she half-crouched behind the far side of the sensor station, pointing her Sunbeam laser pistol at the opening. Flanking the doorway, Adepts Lantos and Yuen pressed themselves against the cover of gee-chairs, likewise covering the command center's sole access with lasers of their own.

The bridge was nearly black. Every monitor within was shut off and every console light had been deactivated or covered up by whatever spare suits and duty robes they could find in the emergency lockers. In the dark, airless chamber, Inagi quickly found the sound of her and her crewmates' breathing deeply disturbing, but she resisted the urge to switch off the comm channel they shared out of tactical necessity. Blake willing, she prayed, the maddening wait for their enemy would end before she went completely out of her mind.

The defense plan was simple enough: the moment that hatch opened, all three of them would fire at any form darkening the doorway—and keep shooting until all that remained were light and corpses. Voiding the bridge would force the intruders to fight their way through a windstorm, only to risk a final death from asphyxiation if they weren't prepared for it.

Of course, Inagi wasn't about to put all her Eagles on that strategy alone. There were any number of ways these Housespawn scum could acquire vac suits or breathing masks on this ship. Hell, every crew deck had to have at least three lockers stocked with emergency-grade safety gear, just in case of a hull breach or coolant leak. None of that would be combat-grade, but she'd insisted on lasers over needlers anyway. If the results were hits guaranteed to breach an enemy space suit, she could accept the risk of a missed shot or two popping open whatever utility lines they might hit along the corridor bulkheads.

The hatch opened with a gentle rumble Inagi felt, but could barely hear. As the door slid into its bulkhead, a blast of smoke rushed inward—smoke tinged green and black in the light that spilled in with it. Inagi felt a strange sense of wonder that these intruders would truly expect *tear gas* to work in a vacuum.

Lantos and Yuen started firing wildly, their lasers flashing blindly into the green smoke storm to add an irregular, reddish strobing effect to the surreal scene. Inagi fired a heartbeat later, but the buffeting force of smoky air spoiled her stability; her first shot actually struck the ceiling just above the hatch.

Only then did she make out the strange shadow that sprang up in the doorway, for just a moment. Bigger than a grenade, but much smaller than a human, it spun in a wild arc on what looked like a jet of white steam. Careening off one of the command center's arresting columns, the black canister whirled right toward Inagi. Instinct sent her diving for cover again. The console shuddered against the jarring impact.

"The hel—!" Lantos spat into the channel, followed by a strangled "Ack!"

Something fast, small, and hard struck the deck less than twenty centimeters in front of Inagi and ricocheted with a muted, metallic clank. She flinched back.

"Shit!" Yuen yelled. "Captain, I'm h—aoo!"

Inagi's eyes went wide. The silence that followed was even stranger and more nerve-wracking than the breathing that threatened to drive her crazy mere seconds ago. Instantly, she realized she was alone, coiled into a near ball in the shadows behind a bridge console. Hazy puffs of whitish smoke stretched and scattered about her only to vanish into the air vents just as quickly as they appeared, the thrown extinguisher sputtering out the last of its foam.

Over the ever-present thrum of the ship's engines, Inagi felt footsteps thumping on the deck. The intruders were coming in! Shaking off her surprise, she quickly keyed her comm to another channel.

"Engineering, Inagi!" she hissed urgently. "The bridge is lost. I say again, the bridge is lost! Set Condition O—!"

A tall, wiry man in crew coveralls stepped around the console right in front of her and froze there, a slugthrower in one hand. Despite the dim lighting, Inagi could see enough of the face behind his filter mask to know he wasn't one of hers. Instantly, she raised her weapon and pulled the trigger—

Her life ended in a blinding flash before she ever knew if her shot found its mark.

THE SANCTORUM
CITY OF HOPE
JARDINE (HERAKLEION)
FREE WORLDS LEAGUE
8 NOVEMBER 3067

Specter Precentor Omicron Apollyon, commander of the Master's Hands and de facto governor of the thrice-blessed world of Jardine, stared out the northern window of his office with infinite regret. Before him stretched the false ruins of Hope, its streets concealed beneath camo nets and a canopy of trees and vines arrayed just randomly enough to look natural from the air. Beyond its boundaries, the semi-tropical forests covered most of the landscape, stretching out toward the distant mountains and cut sharply only by the line of the Providence River. To the northeast and east, Apollyon could see the gray-white fog rising from the nearby geyser fields, and idly noted how easily their mist blended into the gray skies above. Already this morning, a drizzling rain was falling across the valley—as if the world itself shared in his sadness.

The smell of ozone lingered in the air, and his true arm still tingled even as he flexed and relaxed the fingers of his true hand. Glancing down, he noticed the blackened stripes crossing his palm, and used his frail hand to rub at them experimentally. A little of the carbon scoring came off, but the heat-scars from his now-retracted grapple cable remained clearly visible. Closing his eyes—both true and frail—he inhaled deeply, holding his breath an extra second or two before trusting himself to speak.

"The cancer has touched our very heart, my old friend," he finally, quietly said. "Or, perhaps, it has been here all along, silently growing while we ignored it."

The man he could still feel standing behind him said nothing.

"I have prayed," Apollyon went on. "In all my years, I have prayed that this day would never come."

When silence again was the only reply, Apollyon turned slowly.

Administrator Ogima Lunalla's face was white as bone, his eyes glued to the still-smoking shell of lifeless flesh now draped across Apollyon's desk. The body was cooling rapidly, its twitching finally ceased. Through his true sight, Apollyon knew the man—Uku—had died almost instantly. The jolt, delivered to his heart by the equipment stowed within Apollyon's true arm, carried more than enough current to get the job done. But it took the traitor's brain and nervous system a full ten seconds or so to catch up with his expired heart.

Ogima, standing less than half a meter from the man when the attack came, felt some of the shock himself, and stepped back, but not before a thousand strands of his short hair shot up in all directions. Still charged, they remained that way even now. Hope's civilian administrator hadn't moved a muscle since Uku's execution, but through his true vision, Apollyon could see he was unharmed.

"Ogima," Apollyon said. His voice, soft yet commanding, caused the other man to flinch, but that was all.

"*Ogima!*" he repeated, much more forcefully. "Are you listening to me?"

Like a cadet struck by his superior officer, Ogima instantly snapped to attention, his gaze finally tearing away from Uku's corpse. "Y-yes, Guardian Master!" he croaked. "I hear you!"

Apollyon briefly glanced at Uku before turning his sympathetic eyes back to Ogima. "I know your pain, my friend," he said. "This is a terrible loss to our community, but we will move on. We *must* move on!"

"Yes, sir!" Ogima answered, his voice still shaky. "We shall!"

"Then purge your doubts, Administrator," Apollyon snapped. "Let none hear it in your voice, nor see it in your eyes—lest we suffer more like *him*! Our time is near, Ogima, and we need you to help see it through. The Promise is upon us, and all we have done here has been for our people—for *all* people."

At that, Ogima finally managed to look up and meet Apollyon's gaze head-on. Fear remained deeply etched on the administrator's face, but the signs of recovering self-control came through in his stance, and his voice. "What, then, are your orders, my Precentor?"

Apollyon nodded gratefully, but his expression remained grim. "Our home has been compromised, my friend," he said. "And I fear this time, with so many of our brethren called to station, we may not be able to staunch this wound to our most cherished of havens in time."

"The Lost will find us," Ogima said. It wasn't a question.

Apollyon stepped around his desk, Uku's remains already forgotten, and placed a fatherly—frail—hand on Ogima's shoulder. "I shall contact the Master," he said, "beseech him for guidance, and for mercy. But I fear the Protocols of Karpov are clear enough..."

Ogima's eyes narrowed and fell as Apollyon's voice trailed off into uncertainty. "May all the gods, in all the heavens have mercy on us," he whispered.

Apollyon said nothing, but gave Ogima's shoulder a gentle, momentary squeeze before pulling his hand away.

CHAPTER 9

"Now, stowing away, pulling the old bait-and-switch, and the good old frontal assault are all nice ways to score a ship, sure. Pirates and House militaries use these tricks all the time to subvert a transport for whatever strategic goal they have in mind. But most folk in these cases prefer to take such care in situations like these that a cool-headed captain has a good chance of countering them. The presumption is that your attackers want to capture your ship and use it when all is said and done, so even if you're outgunned, simply running and/or jumping away will do the trick.

"But what happens when your attacker doesn't really care what they might break while trying to capture your ship? For many covert missions, even the mutual destruction of both sides can be considered an operational victory."

—TIBOR MITTERNACHT
AS QUOTED IN *"CHANGING THE OBJECTIVES* (PART 2)"
(WARRIOR DIGITAL PRODUCTIONS, SOLARIS VII, JUNE 3061)

K-1-CLASS DROPSHUTTLE *STILETTO*-7
JARDINE (HERAKLEION)
FREE WORLDS LEAGUE
9 NOVEMBER 3067

On the aft viewscreen, the *Leopard CV* appeared as little more than a dense collection of blinding suns, looming ever larger as the DropShip's tail engines continued to burn for deceleration. From the angle of camera, *Stiletto-7*'s own drive flare—minute in comparison—was visible as little more than a glare stretching across the image's lower-right quadrant. Assuming their pilots were competent enough, the two ships, still separated by hundreds of kilometers of void, would reach each other in just ten minutes or so, at or near a relative velocity of zero.

To this point, Precentor Damien Lucille and his crew maintained the charade they committed to six days ago. Through the voice modulator Lamashti had programmed, Adept Rumiko sent to and answered hails from the *Kaylin* as if she were Doctor Brooklyn Stevens herself. When the *Kaylin*'s commander—a cocky man named Anton Hara—failed to mention the second JumpShip himself, Lucille had Rumiko fish for some information on it. Hara's response was coy, teasing "Stevens" about losing track of her own people, and feigning ignorance of their whereabouts as well.

The news was like a dagger in Lucille's heart, proof positive that the real Stevens had indeed managed to elude capture, and that her crewmates were hard at work on an effort to rescue her. In the first moment of solitude he could find after that discovery, Lucille prayed to God, Blake, and Apollyon himself for the universe to find a way to bring those defilers the swift and bitter end they so richly deserved.

In the meantime, his journey continued toward the unknown factor of this second group of House-spawned violators—and the orders remained unchanged. As the hours and days continued to crawl by, Lucille focused on that, hardening his resolve and planning the assault.

Now merely minutes from the moment of truth, he knelt behind the shuttle's copilot station, the bulk of his Purifier battle armor—lacking only its helmet and forearm modules—taking up the space where ordinarily there would be a standard gee-seat. At the pilot seat beside him, similarly clad, was Adept Rumiko, controlling the craft's final approach with the deft touch of her haptic-gloved hands.

To Lucille, these final maneuvers felt disturbingly quiet. Although communications between the two ships' pilots remained open, it sounded to his true ears as though their instruments did all the talking for the past few hours, whispering data through the void in the elegant language of machines. Rumiko's last voice transmission from "Stevens" was met with the barest of acknowledgment; Hara's usual snide banter was entirely absent. Even with all the EMCON protocols under which Jardine's space crews operated, Lucille found this lack of chatter particularly conspicuous.

That was, until an alert sounded on his console.

Lucille spotted the flash of smaller lights for only a fraction of a second on his rear-view display, breaking away from the massive flares of the Kaylin's engine. Glancing down at her radar screen, Rumiko blinked her oily black eyes in the closest expression she had to surprise since the destruction of that Wayward camp back home.

"Fighter launch," she said. "Two craft. *Lightnings*."

"As escort?" Lucille wondered. "At *this* stage?"

"Could just be clearing space for us," Rumiko suggested.

"*Two* spaces? For a shuttle that can't even fit in one?"

Rumiko frowned and reached out to key her microphone, when another alarm sounded, this one the insistent, ominous beeping of hostile tracking systems. Lucille's true hearing picked them up at the same time as distant radio pings, finding range from two hundred klicks away, while scrambled electronic transmissions buzzed at each other in the dark.

Lucille's mind screamed as a fresh surge of rage welled up inside him. *How did they figure it out?*

"That's close enough for now, Doctor Stevens," Hara's voice suddenly came through the speakers, dripping with more contempt than Lucille had heard in the entire flight to this point.

Lucille arched an eyebrow, shot a glance to Adept Rumiko, and whispered, "Demand explanation."

Rumiko nodded and hit the mike. "What's the meaning of this, Hara?" she snapped, enhancing the performance with a well-practiced Germanic accent.

"Let's just say our mutual employer knows you too well," Hara replied. "And I'd like to be sure where we stand before you set one dainty toe on *my* ship."

Lucille couldn't help but smirk at that. *Leave it to good old-fashioned paranoia to ruin a perfectly mundane working partnership!*

"Where we stand?" Rumiko echoed, maintaining her pretense. "You can't be serious! We *stand* in hostile territory, with an enemy DropShip outmassing both of us barreling right this way!"

"A ship *I* can outrun forever, my dear. But I'm willing to lay odds you're just a few one-gee days from fumes in that little tub of yours."

Rumiko turned away from her instruments and favored Lucille with an expression that blended mockery and contempt. Only the slight flicker of reflected cockpit lighting made it possible to see she was rolling her all-black eyes like an exasperated teenager. Lucille gave her a knowing nod and a "move it along" gesture that sent her back with a scowl.

"What do you want, then, *Arschloch*?" she snapped.

"Such language!" Hara deadpanned. "Do you fellate your lovers with that mouth?"

Rumiko didn't even have to fake outrage now. "Oh, you *Mutter Fi*—!"

"Whatever, Stevens! Bellamy here tells me its customary for you explorer types to record all your discoveries on your ship logs, and you—being the *professional* you are—almost certainly still do so. He also believes, given your past issues with the company, you and your crew will try and play hard to get with that data once you're all out of danger. Maybe you'd even go so far as putting some kind of kill-switch on those files—you know, just in case."

"Of *course*," Lucille mumbled through his teeth. "Why stop at mere paranoia when one can go all the way to double-crossing?"

Rumiko, her expression now twisted in a mask of pure disgust, closed the mike and turned to him. "Blake preserve us!" she hissed. "To think the Promise is meant to save even dregs like *this* one!"

"At least we won't need to save him in particular," Lucille assured her. His hands were already on the console ahead of him, armored fingers hammering away at the keys with remarkable deftness while he simultaneously paged through the shuttle's utilitarian database. "But he does make an inconvenient request. It would be easy to simply fill a few records with pure gibberish, but these frails will certainly inspect them before they let us close."

"We don't have all day here, Doctor!" Hara's voice crackled through the speakers.

"Say the word, Precentor," Rumiko growled, "and I'll ram this shuttle straight into one of their flight bays before their flyboys know what's happening."

"Not just yet," Lucille said, now typing at blinding speed, eyes glued to his screen. "Keep up the act and stall. They won't shoot as long as they think they can give them something. Perhaps we can bluff them with 'encrypted' files..."

Rumiko grunted.

"And get ready to button up if they call it," he added. "One way or another, we are *taking* that ship."

LEOPARD-CLASS DROPSHIP *KAYLIN*
JARDINE (HERAKLEION) SYSTEM
FREE WORLDS LEAGUE

Ever since the *Kaylin* had separated from her JumpShip, Nathan Bellamy's mere presence on board the DropShip had been a thorn in the side of her captain, Anton Hara. Although he'd tried to leave the IE liaison behind, Bellamy once again surprised him by displaying enough backbone to insist on coming along. It was critical, he declared, that Stevens be "debriefed" by her employers as soon as possible, and he wasn't about to leave *that* job to the hired help.

Bellamy now stood on the *Kaylin*'s bridge, keeping his magslips firmly on the deck while clinging to one of the handholds beside the DropShip's comm station, where he was studying the data scrolling across one of its monitors. The dark gray coveralls he wore in place of his usual suit today gave him an almost respectable look, like someone who actually *belonged* aboard a mercenary spacecraft, rather than a mere passenger. He even kept a sidearm strapped to his hip now, mimicking the habit shared by every one of the *Kaylin*'s bridge and fighter crewmen. Hara had to admit that Bellamy's manner and bearing were finally starting to show some serious acclimation to spacer life.

"Hell," he once thought aloud to his exec in a moment of wry amusement, "another month or two, and that guy might even pick up enough jargon to really blend in here!"

"Perish the thought," Lenard Bryce deadpanned with a semi-scowl. "If that happens, we'll need to kill him lest he evolves any farther."

While Bellamy continued to study the comm station screen in silence, Hara and Bryce stood near the bridge's central hub, where an all-purpose display table was installed that normally served as a navigational display. Right now, however, the scratched and age-worn screen projected a tactical map of the surrounding space a scant 500 kilometers around the *Kaylin*. At this scale, the DropShip itself appeared as a fat green oval with wings, anchored to the map's center. Adjoining arrows and telemetry data showed its present velocity, heading, and relative position within the planetary system.

A little less than 100 kilometers to the DropShip's port and trailing a bit behind was a smaller red circle icon representing Brooke Stevens' K-1 DropShuttle. Its own telemetry and heading arrows described a course that currently ran roughly parallel to *Kaylin*'s, give or take five to ten degrees. Between the two vessels drifted a pair of slightly smaller wedge-shaped icons. Painted in the same shade of green as their mother ship, these fighter markers currently maneuvered to close with the shuttle while simultaneously keeping pace with both ships.

The fighters would be in firing range soon, waiting on orders from Hara to either go weapons free or assume an escort position. Orders that right now were being held up by the silent liaison still hovering over the comm station.

Bryce cleared his throat softly, drawing Hara's attention long enough to throw him a look and a palms-up gesture that said it all. *What the hell are we waiting for?*

Hara nodded and turned around. "Mister Bellamy," he called out, "talk to me. Is this what we're here for or not?"

Bellamy seemed reluctant to turn away, but when he did, his expression telegraphed his annoyance. "No," he shook his head. "I don't think so. It looks more like gobbledygook to me."

"Could it be a cypher?" Bryce suggested.

Bellamy glared at him. "If so, it's nothing like anything IE uses."

"I'd presume Stevens doesn't exactly play by all the IE rules," Hara said. "Otherwise, she'd still be wearing your logo, right?"

Bellamy's face didn't even redden. Instead, he shrugged and said, "Maybe, but I've seen coded transmissions before, and this one looks more like what you'd see if you sat brain-damaged toddlers at a keyboard. My gut says she's pulling a stunt."

"Bitch move," Hara grumbled, then addressed the crewman seated beside Bellamy as he moved toward the comm station. "Jacoby, get her back on the line for me. Len, tell our boys to get ready for a warm-up."

Jacoby gave a curt "aye" and went to work, tapping open the mike at his station and patching it into the nav channel already connecting *Kaylin* and Stevens' shuttle. A secondary channel, beaming to the two *Lightning*s of Fyre Wing, shunted from the comm station to the tactics table, allowing Bryce to relay commands out of earshot.

Bellamy stepped aside, once again demonstrating his growing intelligence by not questioning anything.

"Stevens," Hara barked into the mike, "do you really think you can bullshit us?"

"Why, what*ever* do you mean, Captain?" came the woman's snarky reply.

"You know damned well what I mean. Do I really have to have my pilots explain to you that we're not messing around?"

Stevens' voice turned ice cold. "You wanted my files," she said, "you got them, *Saftsack*. Did you really expect me to give up all my cards so easily? Let us dock, and I'll hand you the code key."

"Bellamy here doesn't think—"

"Cap!" Bryce suddenly hissed loud enough to be heard. Hara whipped his head around. "Something's off! I've got gun-cam images from Fyre here; that shuttle's pristine!"

"Pristine?" Hara echoed. For a moment, he wondered why that would matter—but only for a moment.

"What does that mean—?" Bellamy started to ask, but Bryce drowned him out.

"She's flipping, sir!"

"Weapons free!" Hara snapped back as he shoved himself violently away from the comm station and spun toward the table. "Signal weapons free! Sound red alert!"

"Captain Hara!" Bellamy shouted, mere moments before all the bridge lighting switched from fluorescent white to glaring red, and the angry sound of *Kaylin*'s combat alarms blasted throughout the ship.

"Stevens supposedly crash-landed on that planet, Mister Bellamy," Hara yelled back, "but that shuttle out there is undamaged! I don't know whose ship that is, but I know a trick when I see one!"

On a plume of plasma fire several kilometers long, the K-1 class DropShuttle blasted forward the moment its broad nose cap fully swung about. Lighting its engines for maximum thrust, the 200-ton small craft shot from relative-zero velocity to three-gee acceleration in under a minute, while jets of extra maneuvering thrust set its ovoid hull into a corkscrewing roll.

As soon as the shuttle came into range, the two *Lightning* aerospace fighters approaching it opened fire, unleashing streams of high-caliber shells and bolts of coherent energy in near-perfect unity. All but invisible in the void, the weapons tore through space and raked the shuttle's hull. Shards of armor blasted apart and vaporized under the assault, but the craft forged along unhindered.

Halfway to its target, the whirling shuttle let loose with its own weaponry. A spread of missiles and lasers shot forth, lashing out at *Kaylin*'s aftward flank. The long-range warheads and medium-grade missiles all struck home, but against the superior armor of the 1,900-ton DropShip, their impact was barely a nuisance. Instead, the larger ship lit up its own maneuvering thrusters, rolling and twisting about to face its attacker.

Clouds of missiles, lasers, and bolts of high-energy particles flashed from *Kaylin*'s weapon bays, all aimed at the incoming shuttlecraft. A sudden blast of thrust from the DropShip's main engines added new momentum to her course, throwing it out of the barreling craft's direct trajectory. In mere seconds, explosions of armor splinters, briefly illuminated by flickering bursts of red and blue light, blossomed across the shuttle's broad, blunt nosecone.

And still, the smaller ship came on, turning just enough to match *Kaylin*'s movement.

By the time the fighters—now racing up from behind— could bring their own weapons to bear again, nothing in the universe could stop what came next. But that didn't stop them from trying anyway.

The collision came amid another furious volley of weapons fire from both the *Lightning*s and their mothership. Although the tiny K-1 craft weighed barely more than one-tenth of *Kaylin*'s mass, it plowed into the DropShip at over 6,000 kilometers per hour, striking the broad side of her hull just a meter shy of her aft-starboard launch bay.

As the shuttle disintegrated, *Kaylin*'s hull nearly crumpled from its impact. The ship immediately went into an awkward tumble, spewing atmosphere and wreckage from the rents in her outer hull where whole spans of reinforced armor had been mere moments before. Flashes of cerulean light and glimpses of orange fire flickered amid the expanding cloud of debris, but quickly vanished as the last of the air bled out into space.

The *Kaylin*'s thrusters sputtered out, and even her running lights went dead for a few moments as the fighters of Fyre Wing coasted past above her, but only for a few moments. Then the thrusters fired again, and the lights returned as the carrier DropShip began to stabilize herself—mangled, but still very much alive.

Klaxons blared and alarms wailed throughout the *Kaylin*'s command center, while several monitors blanked out or flashed warning messages in blinking crimson. Clinging to one of the handrails affixed to the central table, Hara pulled himself up from the deck and found Bryce already standing across from him. Bryce held a hand over his nose and mouth, and blood dripped from a cut on his right eyebrow. His glasses were nowhere in sight, but that didn't prevent him from taking note of his captain's questioning look and nodding curtly.

Assured of Bryce's health, Hara swept his eyes around the rest of the bridge, finding the rest of his crew still alert at their stations. Jacoby, at his comm station, pressed one ear of his headset to his left ear, while his right flicked across the panels in front of him. Beside Jacoby, Bellamy looked dazed, but still managed to seize the nearest handhold and pull himself away from the storage locker he'd been thrown against.

"Damage report," Hara called out.

"Still updating!" Jacoby shouted back. "Multiple hull breaches on starboard side! Flight Bays Starboard Baker and Starboard Charlie are gone! Heavy damage to aft dorsal and lateral thrusters! Emergency bulkheads and fire suppression systems engaged! Pressure seals in place and holding! Engineering reports we still have main drives and reactor integrity remains nominal, but we have blown power conduits all over the ship! Backup lines are handling the load, but just barely! No casualty figures yet!"

"Cut power to all primary weapon bays; lighten our energy load! And kill the alarms!"

"Aye!" Jacoby snapped.

"Calling Fyre Wing back to escort positions," Bryce announced just as the collision alarm fell silent. His voice sounded stuffy, and Hara looked over to see his brown-skinned exec had taken his hand away from his face so he could fetch the small, wired comm mike he now held close to his mouth. Above the comm, Hara could see just a slight trickle of blood coming from the man's nostrils.

Hara nodded, resisting the urge to try and check his own nose for signs of breakage. "Any sign of that shuttle?"

Bryce looked at the table, then sniffed and glanced over to the crewman on the sensor station—a pale, thin, blond-haired and blue-eyed young man named Vogel. Vogel, sensing his attention, shook his head without turning away from his own screens.

"Nothing," Bryce said finally. "The craft must have broken up on impact."

"The hell was Stevens *thinking*?" sputtered an incredulous Bellamy.

"Stevens?" Hara echoed with a scowl. "No, I don't think that was Stevens at all."

"What are you talking about? You were *speaking* to her, Captain!"

"I spoke to a woman with a Steiner accent, but none of those messages were on-vid. Damage, they said. Damage I didn't see on that shuttle before it came at us."

Bellamy practically bristled. "Who else *could* it have been?"

"Probably the same assholes driving the *Union* half a day behind them, maybe?" Hara snarled, feeling his patience collapsing as he met Bellamy's gaze head-on. "Or did you forget about *that*?"

Whatever defiance the IE liaison had left in him evaporated at that point. His mouth opened for a retort, but closed just as quickly.

"Right," Hara said. "Helm! Set course for our Jumper! We're out of here as soon as Fyre gets back on board."

"We'll have to use the port side bays for recovery, Captain," Jacoby called out. "I'm still not getting any response from the starboard crew, and power's still sketchy there."

Hara locked eyes with Bryce again. The exec nodded before relaying the captain's commands.

"We're just *leaving*?" Bellamy said.

"IE didn't pay us to die here, Mister Bellamy," Hara said. "This mission's a bust. Wherever your wayward girl went, we won't find her by loitering in a hostile system.

"So yes, you fool. We *are* leaving!"

CHAPTER 10

LEOPARD-CLASS DROPSHIP *KAYLIN*
JARDINE (HERAKLEION) SYSTEM
FREE WORLDS LEAGUE
9 NOVEMBER 3067

In the chaos of *Stiletto-7*'s final moments, an outside observer could be excused for failing to notice how the small DropShuttle tumbled around one last time and fired its engines at full blast, as if to halt its own suicide run just before impact. It would be even easier to forgive the same observer for failing to spot several much smaller *somethings* tumbling out of the craft while it did so.

Landing a thousand-kilogram suit of battle armor on the hull of a moving spacecraft—while simultaneously trying not to be killed by the cloud of exploding debris from a ship-on-ship collision near your landing point—was a rather difficult thing. Indeed, by the standards of any military, mercenary, or major intelligence agency in the Inner Sphere, it might even be considered a benchmark of insanity.

But the Master's Hands weren't like any military, mercenary, or major intelligence agency in the Inner Sphere. Theirs was a calling greater than all others: the redemption of humanity, at any cost. Suicide tactics weren't just a last resort; to protect the Promise, they could even be considered standard procedure. And so it was that, mere seconds before impact, Adept Rumiko willingly sacrificed herself to soften their wild charge into the enemy DropShip, in the hopes that at least one of her eleven comrades would survive to complete the mission.

Her death would not have been in vain had even one of the troopers survived to board the *Leopard*, so Precentor Lucille considered it Blake's own providence that he managed to link up with four other Domini in all. Their suits were battered, to be sure, but most remained fully sealed and combat-ready. Only Adept Warren's Longinus had suffered major damage to its systems, having bled out its entire oxygen supply after losing half of its (and Warren's) right arm just below the elbow. Despite this, Warren remained mobile, and had simply held his breath until he could scavenge an emergency oxygen tank from the ruins of the depressurized flight bay he'd found himself in. When Lucille found him, the warrior had just finished rigging up a makeshift apparatus to feed air into his suit straight through the stump where his arm had been.

They now stood in the dark, vacant remains of a mid-ship corridor, just outside one of the ship's emergency bulkhead doors. Lucille's helmet sensors and true vision alike could feel the heat from the other side, and a pressure indicator on the door itself confirmed the presence of breathable air as well. As he reached his armored hand for the emergency crank that would open its locking mechanisms, savoring its icy feel as transmitted to his true senses by his Purifier's neural interface, he turned to face his team one last time.

"Remember," he told them, "sweep and clear all frails on sight, but check your fire for shipboard systems; we need this ship functional enough to rejoin her transport. Adept Kano, you shall proceed aft to secure engineering. Adepts Nonehe and Sakov, take the flight bays and mid-ships. Adept Warren and I shall take the bridge. Maintain radio silence and jam all transmissions once we're inside. Understood?"

"By Blake's Will, it shall be so!" Kano intoned.

"Blessed be," said Nonehe and Sakov.

"For Jardine," Warren snarled ominously.

Lucille gave a nod his armor obediently replicated and started to turn the crank. "For the Master, and the Promise!"

The stench of ozone hung heavy in the air, the latest in a series of annoyances following the false Stevens' suicide run. For perhaps the ten-millionth time in his entire life as a spacer, Anton Hara cursed the ever-unreliable nature of 31st century circuit breakers. The fire that erupted from beneath the nav table was easily enough extinguished, but it killed Bryce's communications with the DropShip's flight deck just as the fighters of Fyre Wing were coming back on board. And—of course!—just as the *Kaylin*'s exec moved to work with Jacoby at the primary comms station, all ship-wide intercoms went down.

And so, for the moment, *Kaylin*'s crew were basically coasting along, but at least the burn back to their JumpShip was underway. Hara took solace in that after the news finally came in from Engineering. In the meantime, Jacoby and Bryce continued their efforts to reach the rest of the ship's personnel using personal devices.

Nathan Bellamy, likely hoping to maintain his own relevance now that he had nothing else to do, stood at the darkened table, staring blankly at its scuffed surface. His low-voiced musings continued, even as Hara did his best to ignore them.

"She *could* still be planetside," he suggested. "Captured, maybe. Or killed, but with her record, that's a bit doubtful. It would explain how they knew enough about her to try and dupe us, but why?"

Hara sighed.

"Right," Bellamy said, as if finding an answer in that. "To protect their secret, they'd be trying to capture any JumpShips waiting for her before they can escape..."

Hara turned to the liaison with an expression of bland irritation, but said nothing.

"But who are *they*?" Bellamy asked. "If Stevens' people knew, they didn't bother to tell us..."

"Fancy that," Hara said flatly.

Bellamy shot him an annoyed glare. "Perhaps we would have gotten some more answers if you'd allowed them to dock, or shot them apart *before* they hit your precious ship, and scavenged the wreck."

"Neither of which was going to happen, Bellamy, as I'm not an idiot."

Bellamy scowled. "I fail to see how any of *this* is better," he grumbled back, waving vaguely at the table.

"You *fail* to see a lot," Hara snapped. "We're in a system you explorer-types have been trying to find for over a century, and someone clearly went through all that time trying to *keep* it hidden. Someone who has at least a fleet of DropShips and fighters to spare on suicide runs like we saw at Shasta and here. Someone who doesn't have any problem attacking JumpShips, Ares Conventions be damned. Whoever they are, they aren't your run-of-the-mill bandits, I can tell you that. We're looking at some House-level operation, of the black variety."

"What, like SAFE?"

"Hell if I know! And to be blunt, I don't really think I *want* to know at this point, because whoever it is has probably marked us already. Your Stevens kicked over a hornets' nest, and now they have our scent too."

Bellamy broke into a smile that Hara instantly wanted to punch off his face. "So *that's* why you're running, isn't it?"

Hara leaned toward the man, coming close enough to make his stupid grin evaporate as he edged cautiously back. "As I said," he snarled through his teeth, "unlike *you*, I'm not an idiot!"

"*Captain*," Bryce suddenly cut in from across the bridge, his voice tense. "We've got trouble!"

Hara straightened himself and turned about, ignoring the flash of rage on Bellamy's face. Bryce was standing just left of Jacoby's chair, his eyes half-squinting, but whether that was from worry or the absence of his spectacles, Hara couldn't be sure.

Bryce held his personal communicator at his side, but Hara could see a flashing glow of red coming from the device. "Something's jamming us," he said without waiting for a prompt. "We can't reach anyone on the ship."

"What?" Hara said, incredulous. In two deliberate steps, he stood over the sensor station. Instinctively, Vogel looked up at him from the seat and gestured silently at the displays. The radar screen showed a cloud of random static, while the external and internal sensor screens appeared completely blank. Reaching over and switching through their inputs changed nothing. "Where is this coming from?"

"Unknown," Vogel said. "Everything's too overloaded with noise for me to even triangulate."

Hara glanced around the bridge to find everyone's eyes on him. Even Cadence—the ever-silent brunette at the ship's helm—had turned back from her flight control boards with a look of concern. Bellamy's expression had also given way to worry. A cold feeling grew in the pit of Hara's stomach and his mouth ran dry. They all realized, as he did, that anything close enough to jam the *Kaylin*'s systems was close enough to be an imminent threat.

But nothing else had even been on the radar once that shuttle rammed them...

"*Son of a Canopian whore!*" Hara hissed under his breath. Pointing at the aftward hatch, he locked eyes with Bryce and barked, "Lock down the bridge! That shuttle wasn't a kamikaze! We've been boarded!"

Bryce moved swiftly, but before he even reached the door, it swung inward with a heavy, ominous *thud*. Before anyone else could react, a huge monstrosity ducked through the opening into the bridge. The hulk was a one-armed beast of a man clad in a badly dented suit of battle armor painted in a mix of bloody red and deathly black. The trooper within wore no helmet, exposing the visage of a bronze-skinned man with vaguely Asian features in what appeared to be a black, skin-tight hood. Although the man's left eye was readily visible under the bridge lights, the other seemed to be covered by a chrome-ringed, green-lensed monocle. Stranger still, his lips curled back to expose what looked like a mouthful of jagged, metallic teeth.

But what truly chilled Hara to the bone was the symbol he saw emblazoned on the right side or the armor's broad chest, scratched up, yet still clearly visible: a downward-pointed broadsword on a field of black. It was a symbol most familiar to anyone who lived or worked among the peoples of the Free Worlds League for the last fifteen years:

The insignia of the Word of Blake.

Before Hara could blink, Bryce reached for the pistol at his side and slid it from its holster. In that same amount of time, the one-armed trooper turned and raised a metallic claw toward him. From a weapon concealed somewhere inside the suit's armored palm, a hail of bullets erupted, impossibly loud within the confines of the bridge.

Blood splashed across the cabin as each round tore through Bryce's thin frame, nearly cutting him in half. In an instant, the man who'd served as Hara's first officer for more than a decade—a man he'd come to trust with his deepest secrets and his very life—was gone.

"*Len!*" Hara's cry was automatic.

"Jesus Christ!" Bellamy yelled, diving forward to put the nav table between him and the monster.

The trooper turned again, his feral snarl unchanged as he stepped further into the command center, and swung his arm about to spray another burst of shells at the forward end of the cabin. Hara flinched and ducked as the shots flew past, only to hear a scream from Cadance somewhere behind him. The pinging of missed rounds echoed about the bridge, punctuated by a loud cracking Hara couldn't immediately identify. As the shooter paused briefly, Hara also became aware of an ominous hissing, but his instinct to assess the damage was overridden as he saw a second form lumbering through the hatch.

The second warrior wore armor that looked more eerily human-like than the first, armor that moved with a terrifying fluidity. Weirder yet, parts of the thing appeared to be blurring, with colors shifting and flowing across several of its more prominent surfaces in surreal patterns. The rest of the battlesuit was bloody red, and its trooper's face hid within a helmet that looked more like a green-lensed gas mask.

As the first Blakist fired again, ripping Jacoby apart where he sat, the second raised a weapon of its own, a giant muzzle that seemed to take up its entire forearm. In horror, Hara realized this cannon was pointing his way, and he pushed himself forward, scrambling toward Bellamy's hiding place. Crimson light flashed overhead, close enough for him to feel its blistering heat, and a sickeningly wet *pop* nearby marked the end of Vogel's life.

A strange, almost dreamlike silence descended upon the *Kaylin*'s bridge, marred only by the buzzing of half-ruined electronics and the persistent hissing of a breached line somewhere near the pilot's station. Hara pulled himself into a seated position next to a wide-eyed Bellamy who—against all his past estimations of the man—now clutched a Magnum autopistol in his hands like someone who actually knew what he was doing. Glancing about while he fumbled for his own sidearm, Hara struggled to comprehend how everything had gone so wrong so quickly. His entire command crew was dead, his ship wrecked and boarded, days away from any safe haven—even if they *could* call for help.

None of this made sense!

"What do we do, Captain?" Bellamy whispered through his teeth.

Hara blinked at him incredulously.

"You surrender," an amplified voice declared before Hara could find any words. *"Or make peace with whatever god you profess to believe in."*

Bellamy sat frozen, his mouth agape. Hara pulled himself into a crouch, turning away from the IE liaison so he could keep an eye on his side of the nav table. In his mind, the tactical situation was finally starting to crystalize, and it was a bad one. Two battle-armored troopers stood now on his bridge, waiting for him or Bellamy to give up or do something even dumber. While both of their suits had looked damaged to Hara, only one trooper—the one with a missing arm and exposed head—could possibly be felled by the weapon in his hand. That warrior, Hara knew, had moved closer to the starboard side of the command center when his friend came in—which meant he might be standing just around the corner from where Hara now huddled. Give or take a half meter or so, it was possible Hara could peek around and squeeze off a clean shot at that monster's head. If he hit, the Blakist might fall, but if he missed...then what?

Hell, Hara told himself, *even if I hit, what next? Try and bull-rush the* other *one-ton battlesuit standing between us and the nearest escape pod?*

"W-who are you?" Bellamy called out without warning. Hara nearly jumped at the sound.

"We are the Guardians of the Promise, frail soul," answered the amplified voice. *"We are the bloody hands of Justice, the bane of the Clans, and the bringers of truest peace. We are the salvation you House-spawned children so desperately need."*

Hara winced as he heard a single *thump*, accompanied by a heavy vibration in the decking. It felt close to him. The starboard trooper was moving again. Had to be!

"I don't understand," Bellamy nervously shouted.

"Your understanding is not required," came the reply. *"Suffice to say, we are the warriors who will save mankind from the shadows, your unseen protectors."*

"Our protectors? If that's true, then wh-why are you attacking us?"

"Because you have trespassed. Your presence here threatens the Promise."

"Our presence here?" Bellamy repeated. "Where's 'here?' We just jumped into this system to—"

"Do not try lying to me, Frail!" the voice boomed now. *"You were in league with the intruders who set foot on our world, even if you* did *ultimately hope to betray them."*

Another *thump*, another vibration. That same trooper, creeping along in his armor, was moving closer. Cautiously, Hara tilted his head just far enough to catch a glimpse of where Bryce's corpse lay stretched out upon the floor. Directly above the body, ominously glaring right back at Hara, stood the one-armed man.

"Okay, okay," Bellamy was saying, his voice cracking. "You're right, okay. B-but this is—I mean, maybe we can cut some kind of...deal here?"

Hara heard and felt two more *thumps*, and realized the warrior who was speaking was now on the move, likely circling along the chamber's port side, toward Bellamy. In his mind, he could almost see it. The aft hatch, wide open, now unguarded, less than ten meters away. *If* he could act before the wounded trooper did, *if* he could land the shot right, and *if* he could bolt fast enough while the talkative one was still dealing with Bellamy...

"A deal?" the unseen trooper asked. *"Do you truly believe you're in any kind of a bargaining position here?"*

"There has to be *something*!" Bellamy pleaded. Hara could practically taste the man's terror now, the bleeding edge of hysteria making his every word sound breathless and small.

"Something your people need! M-money? Information? Con-connections? I—I know people! All over the Sphere!"

"Are you this ship's captain?"

Hara's eyes widened, and he snapped his head around. He still couldn't see the other trooper, but he could see Bellamy glancing back his way, slack-jawed, his face frozen with fear.

"Oh, shiiit!" Hara growled. In that instant, nothing was clearer than the next few seconds ahead, the certainty that Death itself was reaching out for him.

Without another thought, Hara spun back toward the first trooper, raised his weapon, and fired. He was up and running before he could even tell what he'd hit, his eyes on the aft hatch as if nothing else in the universe existed. The blood rushing in his ears all but drowned out the sound of alarmed cries, a shouted command, and the air-splitting *pop* he felt in his chest. Somewhere in all that came a nova of angry red light, which lasted for less than a moment.

Suddenly, his nostrils were overwhelmed by the stench of burning metal. Hara gagged, and found himself on his knees with no memory of falling. Just half a meter ahead of him stood the open hatchway. On the corridor wall beyond that, he noticed a blackened scar he'd never seen before, surrounded by a watery ring of the darkest red. That was when he realized he couldn't breathe, couldn't speak, and couldn't even feel his legs anymore.

Hara reached a hand up to his chest, and looked down to find the ashen edges of an impossibly large hole in his shirt. His fingers, half numb by the time they reached the wound, came away bloody.

As he tried to turn around, gripped by a final compulsion to look out at the stars from the *Kaylin*'s viewports one last time, his vision swam, and the cold, black fog of oblivion closed in all around him...

CHAPTER 11

MERLIN-CLASS DROPSHIP *AGRAVAIN*
RETROGRADE INTERCEPT COURSE (ADRIFT)
JARDINE (HERAKLEION) SYSTEM
FREE WORLDS LEAGUE
10 NOVEMBER 3067

The *Agravain* was dead.

Her fusion heart was cold and inert, her atmosphere-recycling lungs empty and still, while the plasma thrusters that served as her wings and legs sat limp and lifeless. And for all their expertise with spacecraft systems, there was nothing Brooke or Tibor could do about it.

The Blakist DropShip became a Flying Dutchman within minutes after the bridge fell—undoubtedly in a last act of spite ordered by her doomed captain. A powerful rumble announced the destruction of the reactor's containment chamber, and though Brooke was certain they'd all perish an instant later, the all-incinerating nova she and the others braced for simply never came.

Tibor, still clutching the fresh laser wound in his thigh, managed to *laugh* about it. "A fusion plant that actually scrams itself right!" he exclaimed. "The interstellar safety code strikes in our favor for a change!"

But now, a day later, he and Brooke finally had to admit defeat. The damage done to the engines and power plant was simply beyond their abilities. The only consolation left was that however many Blakists were on board after they'd taken

ESCAPE FROM JARDINE

the command center, all of them had either died or fled the ship soon after. Amid the floating ruins of Engineering were two more bodies than had been there during the stowaways' last visit, both shredded by shrapnel from whatever they'd exploded in there. The jettison of a life pod—the second, and last, of the two the ship had been equipped with—followed by the launch of some kind of small craft from the hangar bay, not only carried away whoever else remained, it left Tibor, Brooke, and Alahni with just one other means to escape the dead ship.

"It's a heavy fighter of some kind," Tibor said. "Damned if I recognize the type, though."

"Looks brand new," Brooke admitted. "And sleek. But still…"

They were in the launch control station of *Agravain*'s flight bay, a dimly-lit side-chamber in a large, round, and otherwise wide-open deck. Beyond the station, the bay was occupied by little more than a few giant retrieval mechanisms, some empty stowage gantries, two fighter catapults, and a single, large, red-and-black craft with back-swept wings and a semi-circular tail wing assembly lacking any apparent vertical stabilizers. One of the bay's two wide space doors was already opened to vacuum, its corresponding catapult sprung and empty, while the strange aerospace fighter sat slightly off-kilter on its own catapult, facing the closed door.

With the rest of the DropShip's atmosphere bled out the day before, entering this area didn't cause the same windstorm of changing air pressure they'd experienced when seizing the bridge, but that fact did little to reduce the strange sensation of mixed panic and exhilaration everyone felt upon coming in. Alahni, in particular, nearly hyperventilated in her vac suit and grabbed the nearest handholds for dear life when she saw the yawning void beyond the opened bay door, the starfield beyond silently and lazily drifting by in an endless loop as *Agravain* idly tumbled through space. It took more than a few assurances from Brooke and Tibor to get her to relax and trust the magnetic slips on her feet enough to shuffle-step into the control room.

Emergency batteries kicked in throughout the DropShip within minutes of its engine's demise, casting much of the ship's interior into an eerie red twilight. Most of the computer systems were off-lined instantly, but Tibor found his E-console was still able to reactivate some of them—however briefly—as they explored the derelict. But opening doors was another matter, as the depowered hydraulics for every major hatchway required a lot of hand-cranking to spring them. Even under the microgravity that followed the loss of continuous thrust, the working of these various mechanical door controls, not to mention the constant need to alternate between reliance on magslips and handholds for travel, made for an exhausting day's work.

The lack of sleep and food wasn't helping either. Brooke felt her eyelids drooping, and her stomach growled softly. It took her a few moments to realize she'd just trailed off mid-sentence while she stared blankly at the parked aircraft through the control station windows.

"I know," Tibor said. "It's still a fighter. No fuel expansion system."

"What does that mean, again?" Alahni nervously asked. Brooke turned to her and found the girl's eyes remained glued to the station windows, staring incredulously at the open bay door, and the stars beyond it. Had she not spoken up, it would have been easy to imagine Alahni wasn't listening to them at all.

"It means," Brooke began, "that—unlike a shuttle or DropShip—this fighter will burn a good part of its reaction mass every second the engines are lit."

"Which means it'll be pretty fuel-expensive to slow it down," Tibor added. "Depending on how much that thing carries, the tanks will most likely be emptied out long before we've decelerated from the speed this ship's already moving at."

"Slow down?" Alahni asked. "Why would we need to? The Guardians must surely still be chasing us!"

"Once we get out there," Tibor said through a stifled yawn, "we can start feeding telemetry to the *Sacajawea* to come and meet us part way with one of her other shuttles. But shuttles and fighters aren't really built to dock with each other, so the goal will be to match speeds as we get close. It's dangerous and tricky, especially if you try to do it under fire or in too much of a hurry. But it's doable. So, it's safer the lower you can get your velocity."

Alahni blinked and finally managed to tear her gaze away from the void outside. "But if we still can't dock," she started, "how would we...?" Abruptly, her eyes widened.

"*Ja*," Tibor said. "Exactly. So be careful with that vac suit."

"Well," Brooke muttered, "the sooner we launch, the better. I just hope there's room for all three of us in that thing's cockpit..."

Close to an hour later, after manually cranking open the second launch door to reveal more open space beyond, the last three living souls on the *Agravain* prepared to climb into the confines of a technological marvel none of them had ever seen before. Although designed with up to two occupants in mind, room for a third body in the rear co-pilot's seat was discovered in the form of several redundant control systems that proved remarkably easy to remove.

"Aha!" Tibor exclaimed through their shared radio channel when he found the release mechanisms. "Modular tech! State of the art! I think I've heard of this fighter type after all."

"So this is an OmniFighter?" Brooke asked.

"*Ja*," he replied as he pulled the last power cables free and yanked the secondary gunnery station up from its mounting. "I think it's a joint project the League and the Word started cooking up ten years ago or so. Shame we couldn't secure this thing before they purged this deck; we might have been able to swap out the guns for some more fuel tanks."

"Without a tech crew who actually knows what they're doing?"

Together, Brooke and Tibor hurled the bulky console away, aiming for the far side of the flight deck. Between the microgravity and the DropShip's tumble, the weightless console flew across the flight deck in a way that looked utterly unnatural. Noiselessly, it eventually bounced off a support beam near the empty flight bay's ceiling and ricocheted into a dark recess far out of the way.

"A guy can dream, can't he?" Tibor said. Peeking back into the passenger area, he gave a short nod. "Well, it's not a lot of room, but if I take Alahni on my lap, we both hold the harness straps, and brace with our legs—"

"Whoa, there!" Brooke cut in. "If *you* take Alahni on your lap?"

"What's wrong with that?"

"*You're* the better pilot here, Trouble. It's going to be difficult enough launching from a dead ship without a functioning catapult."

Tibor gave Brooke a wary look that was rewarded by a crooked scowl from her. "Alright," he said with a sigh.

She turned back to Alahni, whose suited form was re-emerging from the launch control station, and gave a short, awkward wave to catch the young girl's attention. "How went your search over there?"

"I finally found what appears to be standard ration packs and some spare emergency ox-canisters in a couple of storage cabinets back there," Alahni replied. "Will there be enough space in that thing?"

Tibor glanced into the fighter's open cockpit once again, then looked back at the Jardinian, who was holding up a narrow metal cylinder the size of a personal coffee thermos in one hand, and a pair of small, foil-wrapped packages in the other. "It'll be really tight," he said, "especially in the back with you and Brooke. But we *should* be able to make it work..."

Once the passengers and provisions were secured, Tibor dogged the canopy and spent the next few seconds hunting and pecking at the various control switches to begin the process of starting up the fighter's power plant and life support systems. A soft whooshing—merely felt at first, and heard only as the internal air levels climbed closer to breathable—filled the cockpit.

"Right," he began, "nobody crack their helmet seals until we're free and clear of the ship and I give the okay. This launch will probably get a little bumpy."

"Bumpy?" Alahni nervously repeated. "How bumpy?"

"The DropShip is actually in a slow tumble right now," Tibor explained. "And its normal catapult launcher is useless without a flight deck officer helping us out, so we'll be relying completely on jets and maneuvering thrusters to keep us aligned with the opening. And since there's basically no gravity with the DropShip because it's adrift—"

"Trouble," Brooke cut in, "can we *not* discuss this right now? You've got this, and you know it."

"In other words," Tibor said with a smirk, eyes and hands still darting across his instruments, "stop scaring the girl. Got it."

"I *can* still hear both of you," Alahni protested. "You know this, right?"

"Can't be helped. I mean, sure, we could keep quiet, but that would probably make it harder to keep you distracted before I do *this*—!"

Slamming the main thrust control forward, Tibor kicked the fighter's gear release and triggered the fuel ignition systems in concert. Instantly, the 85-ton OmniFighter went from a low, idling thrum to the full-blast of three-gee acceleration. Alahni gave a squeak that nearly pierced Tibor's eardrums despite the filtration of his helmet speakers, while he and Brooke each let out audible grunts of their own.

In less than an eyeblink, the fighter vaulted off the deck, through the open bay door, and straight out into open space.

But it didn't do so cleanly. A loud *bang* and a hard slewing of the craft to the right added to the chaos of the moment. Tibor felt himself thrown hard to the left, his helmet rapping against the armored canopy with an ominous *crack*, and Brooke's *"Scheiße!"* at the same time told him he wasn't the only one. His eyes dropped immediately to the damage monitor, where an alert beeped for his attention and a wireframe image painted the forward half of the fighter's right wing in blazing red.

"Trouble?" Brooke called out.

"We clipped the exit!" he shouted back, killing the main throttle with one hand while his other struggled with the flight stick. "Forewing took the hit, but I think we're still in one piece!"

"May God and Blake preserve us!" Alahni's voice mumbled in the background, nearly lost to the din of warning sounds and the firing of maneuver thrusters.

Beyond the canopy, stars swirled about as they continued to spin through the void, their lights outshone only by the occasional flare of Jardine's distant sun and the reflection of the *Agravain*'s derelict hull. Tibor grumbled a few choice curses of his own as he pulled at the controls and feathered the thrusters, but over the next full minute or so, he finally managed to bring the massive war machine back under control.

Killing the damage alarm took another minute after that, by which time Tibor swore he had a migraine coming on.

"Trouble?" Brooke called out again, with wary relief in her tone.

"Is everyone back there alright?"

"I think so. You?"

"Nothing seems broken," Tibor said with a sigh. "At least, no more than it already was."

"We're okay, then?" Alahni asked. "Truly?"

"Heh," Tibor said, finding more joy than he expected in the way she asked. "Yes, *mein Liebling.* We're okay."

"Don't worry, Alahni," Brooke said. "We're in good hands now. You can open your eyes now."

"Oh my god!" Alahni said a few seconds later. "The stars... There's so many!"

"Beautiful, aren't they?"

Tibor felt a smile cross his face as he listened to their conversation, and looked up through the canopy at the eternal night of open space. All at once, it seemed, the tension and fear that had tensed up his every muscle over the past few days just melted away. A sense of immense relief washed over him that he could barely believe possible just minutes ago, as if the weight of an entire universe had finally come off his shoulders—if only for the moment.

"Yeah," he whispered, even though he knew Brooke wasn't really asking *him.* "They are."

CHAPTER 12

To: Bertram Habeas, Asst. Ed., HART, Chekswa School of
    Literature
From: Leuchtend Wahrheit, Dir. of Comms., Dobless
    Information Services
Re: Alliance Handbook Project, Data Correction
Send Date: 5 Dec 3067
Greetings, Professor Habeas:

    It has been brought to our attention that the first
edition publication of your abridged almanac, entitled The
Lyran Alliance Handbook, has already begun its statewide
electronic dissemination. That being said, I regret to inform
you that, upon reviewing the final drafts your team sent
our way, they appear to contain minor cartographic errors
which we have only been able to verify, in their entirety,
in the last few days.
    Miraculously, it appears we would have missed
these errors ourselves, were it not for an astute amateur
cartographer who sent us a written request to verify
our own interstellar maps. It was only then, upon cross-
referencing our charts with the CCS-produced maps
included in your team's publication, that we noticed the
errors at all. ComStar's historical gremlins strike again!
    For the sake of historical accuracy, I am including
data files for the specific maps affected: Post-Age of War
(2571), post-First Succession War (2822), and post-Second
Succession War (2864). I highly recommend that these

updates be incorporated into your electronic distributions of the Handbook *at your earliest convenience.*

If you have any inquiries regarding this or any of our other academic services, please feel free to address them to my office. It has been a pleasure corresponding with you.

—LW, DoC, DoBInf
Ludwigdhafen

EXPLORER-CLASS JUMPSHIP SACAJAWEA
ZENITH JUMP POINT, LORIC
LYRAN ALLIANCE
12 DECEMBER 3067

Strapped into a gee-chair, Alahni shook as her mind and body fought back the intense nausea and dizziness they had yet to grow accustomed to after four consecutive trips through hyperspace. She had found it helpful to keep her eyes squeezed shut throughout the process, though, and while she knew it was completely unnecessary, whispered a thanks to Jerome Blake every time she returned to normal space. This time, her prayer was doubly emphatic, as the jump didn't carry with it the same nightmarish visions of cyborgs and fire that came with the last three.

In the days between each leap, Alahni reflected often on the oddity of Jerome Blake. From childhood, she had been raised to revere him as a savior of mankind, the visionary who foresaw humanity's End Times, and worked to save those he could from the terrors to come. Brooklyn Stevens told her most of that was true to a certain degree, but the story was far more complex than that—so much so that many historians felt the Sainted Blake may have done more to accelerate the Succession Wars than shield anyone against them. Nowhere was this more apparent than in the news reports the *Sacajawea* had picked up after its last jump, with rumors of chaos that seemed to rattle Brooke and Tibor, even after all they'd been through.

It was all enough to make Alahni wonder why she still whispered prayers to Blake at all.

As she felt the last ripples of jump-induced confusion fade away, she opened her eyes to find she was, in fact, still strapped in her seat, within the simple shipboard quarters Doctor Stevens had provided her. Gray-painted walls of metal surrounded her, broken mainly by a simple hatchway facing the ship's main grav deck corridor, and the porthole-simulating monitor affixed to the opposite wall. Lit by a quartet of bright yellow pseudo-fluorescent bulbs recessed into the ceiling, the chamber came with thin, deep blue, wall-to-wall carpet, a pair of simple-yet-comfortable fold-out single-sleeper cots on the aftward side, and the utilitarian computer desk which Alahni now sat before. A second door to the chamber, fashioned from some form of synthetic, laminated wood, stood closed on the room's forward side, beyond which was the washroom she shared with the cabin next door.

Brooke's cabin.

Ever since their escape from Jardine, the first Lost Ones Alahni ever met had been nothing but protective and considerate. But while both Brooke and Tibor did their best to keep Alahni safe and help prepare her for the realities of a life beyond her Wayward tribe, the attentions of the former often felt more like the doting of a mother toward her child. In fact, during the first week after their first jump, Brooke's visits to her cabin "to check up on her," started to feel almost smothering— until Alahni finally asked if Doctor Stevens had any kids of her own. The older woman seemed almost ashamed at that, and her visits declined noticeably in the following days. And while her warmth toward Alahni never truly waned, when she did come by, she maintained a certain distance, as if there was now some form of invisible barrier between them.

All in all, it was a little bit awkward at times.

Tibor Mitternacht, meanwhile, had assumed more of a mentoring role, answering Alahni's questions about history and technology in the Inner Sphere while also showing her around their wondrous jump vessel. He also filled in some of the blanks about how the various Succession Wars and the Clan Invasion had unfolded while Alahni's people lived their lives off the map. His explanations were remarkably candid, neither praising nor condemning the horrors of history, and those who brought them about. His dry accounts simply told her how things happened and why, so far as he understood them. They were certainly less dramatic than her own versions of the past, as she told them to entertain or educate the youth of the Shrouded Forest. (But she tried not to dwell on that too much now—at least not outside of the quiet moments when she had the time and privacy to grieve for those left behind.)

Reaching up to her sternum, Alahni pressed the release on the chair's harness, and pulled the straps off her sides. Retractable cords pulled the harness the rest of the way, minimizing their presence by coiling the straps along the chair's back and underside, where they'd remain until needed again.

Clicking the heels of her mag-shoes together, Alahni felt her feet being tugged toward the metal plating beneath her quarters' carpets, and gently pushed herself away from the chair. For her, learning to stand and move in microgravity had been a crash course ever since those days spent on the *Agravain*. But then again, she had to admit it was a lot less stressful than relying on sheer adrenaline, fear, and willpower to keep herself running around, climbing ladders, and fighting hostile Guardians on a ship burning hard enough to make her feel like her weight had doubled. Thanks to some patient tutelage from Brooke, Tibor, and the rest of *Sacajawea*'s crew over the last month, she could now maneuver comfortably in the null-gravity conditions that perpetually characterized JumpShip life outside of a spinning grav deck.

These newfound skills enabled her to rise from the desk chair and half-walk, half-float to the outer wall, and its window to eternal night. (Indeed, although all of *Sacajawea*'s living quarters occupied the bulk of the ship's grav deck, and thus approximated 0.7 gravity most of the time, Tibor had explained to Alahni early on that Captain Pohl always kept the rotational systems disengaged for half an hour before and after each jump, as a safety precaution.)

Projected on the porthole-monitor was a universe of stars, not a single constellation of which Alahni could identify. As beautiful then as it was when she truly stared out from the cockpit of that stolen aerospace fighter, the darkness of the void nevertheless also chilled her to the bone. For weeks she had marveled at the view beyond *Sacajawea*'s windows, often transfixed by sights these Lost now took for granted. Jardine, her home, was about sixty light-years away by now, but even though she knew what that meant on a technical level, it still boggled her mind to think about it. For most of her life, Alahni's whole world had been a tribe in a patch of forest barely twelve kilometers across, hiding in the shadows of the City of Hope.

But all of that was gone now...

"Welcome to Lyran space, Alahni."

Brooke's voice broke through her concentration, but it still took several seconds to tear her eyes from the view. She stared blankly for a moment, briefly wondering how long the Lost woman had been standing there, and how she missed the sound of either of the doors opening behind her. The strange distance Brooke had maintained over the last two weeks was still there, but Alahni could also sense something else—sadness, or worry, perhaps—just barely evident in her brownish-green eyes.

"This is the Loric system," Brooke went on after a moment, nodding toward the faux porthole. "Home to almost two billion people."

"Are they friendly?" Alahni asked.

Brooke shrugged with a faint smirk. "If one has the money, I suppose."

Alahni blinked. Money was a concept she understood only in the abstract; neither the Guardians nor the Waywards used currency as such. The Guardians received any resources they didn't already have from the other worlds of the Five, while everyone else back home saw to their own needs through sweat and muscle—bartering among themselves for everything else.

"You look nice today," Brooke murmured. "The outfit, I mean. Looks good on you. Glad it fits."

Alahni frowned and glanced down at herself. The wardrobe that came with her new quarters included a selection of casual and work clothes belonging to one of the *Sacajawea*'s former crew. While the synthetic fibers and machine stitching took some getting used to after a lifetime spent wearing handmade garments of hide and spun furs, she couldn't deny their appeal, both in comfort and their colorful variety. Moreover, they even *smelled* different from her old tribal wear, carrying a vaguely floral scent Alahni first took to be from whatever perfume their previous owner favored. (Brooke eventually explained the fragrance actually came from the chemical soaps used in the shipboard laundering system.)

Just before the jump, Alahni had chosen to wear a soft blue vest over a pale gray blouse, with pleated black trousers. But as she took in Brooke's uniform—loose-fitting khaki coveralls, cinched at the waist by a black cargo belt, over a neck-hugging black undershirt—she started to feel strangely overdressed for the day.

"Thank you," she replied after a moment. "It does. Your friend Marissa truly had good taste, I take it?"

Brooke smiled a bit sadly and nodded. "She did, but she didn't show it off nearly as often as you might think. I wish you could have met her."

"She sounded nice."

"She was," Brooke said with a sigh. "She really was..."

An alert echoed throughout the JumpShip, a noise different from those Alahni already identified with the hyperspace jump procedure. It didn't seem particularly urgent, as Brooke didn't tense up or bolt from the room when it sounded, and it faded quickly away, like a single toll of an electronic bell. Brooke's eyes did turn away from Alahni, however, her attention shifting back to the porthole screen. Following the older woman's gaze, Alahni saw what looked like a long metal rod, floating in space, dim lights of red and green pulsing at both ends. It's presence there alarmed her; that JumpShip surely wasn't there before, was it?

As they watched, a flicker of silvery...something started to emerge from one end of the vessel, gradually unfolding like a strange, metallic flower bud. In minutes, Alahni knew, it would form a large, reflective parasol—a jump sail. Now she understood the alarm; it was a signal to the *Sacajawea*'s crew that another ship had jumped in nearby.

After a long silence, Brooke sighed without looking away from the distant craft. Something new had just blinked near the middle of the JumpShip, a yellow spark of light moving ever so slightly downward before vanishing a second later.

"Looks like our *friends* are here," Brooke said at last, with an unmistakably sardonic emphasis on the word "friends." "Get ready to steel yourself for this."

Alahni nodded hesitantly and turned to find Brooke's eyes on her again, but this time there was a new fire in them. It was a look she hadn't seen since Jardine.

Outside the airlock to the small craft bay, Tibor Mitternacht and Lawrence Pohl, each clad in a light duty flight suit, stood in a state of semi-attention. Above the heavy steel doors, the air pressure light glowed a dull, angry red, while a steady hum from somewhere beyond the walls droned on.

They'd only been there for a few seconds now, but already, Tibor could sense the unease in Lawrence's breathing. So he wasn't surprised when the gray-haired JumpShip skipper glanced his way just a few heartbeats later. "You holding up alright, Trouble?"

Tibor looked back at him with a shallow, half-hearted smile. "As well as I can," he replied. "You?"

"Still in shock, to be honest," Lawrence said. "I mean, nukes on the Triad? Luthien gone dark? War on Outreach? What the hell is happening out there?"

"I'm afraid to find out."

The journey from Jardine to Loric had been made under complete EMCON. For each jump, the *Sacajawea* stayed off the communications grid, selecting uninhabited systems along a seemingly random course until they reached Lyran space. It wasn't until their last stop over Giausar that they dared send a message packet to Loric via the local HPG station, so the Interstellar Expeditions agents awaiting them there knew they were finally en route.

Other messages also went out at that time, of course— each one a calculated risk, given the very real possibility that the Word was undoubtedly still looking for them. But the real shock came when they picked up several news packets while waiting for the *Sac*'s jump drive to recharge.

It sounded like the entire Inner Sphere was going straight to Hell. And the Word of Blake was at the heart of it all.

"You don't think we—?" Lawrence began.

"No," Tibor snapped, waving a cautionary hand between them. "Don't even suggest it. This was...something else, something they planned, way before we even took this job."

"Still..."

"Still," Tibor repeated with a nod. He understood all too well. "We're marked. We saw a secret they've been hiding for generations. And something they haven't unleashed yet. Something maybe the rest of the universe doesn't know about."

"That's why Brooke asked you to send the worm?"

Tibor nodded again. Of the data packets they'd sent back at Giausar, that bit of code he put together was probably the biggest gamble of them all.

Lawrence sighed and gave a weak shrug. "Then I hope it gets where it needs to go."

"So do I," Tibor admitted. "So do I."

With a faint hiss and a heavy *clank* of metal on metal sounding from somewhere inside the walls, the air pressure light flashed a cool green, signifying that the bay beyond finally reached the right pressure and oxygen content to safely enter. Tibor gave Lawrence a stern nod, and saw it returned in kind.

Their game faces came back on just as the door opened, revealing two men in identical black coveralls. Each of their uniforms was adorned with the simple "*IE*" logo of Interstellar Expeditions, stitched into the outer fabric on each shoulder.

Behind the two men sat a plain, gray, S-7A shuttlecraft "bus," securely clasped and held to the deck by the bay's retrieval boom. Aside from a simple registry of seemingly random numbers and letters stenciled just behind its forward canopy shields, the craft was unmarked. Tibor figured it for a rental.

The man who approached Tibor first was easily recognized between his ultra-short blond hair, pastel blue eyes, fair skin, and a face so broad it was almost flat. Doctor Henry Croft's expression was pensive, almost sheepish, as he extended a hand toward Tibor...who left him hanging for an uncomfortably long time before he accepted it.

"Mister Mitterschmidt, Captain Pohl," Croft began, "on behalf of Interstellar Expeditions, please accept my profuse apologies for the behavior of Doctor Bellamy and the mercenaries under his command. You and Brooke, of all people, surely must understand how the lure of the unknown can sometimes drive some of our field personnel to foolishness."

"Foolishness like that should be fatal," Lawrence snarked.

"I'd say that in this case, it possibly was," Croft said. "We have not heard from Bellamy, Captain Hara, or any of their expedition since we became aware of your situation."

"Small comfort," Tibor deadpanned. "I'm sure Doctor Stevens and myself would've loved to *thank* your boys personally for all their little stunts."

"Their stunts at Jardine, I take it?"

Tibor gave Croft an empty smile, but held his tongue and gestured for both men to follow him and Lawrence to the grav deck. At this point, Croft would just have to wait to see Brooke if he wanted the details.

As the four men half-walked, half-floated through *Sacajawea*'s corridors, Croft tried to make small talk with Tibor and Lawrence several times, while his own companion—a dark-haired, middle-aged, and slightly heavy-set man wearing tinted glasses—remained utterly silent. After getting only the briefest possible replies, he finally gave up halfway along.

The conference room Brooke had selected for this meeting was smaller and blander than the one usually reserved for mission planning. Instead of a table for ten surrounded by just that many synth-leather chairs, with bookshelves and starmaps lining the walls, this chamber housed a small, metallic, wood-veneer table flanked by four metal seats covered in faded black fabric. There were no bookshelves in here, beyond those hidden behind the doors of a small row of cabinets just as dull and gray as the otherwise unadorned walls. Off-center on the table stood a small trideo projector, held in place by magnetic feet. The air in this underused room smelled a bit stale, with hints of ozone and the dry odor of dusty, neglected heating elements.

At the far end of the room, closest to the holo-projector, stood Brooke Stevens and a young woman whose strangely exotic Polynesian beauty and intensely curious stare clashed with Brooke's comparatively more mundane Anglo-European features and the perturbed expression she turned Croft's way as soon as he entered.

"Doctor Croft," Brooke began sharply, "I hope you realize how easily we could've blown you out of the stars before your shuttle even docked here."

"Absolutely, my dear," Croft managed with a mirthless smirk. "But you've never been one to blow a deal at the last moment."

"And who says we even have a deal anymore? Those flunkies you sent along to help us made some pretty underhanded plays out there."

"And, as I have already told Tibor and Lawrence here," Croft gestured vaguely toward the two men, who now stood off to his left, "I apologize for that, both personally and on behalf of IE. In fact, prior to our jump to this system, I managed to convince upper management to authorize a doubling of your payment and cover any repairs your ship requires at this time. Of course, that's all provided you have evidence of a mission accomplished."

"Heh," Brooke scoffed. "We picked up their radio chatter, you know. Your mercs tried to scare my crew off by broadcasting their position in a system they knew to be hostile so they could try and take me and our data at gunpoint."

"You and I both know greedy men only get that bold when they see a prize in reach, Doctor. You can't tell me you *didn't* find Jardine."

Brooke stared at Croft for a long moment, then allowed herself a crooked smile. "Oh, you're too good for IE, Henry."

Brooke pulled one side of her coveralls open and reached inside while Croft's eyes intently followed her every move. From an inside pocket, she withdrew a data chip, flourished it briefly, then set it into the projector.

With a soft *beep* and a nearly inaudible hum, the device sprang to life, and the glowing, holographic image of a star system materialized above the table. Text call-outs flashed quickly in the field, spilling out solar data, highlighting jump points, and flagging the various warning buoys before, finally, one world flashed in brilliant green, and suddenly exploded in size until it dominated the entire field. Beneath and alongside the slowly rotating orb, statistics on everything from axial tilt and orbital distances to atmospheric composition and magnetic field ranges scrolled by on rings of text.

"Jardine," Brooke said. "Right where we left it."

"And where might that be, exactly?" Croft asked after a moment. "For that matter, how can you be absolutely sure it *is* Jardine?"

Brooke tilted her head and arched an eyebrow before reaching out to switch off the projector. Ejecting the chip, she tucked it back into the same inner breast pocket it came from while a thin smile crossed her face.

"We lost a crewmember, a DropShuttle, and a *Possum* landing on that planet, and I can't count the number of times some bionic psychopath nearly killed Trouble and me both. But you can verify the log data we compiled in this chip from the *Sacajawea* and the DropShip you guys lost on Shasta. Not to mention the detailed navigational data we managed to salvage from the Blake DropShip we snuck aboard to get off-world. I can also offer our full vid-statements giving you complete accounts on everything we found there to verify that, yes, that *is* Jardine.

"But the hardest evidence we have is staring you right in the face right now," Brooke finished, with a gesture toward the young girl beside her. "Doctor Henry Croft, meet Alahni, Keeper of Tales for the Shrouded Forest Tribe on Jardine. Alahni...?"

Alahni nodded to Croft without saying anything, her expression apprehensive. Brooke reached into another pocket on her jumpsuit, withdrew a syringe, and extended her free hand toward the girl. Alahni raised her right arm and pulled back her sleeve, exposing even more of her flawless brown skin.

"This won't hurt a bit," Brooke whispered to her as she expertly found a vein and poked the needle into it. Alahni winced and frowned. "Whether they do anything to us or not," she began while she worked, "most of the micro-organisms found on any life-bearing world get into us as early as the womb. That's basic xenobiology..."

After filling the syringe with Alahni's blood, Brooke fished a small bandage from her pocket to cover the wound, and gave the girl a reassuring smile as she did so. Turning to Croft, she popped the now-filled vial off the needle, and casually flicked it toward him. All eyes in the room watched as the vial, granted the unnatural weightlessness of microgravity, tumbled slowly and strangely through the air in Croft's direction.

Although Brooke's aim wasn't perfect, Croft barely needed to stretch his arm out to capture the incoming missile. Once he had it, he shook the tiny vial and watched as the crimson fluid inside sloshed about, before making a non-committal "hmm" and handing it to his companion. By the time he looked back, Brooke's gaze was already on him.

"I'm sure John will be able to verify Alahni's blood will show markers unique for microbes indigenous to Jardine. Check any records you like, though I'd recommend you avoid anything sourced by ComStar or the Word."

Beside Croft, "John" let out an inquisitive "hmm?" at the sound of his own name.

Croft smiled, but only for a moment. "I know your rep, Brooke," he said. "I don't doubt what his tests will find. You're no con artist."

"Then you also know full well I won't be giving you this data chip, or even one scrap more about that world until you agree to a bit more than a pay boost and ship repairs for me. If Hara or Bellamy hadn't managed to get themselves killed before, they'd be able to tell you what I'm saying right now. The planet's hot, hotter than IE can probably even imagine."

"I'm definitely getting that impression right now," Croft conceded with a sigh. "Alright, Doctor. What's it going to be?"

"First, it's going to be *triple* my standard fee, not double, and I want half up front. Second, your people will fix my JumpShip free of charge. Finally, I want a ship sent to Donegal by no later than next week—"

"Donegal?" Croft blurted out. "Haven't you heard—?"

"—*where,*" Brooke continued with intensity, "it will meet a shuttle whose occupant will tell the crew where to go next. We will meet your ship at that second destination. Do not ask that individual any questions beyond that, and don't try anything shifty."

"We're not a taxi service, Brooke."

"You are now, because only *when* that's all done, will I hand over this data. Trust me; it's *that* important."

"And after that?"

"After that, you pay my crew the rest of the money you owe us, and we part company."

Croft hesitated, but never broke eye contact with Brooke. "The deal," he said at last, "was for Jardine and *all* evidence of its existence. We'll also want the girl."

An outraged gasp escaped Alahni's lips, and she took a reflexive step back away from the table, her eyes darting back and forth between Brooke and Tibor. Brooke laid a reassuring hand on her shoulder and narrowed her eyes on Croft.

"She's not property, Doctor," Brooke snapped, "and I'll not subject her to your likes. You have all the evidence you need in that blood sample and the data chip I'll give your people at the rendezvous. Take it and be happy."

Croft sighed again, lowering his eyes a moment, his mind clearly racing for an answer. A bland smile found its way to his face by the time he looked up again. "Counterproposal," he said. "I'll do all you ask, and even *quadruple* your pay for this mission, if you and your crew come back to the fold. You found Jardine; I don't need John to finish his analysis for that. IE could use a woman like you, and I think you'll find our new long-term employment options much better than those you left behind."

Brooke gave him a lopsided grin and shook her head slowly.

"Think about this, Doctor," Croft cautioned. "In case you haven't heard, the Word has gone mad lately. They're on a warpath, and no borders or treaties seem to be stopping them outside of Marik and Liao space. If they really do have the stake in Jardine you're implying, you're surely on their radar as well. With IE, you'll have more protection."

"Takes a lot of nerve to offer that after what we've gone through, Croft," Brooke said coldly. "The deal stands as I phrased it. Full repairs, triple pay—half now, and half when we rendezvous with my...associate. Botch this, or sell me out to the Blakists, and not only will you never see this data, but I'll see to it you and everyone you care about will find yourselves floating in the void.

"Take the deal, Henry, or screw you guys. We're going home."

A tense silence hung over the room. Alahni, her eyes still wide and worried, glanced at Brooke, comparing her defiant glare to Croft's sour expression while the two fought their wordless battle of wills.

Finally, after what felt like an eternity of seconds, the older man blinked, and tipped his head in defeat.

"You're playing a dangerous game, Brooke," he said, "but fine. Have it your way. And may God have mercy on your soul."

"One way or another," Brooke told him, "I figure we'll see soon enough."

EPILOGUE

My dearest Tyler,

I hope this message finds you well. I have so missed you in these past many weeks, and as I write you now, I can only beg for your forgiveness over and over. I have been away for so long—too long. I don't dare say more at this time, but I beg you now to pack your things. Call it excess paranoia if you will, but while I may take my chances with my life, I refuse to do so with yours.

So, while I know this is going to come as a great inconvenience—and I can hear your outraged "I told you so!" from here—I think it's time for that little contingency we talked about. Take only what you need, Love, and whatever you need to handle the trip, wait for me at the rendezvous. I will find you there soon.

And when I do, please set an extra place for dinner. There's someone I want you to meet...

(SIGNED) BROOKE

SCOUT-CLASS JUMPSHIP *BROKEN KNEE*
ZENITH JUMP POINT, SKYE
LYRAN ALLIANCE
12 DECEMBER 3067

So many promises, so many dreams, now lay in ashes. Ashes Apollyon could virtually taste as he regarded the holoprojector in front of him. There, rendered in faithful, high-resolution detail, floated the image of his greatest friend and mentor.

His Master.

The man, who once bore the surname of a House Lord, who'd eschewed his throne for the true power of knowledge, whose foresight had helped guide the faithful through some of the darkest days of this new era, sat behind a desk of polished obsidian in a chamber of dark gray shadows. His face was a mask of scars not unlike Apollyon's own—most earned from the treachery of his own kin—and what remained of its original, frail flesh was weathered and worn by age. From the ruddy, warped half of his face, where no hair grew, his true right eye blazed in angry red from a socket of gleaming titanium, while its more expressive companion, reinforced by implants far less overt in nature, stared into the camera with no less intensity beneath a grey eyebrow now arched low in frustration.

With the hood of his bone-white robes thrown back, the Master's half-head of wispy, silver-gray hair was clearly visible, mostly swept back in neat formation, save for the few errant strands scattered about here and there of their own accord. Thin cables peeked out from somewhere behind his right ear, before snaking back again to disappear somewhere within the collar of the red-and-gold tunic he usually favored these days. A faint, warm glow showed near the right side of his chest, betraying activity from the filters of his true lungs. Though his sullen, pensive speech had been unimpeded by their efforts, the first of the Master's Hands knew when his liege was struggling to breathe. It pained Apollyon to see him this way.

"My friend, rest assured that I am well and unharmed. The treacherous Dragoons never breached my sanctum grounds, and none of their number escaped our wrath. Nevertheless, I have enacted our most prudent contingencies. We shall ensure these Clan-spawned curs pay the ultimate price for their hubris."

Apollyon clenched his fists as a new wave of rage passed over him. The Wolf's Dragoons were among the first worries he'd expressed when the Master chose to journey to Terra. But the true heart of the Word would not be swayed for such petty concerns. Even with their ill-gotten homeworld a scant two jumps away from the sacred havens of Terra, the Dragoons could pose no credible threat to the Master or the Promise—at least, none the Word was not well prepared to encounter now that the time of the Third Transfer was nigh.

But then that foolish relic on Outreach had to go and slip his leash too soon. Had Wayne Waco not managed to get himself killed taking out the hated Jaime Wolf, Apollyon would have commanded his finest to do the deed himself. And now, years of careful planning to deal with the Inner Sphere's Dragoons problem as surgically as possible had been scattered to the winds—at the very *worst* possible moment in history!

"Because of this, and the crises brought down upon us at the capitals, we are forced to reallocate our assets for the time being..."

Another wave of rage crashed down on Apollyon as he fought to keep his focus. Another fool, closer to the Word's heart, heralded these "crises" his Master spoke of. Cameron St. Jamais and his Sixth of June had long impressed the Word's true leadership with their fierce loyalty to Blake's legacy—but even in these traits, Apollyon always knew they paled in comparison to the selfless dedication of his Manei Domini. St. Jamais gave him pause, in fact, for his obvious and overt ambition. Where the Hands served for nothing greater than Blake's Promise itself, St. Jamais's efforts to climb the Word's ranks were crass and vulgar.

But even Apollyon could not believe it when the Word's Precentor-Martial managed to foul up *everything* when it mattered most, and sent the Promise itself careening into the pits of chaos!

That the Master did not immediately demand St. Jamais' head on a platter at first confounded Apollyon. But when he eventually sensed the reason such a fool had been left in the very visible position he'd so brazenly sought, his confusion gave way to prayers that he would live long enough to witness the man's inevitable reckoning.

"Your hunt for those who violated our paradise has raised attentions elsewhere, my friend, and for this reason, you must see it through to the end. I have, in the interim, sent new orders to the rest of our Shadows, which you will find in the data file I'm attaching. I have also sent orders to Erinyes, whom you shall rendezvous with once you have ensured your mission's success. As much as it pains me, my brother in Blake's Wisdom, the Karpov Protocols must be observed if any of the Promise is to survive."

Apollyon's mouth went dry, and he felt his own breath catch in his lungs. The Master's words, though anticipated, were like a vibrodagger to his gut. He closed his eyes—true and frail alike—and instantly envisioned the fires that would soon engulf everything he once held so dear. But where the orders and the image might have brought another man to tears, Apollyon simply let out a long, controlled, regretful sigh, and willed his heartbeat to slow down again.

It would be done. For the good of all, it would be done.

When Apollyon opened his eyes again, the Master's image was gone, replaced by the glowing broadsword insignia of the Word of Blake. He blinked sadly at the image, unable to remember any of the Master's final words before he'd signed off on this message. Had he said anything at all after confirming the dreaded Karpov Protocols?

For the first time in decades, Apollyon felt unsure of himself. There was so much he wanted to say to the man in the holovid, but that would have to wait. There was too much that needed to be done right now, and the Master's Hands would need to be ready.

Apollyon ejected the chip from the holovid reader and closed his frail hand around it. With one more deep breath and a moment of silent meditation, he forced his mind to re-center itself before he finally reached over the communications panel beside the holoprojector.

"Precentor Lucille," he called into the device.

Damien Lucille replied instantly, as if he'd been hovering over his speaker all along. "Yes, Precentor?"

"Stow the sails and initiate jump calculations."

"Acknowledged, Precentor," Lucille said. "Our course?"

"Unchanged," Apollyon grimly told him. "Our course remains unchanged."

Lucille's response came after the briefest of hesitations, but his voice resonated the same gravity as the orders he'd been given. "Understood, sir."

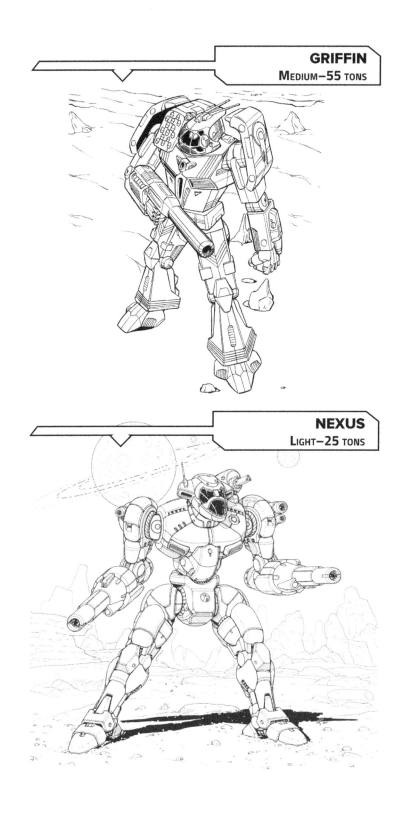

GRIFFIN
MEDIUM—55 TONS

NEXUS
LIGHT—25 TONS

OWENS
LIGHT—35 TONS

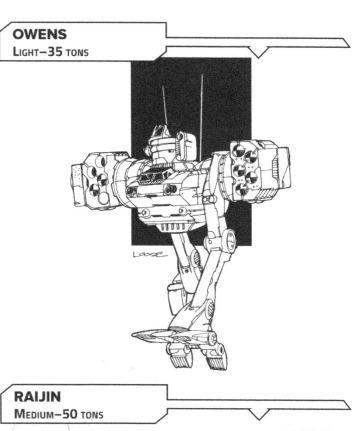

RAIJIN
MEDIUM—50 TONS

MORE BATTLETECH FICTION BY HERBERT A. BEAS II

If you enjoyed this *BattleTech* novella, you can find other stories by Herbert A. Beas II in the following books:

THE HUNT FOR JARDINE
(FORGOTTEN WORLDS, BOOK ONE)
BURIED IN THE ASHES OF WAR...

Freelance explorer and treasure hunter Dr. Brooklyn Stevens has made her career finding lost artifacts from Inner Sphere history, but during the waning days of the FedCom Civil War, a job offered by the academic organization known as Interstellar Expeditions affords her the chance to pursue the find of a lifetime: a missing planet, one lost in the ravages of the brutal Succession Wars.

But the world of Jardine did not only die in fire—it was erased from stellar maps entirely, and Brooke's employer wants to know why.

She must hunt down the only known link to this forgotten world: a dangerous predator native to Jardine, whose initial discoverer was silenced under mysterious circumstances. Someone wants this planet to remain buried—and they will go to any lengths to ensure that Brooke's quest to uncover the truth of Jardine's disappearance ends in tragedy.

FINDING JARDINE
(FORGOTTEN WORLDS, BOOK TWO)
UNCOVERING THE SECRETS OF A LOST WORLD...

Interstellar explorer and freelance treasure hunter Dr. Brooklyn Stevens has made the find of a lifetime—an entire planet thought lost for centuries. Jardine was supposedly wiped off the maps of the Inner Sphere during the hard-fought Succession Wars, but the verdant forested world she and her adventuring partner just crash-landed on tells a much different story.

And so do its inhabitants. Dr. Stevens and her partner soon find themselves between two very different groups: one whose members are an unholy amalgamation of man and machine, the other a hardy group that lives off the land. Both groups are soon after Stevens and her knowledge about Jardine—one side to protect the planet from those that would seek to reclaim it, the other intent on killing anyone who knows of its existence. Caught between both sides, Brooklyn must uncover the mysteries of Jardine...and stay alive long enough to tell the universe about it...

WEAPONS FREE
(BATTLECORPS ANTHOLOGY VOLUME 3)

This volume features "Growing Up," in which the would-be Baron Hasseldorf must win a duel on Galatea to earn a command position in Kirkpatrick's Bandit Killers.

FIRE FOR EFFECT
(BATTLECORPS ANTHOLOGY VOLUME 4)

This volume contains two stories by Herbert Beas. The first, "Case White: To Serve and Protect," is set during the climactic Case White operation, where a TerraSec officer learns the difference between upholding the law and fighting a war. The second story, "Forgotten Worlds: The Hunt for Jardine," follows treasure hunter Brooklyn Stevens in her quest to locate one of the Hidden—rumored secret planets controlled by the fanatical Word of Blake.

BATTLETECH ERAS

The *BattleTech* universe is a living, vibrant entity that grows each year as more sourcebooks and fiction are published. A dynamic universe, its setting and characters evolve over time within a highly detailed continuity framework, bringing everything to life in a way a static game universe cannot match.

To help quickly and easily convey the timeline of the universe—and to allow a player to easily "plug in" a given novel or sourcebook—we've divided *BattleTech* into eight major eras.

STAR LEAGUE
(Present–2780)
Ian Cameron, ruler of the Terran Hegemony, concludes decades of tireless effort with the creation of the Star League, a political and military alliance between all Great Houses and the Hegemony. Star League armed forces immediately launch the Reunification War, forcing the Periphery realms to join. For the next two centuries, humanity experiences a golden age across the thousand light-years of human-occupied space known as the Inner Sphere. It also sees the creation of the most powerful military in human history.

(This era also covers the centuries before the founding of the Star League in 2571, most notably the Age of War.)

SUCCESSION WARS
(2781–3049)
Every last member of First Lord Richard Cameron's family is killed during a coup launched by Stefan Amaris. Following the thirteen-year war to unseat him, the rulers of each of the five Great Houses disband the Star League. General Aleksandr Kerensky departs with eighty percent of the Star League Defense Force beyond known space and the Inner Sphere collapses into centuries of warfare known as the Succession Wars that will eventually result in a massive loss of technology across most worlds.

CLAN INVASION
(3050–3061)
A mysterious invading force strikes the coreward region of the Inner Sphere. The invaders, called the Clans, are descendants of Kerensky's SLDF troops, forged into a society dedicated to becoming the greatest fighting force in history. With vastly superior technology and warriors, the Clans conquer world after world. Eventually this outside threat will forge a new Star League, something hundreds of years of warfare failed to accomplish. In addition, the Clans will act as a catalyst for a technological renaissance.

CIVIL WAR
(3062–3067)
The Clan threat is eventually lessened with the complete destruction of a Clan. With that massive external threat apparently

neutralized, internal conflicts explode around the Inner Sphere. House Liao conquers its former Commonality, the St. Ives Compact; a rebellion of military units belonging to House Kurita sparks a war with their powerful border enemy, Clan Ghost Bear; the fabulously powerful Federated Commonwealth of House Steiner and House Davion collapses into five long years of bitter civil war.

JIHAD
(3067–3080)
Following the Federated Commonwealth Civil War, the leaders of the Great Houses meet and disband the new Star League, declaring it a sham. The pseudo-religious Word of Blake—a splinter group of ComStar, the protectors and controllers of interstellar communication—launch the Jihad: an interstellar war that pits every faction against each other and even against themselves, as weapons of mass destruction are used for the first time in centuries while new and frightening technologies are also unleashed.

DARK AGE
(3081–3150)
Under the guidance of Devlin Stone, the Republic of the Sphere is born at the heart of the Inner Sphere following the Jihad. One of the more extensive periods of peace begins to break out as the 32nd century dawns. The factions, to one degree or another, embrace disarmament, and the massive armies of the Succession Wars begin to fade. However, in 3132 eighty percent of interstellar communications collapses, throwing the universe into chaos. Wars erupt almost immediately, and the factions begin rebuilding their armies.

ILCLAN
(3151–present)
The once-invulnerable Republic of the Sphere lies in ruins, torn apart by the Great Houses and the Clans as they wage war against each other on a scale not seen in nearly a century. Mercenaries flourish once more, selling their might to the highest bidder. As Fortress Republic collapses, the Clans race toward Terra to claim their long-denied birthright and create a supreme authority that will fulfill the dream of Aleksandr Kerensky and rule the Inner Sphere by any means necessary: The ilClan.

CLAN HOMEWORLDS
(2786–present)
In 2784, General Aleksandr Kerensky launched Operation Exodus, and led most of the Star League Defense Force out of the Inner Sphere in a search for a new world, far away from the strife of the Great Houses. After more than two years and thousands of light years, they arrived at the Pentagon Worlds. Over the next two-and-a-half centuries, internal dissent and civil war led to the creation of a brutal new society—the Clans. And in 3049, they returned to the Inner Sphere with one goal—the complete conquest of the Great Houses.

Made in the USA
Monee, IL
08 October 2024